KORP
and the
THINKER

A MOLECULE OF CONSCIENCE

KORP
and the
THINKER

A MOLECULE OF CONSCIENCE

PART ONE
ORLY CASTRO A.

To
Sally-Anne
Thank you for your patience and support.
And to our children
Daniela and Debbie, for lighting up our lives.

Acknowledgements

I have dedicated this work to our students in our Spanish class and to you, the readers, who, in one way or another, have influenced the execution of this book.

To Kate Offer for inspiring me; Jill Atkins, our first student, for all her support; Lorna Polke and Denise Collins for their perseverance and persistence in studying week after week; Peter For for his outstanding dedication and commitment; Sarah and Hollie Villafuerte Richards for their wonderful friendship and commitment; Faith and Emma Taylor for their devotion and love; to Alex Budding for his extraordinary commitment and sense of responsibility; and Rufus and Thea Cobbald for their extraordinary dedication. To our former students: Stewart and Anna-Claire Cusick, Anita Brinkley, Sophia and Edward Wilson, George McCathie and Sam Hunt.

To our new students: Isaac, Reuben, Henry and Jonny Stenhouse; Natalia and Amelia Lewinska; Tim Holt-Wilson; Susan and Derek Rose. And to all those who have attended our courses, thank you for your support.

I also dedicate it to you because you took some time to transform it into precious moments to spend with me. These experiences and memories are my refuge and protection when the days are grey, cold or sad, and they are the bright light that shows me and reminds me of how beautiful the path of life is. Without you, I would be like an empty seven-star hotel built on Mars. You give my life meaning.

To my father, Rufino, and my mother, María. To my brothers and sisters, Efraín, Beto, Vicente, Dorita, Ruth, Sarita, Ariel and Andinita. I take them to heart.

To my friends from Step Carachipampa Bolivia 90: Clare Cole, Julie Noble, John Cowan, Roland Brown, Orlando Saer, Jacqui Kemp, Olivia Cunnington, Emma Stanhope, Emma and Mathew Pickard, Louise Leat, Anna Hanton, Jono Shimwell, Norton Murdoch, I love you guys.

To the international community of Latin Link, thank you for all your support.

With special affection to my Latin American family in Ecuador – Carlos Vázquez, Cristina Rosero, Carlos Varela, Jaime and Melcy Gonazaga, Mario and Paty Sylva, Luis and Konny Eguiguren, Debbie Sylva, Carlos Cadena, Jimy and Maritza Gonzaga; Argentina – Alejandra Wolff, Nancy Marreta; Bolivia – Aurea Choque, Hernán Gonzales, Elisa Canqui, Juan Ancalle, H. Marcela Cayoja and Virginia Oros; Paraguay – Sonia Duarte; Colombia, Carlos Aranguren; Mexico – Gama Canul; Costa Rica – Melvin Alvares; Chile – Ramón Huerta and Magaly Berrios and Perú Luis Sanchez.

To my friends in the Diss region: Gareth Newberry, Heribert and Kathryn Westerveld, Jenny Goater, Mark and Bridget Lanchester. Justin, Amy, Joe and Lily Cossey; David, Tim Clarke; Hope Church and Graham Blake.

Special mention to Susan Holloway; Avril and Alan Mackay; John and Brenda Hart; Alan Tower; Esteban Andrade; Kate Henry; Katy Griggs; Andrea Gardiner; Tim and Elsa Pawson; Rosy and Philip Beales; Fredd, Mary, Paul, Jo, Lizz Kerridge; David and Carolyn Matcham; Richard and Christine Spall; Jairo and Wendy Lopez; Bob Vogel; Remigio Ancalle; Max and Martha Cayoja for all their support.

Preface

There are human beings out there who, just by saying a positive comment, can ignite gigantic fires in the forests of people's imagination. Frances Burrows was one of them.

One morning, at about 10 am, someone knocked at the door of our house in Diss. I wasn't expecting anyone that day; when I opened the door, I saw this woman looking for me.

"I have this address where someone teaches Spanish. Is this it?" She said it in perfect Spanish.

"Yes, come in," I replied, surprised by her level of Spanish.

After a long talk about where she had learned and why she wanted to know more, we agreed on a date and time for three months of lessons, once a week. After three months, I thought she would say 'thank you' and 'bye-bye.' Instead, she said, "I am enjoying my Spanish classes. I want to keep learning, but can we change the day and time?"

"Yes, of course," I replied, showing my complacency.

By this point, Frances needed a book to read and comment on. It was then that I thought of the idea of writing. By then, I was writing minor stories about different subjects for her to read and comment on in class. I realised she immensely enjoyed it when the stories involved politics, science, economics and hope.

'This time, I should write something that covers these topics,' I thought to myself.

It took much work to decide where to start. A name for a story came to mind: Estela. A girl who wanted to know who her father was; one day receiving a letter with the most beautiful news about him, embarking on this trip to meet him, etc.

After reading Estela's story, which had thirty pages, Frances said, "I enjoyed reading Estela. Where did she come from?"

This question opened up yet another door because, in the story, I didn't give details of where she had come from, so I answered her, "I think we will find out where she came from and who her relatives are in the next book we read."

Frances' understanding impressed me so much. After reading the stories, her comments challenged me to write something more profound and full of adventures; this is when I began working on the novel.

One morning, when walking to the supermarket, I saw that hundreds of cars had driven over this credit card on the road; it was dirty, wet and scratched. I thought, 'What can I write about this card?' because I had listed the characters and scenarios for Frances' story that week.

At home, I put the scratched, semi-destroyed credit card on the list, thinking how powerful a credit card was when new. The next day, when preparing the lessons for my other students and searching for some images, I spotted a picture of a man who was sitting and thinking. I liked the idea of thinking: 'The Thinker' also went on the list.

By then, I was growing strawberries in the garden of my friend Jenny, a renowned artist. Her garden had many things made of wire: horses, dragons, people, etc. I saw a silhouette of a person made of wire and added it to my list.

To cut a long story short, I created some scenarios involving most of the items I had put on my list, plus the three things mentioned above, and then the main character's name suddenly popped into my head.

I was the regional coordinator for the charity I worked for, my second job, which sometimes involved travelling by train to the rest of the country. Hence, the train became my primary transport vehicle and where I could finally put the idea of the book on paper. I was under pressure because I had to present something to Frances for her to read.

Two weeks after Frances' question, 'Where did Estela come

from?' I started writing the prequel to Estela's story, which is how the KORP tale began.

In my hometown of Diss, I visited different writing venues: the library, restaurants and coffee shops, car parks, The Corn Hall, St Mary's Church, the train, and many train station platforms. I kept the secret from Frances that I was writing the weekly pages for her Spanish lessons.

After two years of Frances reading KORP and me writing it, she told me she had cancer and had to have chemotherapy. This news was understandably very upsetting, so I tried to make our lessons upbeat: to make her laugh and encourage her to fight back by saying that it was not the end of the journey and that there was always hope. I also took KORP in that direction but didn't tell her I was the author.

As the days passed, she was no longer a student, and I wasn't the teacher. We were friends learning and discussing this character's story in class.

There were weeks when Frances couldn't attend lessons because of her illness and treatment schedule. When she returned, we continued reading the story of KORP from where we had left off. Funnily enough, we read the last pages almost precisely three years from the day she first made her comment and when I began writing.

After reading the final chapter, she asked me, "I enjoyed reading this book, which also challenged me greatly. Where can I get a copy of it?"

I had no choice but to reveal the author to her; she was so grateful that someone would do something like that for her.

Immediately after we had finished reading part one of KORP, I began to write part two. We had read almost three-quarters of part two when her health declined. She stopped coming to lessons, and I visited her at her house many times, where we talked a lot in Spanish.

One day, whilst having a coffee, I said to her, "I will publish KORP Part One, and then you may have a proper copy."

In response to this comment, she laughed.

"You don't believe me, do you, Frances?" I replied. I could tell when she was mocking me.

Months later, after saving enough money, I sent the book to Spain to be edited. I then contacted some publishers. Months later, I had ten copies of KORP Part One in Spanish. I took one for Frances. I knew she was still having trouble because of her health and that this would be a welcome tonic. After knocking on the door and entering, I received a plate of biscuits and a cup of excellent coffee.

"I have a surprise for you, Frances," I said happily.

"Are you going to be a father again?" she replied, laughing.

"Of course not, Frances, not at my age. Don't be so silly!" I replied, laughing at her comment.

Then, I took the book from my bag and placed it in her hands.

I will never forget her face when she looked at it and dug through the pages. She was motionless and couldn't quite believe it; she hugged me with a big thank you.

After that, I went back a few more times to visit her. We once went to Ipswich to have coffee in the library – Frances's favourite place – with her sister Miriam, who had come to Spanish classes occasionally.

Months later, I received a card with the news of her passing.

I miss having our discussions and hearing her comments. After all, we had lovely times learning Spanish.

*'Everybody deserves a miracle in times
when the system has crossed the boundaries of human rights and dignity'*

1. Thumbs-up

As on Earth, so in heaven.

Two young men struggled fiercely to immobilise him; finally, after a long battle, they exerted much effort to hold him by the arms. A third man was standing in front of them, looking at the whole situation with the attitude of a mocking lout, who, smiling, gave the man a thumbs-up as if to say, 'Forgive him for now'.

These three young men always intended to see him on his knees, begging for mercy but had tired of trying. One of them said, "That's enough. We'll try another day, and we still have plenty of time to break his will."

As they laughed sarcastically at him, they let go of his arms. Stepping over the small puddles of water (stained with drops of blood), the three of them fled at lightning speed, and the echoes of their footsteps followed behind them until they disappeared from the basement of that old building. The place appeared abandoned and poorly lit.

After the three left him alone, he tried to fix his hair; he put on dark glasses and stood there looking straight ahead with his head held high, like a fighting cock. With his shirt and coat still messed up from the incident, he had watched as his three abusers ran away from the scene. He fixed his shirt, and seeing that his perpetrators had disappeared, he made an obscene gesture with his hand. With careful and anxious steps, he cleaned the blood off his wound and headed in the opposite direction. He looked back to ensure no one was following him.

The following week, he would take his final university exam.

He had vowed to get high marks in the final exams because he had promised his parents that one day he would make it.

"I will finish my college career with my head held high," he had vowed to them.

Arriving at the door of his house, he was still bleeding from the wound. Once again, he hastily fixed his shirt and hair. He went to his room and strolled to the corner. Next to his bed was a seat stacked with books, magazines and old newspapers. He bowed his head in reverence in front of his poster of The Thinker and, with a broken voice, said, "Colleague, let me sit down."

He sat on the stack of old books and magazines in the same position as his colleague, The Thinker. Closing his eyes as the adrenaline drained from his veins, he rested.

After several minutes of being in the depths of his mind, he turned his thoughts to look for something: a formula, a method, a way to free himself from that humiliating situation that tied his hands, his feet and the heart of his soul.

He had carried that burden from the first day he set foot in primary school through high school until that morning at university. That mockery had become a heavy rock on his back and would not let him live in peace. Besides carrying a dose of the deadliest poison in its belly, that whip had a name and surname: bullying.

Sitting on his makeshift stool and immersed in a thousand thoughts, he designed a tactic – a strategy – to escape his enemies. There were three of them, and he was alone.

He noted that there were many ways of waging war.

"Some use the strategy of infiltrating their enemies; others join the enemy and, being in their midst, annihilate them."

Perhaps he was thinking about the Trojan Horse story. He did not like that idea because it implied that he would have to go to his enemies. He planned it this way: "How about if I make them come at me, and when they are close enough, I can destroy them?"

This last idea left him feeling satisfied with himself.

He urgently created a bait to attract his three abusers towards him, where he would wait to strike them down. On personal principle, he would never go to them, never.

"Why and what difference does it make?" (The Thinker)

It made a big difference for him because that was how he was; he was too proud, and this was his way of looking at the world.

His name is KORP, the human being who manipulates circumstances so that they always favour him or are centred on him; he is the type of person who likes to control life events to take advantage of them – the unbreakable. He is a human with extreme determination, excessive stubbornness, an obsessively capricious will, and, above all, pride.

***

The hours passed, and KORP continued sitting on his makeshift stool beside his poster. He struggled with the plan of how to get his three perpetrators to come to him. After several minutes, he imagined a table with some water lying on the surface in the centre, asking himself, "How do I make that water come to me?"

Analysing the image, he said, "If I want that water to run towards me, I must tilt the table towards me; only then will I get the water to run towards me."

He continued thinking about the image. "Without the table, there will not be a way to control the direction of the water; therefore, I must have a table." He then called the table a system or a systematic way to control or a controller. He put together a strategy and then prepared the bait for his three perpetrators to come to him.

As these three bullies had made his life miserable for many years, he was determined to take revenge. Also, one of them was to blame for his break-up with the only love of his life: his beloved Kate. Because of this, his relationship with Kate became an ordeal for both, with several sad episodes of torment and thousands of harsh edges.

After many hours of sitting while thinking in The Thinker's position, he determined to complete his university studies with his head held high and to leave these three bullies on their knees.

***

Weeks later, it happened just as he had planned: he set the trap and stepped out on the trail of his hunters to spread his net for them. When the three walked towards him, they fell into his net, and he ruined them utterly. Two ended up in jail, and the third, who caused Kate to leave the stage of KORP's life, fled abroad to hide.

***

After years of intense university studies, KORP graduated as a biologist and cybernetics engineer with high honours and brilliant marks. People admired and respected him at the university; he was a genius and a star student. No one noticed that his three perpetrators had bullied him at school for many years. He had to learn how to surf in the sea of life to get ahead.

Since childhood, he had been a tenacious person. He had many skills and high expectations in life. Above all, he preferred to avoid being at the bottom or in the last place of anything. These expectations pushed him to try for success in a universe filled with millions of challenges and opportunities.

Through the years, KORP developed a temperate, competitive and efficient attitude towards work and was looking to climb to the top in every aspect of life. That yearning to climb up – constantly climbing up – became his lethal obsession. He sometimes shouted to his collaborators, "Someday I will get above the top!"

Because of that statement, many thought he had autism – or was it just a part of his strange way of being? I don't know.

From a very young age, he was an excellent opportunist. He never let opportunities pass him by, and with all kinds of means, he always looked for ways to tackle them, making the most of them, especially those he knew he would benefit from, whether for respect, money, reputation, time or whatever. Whenever people offered him job opportunities, he accepted them. No matter how insignificant they were, willingly he would do the job. For him, earning money was the most important.

His abusers bullied him because they were eager to see him on his knees, begging for mercy. Intending to break his furtive and defiant gaze, they tried until his last day at university, but failed. They wanted to make him look at the ground, but this was impossible because of his will of steel.

***

Being in The Thinker's position helped him give free rein to his mind, which was like a wild and untamed horse. In the depths of his thoughts, KORP frequently played and debated wars. Because of the torture he suffered from his abusers and his family experiences, life was a war for him.

His parents took him to the capital city early for his education, under the illusion that their son would become someone significant. Unfortunately, when he reached adolescence, they divorced. From then on, they left him alone to his fate; they had financial resources but did not give him time or moral support.

Despite these developments in his life, he promised his parents he would not let them down. In the last week of his academic exams, he kept that promise. He finished his education with his head held high and top grades; despite being bullied, he never gave up. It may be too much to say that he was lucky to have completed his education.

KORP made an exceptional heroic demonstration of surviving bullying; he was a miraculous example of resilience and courage. He was not the only one who endured that hell, but he was the only one who made it to the finish line so boldly.

But, as with everything in life, some experiences also bring unfortunate consequences. He also did not emerge unscathed from this tortuous bullying experience. That scourge left too deep a mark on his life – destroying, obliterating, searing and eliminating his conscience. Bullying scarred his life and soul deeply.

Because of those dark traces in his soul, KORP could not distinguish between good and evil. He couldn't differentiate between forbidden or permitted actions.

"It was difficult to determine if he ever had a conscience. I dare say that he followed his instincts when deciding on daily life. Bullying erased his conscience systematically and with unprecedented surgical precision until there was no trace. His soul was dark as night, like a bottomless, formless abyss."
(The Thinker)

***

KORP was more eccentric than eccentric; people loved and admired him for that. Most of all, they respected him a lot. He was an attractive eccentric when he was younger, perhaps as a teenager. His eccentricities complemented the gaps left by 'normal' people. He became the centre of everyone's attention, but he couldn't see that fact. Almost always, at parties or social gatherings at school or college, people had their eyes on him, and this infuriated his abusers. Not that he sought attention; he just existed. He aroused natural empathy in others. Perhaps fate? Perhaps, but he always attracted his classmates' attention – his abusers did not.

The long hours he spent thinking in his colleague's position, The Thinker, had also taught him to see life from another perspective. He did not always take off his clothes to meditate, but when he did, it gave him great pleasure, or rather, rest. It was the only thing that calmed him down and assisted him in recovering from his bullying-related emotional breakdown. Being in The Thinker's position enabled him to create a black hole in his emotions. In that position, he digested the agony of the trying hours and the depressing taste brought on by bullying; in that position, he drank in much suffering – the effects of that misfortune's loneliness. Also, spending long hours in that position helped KORP prevent darkness from affecting his will and desire to live as an average human being in his own right. To be in that seat, made of piled-up old newspapers and magazines, helped him transform that scourge's heavy burdens into light ones and incinerate all the brutalities his abusers poured on him daily, week after week, year after year. In this position, he would build an empire that he would control, using the table image as an example so that the water or the lives of its inhabitants would always flow towards him.

He would name his empire the KORP Empire.

From the beginning, I want to clarify that I am not justifying the reasons behind his decisions or his intentions. I am not justifying KORP's actions. It is sacred to think everyone is free and responsible for their choices or actions. I assume that, as adults, we will understand this.

***

For KORP, as he had no conscience, the wars of life were without barracks, human rights, referees, allies or any help. He convinced himself that life was tough, and that there was no other life than the one he was living. 'To get ahead and be happy, one must come face to face with destiny to continue climbing to reach the top,' he thought.

To begin with, he lacked human relationships. Inwardly, he was like a flat man, without facial features, more like a silhouette. For example, he never reciprocated when someone extended his hand to greet him, showing empathy. He needed help to decipher whether this action was a greeting. He left millions of people with their hands outstretched.

His human relationships were never human; instead, they were those of interest and opportunism. He would look sideways if a relationship or friendship did not benefit him. Beyond the irises of his eyes, you could tell that his soul was cold, so he had a sweet, deep, but abysmal gaze.

Height: medium tall; brown hair; thick eyebrows; cat-like green eyes; and full lips. His shallow, sweet, seductive gaze captured any frozen heart. His lips drew an angelic smile that broke animosity barriers and incited friendship, qualities he did not realise he possessed.

Physically, he was in good shape because he devoted himself to the gym. His attractive masculine features, both facially and physically, provided a pleasant camouflage and refuge for his darkened soul.

Since his childhood, he had had a nose for success. He didn't care how, but he always prevailed. A winner's soul, perhaps? Maybe. Winning was so meaningful in his life. He wrote his own rules, with which he subtly manipulated the circumstances of his life and later his business, all for one sole purpose – winning.

He had hundreds of habits for different occasions and purposes to sense reality, such as standing on the sidewalk after leaving his house and inhaling the air deeply before going in any direction. Doing this entrenched him in the path of his freedom, a space where he existed on his way and in his time. A place where his rules and existential norms ruled, which he called 'the sacred cathedral of my personal space'. The area where he freely grazed his free will.

He knew what he wanted and tried to always walk in that direction. His sociability, when necessary, contributed to his popularity. Still, instead of avoiding crowds, he enjoyed having his personal space. In that solitude, he gave free rein to his desires, tastes and instincts, making his walk more solid. He preferred not to have his options limited by others; he hated it when someone told him what to wear, eat, drink, and where to go or do: he was the lord and the master of his decisions.

KORP always relaxed and entertained himself and had favourite places, days, events, activities to go to. Of course, his favourite day was Friday because he knew that two days awaited him, which would let his instincts be free. These instincts were like wild horses that needed freedom's wind bathing in their coat. Also, he saved some weekends to hang out and have fun going to different nightlife centres. Being there in the vast concrete jungle, he took part in all kinds of contests for risk lovers, which was a way to feed his social side and capture people's attention. There, he had a lot of fun, and above all, he enjoyed dancing. Several times, he had saved himself from food poisoning in the Mexican chilli-eating contest or had ended up in the hospital after participating in the 'one-shot' competition, which was a contest to find out who was the strongest or the most macho man, drinking the most glasses of an extra-strong liquor that tasted like anything but liquor.

His curiosity was the vehicle that transported him to try or discover the secrets of the deep side of life; in this way, he learned and became convinced of things in the objective world. Sometimes, it pushed him to walk in extreme environments, exposing him to severe dangers. For example, on one occasion, while studying biology and trying to do the most exciting experiments in class, he needed to know how deadly snake venoms were. It was not enough to read the books on the subject; he needed to experience it himself. Breaking the law and putting his life at risk, he entered the forbidden forest. The most poisonous snakes in the area lived there. First, he went with the idea of just taking some pictures of those animals. However, after taking splendid pictures, a giant snake bit him after he reached his hand into its cave out of curiosity. The venom was lethal. Doctors evacuated him immediately but, on the way, pronounced him dead. Still, miraculously, he breathed again after two minutes. When he heard what had happened, he said, smiling, "The wild grass never dies."

Another thing he adored were the libraries. They were his science and knowledge monasteries. There, he found the resources to feed his ideas. To know or to know more was for him like honey on the tip of his mind's tongue; it nourished his brain's neurons. He enjoyed navigating with passion and ecstasy along knowledge's magical, powerful and invisible paths.

He sought adventures in the known world, the unknown world and the dimensional world.

When he had free time, he became a fanatic UFO hunter. 'This human had encountered extraterrestrials who took him to their ship.' Sometimes, he had conversations like this with people that left one simultaneously perplexed, impressed and dumbfounded. From KORP, you could hear extraordinary, extravagant, off-the-record, outlandish and extrasensory personal experiences. Because of that, people sometimes didn't take what he said seriously. They thought he had experienced hallucinations. He was indifferent and always remained indifferent to people's opinions and comments about him. He was happy in his own skin.

By nature, he was a dreamer. Ordinary people would say he was a daydreamer. In The Thinker's position, he developed a peculiar 'sixth sense'[1] to understand the surrounding reality. Logic made little sense to him. Instead, he could not find answers in the logical but in the illogical, extraordinary and his mind experiments.

Sometimes, he found answers to his concerns in the most unexpected places or reasoned unusual situations from which he took conclusions to guide himself as he walked. For example, while reading a book of famous sayings or phrases, he wanted to understand the concept of 'running against the current'. To do so, he visualised an athletic race with hundreds of participants, of which he was one. When the starting pistol gun sounded, he started running from the finish line towards the starting point. In contrast, the other participants ran towards the finish line. Halfway through the race, he was in the middle, running against the enormous crowd. Thanks to that image, he could better understand the phrase 'running against the current'. He did such mental exercises because KORP believed thinking was free and sacredly respected freedom of thought. That way, he discovered how to look at life from another perspective.

KORP avoided personal arguments or lengthy discussions with people. Not because he ran away or was a coward, but because people would not understand his thinking or reasoning behind his statements. He knew that very well. Sometimes, when he explained his point of view, people thought he was mocking them.

Because of how things worked for him, he always struggled when faced with the new truth about something he had already created or had assimilated as truth. If he learned that the world was square, for him, it was fair; and if someone came and told him it was not square but round, this new concept would derail him from his position. He would get lost, deviated or disoriented. He had to be one hundred per cent sure this was the truth when

---

1. **Sixth sense:** He had a special feeling that doing something was right. He secured situations that weren't clear to him through this feeling. This sixth sense helped him make big economic or commercial decisions. Most of the time, his good decisions came from there.

learning something. Besides his colleague, The Thinker, no one else knew about this personal problem in his life.

"Perhaps for that reason he expected others to come to him? I'm speculating." (The Thinker)

Yes, that is right. Also, KORP created in his mind scenes of theatrical dramas from which he generated his mathematical formula for life. He named these scenes, images and ideas 'my avenues' and were his formulas or codes of life. They consistently guided him as he walked along, and he applied them to time management in his daily activities.

He was a natural philosopher and a great fan of the Greek and other classical philosophers' cultures. Even on subjects incongruous for 'normal' people, he enjoyed philosophising. Sometimes, he would picture himself delivering philosophical lectures in immense Greco-Roman arenas or dressed like a Greek philosopher.

When KORP was alone, he pulled out the philosopher's costume he had used as an actor in a school play, where he had played the Greek philosopher Thales of Miletus with his saying, 'The greatest thing is space because it includes everything'. Dressed in that robe, he philosophised about space in front of his audience, The Thinker, his colleague.

While travelling, he had become accustomed to mental relaxation by repeating phrases, sayings or slogans. These were mental exercises that he did after a tiresome workday. He sometimes played with words, formulating whimsical and fanciful terms that years later became part of the fine print of his business contracts. For example, if he said, 'Where there is a way ...', he would complete the rest of the sentence himself: '... there is an opportunity to do extraordinary things, find solutions, win and not lose, embrace peace and not war, find love, achieve success, give someone hope, do something good for the planet, enjoy life my way, love someone' and thousands more.

KORP never doubted himself or the formulation of his pathways. If unsure, he would sit in the same position as his colleague, The Thinker, and meditate for many minutes or hours. Then, he would only move or leave his corner if he was so sure.

"I would dare say that the day KORP says he needs a second opinion will be the day when he will be in trouble – deep trouble. I can assure you he will be in severe trouble." (The Thinker)

Definitely. Another thing KORP loved to do was gamble, of course. Gambling was his delight, the fragrance that recharged his five basic human senses, and his 'particular sixth sense', with super exciting energy. Betting houses were his favourite shrines where, by playing, he would challenge fate. He knew all the gambling halls in the city. However, he resorted to those places where only the most reckless people bet on things of extreme value, even their own lives.

Once, in a bet, he lost his only car. This loss caused him grief for several weeks. Nothing could replace poor Percy, the name of his beloved car. He had told his colleague, The Thinker, "Percy has a unique smell," and he would not replace it with another. As it was, he never had a car again; instead, he had a motorbike – a Vespa.

Likewise, on a bet, he almost lost his house, too. He kept it, thanks to the lightning strike that hit the area on the gamble day. The lightning was of such magnitude that it cut the entire city's electricity for a few hours, and they had to suspend the game. He was fortunate.

"I sometimes suspect that was how he lost Kate: betting on her in the game to determine whether fate wanted them to be together. From time to time, as the consequences of bullying, KORP had these kinds of suicidal tendencies in gambling games, where he would risk his most valuable belongings or things to find out whether fate wanted him to possess them." (The Thinker)

It would be a lie if someone said KORP was poor and gambled to win easy money. He kept his parents' inheritance in two safes in the basement of his house; one was full of gold, and the other was full of jewellery and money that he had never spent because he never needed it. He loved being independent.

At an early age, he learned to work. Just after his tenth birthday, he worked in the central market of his native town.

People knew him as a Land Rover,[2] a nickname in that place. As I mentioned, he was passionate about his work and full of the will to get things done. So, he worked as a newspaper distributor, messenger boy, shoeshine boy, food delivery boy, and even as a weeper.[3]

You may ask, 'So why didn't he gamble the money he had in the basement of his house instead of betting against his car or house?' The answer is simple. That's how **KORP** was: he liked to challenge, to defy destiny; he delighted in playing with fire. It was his way of checking his luck. His life needed to know if fate was on his side.

Sometimes, guilt arose from within him, pushing him to think that life despised him and was not with him. To certify that wasn't the truth, he needed proof from destiny, and in gambling, he convinced himself of this. For that reason, winning was crucial for him; it was the only way to ensure that life was at peace with him.

At the weekends, after spending all night in gambling houses, he returned home with all kinds of gold objects, such as watches, rings or any valuable thing; some of them he won in gambling and others he stole from drunkards. I am not joking! And he justified himself in front of his colleague, The Thinker, by saying, "I didn't steal them; I simply picked them up from those who didn't need them."

The idea of saving and hoarding also fascinated him. He maintained that 'one should accumulate as much as one can; then, and only then, can one get through the winter'. He got that idea from his hamster. He admired how his hamster, naturally and

---

2.   **A Land Rover** is an off-road vehicle. People on the market didn't know how to pronounce it or what it meant. It became a colloquial word and referred to someone who was an outstanding worker.

3.   **Weepers** were women who worked at funeral parlours, and their job was dramatising. In the towns or cities, making the most significant impression of someone's death was customary. When the victims had no relatives to mourn them, the funeral parlour hired women to accompany them in the wake and then go behind the coffin on the way to the cemetery, and all along the way, they were to mourn dramatically; it was their job. In KORP's world, there were various companies of weepers, depending on their pockets. Sometimes, in the absence of women, they hired men and disguised them as weepers.

spontaneously, hoarded as much food in its mouth as it could hold, like other animals in nature.

Another thing he took meticulous care of was his shoes – perhaps with excessive devotion. For him, his shoes should always be clean and shiny. He mystically believed one could tell a lot about a person by how he cared for their boots. If one didn't clean their shoes properly, they might as well have opened their mouths to reveal where they had been the night before. The footprints left by shoes were mighty messengers and mute witnesses.

Another habit he developed from childhood was that he never lowered his face when he walked, especially while being involved in a fight or just after coming out of one. It didn't matter how big the opponent was; he controlled his gaze and held his face high. He had learned the face-up attitude at the market, where he had worked as a child. In that place, he offered or performed various services from a workspace allocated to him, from helping carry shopping baskets for older adults to taking messages between traders or looking after the stalls or shops. Adults working in this market also had to contend for their place with people experiencing homelessness; in these disputes, they sometimes had to use force to get their jobs respected. Some adults would sometimes arrive too drunk to work there and start chaotic scenes, forcing the police to intervene. KORP would also stand up bravely against these men to protect his workspace. If someone caused him trouble, he would stand in front of the person with a raised face and stick out his chest like a fighting cock, determined to protect his workspace. He fought with all kinds of people of different ages because there were not enough jobs for all of them.

Thankfully, no one harmed him; the shopkeepers cared for him, too. Sometimes, they fed and protected him so no one would hurt him in that hostile environment. He was not the only child who worked there – of course not – but he was one of the few who worked and studied simultaneously. He often sat, listened to shopkeepers' children read, and helped them with homework.

The shopkeepers advised him not to be like some working adults, who mostly spent their money on alcohol or prostitutes.

They suggested to him, 'When you grow up, you must become someone significant, someone who reaches far in life, someone who stands high up,' pointing to the top of the tallest building in the area.

No one could tell what the atmosphere was in his house, starting with his name, which sounded more like an acronym, making people curious about what it meant. Not even KORP himself knew; only his parents possessed this secret. Maybe one day, someone will reveal that secret to us. Who knows? Women in the market sometimes gossiped about his background; they said his parents adopted him, and some boldly said he was an illegitimate son. Some even swore they found him in a box because his biological father wanted his mother to abort him. Still, she escaped, gave birth in secret, and left the baby in a box at the door of a nursing home. I think these rumours were just market gossip. No one knew the truth except his parents.

Despite having younger siblings, he was always alone. His parents cared for him at this age because he was well-dressed and well-groomed, and his shoes were always clean and shiny. He appeared to be an intellectual, contrasting with his market work. He never brought his issues with bullying at school to his job at that young age; this was his rule. Instead, he consumed them at home in front of The Thinker. Whenever his tormentors bullied him at school, he stayed for hours in his corner at home. Closing the curtains in his room, he devoured the pain like biscuits while crying.

***

He maintained a disciplined and dedicated approach to his studies throughout his university years. He never left things for tomorrow as an avowed enemy of procrastination. To prevent stress, he would finish the work for the next day in advance. During one of his classes on philosophy, he heard that 'the present time' had only twenty-four hours to exist. This idea made him think of time from a mystical perspective. He said that to make the most of every hour, every minute and every second of the present time, one must live as if it were the last day of life.

That talk affected him so much that he assimilated it as absolute truth. From that moment on, it drove him to squeeze every second out of each daytime to make the most of things. Since then, he become obsessive about time management, so much so that he considered adopting it as his god. He admired the sound of ticking clocks; they made his mind travel in every direction of the universe.

Since his abusers were out of the way, he enjoyed life when and how he could; he had spectacular days and always made time for social activities with friends from school, university or his neighbourhood. He tried to take his mind off his loved one, filling his thoughts with things that were, as he called them, productive. He did this to ease the pain of Kate's absence.

When he was younger, he did baffling teenage things, too. Together with Kate, two years before she left, they were members of the Open Mind club, with whom they organised many activities that drew university student crowds to free themselves of … no one knew of what, but they did it. This club imposed many social activities on the community of students. Some activities were charitable; others were too liberal and excessive, for which they were always in trouble with the city municipal authorities who monitored them.

For example, he and Kate, plus some of his classmates who were members of this club, had to sleep in prison cells for two nights after they imposed a university-wide 'Mankini Day' activity to raise funds for the city's Adolescent Rehabilitation. This activity forced the university to close its doors because of a lack of modesty. However, they raised a lot of money for the rehabilitation centre. Both were involved in extreme activities like this one, but always with beneficial ends, which balanced their extremisms under the motto 'End justifies the means'.

At university, he had knowledgeable teachers and learned much from them about science, physics and robotics, but biology was his all-time favourite topic.

***

Since he was a child, he had developed existential questions. When he worked in the market, he stared at the meat of the animals sold by the butchers. They sometimes brought whole animals and hung them up to be cut up for customers. Looking at these animals, he wondered and tried to understand where life's power rested. With that question in mind and looking for answers, while he studied human biology in college, he dissected human biological systems, like the cardiovascular system, nervous system, etc. Then, he displayed them separately in crystallised transparent human gel bodies so that you could see nothing but the human system inside the human gel body when viewed through the light. They were fascinating specimens! For example, if he displayed the cardiovascular system in a crystallised gel body, through the light, one could visualise the heart, arteries, veins and even the tiny blood vessels distributed throughout the body with high precision. One could see where and how far the veins and blood vessels extended.

His country's most prestigious medical museums and national galleries exhibited these biological samples. He won a national prize for these works: a scholarship to study biology at a university. Please don't ask me where he got these biological systems; I don't know. But were they from real people? Yes, they were.

He loved the constitution of the biological bodies of living beings. Their collaborative working style captivated him. He concluded that "the human body is the function of several biological systems amalgamated by the first breath, united by the force of life".

Above all, he loved studying human cells, calling them 'micro-fantastic biological factories' or 'tiny biological factories'. He believed that cells, with their complex and precise genetic architecture, couldn't appear out of nowhere. Still, some intelligent force or power has designed them. Fantastic pieces of genetic engineering rebuild the human body and sustain living beings' biological structure, limited only by time degeneration: ageing.

Ageing, for him, was a setback that he could not understand how or where it came from; he associated it with death. So, studying the regeneration of the human body became his particular Pandora's Box. When he thought about the revival of the human body from cells, the hairs on the back of his neck stood on end. He said, "Studying cell regeneration means entering a sacred field reserved only for those who dare defy death."

***

After finishing his university studies, he immediately devoted himself to inventiveness, aiming to enter the business world. For him, that was very clear. After all, he studied two science degrees: biology because he was passionate about it and cyber robotics engineering because he wanted to make money.

On the day he graduated, he started his company. He hired some of his classmates and, with them, set up a small factory to invent and produce cybernetic products. Some people he hired stayed with him until the end of his days; they also became world-renowned scientists.

He invented some original and unique products, but perhaps some were too eccentric, which once almost cost him his company's closure.

When creating his inventions, he had no limits, religious beliefs, modesty or prejudices; he was neutral in his views. He invented things to make people happy or to fill them with pleasure.

Some of his inventions caused such a stir in society that some people complained, calling the radio or the authorities to do something about it. They felt his products invaded their personal space when he advertised them on television or the internet. But other people were grateful for his other products because they provided solutions to their needs.

Domestic robots with animal morphology gave his company a boost. They were small interactive robotic animals that spoke or made animal sounds, like an EL-Xsa,[4] but without the internet. Sunlight recharged them, and they only required window light. These robots were called 'Kanimal'.[5] They became the favourite products of older adults and children because they were attractive, looked almost tangible, and were practical. They did not eat or need an outhouse. For example, if the Kanimal was a cat, this cat looked real and walked around the house; if the owner wanted it to meow, they programmed it to meow, etc.

In a short time, he created many products that quickly did well in the market, and people liked his Kanimal brand, which became famous. He also made high-quality products that the public could wear, like thermal K-jackets. The sun's rays heated these jackets, which do not need batteries. Also among these products was a military favourite: the TSIK-7 Intelligent Symbiotic Suit. These suits were uniforms explicitly made to protect soldiers when deployed to war. He made them from a strong, lightweight, super-flexible material that resembled a motorcyclist's uniform. Once the soldier wore the suit, it attached itself to the human body through sensor-biological-cybernetic transmitters. Its function was to start a dialogue with the human body's immune system, thus beginning the symbiotic process. These transmitters were flexible tubular filaments inserted through the pores of the skin of the arms and legs. Once inside the pores, they read the person's immune system and established a symbiotic health number. The symbiotic health number was one hundred if the person was healthy. The number one hundred stated that the soldier's bodily functions, i.e. body temperature, heart rate, respiration, blood oxygen, etc. were in average condition. KORP incorporated morphine, penicillin, paracetamol, antibiotics or vitamins in the helmet and the overall jacket. The suit would instantly detect any wounds or illnesses in a soldier through the symbiotic health number, which, in this case,

---

4. **The EL-Xsa** digital interactive equipment has programming that enables it to answer specific questions. It is a robot that works when connected to an internet provider.
5. **Kanimal**: A robot with animal morphology, almost independent, interacted with the owner as a pet. They programmed these robots to behave like natural animals.

would be lower than one hundred. Then, through the sensor-biological-cybernetic transmitters, the uniform automatically supplied the body with the medicines until they reached a medical centre. These suits saved many soldiers' lives, especially when conflicts were in remote areas.

In inventing the TSIK-7 symbiotic suits, KORP merged biology and cybernetics to form a revolutionary science called Biodermatik.[6] He turned this revolutionary scientific discovery into art to create mechanisms to protect the human body.

"It would help if you told our readers how KORP discovered the Biodermatik base materials." (The Thinker)

Of course. An older adult sometimes left food or homemade sweets for KORP. When he came home, he would find the food in the driveway. He wanted to know who the person was. One day, he worked from home and, looking through the window, saw her. She was his neighbour who made the most noise in the neighbourhood. This older adult suffered from a disease in one of her lower limbs, made clear from the way she walked. Seeing her through the window, KORP realised the pain she suffered every time she took a step. To ease the pain, he designed special equipment to help her walk. While creating the materials for this equipment, he discovered certain materials were malleable and compatible with other materials when reduced to molecular size. He alloyed them with other materials, achieving several new materials; some were super-strong solids, and others were super-flexible and super-strong. Also, these new materials were compatible with the bone and muscle structures of the human body. As a result, he decided that replacing the diseased limb's bony portion was more practical than creating the equipment. He and his team of scientists managed, through these materials, for the older adult to walk normally

---

6. In the KORP world, **Biodermatik** was the science that amalgamated biological elements in humans and animals with synthetic materials. For example, when they replaced limbs that a soldier lost due to an anti-personnel bomb explosion, through Biodermatik, the artificial limbs were attached to the human body like a natural limb, even in the skin, in such a way that there were no traces of being manufactured. It was a science that offered much hope in reconstructive medicine.

and without pain. Since then, little by little, he has perfected these nano-bio-robotic materials and called them 'Biodermatik materials', thus starting this new science. It was a gigantic step towards reconstructive medicine, which catapulted him as the father of this science.

Besides his symbiotic suits, he perfected his robotic technology. He based his robotic creations on the mechanisms of the human body, from which he got ideas for creating Biodermatik limbs.

As you can see, his tendency to attack or evade bodily degeneration was genuine, and his determination increased daily.

***

Many people preferred KORP inventions. Gradually, his products replaced those of his competitors in both local and national markets. Eventually, the government of his country, through the military, became his biggest customer, with whom he signed large contracts to supply his symbiotic suits to the National Army.

Years later, thanks to Biodermatik science, he amalgamated natural and synthetic skin. From then on, when he replaced legs or arms with artificial limbs, they looked so realistic. You couldn't tell if they were natural or synthetic skin. The synthetic skin joining them together contained no marks or scars. They were fantastic!

Such discoveries earned him prominence in the country's Academy of Biological Sciences and Nanotechnology. In turn, KORP made a place in the heart of science and history books. In addition, the military opened its doors for him to use its scientific facilities, where he advanced his knowledge and research on molecular management and manufacturing atomic devices.

As his fortune and fame grew, he ventured out more often to travel the world with the military. He enjoyed travelling on warships and visiting military conflicts around the globe. While in the war camps, he closely studied the situations where soldiers exposed themselves to danger to improve his symbiotic suits.

On one of these visits, his military client invited him to a village severely suffering from the ongoing conflict between family clans. This military customer wanted to protect his soldiers with a product safeguarding against anti-personnel bombs. He had an experience that would mark him in those lands for the rest of his life. It may be worth mentioning.

In that village, his client took him to visit an old hospital where doctors treated wounded soldiers. Many had lost some lower limbs, such as legs or feet, because of anti-personnel bomb explosions. He took several photographs to study the wounds and, together with his team, made diagrams to replace them with Biodermatik limbs. One morning, as he left that old hospital tent, his gaze fell on a gigantic, polished statue carved from granite stone. It was a statue of some god or deity carved in the human form of a warrior. The figure was full of tiny holes and bumps, a sign of several attempts to knock it down.

This statue made a big impression on him. He walked around the effigy, admiring the face, the physique and the posture. He put his fingers over the holes and marks left by attempts to destroy it. The statue seemed determined not to budge, for it had a defiant attitude and was gigantic. KORP admired the figure greatly and said, "Whoever it is, this stone titan is bold; neither blows, bullets, rain nor wind can stand against it."

"It belongs to the age of Victorious Cultures," replied the doctor who accompanied him.

As KORP looked at the statue, the doctor told him this story:

"Heaven and Earth were at war once. In their eagerness to restore peace, the gods built a golden ladder so that both humans could ascend into their presence. In addition, the gods could visit to see how the Earth was doing. As they walked on Earth, some gods fell so in love with the beautiful human maidens that some took them for themselves and procreated with them. From this union were born people of mighty stature, demigod titans, who became mighty heroes on Earth. These demigods founded colossal civilisations, empires and magnificent Victorious Cultures, which endured for many years. Over time, through their strength, these powerful beings imposed their will on humans across the Earth. They corrupted the land by shedding innocent blood.

"The blood of the humans cried out for justice to the gods, who grieved for what had happened, banished the demigod titans, confining them to the farthest mountains and darkest deserts of the Earth, to avoid further shedding of innocent human blood. The demigods planned an invasion of the gods' home because of this punishment, which infuriated them. For this invasion, they would use the golden ladder under the motto, 'As on Earth, so in heaven'.

"The plan's boldness alarmed the gods when they learned about it. Then, after a heavenly council decision, the gods destroyed the golden ladder to stop this plan. Some gods protested this decision because of their children on Earth, but this did not prevent its destruction.

"The gods watched in sadness and helplessness the destruction of the golden ladder, and they promised themselves that one day they would replace it with a robust ladder difficult to break; this ladder will restore heaven's relationship with Earth forever.

"Shortly after the destruction of the ladder, the demigod titans built a tower to reach heaven. As they built, they repeated, 'As on Earth, so in heaven.' Seeing the tower under construction, the gods whispered to the wind, 'Send a hurricane to destroy the tower.' The hurricane did not match the demigod's determination and gave up its attempt. The gods spoke to lightning, which also succumbed to the tower's strength. Then they spoke to the fire, which fled in terror before the demigods' steadfastness. The gods ordered the rain to flood the Earth with no other remedy. Rain opened the fountains of the heavens and the Earth. In a few days, it covered the entire face of the Earth above the tower and the highest peak, killing the demigod titans. Only one family of humans and hundreds of animal species survived in an ark from this universal disaster.

"This statue is from that time; not even water could knock it down," said the doctor as he bowed his head to the statue while KORP touched the feet of the colossal stone titan. The figure held a finely carved sword pointing at the sky in defiance, and the other hand raised its fist. Its face showed hatred. It was about a hundred and forty-seven feet high.

"Fascinating," said KORP, and he left the scene.

The ladder tale and the gods descending from the sky piqued KORP's interest. He soon returned to this area to learn more about this historic land. During his stay in this hospital, he set up a laboratory in the region near the Stone Colossus area.

While there, he visited and learned about the Victorious Cultures and was deeply involved in the regional wars. His aim in revealing himself to danger this way was to study how soldiers involuntarily exposed themselves to high risks at war. In these high-risk situations, he perfected the manufacturing of symbiotic suits, which he complemented with better applications and more protection possibilities. While offering his scientific services, he also learned more about the demigods' history and collected archaeological material. The artefacts that former empires had left behind in those regions shocked him, and he admired the magnificence and power they once possessed.

Amid these experiences, he associated victory with complete regeneration. He said, "Without complete regeneration, there is no victory. For something to regenerate, you must subject it to degeneration, and from there, something will begin its regeneration, the fruit of which will be victory."

He based this conclusion on biological cells' efficient work when repairing wounds. He felt that the spirit and traces of the gladiatorial demigod titans still regenerate history. They were permeating the electromagnetic space of these geographical regions with their strength.

Sometimes, he would sit at the feet of the stone titan and converse with him as he did with his colleague, The Thinker. These journeys inspired him. They motivated him to cherish the idea that he would one day raise his own Victorious Culture, his empire. 'An empire whose glory leaves deep and unforgettable traces in history, so that one day people will remember it with admiration. Like these Victorious Cultures, it will be an empire whose memory lives forever,' he thought.

2. Building an empire

Actual politics lies in the art of governing well.

KORP matured and learned much about human relations, commerce and industry as the years progressed. But he could not change his personality; this was impossible for him to change. He solved that problem this way: he memorised all the steps to deal with people and then put them into practice. Every step he took in that direction was slow and painful, but accurate. By doing so, he finally got into the heart of his country's government. Soon, his company became a significant asset to national defence thanks to his symbiotic suits, Biodermatik products and his 'developed ability' to relate to people.

Travelling through the political world, he watched the actions of these rulers closely and how they managed the reins of their country's destiny. He could see for himself how murky this environment was. The public knew well that politicians made decisions that benefitted themselves, or almost always. This corruption was an open secret that made people wonder if it was true.

"These are acts of blatant and undeniable corruption by national leaders," said many people as he delved deeper into this matter. These rumours led KORP to visit the Treasury Department for the truth one day. When asking for information about the contracts the government awarded in the region, he discovered many politicians laundered tax money through their companies by signing dubious agreements. He wasn't sticking his nose where he shouldn't, but his obligation was to know the truth.

He was a citizen and wanted to be responsible for his country. Any citizen could find out about their tax money in these dependencies.

Another thing that knocked him on the head were the laws the government dictated. These laws carried thousands of unnecessary bureaucratic requirements written as riddles that were challenging to interpret. These laws negatively affected his company and most businesses because of a lack of transparency.

He sometimes left government offices pale because he felt bullied by the extreme bureaucratic system in those places. However, he clarified that his company's contracts were transparent. Since he, too, benefitted from the contracts he signed with the military, he overlooked these trespasses.

On one occasion, the government invited him to present a project to improve the sophistication of war material for national defence. It was a very ambitious military project by the government; by then, his company was already working on atomic-molecular projects. KORP had successfully developed war material whose explosive-expansive range was above that of the conventional bomb. Later, he called this war material 'mushrooms'[7] after the shape they produced when they exploded. The government wanted to buy these 'mushroom atomic bombs' as part of its geopolitical security doctrine.

The poor guy left that meeting shaken, furious, frustrated and pale because of the ministers' proposal. Since then, he had preferred to bide his time and decided, for the time being, not to return to government offices because they insisted on laundering the money from the overpricing of that project through his company. It was a project whose cost overrun well into fifteen figures.[8] He left that meeting with no desire to do more business with these politicians, only when there was a change in government. "I don't want to waste my time," he muttered.

"One of the main reasons for rejecting that proposal was that he discovered it was a trap. Many companies and some MPs wanted KORP to stain his hand with dodgy money for them to take his military contracts." (The Thinker)

---

7. **'Mushrooms'** refer to atomic bombs.
8. **Fifteen figures**: equivalent to £100,000,000,000,000.

***

"Tell me, who do you work for?" (The Thinker)

There was a time when planetary economic reality suffered a severe setback. Not even KORP's country escaped from that disaster. In its eagerness to close the inflation gap, the government created new taxes and put the burden of inflation on large companies, including his own.

Since profits were only enough to pay taxes, many industrial companies closed their local operations; some moved to lower-tax countries. Only this would make a decent profit. There was no alternative.

KORP was not one to walk away. So, over this injustice, he stood up to the government like a fighting cock. He did something no person in business would do for fear of repercussions from the government itself: he invited himself to a meeting in the Senate to intervene. This is one of his eccentricities. In situations like this, he was never orthodox. In the Senate, he had a severe discussion with the members of the parliament about the need for more transparency in the country's economic reports. He demanded explanations of how and where the government invested the tax money. At that meeting, no one could give objective reasons or explicit descriptions of how and where the money was being spent (he knew precisely where the money had gone). In his intervention, he demanded that they be obliged to recount the whereabouts of these resources, and soon. It was a heated meeting, no doubt. It shook the too-big coat sleeves of the ruling politicians of the day. The news media across the nation and abroad covered KORP's intervention live. Early the following day, the government published, in the local press, an obscure and unconvincing list of works executed in the country and little-known regions, including the blessed overpricing. Above all, it also reversed the government's decision to increase taxes on the country's large companies. That same day, also on the front page of the press, a photograph showed him speaking in the Senate. It had this headline: 'KORP, the champion of the nation's economic rights.' This headline did not please the politicians of the day, who had left him alone for the time being. However, since then, they looked for an opportunity to remove him from his business relationship with the government and the military at any cost.

New regulations adopted by the newly elected government were another instance in which politicians tipped the balance in their favour. It was where they rubbed their hands to catch a fish in troubled waters.

They had many tricks or formulas encrypted in the new government decrees to amass their loathsome fortunes. One trick they used was this: each new government paralysed the projects the companies had been carrying out for the previous government; then, the new government forced the companies to update their existing legal situation with the state. In those newly created legal status arrangements, corrupt politicians applied their robust magic laws for personal gain.

These economic recipes only increased the anaemia of the country's poor and ailing economy, and the country became even more flawed. Legal companies and businesspeople viewed the new government negatively since they applied the same recipes and offered no benefits to anyone except themselves. This problem was like a broken record: it repeated repeatedly.

Sadly, ordinary citizens and the most vulnerable people could do nothing. However, they took the most damage from this outrage and these painful blows. The same corrupt people had entrenched themselves in the strategic places of the parliament. They always won because they had the upper hand. These critical situations in his country made him seriously consider a political career. He strongly identified with vulnerable people. He remembered the destitute people sleeping at the market door, the children who worked, and people experiencing homelessness who slept on the streets. 'What am I waiting for?' he asked himself.

***

In his thirties, while his companies brought him worldwide fame and fortune, he returned to the land of Victorious Cultures. He wanted to observe and learn more about politics. While there, he often visited the Stone Titan Statue site. He noted the stories people told him about the glorious past of these regions.

In these foreign lands, he also became more deeply involved with geopolitics. His products reached markets outside his own country, where orders were larger. By then, he had also manufactured weaponry for war, especially explosives. He wanted to know how his products would affect political realities in global conflicts. He also wanted to know what regulations he should implement or to whom he could or should not sell.

War became more acute because this territory was rich in natural energy resources, and some parts of these areas were now under the control of the enemy. The law of the jungle applied the direction of the strongest. His client was weaker than his neighbours, so KORP offered to help him; then he became fully involved in the conflict. He sent hundreds of mercenaries he had hired using a guerrilla warfare strategy. They did a good job and recaptured the lost areas quickly. He also joined the front lines, assuming command of a Red Hawks platoon.

"Such situations excited his curiosity and enlivened his perception of life, making him feel special. It was as if he planned to die, but only for a few seconds, and then he would return to life again. He was curious to cross the barrier between life and death." (The Thinker)

As happens in war, he was once seriously wounded – mortally wounded. The enemy captured him and interned him in a concentration camp for war prisoners. The enemy did not realise who he was. His advisers instructed KORP not to reveal his true identity from the beginning to avoid danger. So it was: the enemy never knew who he was.

In that concentration camp, he was left to die with a bullet in his leg; in the flesh, he put his symbiotic suit on to test it. Amazingly, he survived thanks to his symbiotic suit. He pretended to be dead, and on the day of his burial, a family took him out of the area alive and cared for him in a house in the middle of the countryside – out of the way of conflict – until his wounds healed and then returned him safely. After he had recovered from his injuries, destiny placed him back on the rails of his life's purpose: to build his empire.

Back home, he worked alongside his colleague, The Thinker. He drew objective conclusions about the internal affairs of his newly formed empire. He noted significant changes in education, health, law, defence, culture, religion, etc. These conclusions led him to refine the principles, values, rules and concepts governing a nation, country or empire. 'An empire?' he thought.

He felt that, by establishing a different political system, he could change his country's political structure from the inside out: "It must be a structural change from the core, from the principles, from the laws, from the regulations, from the small print," he said.

At the end of each day, he returned enthusiastically to his favourite corner of the room, his laboratory of ideas. He would lock himself away for long hours to chat with his colleague, The Thinker. He would write his plans and read them aloud for him to hear: "What do you think about this? What do you think of these reforms? Do you think this is what the people need?" he would say. Sometimes, he took off his clothes and took the same position as his colleague, The Thinker. In that position, he indeed rested. "It must be a change in the rules, a change in the modus vivendi of this old government system, a change to the current structure to replace it with a resilient, durable and prosperous structure," he concluded.

"A structure that preserves the interests of all the country's inhabitants equally and is immune to those who use the system for personal gain. A system where those with the least have a decent roof over their heads where they can spend the night. In addition, they have a place to quench their hunger and thirst," he pondered.

He closely identified and associated the word 'change' with 'regeneration' when considering changing the essence of his country's government system. For him, 'regeneration' summed up a profound structural change, a new birth at the zero point where life's force begins.

"Under the principle of regeneration, I will improve the reality and circumstances of my country, plagued by ongoing corruption and constant social and economic instability. Our nation would integrate into the river where limitless financial resources flow," KORP said while planning to build his empire. His mind created an almost unreal world for his country, envisioning a way of life impossible for 'normal' humans to achieve.

He stretched ideas for his empire like pizza dough to accommodate as many probabilities and positive possibilities in designing his new imperial structure as possible. Above all, he left nothing to chance. 'That change must not be chameleon-like or superficial. It must be a big change from the root, from its very foundation,' he thought as he brought to mind the principle of human cell regeneration in the affected areas of the body, which rebuilds and renews the body.

'In and from that depth, the cells create a regenerative miracle,' he thought. He shook his head at the beat as the hours passed to space music's rhythm. He made those innocuous head movements as his senses worked to create new things in his mind.

Little by little, he envisioned monumental buildings, highways, educational centres, hospitals, sports centres, significant recreational areas and gigantic industrial centres on land and in space. They were so real he could almost touch them. "An empire where people need nothing," he said aloud for his colleague, The Thinker, to hear.

In just a few years, KORP accumulated much wealth, profoundly influenced public life and became powerfully influential worldwide. He positioned his company as the dominant arm of his country's military capability. They awarded him the rank of general for his contribution to the nation's military. In time, the shadow and heat of military power would be his symbiotic protective suit for his political and geopolitical career.

His close relationship with the military opened his eyes and helped him look beyond his reality. That influence gave rise to a deep, perhaps too radical, patriotism for his nation, making him a nationalist.

With this new feeling, he put his country first in his global vision. This patriotism gave him a sense of national pride. He had an intense desire to grasp a prosperous future and bring it into the present reality of his nation as his new challenge. That also implied changes in several aspects of his existence: first, he had to capitalise sincerely on his knowledge of his nation's political reality; then, he had to work on his personality so that he would no longer leave people with their hands outstretched when greeting him. He would have to learn to be empathetic with people, even if inside he remained as cold as ice. He needed the human side to be a skilful politician. This last aspect was the most challenging part of the job.

KORP exhibited a lot of patience and methodism when learning political aspect, which gave him a tremendous advantage; however, he did not believe in the far-off future for his country. For him, the future had to be seized and brought forward to the present reality, where he existed as quickly as possible, just as he took opportunities. He suffered from the idea of a prosperous future that seemed too distant, utopian and unattainable. It made him sick to think of the future that lived in the clouds, the magnificent future that lives on in the flattery of charlatans, or the glorious future that lives encrusted in the unfulfilled promises of rulers, or the future that, when you want it to come to you – as soon as you touch it – vanishes like soap bubbles and has no intention of being realised.

He mocked the future sold by charlatans – the lawmakers and MPs in his country – saying, "I compare it to a super-exquisite apple hung on a stick, held by a rider and placed in front of his horse's nose. Poor horse! No matter how fast it runs, it will never reach that super-delicious apple because this is the idea. That is how rulers, MPs and lawmakers designed our nation's future. No matter how hard our generations try, they will never reach that prosperous future, so that they will bear the pain produced by that maliciously designed governance system. Our children need not suffer; we are here to pave the way for them. It is our duty. Like the horseman, politicians kept the apple on the stick in their pockets to exploit the poor horse's strength. That is how they use your shoulders to build their wealth."

Whenever he published something in the press, he referred to the situation in the country with a language that attracted attention from politicians; this was his intention. Gradually, some political parties approached him for private talks, chose a place away from cameras or microphones, or invited him to play golf. They would tempt him with persuasive proposals, saying he could make a handsome profit if he joined them. In these meetings, **KORP** studied them and learned from their ways. These rulers could smell the power and security emanating from his personality, so they sought at all costs to have him on their side as an ally. They enticed him with significant corporate business opportunities to provoke a smile or nod of approval on his face, but to no avail. Instead, he just watched them coldly and studied them.

Also, he was always loyal to his political party. Although he was not as active as most members, he still supported his co-idealists, who helped him in business relations with the government and globally. Therefore, he would not abandon them because he gave them his promise, and **KORP** always delivered what he had promised.

***

As his success spread, so did the rejection of his companies locally and globally. It was logical, and that is geopolitics. As the core grows, it makes its neighbours' space uncomfortable because of that growth. It is simply the natural effect of increasing. Many were jealous of him because of the position he had achieved in the military; they called him General **KORP**. His critics said he was too young to hold that rank. The government and the army needed him because he was the only one who stood up for the entire nation's interests. The military viewed **KORP** companies as strategic subjects.

In every national election, national leadership candidates requested a special meeting with him. If elected, they also asked for his support. At these meetings, he also almost ordered them, if elected, to respect the contracts he had signed with the government and the military.

"Conflict of interest? It was not KORP's decision that his companies occupied a primordial place within the government; it was the pure and sovereign decision of the government itself and the military, who had no choice. In war, national security took priority over any political argument." (The Thinker)

***

"A smile is the most effective antidote to melting the ice on people's faces; it emits an irresistible warmth." (The Thinker)

Within a few years, he became well-known in foreign policy as well. Some embassies or diplomatic representations gave him space to open a commercial office in their home nations to sell his products. He gained the admiration of many kingdoms for his contribution to science and cyber technology.

They also wanted him to introduce Biodermatik science into the university curriculum, and they invited him to talk about it at the parliaments. In these talks, he warned of anti-personnel bombs' destructiveness and advocated their elimination forever. In addition, he brought up the dirty wars that expansionist nations are still engaged in. He saw this type of bomb as part of post-war cannibalism.

Over time, he solidified his prestige and global presence. His military inventions were increasingly ambitious and sophisticated, primarily national security-related ones. Seeing how the market for his products was growing, he embraced it as an excellent opportunity to secure more commercial space. He also studied theatre, where he tried hard to appear charismatic in his human relations, albeit with difficulty, but somehow he succeeded. Having a global presence was vital to him.

Over the years, he learned to use patience methodically to execute any of his plans, even industrial and commercial ones. When he envisioned a goal, he planned it and walked towards it with much patience, step by step, little by little. Until that point, patience was his greatest virtue; with it, he had learned how to tame and control time. He said time was his favourite space vehicle. He immensely enjoyed controlling time in his way, so much so that he became highly proficient at it. For example, he could guess how much time had passed from his last action to the present, even in seconds, which is why some say the devil possessed him.

Above all, he did not waste time; he believed that 'the present time' had only twenty-four hours to exist. Over the years, what everybody expected happened: time became his god. He loved clocks to the extreme, so much so that, in his factories, he had hung incredibly stunning clocks to which his workers had to bow in reverence.

While on his journeys – when he visited the world's capitals in the high-income countries – he admired cathedrals. Sometimes, he could spend hours sitting there watching the ornaments they held. One day, impressed by the beauty of one of them, he bought the plans and made some changes to them. Choosing his finest property in the city, he had his famous Cathedral of the Clocks built in honour of his god Time.

For the architectural construction of this cathedral, he employed fifteen thousand people who worked in shifts twenty-four hours a day. It took two years to complete. It was an architectural marvel designed to house an infinite number of clocks that he had ordered from all four corners of the world.

The Cathedral of the Clocks was imposing, delicate and elegant. It had Gothic-medieval characteristics, with endless details carved in marble and exquisite stones. It was like a sanctuary whose front wall was the history of clocks and how they worshipped their god Time. Both the capital city and the nation declared it a heritage site. If one goes there, one has to light a candle and a fragrant-smelling stick as a sign of reverence for the god Time. He hired a religious sect dedicated to time study, which held intercession and worship ceremonies. Was this all part of his eccentricity? It may be part of his outlook on life.

***

For KORP and his companies, his thirties were the golden age, and he drifted in and out with the country's armies as the great protector. His favourite transports have always been and continue to be the gigantic and majestic warships; he called them 'steel horse riders' for the way they broke the waves and the wind in the sea.

His products continued to make their mark on the market. His symbiotic suits and the Biodermatik products and weapons he invented became more sophisticated. The newly developed weapons intended to deter the enemy; they neutralised enemy weapons without firing a single bullet. Many of these weapons worked with electromagnetic pulses that emitted heat capable of destroying the electronic control of enemy missiles, ships, planes, drones, satellites, etc. All these contributions meant hope for his country.

With his inventions and 'charisma', he quickly befriended politicians and was soon in a senatorial seat. His creations enabled his government to achieve regional military supremacy and a strategic place in world geopolitics. In addition, his country became a member of the World Peace Group.

His position as a senator did not prevent him from leading the army. He attended parliamentary sessions through a hologram. This prestigious political position also brought him authority and credibility in the eyes of the public. His voice became a reference point, and his words were believable. He did what he said and lived by what he said. Everyone talked about him: 'KORP will do what he says.'

He was always in the press with news of the latest technological inventions or famous KORP tips. While he kept pushing up, he didn't stop there. He only had one goal in life: to get to the top. He was determined and said to his collaborators, "No matter what, wherever I am, I will always get to the top because that is my place, my destiny."

For him, that was the place of genuine success, synonymous with the ultimate victory or the last sign of destiny – the ultimate glory, the last sign of fortune.

***

"One wise decision taken on time is worth more than a thousand super decisions made off time." (The Thinker)

He marvelled at the night sky lit by millions of stars one night as he peered out of his house's window. He searched himself for the willpower to give the final push to decide. To decide what? Take the decisive step towards establishing his empire. It was something he lacked that prevented him from achieving that goal. Maybe he needed more inspiration. Maybe. He took out his notes and his book, where he looked for the 'KORP Empire Layout' section in the notes. He began to read and reflect on the words he had written.

As he recalled, he occasionally looked out the window and wrote more. That night, he was so focused on reflection that time slipped away like water through his fingers. He left there in the morning. In his notes, he explicitly mentioned a new era on the planet, which he linked to the birth of his empire. He did not have a clear vision of when the day of that birth would arrive. Still, he had a strong feeling that this was on the way, so he agonised over the thought of not being ready if that day came at that instant. Although he had carefully written his plans, they were still subjective to him. He sought to solidify or bring these ideas to life, but needed to figure out where to start.

His empire's building formula, or structural equation, had the whimsical shape of a four-sided inverted pyramid whose central vertices met at the bottom, on which rested the surface, or fifth side – a kind of square funnel with a lid. He got this idea from the principle used by the antlion in the desert to hunt. This ant makes a funnel in the sand and hides at the bottom to wait. When an insect falls into this funnel, gravity pulls the victim down to the bottom; unable to escape, it becomes easy prey for the hunter.

KORP summarised his future empire's theoretical and structural formula in this pyramid. He described it this way: "Knowledge, Strength, Power and Absolute Control make up the four sides," and the fifth side or the surface he called the Imperial

Social System which he associated with the table with some water in the middle, which he always visualised.

He said that there was no Imperial Social System or surface without the four sides and he emphasised that the apex of the pyramid should be facing down because that made the surface tilt more efficiently and in the direction he wanted. It was the lightest and simplest way to manipulate the existential context of its inhabitants.

"This way of structuring the KORP Empire leaves me with several concerns. How does he know this way and formula will work when establishing his kingdom? It may be his old habit of defying fate in a game of chance. Or maybe it was a premonition?" (The Thinker)

Despite these conjectures, he inverted the pyramid, positioning the primary vertex downward for all events in the empire's life to descend to a single point via gravity.

'The day this happens will be the most glorious day of my life,' he thought. That was his wish.

He decided that, during the construction of his empire, the pyramid should be in a natural position, with the primary vertex facing upwards. He meant one had to earn merit to build it – that every way of organising things during the building of his empire should be in the shape of a pyramid. "Once I've finished building it, it will be the time to invert it," he said.

***

Many of history's greatest heroes never imagined ending up as the head of an empire. Some never dreamed of establishing a kingdom in their lifetime. Some became circumstantial emperors by inheriting an empire. Few designed and built their empires.

On those sheets of paper, KORP predestined its future. He was ready to launch it when the time came.

When he did things, he did it in this way: first, he planned everything thoroughly and then put it into practice. He was meticulous, detailed in his calculations, down to the millimetre. The precision that he exhibited was impressive. Then, he relied on those predestinations to walk. Those plans were like tracks, and he was on the train. He would say, "I need to plan my life this way." Every project, every goal and every idea he prescribed for himself was his path, destiny and North Star.

KORP emphasised that leaving his plans written this way helped him manage his life freely through his avenues. He said, "Without my avenues, I would wander aimlessly and without freedom, like a cloud blown by the wind from side to side. I would also walk like the dry and light leaves that always follow the wishes of the wind."

That was KORP, that human being who, when setting a goal, runs towards it no matter how long it takes to achieve it. Because he doesn't want to remain on the sidelines, immolated by inaction, and play the martyr for the rest of his life, he always runs toward the aim while carrying the torch of responsibility.

He will still carry the circumstances and experiences on his life's shoulders but when he reaches the goal he will regret none of them, even if they have been sad, withered, full of hate, compassion, pain, heroism, betrayal, unforgettable days, eternal nights bristling with the thorns of bullying or full of beautiful memories, some circumstances defeated, others lived or trapped, enjoyed, buried, tied, forgotten, remembered, decorated, transformed, questioned, repudiated or pulverised.

KORP will march until he reaches the goal. After all, that is what he had decided and predestined in his plans because that was his stubborn character: he honoured his decisions.

When he runs towards the goal, he is also methodical but so organised that he sometimes comes across as remarkably systematic. Still, with the attitude of a cheerful man who moves, tries, persists, picks himself up and wipes away tears, he does not lower his countenance; he always looks forward but never looks back. KORP is courageous and never runs away but faces his decisions; he never stops, never rests, always looks for solutions and only cares about reaching the goal, no matter what, no matter how. He makes mistakes but doesn't regret them; instead, he learns from them. He learns new things, plans, listens and puts what he knows into practice.

He had many followers on social media and in the press, whom he fed with his KORP tips and advice. "The key is to keep walking, no matter what," he told his supporters. He applies this reasoning to almost all his actions: 'Set a goal and walk towards it.'

"Planning to build an empire is a noble and perhaps romantic dream. However, walking towards it is revolutionary, bold, ambitious and extremely admirable. It will fascinate if KORP succeeds." (The Thinker)

3. Global crisis

Disrepute stains are like hot iron marks left on a garment. They stay forever.

The military was in and out of the country with General KORP. However, this did not prevent him from doing his job as a parliament senator; he continued attending Senate plenary meetings via holograms. His political party adored him more and more. There was something about him that appealed. Maybe the influence of his money or power? Maybe. It was like such a magnet.

While KORP companies were growing more robust around the globe, relations between countries were weakening. In a short time, the world's situation changed radically. New kingdoms and global powers arose, some with a predatory thirst and expansionist ambition. Others took their dominions into their neighbours' backyards, beyond their borders and continents.

Ruthlessly, the new global powers unleashed their devastating geopolitical expansionist machinery. Many countries, guided by their ancestors' wisdom, claimed to have inherited vast territory regions in every corner of the planet, even on the moon. With that argument in mind, which was just an excuse, they decided it was time to reclaim them. To that 'divine' end, they launched a voracious arms race.

The more skilled geopolitical experts annexed newly gained territories to their domains, while others gained new allies across the seas. The rise of these global powers also triggered a global shortage of raw materials for the arms industry; KORP was not exempt from this situation. Thousands of companies desperately sent their scout agents to find raw materials worldwide for their industries.

In every corner of the planet and across the seas, peaceful, friendly countries – rich in natural resources – only needed technology to industrialise these resources and generate work for their generations. Many powerful kingdoms established industrial and geopolitical alliances with them, so powerful monopoly trading blocs had formed, which, once established, ruthlessly depleted the natural resources of these friendly country allies.

Also, giant multinational companies would chase these friendly allied countries to convince them to do business with them because of their thirst for raw materials. Other global companies did not negotiate with these friendly governments. Still, they staged coups and took over the country, plain and simple. People who fell into the hands of these technological predators suffered tragic consequences, and they even lost their human rights without mercy if they stayed there or had no choice but to find a new place. Sadly, this was the reality of doing business with these giant industrial predators.

KORP was more sincere and direct in negotiating for raw materials. He carried a full array of his 'Toys'[9] on his steel horse riders to bend the will of any friendly allied countries. At the sight of the KORP weaponry, many countries knelt to accept the swap. It would make their mouths water if their armed forces possessed such weapons. "Let it all be in the name of national security," their national leaders retorted before signing the agreement.

With this way of trading, little by little, KORP patiently planted his Toys worldwide. By then, he had developed the next generation of his 'mushroom bombs' that, by manipulating the nuclei of atoms, produced destructive effects of catastrophic magnitude. These Toys were not simply guns or hand grenades; he

---

9. **Toys** refers to the war weaponry KORP manufactured. The types of artefacts he manufactured for the war were technologically advanced to stop an invasion from neighbouring armies.

called them his favourite 'thermomushroom bombs'.[10] The heat[11] and the craters these bombs left on the earth were massive when they exploded. In that way, he ensured national security for a long life for his companies.

KORP was the most benign of his friendly allies in this technologically predatory race reality. As a strategist, he always tried to be miles ahead of his competitors.

Did you notice I wrote miles ahead instead of steps forward? Because it was true, he had foreseen how to prepare for a world crisis long ago. He also expected the energy shortage by secretly building two industrial helium-3 plants on the moon; by then, because of the lack of oil energy, helium-3 had become an essential energy source. He travelled several times to the Earth's satellite to advise on these plants' construction. He would disappear from the world, pretending to be on holiday. When he returned, he said it was his favourite holiday; by this, he meant how beautiful our planet looked from space.

People noticed a change in his personality every time he returned from the moon. Those trips influenced his character: they made him more empathetic with people, so much so that he would go out and talk to people in the streets or town squares; sometimes, he would sit and play chess with children, young or older people, in the park while he chatted with them.

His country's government knew about these industrial plants on the moon. However, they were not trying to stop him because they also had access to a piece of that pie; they even helped him with logistics, letting him use some of the launch pads of the spacecraft carrying supplies to the moon. His government handled

10. **Thermomushroom bombs** refers to thermonuclear bombs, they can be hundreds or even thousands of times more powerful than atomic bombs. The explosive yield of atomic bombs is measured in kilotons (one kiloton equals the explosive force of 1,000 tons of TNT) while the explosive power of thermonuclear bombs is frequently expressed in megatons (one megaton equals the explosive force of 1,000,000 tons of TNT).
11. **The heat**: During the period of peak energy output, a 1-megaton (Mt) nuclear weapon can produce temperatures of about 100 million degrees Celsius at its centre, about four to five times that which occurs at the centre of the sun.

the whole situation as a 'Top Secret'. These trips to the Earth's satellite made him feel closer to the universe.

As there was nothing hidden under the sun, the media published a selfie of KORP on the moon; this news scared the multinationals to death, as it showed his power. He appeared on record in the press, saying it was fake news and distracted public opinion with other fake news. The experts analysed the picture and declared it authentic. Faced with unavoidable evidence, he could not deny it. He had no choice but to make his helium-3 industry on the moon known to the public. Since then, global economic power groups have openly opposed him after they learned about his helium-3 industry on the moon and published articles to pressure him to decline that project. Also, local powers were concerned about KORP's presence on the moon, especially those groups against him since he began business dealings with his country's government. They claimed that the government favoured KORP companies over national companies. But they wanted to avoid seeing the substantial benefits he provided for his country's economy. He made more profit for his country than all the other companies combined. That was an indisputable, proven, factual fact. Remember, he was a nationalist.

Perhaps it is an understatement to say that KORP was the only one that invested his capital in his own country and did not secretly invest in those places called tax havens, places where most of the country's companies had their money invested because they did not want to risk investing in their own country, which, to justify their inconsistency, they claimed was a poor and insecure country.

These solid economic opposition groups launched a deceptive smear campaign against him on every level because, in their eyes, they had legitimate reasons to do so. Cowardly hiding behind the scenes, the newly formed cross-border global powers joined that dirty war because they claimed, "With KORP out of the way, we will have more freedom." Then, these transnationals bought up goods and services to take over strategic places in the country's local commerce, thus becoming owners of the big commercial chains like written media, from the giant printing presses to the television media, pharmaceutical industry, trade in minerals, clothing, goods and services; land and space tourism trips; supermarkets; and a long etcetera. They monopolised local commerce fiercely and brutally, so much so that an oppressive, totalitarian and terrifying monopoly reigned in local business, suffocating medium and small industries. KORP said nothing at first because he respected free trade principles.

The other hidden reason these new transnational powers allied themselves with KORP's opponents was that they were investing a lot of money and resources in Mars in alliance with the Society of the Continents, which had a lot of experience with Martian soil; it was a mining company – perhaps the most powerful on the planet. It was a strange partnership, but the genuine interest these companies had in Mars was in something other than space tourism. Instead, they discovered rare minerals not found on Earth, which were essential to the space industry.

Mining projects on Mars would generate a lot of money for these companies. It was only a matter of time. So, they quickly formed a united front because KORP was hot on their heels, and they had to act soon. These gigantic monopoly business corporations that opposed KORP had many tactics to get someone out of the way. The trick that always worked well for them was smearing based on lies. They used this fear argument to discredit him: 'If KORP ever gets his feet on Mars and into space commerce, it will be the end of our companies'.

He never interfered with the business of his detractors on Mars or anywhere else on Earth because the universe was infinite for him.

In the moon industry, he was the only person to step foot. The moon was a tough nut to crack despite being close to Earth. However stubborn he was, he promised to do it. It was not true that KORP owned the moon. He never said it belonged to him. He firmly believed in freedom of trade on Earth and in space.

***

As the days passed, this fake news circulated:

"KORP has taken ownership of the moon and space commerce and is planning to sell lunar land for mining."

His opponents planted this ridiculous lie efficiently through the media and print media. They stirred up the masses to revolt against KORP all over the planet.

In many regions of the country, small companies associated with him shut down their business operations for fear of reprisals from these big global powers. His opponents also recruited unemployed people and vandals. They sent them to protest and spread chaos strategically, charging for every hour of protest. In addition, some protesters displayed banners that read: "No, to the moon's monopoly, yes to global trade freedom."

Some influential companies from other continents also disseminated fake news in those latitudes, then across borders and seas. KORP's enemies also spoke negatively about him. All these well-orchestrated, slanderous demolition apparatuses rolled like a steamroller or combine harvester, cutting through people's thinking and leaving them stunned.

"KORP's government dealings were not shady. He sold his inventions, and it was a commercial business. The government also knocked on the doors of KORP companies as a sovereign client, like governments at the global level." (The Thinker)

It is true. There are records of these, such as these:

"Government modernises national defence: KORP wins the tender." *Cybernetic Daily Press.*

Hundreds of press releases in print and television media testify to this business relationship.

Another point in his favour was that the government bought weapons from KORP and resold them outside its borders because he permitted them. Sometimes, the government was involved in shady business to make more money by selling these products outside the country. Although the press blamed him for the government's mess, he did not interfere in these negotiations. He stressed: "Everyone handles their actions."

Outside his country's borders, he was free to do business as he pleased, and his government was not responsible for him either. They were his rules.

Before signing business contracts, he wrote the details of these agreements in the fine print. That way, he was free of any responsibility or misunderstanding. He was in the habit of being very careful. He knew how cumbersome a poorly signed, half-signed or dubious contract could be. The government also reserved the right to sell KORP products outside the country. Buying and selling those products was in the government's interest because selling them at prices that brought more money into the national financial coffers meant progress for the country. Also, several countries offered to pay what the governments charged them. So, in some regional or global military conflicts, military forces used KORP weapons against KORP weapons.

***

Even though political incidents continued to plague KORP, they didn't stop him from developing even more products. He had created hundreds of products that blew up the market. However, inventing and investing in the weapons industry made him more profitable, so he fully engaged his companies.

He followed his old habit of participating in military conflicts to find ideas for upcoming inventions because he saw how quickly technology had changed and armies had upgraded their arsenals. He needed to secure his leadership in this matter.

Many times, he would play chess alone and enlist top players to challenge. From these games, he got the inspiration to manufacture his Toys. He also surrounded himself with a small army of strategists and mercenaries besides his army of scientists. They helped him recreate virtual situations to get a closer perspective on battles. He recruited the most talented Cybernauts to form a cyber army. Many were experts in virtual animation who had brilliant ideas and helped him draw technical blueprints for his inventions. Some were former government workers.

These people knew him very well. Over time, they became like his family and cyberwarfare advisers.

He had also exploited his knowledge of cybernetics and biology to benefit the arms industry. He realised this industry was like 'the goose which lays golden eggs'. Thus, he grew as a manufacturer and supplier of more sophisticated weapons, including space weapons. His Toys were the pinnacle of quality and efficiency.

He always stressed that these weapons were purely for deterrence.

***

As the days passed, conflicts grew and raw materials from friendly allied countries also became scarce. As a result, companies had to drive further away to find them. The strange thing about this situation was that the opposition bloc was also looking for raw materials in the same places where KORP already had a presence, stirring the waters again. They did this intentionally.

Several questions arise: Why were these oppositional powers looking for raw materials in the same areas where he had already operated? What were their intentions? Perhaps they wanted to disturb his sleep? It is challenging to know.

Raw materials were still plentiful across the seas; it was a matter of negotiation with the countries of origin, no doubt. In many countries, there was also an openness to friendly negotiation. It was just a matter of sitting down and talking.

As I have mentioned before, there is nothing hidden under the sun. Gradually, the purpose of these opposition groups' actions became clear: they were trying to dirty KORP's name through confrontation. They made ridiculous excuses about not looking for raw materials elsewhere. They openly said that the planet was for everyone, and everyone had the same rights to exploit raw materials wherever they wanted.

"It is difficult to open true intentions. They are like safes with no access key, which makes it difficult to open." (The Thinker)

At the beginning of all these problems, KORP attached little importance to them. He had faced very similar situations in the past. But as the days wore on, the protests and acts of provocation towards him became more heated, aggressive and poisonous, and the press continued to report on them. The front pages of the newspapers carried headlines like this: "Protests against the KORP monopoly continue."

The Society of Continents had bought advertising space on prime-time television to broadcast protest news; this was one of the apparent signs of a plot. The protesters, who were mostly unemployed people, stationed themselves at strategic places in the city to force security personnel to meet them. It was in these encounters that, taking advantage of the confusion, the vandals would leave fatal victims among the security forces with their firearms, and both local and international television would broadcast these scenes live to add to the drama. In those days, protest news against KORP was in the press almost daily.

But as a sign that destiny still stood by his side in these dark days, KORP received the fantastic news that finally pushed him to establish his empire.

It was Sunday morning, and he was well-dressed to attend the leading service at the Cathedral of Clocks temple. Two of his private agents approached him without warning. He was in a hurry because he wanted to arrive on time; he was the primary guest.

"We know this woman is Kate. Sir."

"Where did you get these images from?"

Showing KORP some images on his mobile phone, one agent excitedly said, "From the Expeditionary Agency, sir."

The agents gave him all the detailed information they had collected, and the news was accurate.

"I thought she was dead!" said KORP, overwhelmed.

"She is alive! Sir. Her DNA tests are inside these envelopes, and everything matches. Also, this is her address in the city where she currently lives. Sir. She changed her details for obvious reasons."

KORP remained silent for a long time. He then turned his back on the agents and put his sunglasses on so they wouldn't see him crying.

After this private agent had located Kate's whereabouts, KORP longed to see her again. Even if it only lasted for a moment, or if it meant turning a second into a day to spend time with her, he was ready to do it to enjoy her presence. After hearing the news, a magical spark ignited in his heart. Hearing this news brought him joy and genuine smiles for the first time in a long time. Kate had now given him a reason to exist.

When they dated each other, they promised, "To the end of the universe."

Oblivion was an exhilarating feeling that threatened that promise, one that he had to fight against for almost every day of his existence. He did not want to forget her at all. He loved her too much to lock her up in oblivion. On the palm of his right hand, he had a tattoo of the letter 'K' and kissed it whenever he saw it.

They were both in the same class at the Faculty of Biological Sciences. A few months into their third year, when Kate had just disappeared, she didn't say why and didn't communicate with anybody; even the university authorities didn't know her whereabouts. 'She took refuge in the absence behind the ellipsis,'[12] leaving KORP stranded. From then on, he assumed that someone had either kidnapped her or killed her. He had tried everything to get her, but nothing had worked. He always wanted to convince her to return to him, but he had to find her first. In the end, he hired private agents to search for her. These agents tracked his beloved's whereabouts by land and sea for months, even years, but to no avail. Finally, after much effort, the agents' persistence paid off. That day, the agents sent him conclusive evidence that Kate was alive and that they knew where she lived.

In the agents' pictures, Kate is leaving the school. Three teenagers accompany her. Her hair is short and dyed black, but her smile and eyes were the keys to knowing it was her. After receiving the news, he didn't sleep well at night. He thought about her too much. Knowing she was alive gave him life, too. That news brought warmth back into his icy heart.

---

12.   **She took refuge in the absence behind the ellipsis** refers to a partner who disappears without explaining but still carries a big surprise.

"KORP was happy to love her. I dare say that nothing in the universe produced that effect in his life. I recognise his facial expressions well. Whenever he took Kate out on a date, he returned to his room with such happiness that he melted like ice cream, and his face completely transformed. When he found out she was alive, he was so happy that he almost gave me the impression that they were together again." (The Thinker)

The news that Kate was alive again gave him a sense of purpose; it was like a balm of miraculous oil on Kate's absence wound. Until that moment, he had consoled himself by looking at his only photograph of her. The news of her whereabouts had awakened an extraordinary illusion inside his soul – the illusion of her return to him.

He liked the idea of moving to live near her area to feel her warmth. The night after hearing this fantastic news, he dreamed she had returned; the next morning, he woke up happy with the illusion of seeing her that day. However, as the evening fell, he felt despair and sadness because the day had ended without him seeing her. It was as if love, fate and Kate were all playing hide-and-seek with him and his heart.

Whenever he remembered her, KORP couldn't explain why he suddenly became someone he couldn't recognise. When he thought of Kate's return, his essence changed into that of plasticine, ready to become anything in the hands of the person who had once said to him, "I love you so much!"

Those memories held too much power and magic over him, so much so that they made him forget it had been almost two decades since he had last seen her.

This news also strengthened his dying hope, fuelling his passion for her. Sometimes, he would rehearse a brief speech, imagining she had already returned and was sitting on the sofa at home, listening to him. In his speech, he would first apologise, explain why, and justify his mistakes, mistakes he thought he would have made, and errors that would have been to blame for her departure. But despite those mistakes, he still clung to Kate's forgiveness.

Inside KORP's abysmal soul, there was still space, a sanctuary only Kate owned. She alone held the keys to that sacred orchard. If she wanted to, she would enter without asking for his permission, and he would allow her to. It was an extraordinary, sentimental love dance performed in a paradise that remained intact.

Under pressure from those close to him and beset by loneliness, he had tried to enter a loving relationship several times since Kate left, but it had been unsuccessful. In his life, no woman could replace Kate's kisses. Her love had the magic formula for him to be alive. Kate's traces were singular; her steps were exclusive, her prints were indelible; her scent was unmistakable. She was the only key left in this tiny space of his soul to open his heart where the marks she left there were too deep, but he kept them there for as long as possible, as they were marks of love and more robust than pain. He went to superhuman efforts to preserve these traces of her there. This infinite love attached him to her for life. He pleaded Kate would always be his soul love through inaudible prayers or cries. Despite this, he tried not to extend his hands to greet these feelings. However, he always found it impossible to do so because he felt too weak in reality's face; he loved her too much to ignore her.

"Dear readers, let me make a point here. In Kate's presence, KORP was like butter, and she was the heat; with her gaze, she melted him. Maybe it's a distortion of his character? I don't know, but it was true. Kate's gaze hypnotised him." (The Thinker)

KORP knew his avenues governed his life, and he had to follow them. Despite this, he healed the wounds and pain caused by Kate's absence with tiny droplets of a balm called 'I still love you'. He kept those droplets in a glass jar and stored them deep in the universe of his soul: his silence. That secret place where no one but him could reach. Only his colleague, The Thinker, knew what he kept inside his silence safe because sometimes, while he slept, he talked to her or named her in his dreams.

The news that they had seen Kate alive and the love he still felt for her was a lamp whose light and warmth gave him enough willpower and strength to build his empire.

He would do it for her.

4. The Force of Freedom

Without freedom, humans wander like corpses in space.

One Sunday morning, KORP stayed at home to rest, relax and have breakfast while watching television. Street protests against his companies dominated the news on almost every channel. After finishing, he wanted to look closer at the street protests his opponents had organised daily in front of television cameras. So, he called his advisers to find out which area of the city the protests were taking place on that day. Putting on casual clothes, a cap, his fake moustache and dark glasses, he set out to find the place; he asked to be left alone. He always travelled with others; for his safety, his advisers and bodyguards always watched him, albeit from afar.

When he arrived at the scene, he found a mass of angry people shouting and carrying banners; they complained aggressively. He got out of the car and mingled with the crowd. Walking among them, he felt a presence that forced him to leave the place quickly because it shocked him.

Arriving at his mansion, he did not respond to the guards' greetings or look at the people guarding his house or the staff working inside. His face was pale with worry but pale as if he were ill. Something had struck him in the protests.

"Knowing KORP, I would say he wasn't worried about the protests or the banners; he never worried about anything unless it was something frighteningly profound or, above all, threatened his freedom." (The Thinker)

Yes, I am with you. What happened that day as he passed through the middle of the protests was that he smelled a familiar presence in the air. This scent had activated his cells to be alert and defensive. The stench of those with bullying in their genes had returned.

Every time he faced bullying from his perpetrators in the past, his body suffered and passed through shocks, just like this day. His physique prepared this way to withstand the screams of hatred, the taunts, the electric shocks of batteries on his tongue, the stones thrown at his legs, the food stains on his new shirt, the punches, the constant threats, the obscene hand gestures, the beatings, the continuous words of inhuman degradation that his executioners poured on him, the persecutions on his way to school, the social marginalisation situations, and it continued.

Entering his bedroom, he looked for the corner where he had cried after his mistreatment at school. His corner, where he gnawed at his nails in pain, where he had wet himself through fear of his three tormentors; the corner that helped his soul become like a black hole that got used to devouring pain as if it were a biscuit; the corner where one day raised his countenance – where he had resolved and vowed to defeat his three enemies.

That corner sheltered him. He sat on his stool next to his colleague, The Thinker, and this is what he did when he was a child, a teenager, and, at that moment, a young adult. He was concerned to the core because the bullying phantom had returned. The spirit he had bravely faced as a child was present again. Until now, KORP had been safe, convinced that he had eliminated them.

It was undeniable: the scent of his three enemies, invisible for now, had returned. They stalked from the shadows like wild hyenas. The demonstrations and protests had left their mark that day.

After making several calls to find out who was behind these protests, he suspected his three ex-oppressors were part of this plot as well. They owned well-known businesses abroad and allied themselves with powerful opposition groups. Still, KORP did not know this was true, so this visit confirmed his suspicions. He could finally see the complete picture with his three ex-oppressors among his opponents.

That fact opened the door to another crusade in his life. It was not simply a trade war. It was not merely a matter of sending someone to jail. Someone released his perpetrators who were in prison, and they fled without serving their sentences. This new situation was a psychological war without quarters, condemning the loser to drop to his knees to beg, but rewarding the winner by lording it over his defeated opponent for the rest of his life. It was a war of life or death.

His ex-abusers, now free, were extremely angry with him and sought revenge. Even though they had harassed him day after day, week after week, month after month, and year after year, they directed their thirst for vengeance at him as if they were innocent victims seeking justice. How pathetic!

The three of them had each done their part to be at the forefront of these righteous winds because KORP had wronged them.

"Now is the time to stand up to him," these wild beasts mused in their hearts with hate.

Faced with this situation, KORP, for the first time and diligently, meditated on the word 'freedom' because he perceived that his freedom, this time, was being trampled upon, questioned, dangerously threatened with death, and, with it, his life. So, he wrote these questions in his book: What is freedom? Where do freedom frontiers lie? He did not state what freedom was or where it existed, but wanted to know the global meaning and scope of that word. He felt that freedom was a vast concept.

Every time he thought about the definition of freedom, he felt nauseous and wanted to avoid facing an explanation that disagreed with his concept. He did not wish to find an image that contradicted or pushed aside his idea of freedom. KORP loved his freedom because it made him feel safe and happy.

Informing his advisers that he was not expecting to see anyone that week because he was away on holiday, he locked himself in his mansion and isolated himself in the shadow of his colleague, The Thinker.

"It is only natural that as a person matures, he considers his actions more carefully. He first thinks or reasons carefully before taking any decision or action further." (The Thinker)

His room had stayed the same since he had slept there last. His stool was the same pile of old books, magazines and newspapers. He built his mansion around his room. That corner of his house was his refuge, and that mysterious man on the wall was his friend. After greeting with reverence his colleague, he sat in the same position as him – The Thinker.

When he meditated, he had a specific order. First, he reviewed all the information in his mind (his galleries) and then pondered his original questions.

After a few hours of thinking, he concluded everything was in order with himself. He opened his eyes without moving from that position; then, closing them again, he meditated on his planned question: What is freedom?

As he contemplated, images of the infinite universe came to mind, as did scenes he saw when returning from his most beautiful holiday – the moon – because every time KORP came back from there, he predicted that his freedom was going to be tremendous and infinite, the size of the universe, which gave him confidence (a lot of faith) in himself. At that moment, he felt pleased with himself for knowing that his freedom was secure.

'My freedom is secure because it is the size of the universe,' he thought.

There was no conflict about that self-concept at the moment.

As the hours passed in stillness in his mind, he activated his imagination and conducted an imaginary experiment. The purpose of this was to gain a deeper understanding of freedom. In his mind, he constructed a massive hall with a circular wall and a high ceiling. He illuminated and painted its walls, floor and interior ceiling black. On this black background, he drew all kinds of things found in nature on the wall, for example, many animals and plants, rivers and mountains, rocks of all sizes, clouds, the sea and many trees. He also painted on the ceiling comets, stars and planets. Then he said: "All these paintings and drawings represent the present reality where human beings live, and the space in this room represents the universe."

He called this room Space-A.

Then he imagined two people: a masked teenager at the protests and himself. He then put the two people inside Space-A, which lacked oxygen. There, the two people floated, inert and lifeless. There was no movement in their bodily limbs; although their eyes were open, they had their gazes fixed on infinity. They also had motionless facial features and pale skin, as if they were corpses. He left his guests floating in that room and, in the meantime, built another room similar to the first one. This room had the same characteristics as the first one, even the paintings. He called this newly created room Space-B and filled it with oxygen.

Then he moved the two people from Space-A to the newly created Space-B. There, the two people came to life because of oxygen. Their eyes looked at the drawings inside that vast room, but they were still floating because they had no energy or strength to move. After a few minutes, in the middle of the floor in that Space-B, he placed a small torch whose flame gave off an essence of a delightful, exquisite smell, an energiser, a force. He called that essence the Force of Freedom, which permeated Space-B to the last corner. Immediately, the two floating people gained strength, settled their feet on the ground, and walked, ran and interacted. They walked from one place to another with a smile; they were happy, had colour in their skin and looked healthy. The young man uncovered his face as he threw the sign he was carrying in the protests to the ground. They both breathed in the air, infused with that delicious freedom essence. After a moment, KORP extinguished the torch, and the delightful essence disappeared from the room. His guests became inert again and floated like corpses in space.

KORP watched his guests for a long while, then lit the torch again, and the Force of Freedom flooded the place. Suddenly, the two people came alive; they looked happy and interacted with each other, sharing their experiences. He did this exercise several times.

Then, he noted in his book, "The space containing oxygen permeated with freedom produces life, interaction and movement. Where freedom does not exist, people float like inert corpses, whose eyes can only distinguish and see but cannot move."

Then, he closed his eyes and continued his experiment with his imaginary guests. This time, he filled Space-A with oxygen and one hundred per cent of the Force of Freedom and placed the young man there. He filled Space-B with oxygen and only fifty per cent of the Force of Freedom and left his other guest, who was himself, there. He observed their behaviour for a while. The young man in Space-A was happy and had a relatively everyday life; he bathed, ate and rested. He felt delighted.

His guest in Space-B became restless, sad, crestfallen, listless, disoriented and worried. He experienced difficulty breathing, fatigue and a desire to open a hole in the wall to let in more of the Force of Freedom while also sitting down and standing up. Then KORP lit the torch and flooded the place with one hundred per cent of the delicious essence of the Force of Freedom. With this, his guest became well again, very well; he was again happy, super-happy; he admired the painted objects on the wall, made his comments on the drawings, ran with open arms, applauded the stars, admired the planets, interacted with everything in his path, and, above all, smiled. Thus, he ended the first part of his imaginary experiment.

Then he wrote in his book: "There are spaces in the universe and around us that contain different degrees of freedom. Humans become disoriented in areas with less freedom. In those places, he survives and looks for a way to be at ease with himself. Still, he doesn't get it because he feels his life is a burden, despairs, gets tired, loses happiness quickly, and always is in an unhappy mood, disappointed with himself or others; he feels limited and trapped. It is as if he had clipped his wings. Where spaces contain complete freedom, the opposite happens."

At that moment, touching his colleague's poster and still with his eyes closed, KORP inhaled deeply, hoping to feel the oxygen mix with the Force of Freedom. He concluded that the oxygen he inhaled at that moment contained one hundred per cent of that delicious essence of liberty. Knowing this comforted him greatly. It made him feel better about himself. He thought he was in a suitable space. With all his heart, he hoped to stay in this space of his freedom forever.

As the hours passed, KORP remained in his colleague's position – The Thinker. After many more hours, he had asked himself, 'What must we do to reach the space that contains one hundred per cent of the Force of Freedom?'

Gazing into infinity, he saw the two spaces he had built and painted: Space-A, empty, without oxygen, and the Force of Freedom. Space-B was brimming with oxygen with one hundred per cent of the delicious essence of the Force of Freedom. As he saw this vision, newborn babies slowly descended into Space-B, some still with their umbilical cords attached. They were precious, tender and settled delicately on every object he had drawn and painted in that room; they rested on every plant, every animal, every planet, star, river, water, etc.

That vision had a significant impact on him and made him understand many things, so much so that he wrote the following in his book:

"From the moment a human being leaves his mother's womb, he inhales oxygen impregnated with the essence of the Force of Freedom; his cells and anatomy have bathed in that blessed essence. Human beings are born free. Freedom is part of human nature; to be, move and live in this sacred space is his inclination and natural condition.

"In this blessed place, space called the essence of freedom, human can exist, coexist, reproduce, imagine, invent, laugh, cry, feel happy, trace his destiny, express his passion, achieve his goals and design his future. Here he can love, make mistakes, get frustrated, correct mistakes, become a hero, taste defeat or eat the soft bread of victory, discover his strengths and weaknesses, and think freely.

"Here, he gives his opinion or remains silent; dyes his hair the colour he likes or pierces the most unusual places on his body; fills his skin with tattoos, plays with his favourite characters, dresses up as a superhero, or as the villain. In this place, he does the stupidest, the most courageous, the most stubborn, the most bizarre things or does nothing. In this space of freedom, he has beliefs, doubts, or lacks thereof.

"Here he wonders what lies beyond death, what gods there are. He either seeks God or worships things like a stone, a tree, himself, the sun, the moon, animals, a mosquito, an elephant, the hero who defeated death or believes in nothingness. Here, he seeks the truth or prefers to live in lies.

"Here, he works hard, leaving deep traces of his existence to be remembered as a model person or prefers to live in oblivion; he became a UFO hunter or a hunter of illusions. He embraces the ideals of Gandhi, Luther King or Winston Churchill or enjoys Mr Bean's stupidities.[13] This place of freedom is where he embraces the paths of evil or follows the noble ways of good. Is this the environment where he mistreats, cultivates, destroys, loves, caresses his body and fills it with pleasures; roams the world or chains himself to a chair in an office; here, he speaks or philosophises in his mind with the verb to be, to be what one could be, denying being who is and longing for who could become and be what he never wanted to be, or rejects what they want him to be because he would not want to be what they expect him to be and prefers to be what he is: a free human being.

"It is here where he becomes a singer or changes his university career a thousand times, loves peace or war or lives in his fantasies. Here, he decides to become a big or small personality or a Mr Nobody. Also, is this where he dreams of the driest, the wettest, the noblest, the dirtiest, the frustrated, and the spiritual dreams or struggles to make his dreams come true? It is here where he enjoys the most delicious morsel of his work; here he rests and sleeps pleasantly or discovers the bitter bite of death.

"Here he learns to turn the other cheek or clings to the disgusting principle of an eye for an eye; or when he wants to drink something special, he orders the tastiest, the sweetest, the most tasteless, the most bitter wine, or prefers to drink his favourite beer,

---

13. **Mr Bean**: Famous sitcom series; when performing, Mr Bean does things or gets into troublesome situations where he does funny or stupid things to get out of them.

cognac, coffee, coca-mate tea,[14] soda, guayusa-water,[15] mate, tereré,[16] whisky, flavoured waters, or maybe he doesn't want to drink at all.

"In this place, he uncovers the taste of the sweetest, most bitter and juiciest fruit or encounters the forbidden fruit. He can be vegetarian or vegan, or prefer to eat meat, insects, rats, junk or traditional food, the most exotic or exciting snacks, or he eats nothing if he doesn't want to. Here, he will become a flower, an animal, a butterfly, or whatever it takes to capture the love of his life or, sadly, to let her go. Here, he writes the white pages of a new day, corrects his past mistakes, learns to play with fire, and decides whether to burn. He embodies Picasso's creativity, Shakespeare's brilliance and Einstein's genius. Here, he learns to taste the flavour of kisses, to hunt the sublime sensations of caresses, and, with them, to become intoxicated with pleasure until he feels the marvellous ecstasy produced by the electric shock when making love; here, he gives free rein to his basic instincts or struggles to replace them with actions that add more days to his existence.

"In this place, he writes the most beautiful or saddest verses, the flattest novels, the dullest stories and the dullest verses. Also, learns to decipher the lying truths, the verifiable truths, the truth lies, the half-lies and the lying lies. Here, he works mightily to ensure that the journey of his descendants, who carry his precious genes, will be safe, happy, in peace and freedom. Here, he strives to fulfil the purpose of being created from the beginning: procreate and be administrator of the Earth."

---

14. **Coca-mate tea** is a typical drink in Bolivia and Peru. It's a mistaken idea that coca equals cocaine. "The use of the coca plant not only preserves the health of all who use it but prolongs life to a very great old age and enables the coca eaters to perform prodigies of mental and physical labour." (John Pemberton, Atlanta Constitution, 1885)
For Andean people, coca leaves have always been vital. Chewing coca leaves together is a sign of affection and camaraderie. The religious significance of coca leaves is also demonstrated by funeral customs, daily activities, holidays and festivities. It is also used medicinally by individuals. It can be chewed for toothaches or pain in the mouth and throat, applied topically (as a powder or poultice), or brewed as a tea to treat gastrointestinal issues. It also reduces the discomfort of delivery and speeds up labour.
15. **Guayusa** water is a typical drink from across Ecuador.
16. **Tereré** is a typical cold drink from Paraguay.

He also wrote and quoted:

"Freedom is the ideal place where a human can be himself because he is in the right place. A free human being coexists with himself and the nature that has engendered him. Space, oxygen and the Force of Freedom provide the right environment where the human being expresses himself abundantly, without reproach and constraint. But he needs to respond better when these three elements are lacking. Freedom is the space where free will is possible. The place where all the attributes he inherits flourish is where he makes the most of him. Humans are masters and responsible for their own decisions when free, whose consequences are eternal witnesses and paths or maps their descendants will inherit. Freedom is not a right gained with a signature but an inheritance he was born with. Human beings were born in and with freedom; therefore, they are free, and that freedom is non-negotiable. No human being can claim that he can give freedom to another human being; it does not entitle him to it, it is not his right, nor does he have the power necessary to take it away. He only has the right and all the power to respect the freedom of another human being.

"We must respect freedom as a fundamental and inalienable right of the individual, regardless of origin, race, nation or social condition.

"If there were another name for human beings, it would be freedom.

"Neither the geographical nor cultural place of birth alters this factor, this reality: human beings are free, whether they are born in space, on the moon, in the house's corner, in a hospital, on a plane, on a ship, in an ambulance, in a nation foreign to their parents, or any corner of the universe. Humans have every right to walk freely on this planet and anywhere in the galaxy."

At that moment, KORP breathed deeply to feel the Force of Freedom again. After doing so, he felt happy and satisfied. It was a habit from his youth: fill his lungs with that essence so the bullying would not penetrate his will.

He drifted his fingers one by one while still in that position and with his eyes closed. He could feel his muscles once more move free of pain barriers. Finally, he cried joyfully, "Thank you for the Force of Freedom!"

***

Freedom's colour and obstacles

Five hours had passed, and KORP was still sitting in that position. He got up to make himself a cup of coffee. When he came back and sat down again, he closed his eyes and smelled the aroma of the coffee, and as he did so, another question came to his mind: 'What colour is freedom?'

To answer that question, he conducted another imaginary experiment. For this, he used only Space-B from his previous imaginary experiment. This room glowed with the essence of the Force of Freedom. He then placed a small, lighted candle in the middle of the room, whose flame emitted a very light-blue, non-toxic smoke. This smoke permeated the room's air, which became light blue. He then moved his two characters – also from his previous experiment – into that room.

There, his guests walked and interacted with each other without interruption; they were happy and walked all over the place admiring the painted objects. They looked delighted.

After a while, he glanced at the room through the young man's eyes and saw that the air was light blue, just as the young man saw it; then he looked at the room through his own eyes, and the place appeared transparent, without the light-blue tint. He rubbed his eyes and looked again through his eyes, and the sight still seemed with no colour.

Through his eyes, he could not distinguish the light-blue colour of the Force of Freedom. He then noted in his book:

"From my perspective, the perception of the colour of the essence of the Force of Freedom is transparent, whereas, from the young man's perspective, it is light blue." He asked himself, 'Why is there such a difference?' He repeated the same imaginary experiment, and the conclusion was the same. Concerned with this, he put a third actor in that room, "Just in case," he said. For this, he included a police officer who patrolled the protests. The young man and the police officer could see the Force of Freedom in a light-blue tint. However, through his own eyes, he still saw it as transparent.

Tense and worried, he noted in his book, "KORP has deficiencies in seeing the Force of Freedom's colour."

He continued with his imaginary experiment; this time, he put three-dimensional objects in different places on Space-B's floor: rocks, bricks, eggs, puddles of water, etc. He wanted to see these three-dimensional objects through his three guests' eyes. Through the police officer's eyes, the things appeared three-dimensional. Through the young man's eyes, the objects appeared distorted, but they were still three-dimensional objects. Finally, when he looked at the things through his own eyes, they looked flat; they had no height, depth or width; they were like stamps, like flat pieces of carpet, like drawings on paper. When his guests walked into that room, now with colour and three-dimensional obstacles or things, the young man and the police officer would dodge the items as they walked or stop to look at them. Still, when his guest, himself, walked, he moved over the objects without avoiding them, as if he were walking on a flat or patterned carpet.

He noted in his book:

"Within freedom are objects, situations and actions, which I call Complements of Freedom.

"When people walk among these Complements of Freedom, they observe or know their existence and interact between and around them. In contrast, when I see them through my eyes, these objects or complements look flat, like stamps or carpets. I don't have the capacity or algorithm to determine the Complements of Freedom's length, height and depth. Without this algorithm, it is difficult for me to perceive or connect with these Complements of Freedom; this situation has shocked me. Humans call this algorithm 'conscience'."

He notes in his book that "KORP does not have the algorithm of conscience". He deduced that conscience was the light that helped people see the height, depth, length, shapes, limits, colour, dangers and obstacles of reality around us.

The applications he constructed in the absence of conscience were his ways, his laws and his own rules. These applications make up algorithms that help him connect and enter the realm of freedom.

As soon as KORP discovered he lacked the algorithm of conscience, he felt sad because he understood the importance of seeing, distinguishing and appreciating the magnitude of freedom.

He could not deduce why he hadn't the algorithm of conscience. At the bottom of the page, he wrote in tiny letters, "I would like, one day, to have a molecule of conscience." After that, he closed his book.

It was on that day that he realised he was trying to appear normal in front of people.

"This explains why he sometimes – or almost always – did things that in others' eyes seemed eccentric; it was his way of seeing the world and how it worked for him. He had to create a parallel life from which he could better understand others." (The Thinker)

Finally, he balanced 'conscience' and 'freedom' and concluded:

"One can exist without conscience, albeit with difficulty, but not without freedom.

"To live without freedom would be to live in the bosom of a slow death.

"To live without freedom would be to coexist eternally with fear; it would be like sitting under Damocles' sword.

"To live without freedom would be to live constantly threatened by death's sting hidden in the familiar dilemma: to be or not to be.

"To live without freedom would be to die alive, knowing one was born free and destined to be what one is and will never cease to be: a dignified and free human being."

These conclusions gave him more certainty about his life; they deeply grounded him in his right to move about his day-to-day life with no threat.

They also gave him more certainty about his business dealings with the government. These conclusions also convinced him that no one could doubt his life, let alone his freedom. No one had the right to question his space, where he could be himself and have free rein with his creativity to invent things.

"No one may question the space where I believe in myself and to keep walking and growing as a human being," he said.

He also noted in his book: "It is time to eradicate from my life – forever – this cancer of bullying, an evil that constantly outrages my existence."

5. Wounded wing

Slogans are the eyes of politics; without them, politics is a blind race.

A few members of his party emerged from the meeting room smiling. Some commented on the news with great excitement: KORP had finally entered the political fray as a national leadership candidate for the next elections, which would be in two years. So, as a political party, they had all that time to plan and prepare for this challenging political race.

The first step in raising his empire was to become a national leader, a long-awaited plan because this was the main reason he agreed to be a candidate.

Meanwhile, in the outside world, violence and abuse against KORP companies did not cease; instead, they escalated into terrorism. Jealousy and envy drove his enemies to be blind and hostile.

These attacks were called 'soft blows' by his enemies. From the first minute they learned KORP was a candidate for a national leader, the tidal wave of coercive actions against him began. He concluded that no one, absolutely no one, had the right to question his freedom. He got to that level of business relationship with the government on his own merits. No one gave him anything. Therefore, he owes nothing.

But he knew his enemies and exactly where they wanted to be. Still, he would not let them go any further this time and instead planned to get them out of the way, but never revealed the plan. He saw with deep concern how his perpetrators and those mobs were using more aggressive methods against him; they set fire to some of his factories, robbed the trucks carrying his products on the roads, or sank his carrier ships. These actions showed they wanted to finish him as soon as possible because they could not sustain a dirty war for long. They tried to break his business hegemony within the government.

The whole situation was already an undeclared war at every level. KORP would act how he knew how: in a war without quarters and human rights. He devised a strategy that would give him power, and this was to get his country's leadership.

Consolidating his convictions that he was a free human being and realising that he still loved Kate just as intensely gave him the strength to sustain his life in these critical moments. The beautiful and powerful combination of these forces – freedom and love – would make his war possible and take him even further.

'With these two forces in my life, I am complete,' he thought.

Years ago, the political party he was a member of encouraged him to run for national leader. He had enormous support from them, but he felt he needed more time to be ready or sure that he could do it.

KORP never accepted something if he wasn't sure of it first, even if the sky fell. But, just as everything changes in life, it was at this moment that he believed it was the right time, and he was sure of it.

Now, he had to start by taking the most elementary step in politics: to understand the feelings and needs of the masses to know in depth the reality in which ordinary people live.

KORP could not conceive the reason for the fragility of the masses' moods: one day, they were like gentle doves, and the next, they were like furious hurricanes. Such a sudden mood change in the masses kept him aloof from politics. But this time, it was different. He would listen, understand the people, and know their expectations of the government. Finally, he accepted the challenges that come with this obligatory path in politics:

"If I want to succeed, I must take the bull by the horns," he said.

"*KORP is right to doubt the masses. He was not wrong to question the masses' mood. People always react and respond according to how wide and secure their freedom is and how complete their bank accounts with money are; he wanted to know how to make these two variables a constant reality." (The Thinker)*

For the time being, he decided not to get into a fight with his enemies because he wanted to prepare for the leadership elections. He chose not to respond to the attacks; instead, he preferred to wait for them to move towards him. Until the final counterattack, he reinforced factory security. While waiting, he strengthened his social side and human relationships.

KORP felt that there was ample time to explore the social side of the crowds and, of course, learn from them before the elections. He concluded he needed a slogan to sway the electorate to vote for him. He also accepted the challenge of learning to empathise with others, even if it was the most challenging path. However, he would take it on. As you can see, he was trying harder to look and to be empathetic and kind. Although this wasn't natural for him, he tried. Every hour, he whispered to himself not to forget to be compassionate.

So he embarked on a journey to learn more about the masses covered in empathy; this would be the last step before wresting power from politicians and handing it over to himself.

He was determined to stick to his plans. There was no turning back. So far, he had established three sides of the pyramidal structure of his future empire: power, knowledge and strength. He needed the fourth side: total control.

The political situation was messy, so he had to hold elections first. He did not want a dictatorship because that would be political suicide. Then, if he won the election, he would implement his imperial system. He planned to find the catalyst to make it possible for the masses – in goodwill – to accept his government in the long run. That was winning the election democratically.

"That will put me in a strategic situation. From there, I can exercise power in the longer term and under my own rules," KORP said.

His political opponents also planned to establish their political order: an economic dictatorship disguised as democracy, a system geared toward obeying the decisions of a few influential people who manipulated the country's economy through their presidential puppet candidate. Classic.

This political contest for country leadership was going to be fierce.

KORP, knowing the opposition party's plan, embarked on a crusade to capitalise on his knowledge of different social and elementary aspects of the daily lives of the masses. He wanted to know first-hand what the reality of an ordinary citizen was like and what the expectations of a father or a mother of a family were, for people all over the country had been under the leadership of all kinds of leaders in the past and had survived, so they would have many experiences to tell as well.

In his crusade, he joined various societies: charitable, sporting, secret, non-secret, religious, service clubs, golf clubs, political parties, industrial and agricultural associations, financial cooperatives, banking societies and educational institutions. He travelled to every corner of the country. He became a member of almost every social organisation in the cities and beyond.

What was he looking for in these places? He wanted to know and learn. His philosophy was to make the table lighter so that he could manipulate it so the water on the surface ran towards him efficiently, as planned.

Whenever he wanted to become a member of some society, he changed his name, personal details and postal address. He got postal addresses from empty houses where the mail carrier left papers. He got up early to start his journey. Riding his Vespa scooter, he visited places of interest to learn about them. As if looking for golden eggs, he was like a fox. He had no intention of joining these civil societies. Instead, he only wanted to discover how and why they attracted members' attention or acceptance.

He wandered around the law courts, claiming to be a law student. He wanted to be present from the beginning of any prosecution case until the last sentence. Instead, he saw that the law cases stretched over many days because the courts had become labyrinths filled with psychological torture because of corruption. He noted in his book about these justice courts. Strength: the entanglement of laws. Motivation: money. Weakness: corruption at all levels.

He visited secret societies using a false name and half-mask, posing as the 'Count of the Heights'. There, he filmed initiation ceremonies for the newly converted. The splendid and organised way they operated fascinated him, how well they looked after each other and how strong they were. They called themselves secret, but they were no longer secret societies thanks to their defectors. One of those defectors helped him interpret their symbolism, beliefs and aim. He discovered that the membership system in these societies was like an archer's arrow; once shot, it could not return. When he witnessed the oath-taking ceremony, he kept repeating in his mind, 'One-way ticket with no return'.

He found the principle of 'one-way' teaching in these societies fascinating. They walk in one direction only: forward. Almost all were experts in monopolising trade, ensuring a long business life. He noted in his book about these societies. Strength: monopoly. Motivation: to learn loyalty. Weakness: excessive love for money. This last aspect was usually the reason for their division and desertion.

Pretending to be destitute, he visited charitable societies; sometimes slept on the streets to converse with people experiencing homelessness. He came to relief houses, where he ate with them. He found that many rough sleepers were victims of the country's social system and could not afford to have access to a house because they did not earn enough money. Some couldn't even prove who they were because it was damn difficult to get an ID card, bureaucratic and impossible, and to top it off, without an identification card, you were nobody. This situation made him so sad and ashamed that he said, "The government makes a show of defending, caring for, protecting and raising millions in gold coins at charity parties to give homes to endangered animals, but at home, they cannot care for these human beings, whose genes are in imminent danger of extinction."

While at the charity house, he talked to the people who took refuge there. He realised that some were genuinely homeless, but others pretended to be vagrants living on government benefits. He noted in his book about these charitable centres. Strength: compassionate. Motivation: humanitarian activists. Weakness: the need for more deep control of government financial expenditures.

Riding his Vespa motorbike, he visited religious institutions to discover why they were so powerful. He noticed that some of them had no perceived material wealth on Earth. He found that strange, but when he learned the reason, he felt challenged. Also, he heard the tale of the man who had defeated death there. In honour and gratitude for this accomplishment, people paid him significant tributes. This story shocked him. From then on, he wanted to one day beat death, too. He noted in his book about these religious centres. Strength: faith. Motivation: love. Weakness: isolation. KORP wrote of isolation as a weakness because he felt they had a powerful message. Still, they were not interested in letting people know about it.

One day, he visited the government's parliament, which he saw as the heart of his country, wanting to know the fundamentals of its strength and power. He pretended to be a journalist for an extensive news network and made a documentary while learning about them. He wrote about parliament. Strength: a well-crafted, beautiful signature. Motivation: the creation of many decrees to reduce freedom. Weakness: ambition for power and control, combined with failure to deliver on what they promised.

He visited trading societies. To get there, he did not disguise himself or pretend to be somebody, for that was what he was: a business executive. It was like entering his own house. He studied them carefully to find out what their success stood for. After witnessing several business meetings and deals, he noted in his book about them. Strength: shrewd and sagacity. Motivation: money. Weakness: disloyalty to every level.

After several months, he toured most societies and discovered a common trait: fear. It was the perfect base ingredient and the key to mass manipulation. KORP concluded that, in the vast majority of these societies, loyalty was subordinate to fear. People followed or obeyed a cause out of fear rather than belief.

He discovered many societies had mastered using fear as the catalyst for loyalty and manipulation of the masses. Fear of punishment by the laws, established rules, leaders or rulers. Few were those societies where the basis of allegiance was love or the desire to serve a noble cause without personal ambition.

When he discovered what was happening, he was concerned and sensed that humanity deserves better. KORP felt freedom had a small place in most societies he knew and felt that freedom's surroundings were full of obstacles, so much so that there was almost no space to walk or move. Some societies have developed this situation, so people have no choice but to shake their heads to say yes or no because of excessive rules. With concern, he observed that these absurd rules, norms and precepts, often beautifully written or encrypted, reduce the space of freedom, which, over time, become heavy rocks on the backs of their members or partners.

"I repeat, there were exceptions, places where a real and genuine concern for human beings based on love had reflected, but they were very few," KORP said.

He also noted that some societies had rivers of regulations, rules, narrow requirements, dire warnings, etc. In some organisations, they accompanied their friendly human relations practices with security cameras, torture rooms, arrest warrants, offshore surveillance centres, private security via satellite or telephone, hidden cameras or microphones, etc. Seeing all this, KORP wondered where trust was. It did not exist; confidence was extinct or replaced with mistrust and judgement. He deduced that extreme fear subordinated freedom and faith in some civil societies. If one became a member of these societies, one moved from being a happy, free person to being watched and controlled twenty-four hours a day.

Sometimes, leaving these organisations represented psychological and terror-torture. It was the most terrible experience when a member of one of these societies stopped being a member for whatever reason, as sometimes happens. As a result, the organisation punished the person through the infamous 'psychological death while living'.[17] When KORP discovered this situation, he was mightily incensed and said that it was barbaric; humans may have better treatment and care.

In those societies, he found all kinds of ideals, slogans and commands such as 'Progress,' 'Reincarnation', 'Peace', 'For the good of humanity', 'Order', 'Unity', 'Salvation', 'Atheism', 'Immortality', 'True freedom', 'Self-realisation', 'Revolution', 'Anarchism', 'Open societies', 'Becoming god through knowledge', 'Faith in oneself', 'Liberation', 'Perfect state', 'Faith in the true', 'The chosen ones', 'Self-development', 'Humanism', 'Historical hero-worship', 'Divine justice', 'Eternal life', 'Everything is god', 'Dictatorship', 'Life on other planets', 'Extra-terrestrials', 'Transcendence', 'Dimensional portals', 'Outer world', 'Metaphysics', 'Consumerism', 'Time travel', 'Evolution', 'Hope', 'Pantheism', 'Science yes, religion no', 'Materialism', 'Astro-vision', 'Relativism of good and evil', 'Planetary migration', 'Worldview', 'Occultism', 'Prosperity', 'Nothingness', 'Healthy living', 'Sports', 'Body culture', 'Well-being', 'Black matter', 'Rebirth' and thousands more.

After months of searching for information about the behaviour of the masses, he retired to his room to review all the findings and experiences he had discovered. Along with his colleague, The Thinker, he revised memorable, outstanding, comical, sad, joyful, awkward, bizarre, nonsensical, playful, humorous and uncomfortable events he wrote about. He mulled over the conclusions he had reached, then transcribed them on small sheets of sticking paper in different colours and stuck them on the walls of his room, and they filled with these notes. Then stuck them around The Thinker, forming a silhouette of him, stuck

---

17. **Psychological death while living**. There were civil societies where they didn't forgive the deserter, and even his family could not contact him; they could not call him on the phone; if they saw him on the street, they had to ignore or avoid him; and if the deserter had children, the grandparents could not visit those grandchildren for the rest of their lives.

them, covering the sofa, bed, shelves, dining room, kitchen, living room, the floor, the ceiling and everything else inside his house.

When he had finished reviewing all his findings, one could see thousands of notes stuck over every object inside his house. Then he turned off the light and instead turned on an ultraviolet light.

The papers reflected the character of the notes in such a way that one could read them. Finally, he removed his clothes and sat in The Thinker's position, meditating on these writings.

He found slogans made it easier to appeal, convince and attract the masses. Slogans were powerful influencers and made people respond positively, passively and friendly to the causes they promoted quickly and easily. He analysed the how and why of things in these societies. First, he discarded ridiculous concepts, such as 'the relativity of good and evil' or ideals that had neither head nor tail. Then, he moved on to the more revolutionary ones and ended up with the counter-revolutionary ones. He carefully studied the themes applicable to present reality – reality existing in the present moment, not before or after, but now.

He thought further and concluded that, in some societies, people had expectations that extended from the present to the distant future. Their expectations extended to life beyond death and were not only confined to this planet's present reality. They presented life in a continuous present that crosses the barrier of death to continue living in another place called paradise; this idea made him think that this way of looking at reality was unprecedentedly powerful – something like life's journey. In their view, human existence continues after death somewhere, which would be the end of the trip or the last stop. For that reason, they emphasised that the earthly presence was temporary. The foundation of this teaching was faith, which brought hope to the population. This hope made those people move forward and walk through life more positively than usual.

He noted in his book: "We must offer something that gives hope and reaches beyond the present time." He found religious societies were most likely to present this hope. They stressed in their assemblies that death was not the end of everything. In his opinion, the concept of immortality and regeneration, instead of imminent destruction by death, was highly counter-revolutionary. He asked himself, 'Is this the hope people need now?'

Sometimes, he stayed longer to listen to teachings in societies where political slogans, concepts or definitions were attractive; he wanted to know more about them. He would talk to people or seek interviews with their leaders, asking them about their concerns.

In a religious society, the teaching about life after death and true freedom challenged him deeply. That day, he felt he lacked the faith to believe those words.

'If the offer had been to attain the afterlife without having to change the life I lead now, I would say yes, without hesitation,' he thought, relieved with a smile. However, it deeply shook and challenged his freedom, leaving him stunned as he left the meeting that day.

Regarding his conclusions, another concept that helped him was 'prosperity'. 'It opened infinite wealth and value accumulation opportunities,' he thought.

The concept of 'accurate knowledge' made him reconsider his knowledge. He concluded that knowing or having knowledge had no limits; it was infinite. He said, "No one can claim to be the master of truth because truth is infinite."

Hearing about the 'self-realisation' concept positively stimulated him because it reinforced his way of being with himself.

He was unsure about 'the relativity of good and evil'; for him, it was a very forced concept because it taught that death was the ultimate expression of evil. He pondered, "If someone can conquer death, then evil must have also conquered, so it cannot be relative to good."

He marvelled at the concept of 'Resurrection'; for him, it went hand in hand with the idea of 'Regeneration', the reversal of biological cell degeneration into a new body. The idea of the type of blood which makes resurrection possible dazzled him.

'Resurrection is only possible with a different type of blood,' he thought, because he knew life was in the blood.

"Coming back to life after death is bold, brave and categorical; it is perhaps the most powerful concept of all I have heard so far; all other concepts remain small and eclipsed by it," he said, speaking to his colleague, The Thinker.

He also wondered, 'Who is the bravest, most daring one who defies death itself and defeats it? It must be someone all-powerful. Perhaps a god or demigod descended the golden ladder.'

He brought to mind the small figurine of the character who defeated death. People said this small figurine brings good luck and gained worldwide recognition. In addition, many sacrificed their lives for his cause. The adoration that many people had for this hero amazed him. KORP also longed to be honoured and revered this way, so he placed the figurine in the Cathedral of the Clocks.

The faith theory[18] also intrigued him.

KORP continued meditating on the paper notes stuck on the wall. He became heartbroken when he reviewed his visits to government offices and courthouses. He always thought that those who governed a country had a strong understanding of the law of justice and safeguarded the laws. Or, those who dispensed justice were experts in fairness, almost demigods, but sadly, he realised they were mere mortals, humans doing their part. He excused honest and transparent people but condemned the corrupt. He said we urgently needed radical changes in these areas.

---

18.   **Faith**: For KORP, faith was a counter-revolutionary concept too. He said it was the most illogical concept in the universe. He always struggled to understand it. He wondered whether it was a science, a thing, something coming from somewhere subliminal, provoked or a theory. For him, faith was the antithesis of science.

He firmly believed that proof should determine science; something is proven true through systematic study and applied knowledge. Confirmation or verification is needed to accept something as a scientific discovery; the evidence must be tangible and factual. The existence of something without that is a theory.

Instead, they define faith as accepting something accurate and factual without necessarily providing proof. It is assuming something is true without seeing it or needing verification. For example, if someone says, 'By faith, I believe that the world is the product of someone's creation', they affirm that, through faith, it happened that way. Science will say, 'Show me the procedure or the proof to accept it as such', or it will ask, 'Have you been there when it happened?'

KORP concluded about faith: "When understanding or accepting something is too big for the human mind, faith is a good tool to consider." He believed in the causality of things, not randomness. He said everything had a beginning, and there was no doubt about it.

Also, **KORP** stared at his notes about visiting a famous biology and genetic society, where they hold the idea of some beginning that generated things; they keep this idea based on how human cells or these micro-factories operated and consider them too organised to interact by chance. They had the theory that chance is imperfect and generates chaos. But the perfect synchronisation of the cells made them doubt it was mere caprice. He held that theory, too.

For example, the concept of 'true freedom' made him doubt his freedom. For him, his freedom was his true freedom, and hearing about another kind of freedom was a shock that left him pale and intrigued, so much so that he became curious about the difference between these two freedoms. He became curious about experiencing that difference one day. At the end of the page, he wrote in tiny letters, "I would like one day to experience this other true freedom."

He also found that lack of money was one of the main reasons for corruption. He wrote these words on red paper in bold letters: "Eradicate the money-grabbers who monopolise finance and combat the miserly wages paid by their companies."

After visiting all these civil societies, he found that most of their members expressed common discontent about the current global economic crisis. This discovery led him to conclude: 'A kind of labyrinth trapped human beings making them experience a state of dissatisfaction. They feel their space lacks freedom, causing the masses to become volatile, fragile and malleable. This dissatisfaction makes them like gentle doves today and turbulent hurricanes tomorrow. This dissatisfaction also produces emptiness. If there is no change for good somewhere, life is meaningless to them.' He then wrote these conclusions in his book.

"A vacuum meant an opportunity for KORP – a remarkable one. Thus, he assumed he had to persist in gaining the control of his nation's power. From there, he could fill those gaps in people's expectations." (The Thinker)

Finally, he concluded that, at that moment, his primary concern should be how to fill people's emptiness. He should also think about how to fulfil their expectations.

What were people's expectations? The answer was that someone had to raise wages. He knew it from the people he spoke to on his visits.

They told him, "The greed of a few is the father of corruption in our nation, and the miserable wages many receive are the mother."

He excluded individuals who were honest and integral to what they did at any level, so he respected them a lot. He had signed contracts with some of them in his business, whom he held in high esteem. To him, they were like mirrors that reflected truth and justice.

He underlined all those things that tarnished those societies' honour and protected the most valuable things they had.

Then, he created his brand slogan with all the material reviewed, studied and shredded. Strategically, he thought it should be inclusive and embrace most or all people's expectations. His slogan read, "For humanity, let's build our future in progress, peace and freedom towards eternal life."

His advisers told him that the words 'eternal life' were too promising, perhaps unrealistic. Still, he was furious when he heard they wanted to remove them; KORP insisted they leave those words where they were because he did not doubt the algorithm's existence that would make that possible. His political advisers needed to determine whether he was talking about finding the formula for eternal life or what. Later, they learned he meant the hero who defeated death.

KORP travelled to the region where the hero who made eternal life possible lived. With deep sadness, he had to accept that they had deleted the words 'eternal life' from the slogan. He realised there was also a lot of division in the population because of this hero, and he did not understand why.

'In politics, the one who unites forces wins, not the one who scatters them,' he thought. In KORP's view, this hero's achievement was extraordinary and lofty. He said, "Eternal life remains a national priority for research." He would invest more human and financial resources in studying and discovering life beyond death.

Every time he visited the Cathedral of the Clocks and passed by the small figurine of the hero, who had defeated death, he repeated these words: "If you did it, I can too."

The concept 'True knowledge opens the door to immortality' intrigued him profoundly to where he considered replacing the words 'eternal life' in his slogan with it, as that concept also provided significant hope to secret societies. He concluded: "If accurate knowledge brings eternal life as well, then this way or the other, we will arrive at the same destination, and this concept does not divide people so drastically."

One day, he asked the society – where they taught this concept – if they had any measure, value or amount of knowledge required to attain immortality. They could not give him any information about the exact measurement or amount, only telling him he must first accept the terms and conditions for membership in these societies, and then, and only then, would he begin his march to meet the Source of Everything who, to them, was the giver of proper knowledge and, therefore, of immortality. He found the possibility to be very appealing and stinging. It piqued him to know more about the knowledge one received and the amount of knowledge required to attain immortality.

"I get the impression that KORP emphasises that his knowledge is immense and pervasive; he meant all the information he harboured in the galleries of his mind. He then assumed he could achieve eternal life by adding it up, plus what the Source of Everything would reveal to him." (The Thinker)

I suspect the same thing myself.

Of all the subjects learned in those civil societies and social meeting places, his favourite was 'life on other planets'. He would stay learning about this fascinating subject for days in the organisations and societies where they teach it. He discovered that hundreds of space companies and clubs had aggressively explored cosmic space during the terrestrial space age. For these societies, reaching the moon and Mars was child's play; they sent exploratory probes to various planets and moons of different worlds long ago. They even got dimensional spaces where time had an additional value or ran faster. For example, one Earth minute could be equivalent to a year or a thousand years in those dimensional spaces.

"It's certainly a very complex subject; perhaps we should talk about the subject of eternity, a space where the terrestrial time we know doesn't exist," he said with a smile.

The idea of residing on another planet had always fascinated KORP. He would like to create an interstellar fleet linking Earth with other worlds. "This would expand our influence as humanity into the universe, thus fulfilling why we are here," he yearned.

He became an active member of one of these space societies because he found hope there. He dreamt of living on the planet of the aliens who abducted him as a child.

***

After formulating his slogan, he met with his political advisers to work on the design of campaign banners, billboards, TV advertisements and uniforms for young people, who would distribute the propaganda in public places and shopping centres around the country, radio spots, etc. They had a few months of arduous work before the elections.

***

After the government promulgated the official opening for political campaigning for the national elections, his political advisers set the plans in motion.

The artistic designs for his political party banners conveyed futuristic scientific emphasis. These banners featured graphics of atoms moving around the nucleus and artistic photographs of DNA in eye-catching phosphorescent colours.

They printed T-shirts with their slogan divided into two parts: the first was on the front, and the second was on the back. They had caps, armbands with the slogan, etc. The banners had vivid prints of Biodermatik soldiers wearing symbiotic suits and a message emphasising KORP as a synonym for life. People could see them displayed along highways.

The other political parties were just a little behind. They had platforms set up at gas stations or near supermarkets. On these platforms, an army of young people talked to customers about the benefits of voting for their political party and candidates. They also gave away T-shirts and many incentives to secure votes.

At weekends, political parties had their candidates' names and slogans written in vaporous clouds in the sky. The pilots of the planes that did this job were risk-takers; they made a lot of money to do it. These advertisements were spectacular, covering dozens of miles from where you could read them.

The public demanded more proposals to address their concerns during debates to increase their satisfaction. Candidates also worked themselves to exhaustion, so they sometimes had to use doubles. In large venues where the speech platform was far from the audience, they used pre-recorded speeches that stunt performers mimicked. That was clever!

6. From bullying to power

Patience's greatest weakness is impatience.

Now, KORP will show how clear his strategy is and how determined and sure he is about it. In his mind, the complete picture of his empire-building plan was clear. In his will, he had all the guarantees to put it into practice.

Seizing control of his country through a democratic election was the only way to establish his empire; that way, he would get enough power to rid his tormentors for good and forever from a strategic position. Those were both his priorities and his primary plan.

Notably, when he implemented his plan, he never measured collateral damage. I repeat, never: he could not. He was like a horse with blinkers covering its eyesight; he could not see to the sides, only to the front. For him, the critical thing was to get there and accomplish his goal; above all, it was imperative to stick to the plan. It didn't matter how long it took or what the consequences were.

***

As the weeks passed, KORP felt his three ex-bullies' presence and psychological-demonic pressure grow closer. Every time he stood on the pavement of his house and inhaled the air, he could hear their steps, smell them and sense they were close. The stalking of his enemies became a deadly poison. Even if he wanted to, he would not survive this time if it reached his bloodstream. He was under much pressure, but he was ready to respond. He said, "Now or never."

Knowing this, he secretly and in advance planted his mushroom bombs in the countries from which his enemies came; he also planted them in different parts of the continents, in the seas and in space as a sign of precaution. His idea was to pressure them if there was no change of attitude towards him. Pressing the yellow button or activating his mushroom bombs' safety key was only a matter of time.

Also, KORP's friendly countries – sometimes allies on the continents – agreed to support him by guarding or storing his mushroom bombs in their territories, at sea and in space. This way, he had his enemies surrounded. He hid strategically in the shadows and was ready to counterattack when necessary. He had a powerful enemy that never slept, but planned to pounce on him like a hungry beast.

***

With the election days away, he plunged headlong into the home stretch. His political party was happy with its presidential candidate, KORP. His party supported him with passion and care. They wrote of him: "Who is better than this champion, this warrior defender of science, who leads our country on the path to victory? Who has made our country a powerful influence on Earth?"

KORP toured every corner of the country in a relentless and aggressive political campaign. Everywhere he stood, he offered true freedom and progress. He memorised an excellent speech his political advisers had written for him, and a team of international political propaganda experts surrounded him. These advisers gave him a complete list of requirements for his public campaign. For example, he learned how to shape his facial features for television cameras and holograms, made angry facial gestures when he spoke out against corruption or made hand movements with his fists clenched tight when he protested about something. He learned to control the tone of his voice, adopting the voice of a kind and caring father when he offered economic stability.

After many practice sessions, he developed efficient ways of speaking in front of crowds, modulated his voice for radio and press conferences or debates, and learned to control his movements and postures for press photos. He devoted himself – often to extensive lengths – to making his facial features more pleasing, forcing with great effort a bright, natural smile. His make-up artists cast particular shadows on his face to make him look like a clear-headed and sensible intellectual in front of television cameras. Another element they cared about was his wardrobe; his clothes exuded confidence and glamour. It was part of 'media-strategic body language'. He followed the requirements of his political advisers, who were on the other side of the camera.

He also learned to dance to the 'Remove lice from your shirt' rhythm, a viral song in those days. Sometimes, after giving a speech, he asked the band to play it. Raising his jacket, he would wiggle his hips happily to the rhythm of the music and invite the entire audience to dance with him; it was his way of appealing to the younger generations. KORP gave up his existence to win votes.

His opponents did the same and had even welled support from the fourth estate – the press – riding the apocalyptic horseman of lies. They fabricated all kinds of soap opera stories to tarnish his name. The venom of the presidential race wounded the other candidate's weakest part to get him out of the way before election day. It was a savage race.

KORP's speeches were offensive, such as: "Now is the time to clean up the corruption with which they build their rotten riches on your shoulders." Or hopeful like this: "Now is the time to deliver justice to people unjustly imprisoned." Or, more precisely, like this one: "It is time to open the country's economic coffers and enrich everyone. It is your right."

In his speeches, he avoided the terms 'common,' 'social equality' or 'economic capitalism', which sounded like communism, socialism or capitalism. He did not want to copy these ancient ideologies. Therefore, he did not even mention them. Despite positive intentions, these ideologies eventually crossed the line to destroy human dignity, resulting in their demise. Many governments stripped human rights in the name of these ideologies, bringing terrible memories.

People felt disgusted whenever politicians mentioned democracy because corruption reached it too, and people felt repulsed whenever politicians said it; despite offering hope and freedom, many found it subjective, an extremely uncertain possibility. Also, in the name of democracy, many prominent politicians had perpetrated crimes against humanity in his country, whose perpetrators took refuge within powerful and insensitive nations, so KORP cleverly brought up these horrible memories in his speeches to destroy his opponents.

Also, he was precise and strategic in using his time on the campaign stage. When he gave a speech, he avoided long speeches; instead, he got straight to the point, which was his speaking success. People were cheerful about listening to the candidate's voices, but only for a few minutes. Sometimes, in the middle of his speech, he called on someone from the audience to say a few words.

The argument that weakened him the most, which his political opponents used very well against him, was this: "KORP has become the owner of all natural resources on the planet, and his companies prevent access to raw materials throughout the globe, even on the moon. It has also set its sights on natural resources on Mars." That last part about Mars was a complete myth.

KORP countered with this statement: "They have monopolised freedom of the press, opinion and the will for you to decide for yourselves. What they offer is neither true freedom nor true democracy. They want total control over your freedom. The democracy they offer subdues your resolve and free will into absolute obedience to their command. They want to establish a financial monopoly, a dictatorship disguised as a democracy. Working with me means progress and freedom. Your children will have free university education and health care. I will raise wages by one hundred per cent. There will be freedom of the press and opinion, and you will be free to believe what you want."

"KORP's offer was bold. It was the complete opposite of what the other candidates offered. He attacked his opponents with the things they were most careful not to say or offer: first, freedom of opinion and thought, and second, increased wages, because he found that those two factors had produced a huge gap of dissent in the hearts of the masses, and for that reason, the attitude of the people was dissonant." (The Thinker)

He took advantage of the news and turned it into a campaign offer. Everybody knew and confirmed that his opponents and the power groups monopolised freedom of speech, thought and wages. He had the means and the power to turn these variables into permanent features. In his opponents' companies, workers earned secondary wages and that suffocated their families.

"KORP understood very well that a contented heart was the seat of happiness, and happiness stimulated the will powerfully." (The Thinker)

He was acutely aware of the sad reality of most families, where both parents had to work to make enough money to cover family expenses, frequently leaving their children at home on their own.

However, because the power groups controlled the media, they kept this truth in a secret chamber with seven keys.[19]

He knew that by raising wages, companies could never become poorer – a fact he learned when visiting trading companies. The genuine issue with unfair wages was greed, often excessive greed. To make more money, these economically powerful companies designed a monetary system called the 'Fountain of Miracles' to get their hands on the country's financial system. It was a financial equation that supposedly produced economic miracles.

His opponents, who designed it, explained how it works in this way: "It is like a water fountain with two bowls, the upper and lower bowls. When water flows from above, it fills the upper bowl

---

19. **Seven keys**: It was a saying from the story of a king who suffered from anxiety and kept all his treasures in a building with seven rooms. Each room was inside the other and separated by a corridor around it. The safe was in the innermost chamber, and only the king had the keyring with seven keys. Supposedly, it was the safest and most secret place to keep his treasures.

first, which, once filled, overflows into the lower bowl to fill it as well. The water in the bowl is money and the upper bowl is us. The lower bowl is you, the masses, and we all become equally rich."

KORP observed this economic equation: "It works like this: when the upper bowl is about to be filled, efficiently and greedily, these power groups enlarge it so that it hardly ever reaches the lower bowl. Thus, the miracle fountain miraculously dried up its water and did not fill another bowl. In addition, as the water flow is constant, enlarging the upper bowl is also ongoing. So, with each passing day, the upper bowl becomes more significant, and the lower bowl dries up and becomes smaller and smaller than the upper bowl. The savageness of their wealth is based mainly on your sweat and your sacrifices."

He was honest in his speeches and practical in his approach, which fascinated the crowds.

He stood up for the rights of those most oppressed by hunger and poverty. People know that this cause arouses passion and becomes a powerful magnet in politics, attracting people of all political affiliations to rally around it. In addition, it raises immense promises to end this threat to humanity. However, sadly, these promises end up in a drawer in well-written papers. Disparity in the personality of society? I don't know.

His executioners and his enemies planned an accident to remove him from the political race because they realised he was above them in the polls. The plan was to eliminate him in the last political debate; they orchestrated an accident to cause his death. They had arranged for the political discussion to take place in a village nestled in the mountains, near the remote northern borders of the country. There were gold-mining towns in those regions that had expressed an interest in a debate between politicians before the national elections and wanted to meet them up close. After all, these populations contributed much money to the country in taxes and mining royalties. They wanted the press to reach out through the debates and inform the rest of the country about their tourism potential.

The scenery along the way leading to these places was magnificently picturesque. It passed through rugged terrain, tunnel-filled mountain ranges, winding, narrow roads, dreamy lagoons and surreal forest landscapes. KORP didn't want to miss this trip, so he travelled by car for the apparent reason: the scenery. His enemies planned to explode a bomb in the snow to produce an avalanche, covering the vehicle he was travelling in.

Indeed, so they did: they exploded the bomb, which unleashed a gigantic avalanche, and it swept away the caravan in which he supposedly was travelling and half-buried it in rocks and snow. It was a deliberate, cowardly and grim accident. Fortunately, they killed no one, but some of his advisers, including his double, were seriously injured. It showed his bloodthirsty executioners. Fortunately, his bodyguards discovered the trap in time and took precautions. Even though the attack was not certain, it occurred. His double suffered severe injuries, and it took him months to recover.

KORP said they saved his life, and he thanked them. It was strange to hear him give thanks because he never did. He insisted on attending that debate, driven by his never having been there. The things he heard and read about the place whetted his appetite to learn more. On the day of the journey, he reluctantly stayed home against his will. He was furious with everyone, but remained. They even offered a helicopter ride for security, but he declined. After what happened, he stayed away from the press for a few days, making it seem like he had suffered severe injuries from the accident.

As the dark days of the attack against him passed, he sat in front of the television watching the political news, drinking coffee and eating some strawberry-quinoa jam cookies, his favourites. His hamster accompanied him. He insisted on being left alone because he was in shock.

He would occasionally give speeches wrapped in bandages as he had big wounds. That assassination attempt pushed KORP higher in the polls as he got out alive. The entire country said

Providence[20] was by his side.

Instead, to respond to the provocations of the premeditated accident, he used that experience as a lethal weapon to further wound his opponents in his speeches.

After listening to intense debates and watching fierce political struggles to win the elections, finally, the vast majority of the masses – the working classes of the country – understood that if they wanted to improve their financial situation, voting for KORP was the great opportunity they had been waiting for. They would not waste it.

He was a strategist. Until that point, everything worked according to his plan. A few months before the election, his political opponents boycotted his companies abroad even more viciously and shrewdly. They sent infiltrators disguised as prestigious politicians who sabotaged KORP's business relations on five continents to achieve this. They travelled around the countries, saying that "if he becomes president, it will be the end of free trade on the planet".

Many governments bought into the lies and immediately embargoed or banned KORP companies from their countries. Other countries took another more severe course of action: they took away KORP's operating license, which resulted in the death blow for some of his companies. Besides being an illegal act, it was inhumane because it left thousands of his workers' families on the streets.

These actions provoked his anger, but he endured them because the elections were only a few weeks away.

His opponents escalated even further because he did not respond to or react to these insults. They convinced some countries to declare war on KORP's government before the elections. There was no need to go that far, but they did.

His enemies did that because they wanted to weaken him

---

20. **Providence** means unceasing provision. It was one of the hundreds of goddesses worshipped by the inhabitants of the KORP Empire. She was the goddess whose hands were always outstretched with palms upward, giving food or protection.

profoundly by using chaos and anarchy in his companies. The irony of his tormentors and opponents was that they were unsatisfied with all the damage they had already caused him. These people had bullying in their genes, no doubt. Who were they serving? What was in it for them? Nothing would be the answer since, according to the polls, they were losing the elections, so they were only exposing their rotten democratic character. Yet they claimed they sought revenge. He called them hypocrites.

As the elections approached, his opponents stirred the entire planet, forcing the Organisation of Continents – the highest authority for world peace and supposedly neutral – to take part in the conflict. Unfortunately for KORP, that organisation supported the executioners and his political opponents by seizing his companies globally.

This last act of cowardice broke the camel's back. KORP's enemies were sure that this time would take him out of his stride and cause some political slip-up or miscalculation that would change the course of the election. However, he strategically withstood the insult even though he pounded the table angrily when he was alone at home and desired to give them their comeuppance. As he complained in front of his colleague, The Thinker, and Kate's photograph, he cried out in frustration. Only these people listened to him and consoled him.

***

On the week of the long-awaited elections, KORP had a wounded wing, unable to breathe its last sigh of patience. He had his workers wandering the streets of foreign cities with their families left in uncertainty; this frustrated him greatly.

Finally, election day arrived – the nation celebrated by spectating in a tense atmosphere. Most people got up early and went to the suffrage houses to vote. Some did it at home via the internet. What his tormentors and political opponents feared most happened at that moment. Around midnight, amidst national nervousness, the country's electoral tribunal announced he had won the elections. His triumph was overwhelming, and his political party even won the most seats in parliament. These were unprecedented and the last elections in his nation's history.

The entire nation celebrated this victory with great joy. In the capital's major streets, excited people set up stages with music to dance the night away. Many voters celebrated their champion, KORP.

That night, after hearing the news, he climbed a tall tower where he could see the city and beyond on the horizon. Standing there, he listened to the celebration of his triumph and watched as fireworks filled the skies over the capital. He stood at that moment to embrace the solitude and, raising his arms, wept with joy at his triumph and victory.

It followed long months of work and extended, bitter nights of practising and memorising speeches. It was the culmination of years of studying the masses, and KORP wanted to celebrate this special moment with the memory of the person he loved most. Pulling out Kate's photograph, he kissed it and said, "Thank you for always smiling. I promise I will find the way, no matter how, to bring you back to me again, because I still love you."

That moment was special for him. It was a family celebration in his heart and soul. Then one of his political advisers got there, and after greeting him, said, "We're waiting for you, sir."

The man had confetti on his head and all over his body, a sign of a big party celebration. KORP descended the stairs to the main hall, where his friends and political associates were waiting. When they saw him enter, the place filled with applause for the new national leader.

It was also a special moment for his political party because they had put too much on the line. For several minutes, there was a flash and a click. Everybody was in the presence of an eminence.

In the middle of that party, someone proposed a toast, saying, "Long live our brand-new national leader," and everyone shouted, "KORP, KORP, KORP!" It was an extraordinary time for his political party. He took it with humility and respect, even for his political opponents. Still, I couldn't say what he thought about his tormentors then. Then, it was time to give his first speech as the newly elected ruler of the nation. His advisers had put his address on an autocue, and he read it out for the cameras.

Within days of taking office, he raised salaries by a hundred per cent. He declared freedom of the press, opinion and everything. These were his first campaign promises, and he fulfilled them just as he promised. With this gesture, he sealed a strategic alliance with the masses, which would grow stronger over the years.

"Keeping one's word is miraculous; it heals wounds." (The Thinker)

KORP understood very well, from the beginning, the power of keeping promises made to the masses in political campaigns and delivering them.

In the following days, he restructured the entire political system to make it more transparent, applying his orchestrated principle of regeneration from the inside out. He completely reorganised the whole financial system to serve the country. These early reforms made people entrenched in these critical jobs and corrupted over the years very uncomfortable; many left, but immediately, he fired those who stayed before they put their dirty hands over the new political system. The new government found those who had got property through corruption guilty, and they confiscated their property without the option of appeal.

He established community service for thousands of prisoners waiting for their sentences. He ordered the judicial system to speed up their cases immediately.

In the meantime, he reinstated those prisoners with minor crimes by giving them decent jobs and salaries pending their release. It was also a campaign promise. Many prisoners released from jail had the chance to work in road construction jobs with proper wages.

The new national leader proclaimed freedom of belief: the country could believe in whatever it wanted without restriction and declared it a secular nation. He also regularised all undocumented people in the country, giving them residence permits and work opportunities and receiving living wages[21] for their work.

KORP signed a law prioritising people experiencing homelessness and providing help for people without housing. He gave them a home through a 'Safe and Dignified Journey' programme. Also, he restructured the healthcare system by introducing free medical care to those who suffer terminal illnesses as a national priority and mandated access to medicines at cost.

He bought up many small printing presses and turned them into mega-printing houses to stand up to his critics and the fourth estate: the press. He pushed for fair trade with food and other supply importers. Above all, he responded with the same coin to the countries that embargoed his assets abroad; because of that 'hostile act', many countries, supported by the Organisation of the Continents, including his political opponents and his executioners, went into direct war against KORP's government. They wanted to show him who was running the planet, including his country. But he tried to mend his country's relationship with the Organisation of Continents to achieve peace. He did not want to conflict with the world's mother organisation, so he sought peaceful means to settle the situation. However, the world's mother organisation would not pay attention because it had become blinded and deeply poisoned by KORP's enemies' lies.

The verdict was that he had no alternative other than warning those countries and the Organisation of Continents, which still had his assets seized, about the consequences. He warned them he would press the yellow button if they did not change their attitude. His administration gave them clear deadlines for returning his companies to him or facing catastrophic results.

He declared to his advisers, "No one can give freedom to another, and no one can take it away; all that remains is to respect

---

21. **The living wage** was a rule measuring how much someone received for work. People said that, in historical times in the KORP world, companies had to pay twice as much to workers whose partners were at home caring for children because they considered it essential childcare work for society.

it." These countries and hostile groups did not know who KORP was. They disrespected his freedom at every level. His wars had no mercy or respect for human rights. They were unaware he was not afraid to strike back, even with twice as many blows. Instead, they turned a deaf ear to his warnings.

"Being the leader of his nation did not change who he was. He was who he was. Still, he was the same KORP: the one who set a goal and ran towards it without fear; the mighty warrior; he, the one who was clear about his freedom and understood the world in his way and by his own rules." (The Thinker)

In such scenarios, despite who he was, KORP was never the aggressor, but tried to stay out of discussions to avoid conflict.

Also, the Organisation of Continents sent him a request requiring free access to raw materials in the countries where he had businesses. What was the argument? The argument was a whim and nothing more. When you discover the proper reasons, they will surprise you.

"There is no argument since KORP is not saying they cannot exploit raw materials there. He never said that. That is a lie. Also, there were raw materials worldwide, perhaps better than what KORP exploited. However, they were stubborn about him and wanted food on his plate because it seemed more delicious to them, and in that way, they could disturb his sleep." (The Thinker)

So, in the first year of his rule, people were content with their national leader, KORP. Families had enough to live on. One member of the couple stayed home to care for their offspring, and the other worked because one's salary was enough to support the family, as it was an adequate living wage.

But outside his country, the situation was different. Because of this abuse, the Organisation of Continents was still embargoing his companies, which resulted in irreparable losses. Many countries threatened war if he did not stop building industrial plants on the moon. His tormentors did an excellent job of defamation, operating viciously from the shadows. He sought peace with everyone at all costs. No one listened to him.

"This is unjust!" he had claimed.

He retired to his house for a few days, sat beside his colleague, The Thinker, to meditate on his stool, and concluded that a seed must die to sprout a new plant. The next day, he called in his military strategists and asked them what the chances were of escaping unscathed in an eventual 'Mushroom Thermonuclear War';[22] all agreed that the country's underground cities were the safest and its entire population would be safe.

He then ordered his strategist to press the yellow button on the second day of the fourth week of the month (which had twenty-eight days) at 00:00 hours. That would give time to save as much of the country as possible and evacuate its citizens from all corners of the globe to safety. He asked his country's politicians to do all they could to convince the Organisation of Continents to back down from its stubbornness.

His advisers communicated KORP's intentions as soon as possible. They were sure such a decision would convince their enemies. However, nothing convinced the mother of the world's organisations; it was both blind and deaf. The poison went too deep. There was no way to change the determination of his enemies' hearts.

The continents also prepared for the impending war and would fight back with the same mushroom bombs KORP sold.

Knowing what was coming, many nations around the globe prepared for this hell. Because of the Cold War, some countries enlisted in emergency contingencies many years ago. Others reorganised their hideouts and took supplies deep into the earth. In contrast, countries that had never been in such situations thought the news was just another baffling story from politicians who did nothing but talk and talk.

The Armada positioned its warships strategically on the seas to unleash their angels of death, supersonic craft that travelled at light speed and carried death and destruction in their guts.

Little by little, and in a matter of weeks, most humans disappeared from the face of the Earth as if by magic. They left behind villages and ghost towns.

In space, satellites rushed silently from one place to another to comply strictly and faithfully with their orders. Respectfully,

---

22. **'Mushroom Thermonuclear War'** refers to nuclear war.

they also met the enemies' satellites, who hurried to take their positions. None of them could distinguish the concept of 'enemy' nor decipher the idea of 'friend' or who was who. Their looks and attitude were reminiscent of blind automatons. Submissive of their algorithms' orders, they positioned themselves in their strategic places. From here, they would also spew the rain of hell they cradled in their stomachs.

If those 'intelligent' machines could have been the mediators in that conflict or the judges to appease the gladiators thirsty for innocent bloodshed, they would have stopped that storm of torment and carried the deadly poison from their wombs beyond infinite space to vomit it. So, only so, they would have freed humans from that bitter bitterness hell.

KORP's country had nine thousand five hundred nuclear bombs, and the heat emitted by each when it exploded would exterminate any organic being within a one-hundred-and-fifty-mile radius. It was not him who made those lethal weapons. He had only made the latest generation of these dark angels of death. Still, they were even more destructive because of the expansive radius they reached when they exploded. They also penetrated the Earth's surface several metres deep.

"You might wonder why KORP took this matter so far when he had so much wealth and power. And he also controlled his country. Wealth, power or total control don't define freedom. Freedom is possible without riches, power or total control, but wealth, power and total control without freedom are equivalent to death. Substitute freedom may be the worst thing to do. It is singular. They threatened his freedom with death, plain and simple." (The Thinker)

Yes, you are right. Freedom can be effortless and pleasurable, but it brings complex consequences to human life if imprisoned. KORP knew that his tormentors and his enemies had determined to see him defeated and would not rest until they saw him look at the ground; that was a fact. His defence was legitimate in his own eyes. This war was an act of self-defence, life or death.

There was simply no more room in the glass of his patience, and now the water flowed to the ground. His patience had reached its limits and lost its patience like his. He would no longer tolerate bullying – not even now, as the leader of his nation, which he loved dearly; this was the moment he waited for to get rid of his enemies and focus on it. He couldn't measure the consequences of that decision, either. Even if he wanted to, he couldn't.

KORP remarked that if his enemies wanted raw materials on the moon, there would be enough space for everyone, which was true. The countries from which he had imported his raw materials represented a tiny fraction of the total number of countries on the planet, which was also true. So, his enemies only wanted to disturb his sleep and eat food from his plate as an act of bullying.

On the second day of the fourth week of the month, which had twenty-eight days, at 00:00 hours, darkness settled over the Earth and filled it with mourning and despair.

Damn whim!

7. One Way, Only One Way

Even mosquito breathing can sweep away those who lack a sense of belonging.

Some years have passed since the Nuclear War. It isn't easy to describe the world after that event because it was an unprecedented, catastrophic war which stripped from the soul and peace-thirsty heart the last tears of hope. It was too sad. The collateral damage was innumerable. The Nuclear War claimed the lives of many innocent people. As Earth's face faded away, its beauty remained disfigured.

The explosions reduced many places on the Earth's surface to ashes, and their chemical formulas adjusted to one equation: zero life. On that dark day, explosions also stopped the time clockwise. Many people had left stamped against the air, giving them no time to reach their underground shelters. The radioactive heat engulfed some cities and condemned them to wander like dust.

From space, the Earth's skin looked like a leopard's, with vast areas stained black and orange-yellow and others reduced to ash. Dust, contaminated with radioactivity from the explosions, travelled on giant desert sandstorms, polluting vast regions of the Earth and the atmosphere. Each explosion shook the Earth's orbit and destabilised it so much that it was the day the planet cried out its labour pains to heaven.

The war wiped many countries off the map. Many capital cities looked like Sodom, cities after divine judgement. The thermonuclear bombs stripped them of their beauty, pride and glory, covering them in ugliness before being sent into oblivion. They aimlessly wandered and played host to dust and birds of prey. They were unrecognisable.

Also, Mother Nature was so disoriented that she shook her head, trying to overcome the shock. Impotently, she attempted to return the rain to the earth, making significant efforts. However, the dust, wind, sand and ashes spoiled these attempts; she struggled to understand what had happened.

The bombs disrupted immense ecosystems crucial to food production. Like grass to feed the animals, drinkable water fountains suffered severe contamination by radiation. Resolving environmental problems and restoring arable land would be challenging.

KORP's enemies also died, and they lay buried under the eternal shadows of death in the rubble, leaving no memory of them in the land of the living.

***

In the post-Nuclear War era, global geopolitics also underwent radical changes. Geopolitical boundaries drawn by the previous age had disappeared, creating new ones.

The day the floodgates of the underground cities opened, they marked a 'new era' on the calendar. Indeed, the dawn of genesis began in this corner of the universe – another cycle, another spin on the disc of life. Slightly different, but from then on, everything would be a challenge.

With much desperation, time again sped up its needle clock to raise humans' countenance.

When the conditions were right, the survivors emerged from their underground cities and quickly rebuilt on the surface.

Within a few years, they successfully established five significant cities on this side of the Earth. Luz[23] was the most powerful of the five towns. With KORP at its head, that city prospered swiftly and shrewdly. It became a dominion, an influence and a catalyst for

---

23. **Luz** (Spanish) means light.

the new global millennium. It rose from the ashes like a phoenix, proud, powerful and robust compared to the other cities and kingdoms of the planet. Above all, it was full of self-confidence.

The other four cities were close behind, but they had to make significant efforts for their subsistence; their greatest obstacles were the means to find more food and transport. These extreme circumstances forced them to import their supplies from distant lands south of the equator, forcing them to cross the Valleys of Death – vast areas still riddled with radioactivity – and fierce seas.

KORP offered them help, which they accepted, help that, little by little, made them dependent until, finally, the inevitable happened: these cities had to join the jurisdiction of the town of Luz, which led to the formation of the empire he had always dreamed of. He never imagined it would be through Nuclear War, but it was.

He called this upcoming empire the KORP Empire. Its dominion stretched from the Tropic of Cancer to the Arctic Circle. The city of Luz became the empire's capital. These five cities agreed to submit to the KORP Empire's government and pay tribute for protection and food supplies.

***

It is difficult to explain how Earth survived that catastrophic conflict. Still, it was more difficult to explain how KORP's face looked considering these facts. His face reflected a total coolness, as if nothing had happened. His attitude was one of inert complicity in his emotions and coldness in his reactions. This lack of empathy aroused much resentment towards him, especially from people who had lost a loved one.

Despite this distortion in his character, everyone in the upcoming empire loved KORP. The masses loved and respected him, no matter how dark and cold his feelings or face looked. While the nuclear pandemic hit the populations hard, they stood up to the catastrophe. They quickly organised themselves, with their newly appointed emperor at the helm.

What was KORP's success?

"That is a brilliant question. I think it was his government policies that made him successful. His government had consistently kept its campaign promises: raising wages and ensuring freedom of thought, speech and belief. His goal was to make his domain happy." (The Thinker)

Yes, I am with you! He organised a plan to restore the land surface to cultivation. However, at the rate the work progressed, restoring the planet's entire surface would take at least a few decades.

In the cities, there were periods when food was scarce, and the efforts of the people to supply that need were immense. As in the other four towns, Luz rose quickly from post-war calamities. Cities had to build walls around them called Gerikos; they were gigantic, tall and thick, covered in stainless steel. These walls contained polluting dust.

He made good allies in some parts of the planet where the consequences of war were not so catastrophic. These parts still had fertile areas, especially south of the equator. KORP built a solid commercial food bridge from these places to the empire, building a sizeable commercial bridge with his steel horse riders after restoring his ship factories.

***

Wages in the newly formed empire rose constantly, so there was little to worry about as they met their basic needs: security, food and shelter. They didn't need something because they had sufficient purchasing power. Undoubtedly, this strengthened the people's economy, so they soon forgot the past and looked to the future with their heads held high.

In the empire, no matter where you worked or what you did, you still earned a high wage.

His steel horse riders were the workhorses in this post-war reconstruction and consolidation period. Seas became his strategic allies. He had to learn to tame their waves and ride their storms.

Throughout the empire, there was a race against time to

create food autonomy. People crowded the main entrances of the Gerikos in each city. Merchants came in, bringing food and leaving to get more supplies from distant lands. These traders were like miniature ants in front of a hungry giant.

KORP made wise decisions; he swiftly and accurately restored political, economic and commercial strength. He quickly created the new empire's political constitution for security and territorial sovereignty.

The army created the Biodermatik Armada as an elite force. Apart from their sophisticated symbiotic suits, they carried sophisticated military equipment to deter potential threats and deployed them to the newly created frontiers to secure the empire. The emperor emphasised they were to stop potential enemies.

"Holding such a lot of territory, he must keep the spearhead sharp." (The Thinker)

What do you mean by that?

"I mean. The restoration of the planet happened not only in the newly created empire but also out of its territories, where new kingdoms also arose and needed space to grow. That triggered the creation of 'no one's land', a vast territory between the parallel Tropic of Cancer and the equator. Immense deserted land with no ownership. In time, these territories will become the desirable apple of discord." (The Thinker)

***

With each passing day, the freshness on Emperor KORP's face became more intriguing and more worrying. The people who worked near him were sometimes a little afraid of him. He did not express remorse for the consequences of the Nuclear War, speak of the matter, or celebrate any memorial alluding to the subject. However, he wasn't preventing it either.

The emperor did not attend any service or ceremony to commemorate anything or anyone. To many people, this seemed like an inhumane attitude. His advisers tried their best to understand the emperor's behaviour to see how they could support him psychologically. He always replied that everything was fine.

Knowing what he was thinking was getting harder and harder to tell.

He withdrew more frequently to meditate on the position of his colleague, The Thinker, and there he planned his future projects in pursuit of rebuilding the planet. 'For humanity, let's build our future on progress, peace, and freedom.' It was the motto he had written in his slogan, and he wanted to clarify this was still the north to follow.

He decreed that: "We should orient all effort in the empire towards constructing the new home and restoring the planet under this motto – Let it be what one day it was."

***

Many humans found themselves trapped in various parts of the globe, surrounded by places with a high radioactivity concentration, which they called the Valleys of Death. These men and women were fighting for their lives and had no choice but to seek refuge in one of the five cities. However, they had to make dangerous survival journeys to get there. They had to risk crossing the Valleys of Death, dark places where life and death fought against each other like gladiators for humans' lives. These risk-takers were called Time Travellers. These people were refugees. If they made it out of the Valleys of Death alive, they believed to have returned from death to life.

Many Time Travellers fell by the wayside, buried beside their dreams of a better life. Some, willing to continue and put their hands on the chopping block, faced that reality and miraculously reached the imperial cities.

Another big problem was looting. Many communities had to steal to get food. Their favourite targets were the Time Travellers and small communities. Villages that had suffered a direct impact from the war had to survive a complex challenge. Some small villages would disappear because of population migration, leaving them empty. They carried the memory of their inhabitants in the photographs stocked on the walls of half-destroyed houses. Other communities quickly restored their land, cultivated it with hope, and succeeded.

***

After a few years of crisis, the population finally achieved food sovereignty, trade and security. Food flowed through the empire and the planet's cities again.

"Blessed are human beings who, just as they know how to destroy things easily, also know how to rebuild easily. Who gave them that wisdom?" (The Thinker)

KORP quickly re-established industrial trade with distant lands on the planet. Besides restoring his arms industry, he continued making Toys and trading them to strengthen his empire's economy. He rode in and out on his steel horse riders in the army he had now created.

Countries that had suffered collateral damage were resentful of him and walked away or avoided political-trade relations. Only a few offices and properties that eventually became a refuge for Time Travellers remained in the Organisation of Continents. The empire aimed to promote the union of the countries through commerce at all levels. Many accepted this proposal but with suspicion towards KORP.

***

The flow of Nuclear War survivors out of the empire into the five imperial cities was consistent. Instead, some risked moving south of the 0° parallel of the equator, where the devastation would not have been so catastrophic. However, the problem was the distance to get there: it took long months of walking, avoiding pillage or getting out of the Valleys of Death, and sometimes crossing the seas.

"Some risk-takers said, 'I'll never know unless I try', and so they took what they had and joined the Time Travellers' caravans, and miraculously, they made it! Bless them." (The Thinker)

Ultimately, he established that there would be no more elections and instituted a single government, which the masses accepted without question. The parliament called him King Emperor KORP. His coronation occurred in a lavish ceremony in the restored Cathedral of Clocks, and weeks of festivities followed.

Over the years, KORP got an entire generation of young people to idolise him, unite and fight for his cause. They became his proudest supporters. They saw themselves as protective guardians and defenders of a developing civilisation. These people believed passionately in him because they said his government's policies were right. He further strengthened the masses' alliance with his empire with this support.

He established a council of thirteen individuals who executed all his decisions. Each received a cloak of truth and a sword of justice. Most New Council members came from large societies such as Star Trek, Nanotechnology and the Biodermatik Society. They also included relatives and friends who had been close to him since his early days in politics and advisers in his companies. This New Council promised to serve the empire and the world 'for the sake of humanity'. It was their job to represent him throughout the empire.

Finally, he took the last step to merge his power and achieve total control over the masses. This stage was essential to establishing his KORP Imperial System, which involved manipulating the masses without resistance. This ultimate step was what he called the Oath of Allegiance – an act based on a simple decision of the will. To take the Oath of Allegiance, he chose a day on which he organised a significant national event. He invited everyone from the empire who wished to swear allegiance to his kingdom. He also made that invitation appear on newspapers' front pages to persuade citizens.

This event was a public, voluntary act in which the population pledged allegiance to the KORP Empire by repeating this vow three times: 'One Way, only One Way, no return.' It meant that there was no turning back once a citizen swore allegiance. After the candidate had repeated the loyalty oath, the empire declared its adherence to the candidate. As a token of that commitment, it issued a gold-plated card emblazoned with the words written in high relief: 'One Way'. It was like a mighty credit card. After signing the card in front of the cameras as witnesses, the empire passed all the personal information from the card into his imperial software system with a laser pistol.

Also, they tattooed a three-lined symbol on the thumb of the new Citizen Member of the empire, which had special significance. The middle line was longer than the other two and was the figure of a person with outstretched arms whose hands almost rested on the other two lines; this line represented the emperor, and the other two lines represented a woman and a man. The meaning of this tattoo was that KORP protects both women and men. To see the tattoo, the person showed a thumbs-up as a sign to get into the imperial cybernetic system, which allowed the person to go anywhere in the empire with no impediment. The person became an imperial citizen.

The day after that magnificent oath or membership ceremony, in his heart and mind, KORP inverted the pyramid of his empire, with the primary vertex at the bottom. That image was significant to him because it was part of his plan. From then on, all events and happenings in the empire's life would be due to him, by him, and for him.

Once people got a One Way card, they also enjoyed special privileges. For example, they could access financial credit at no extra cost. They could borrow as much as they wanted because all the Imperial Monetary Fund money now belonged to him. So, no matter how much the Citizen Members spent or borrowed, all the money returned to the empire. It circled its financial system.

"If you hold a One Way card, you also can use other credit cards. Members only use the One Way card in the empire's emergency financial situations. If you wanted to buy a house but didn't have the money, you could use your One Way card and problem solved! All with no bureaucratic restrictions. Then you paid a minimal fee with a small amount of interest." (The Thinker)

This act of loyalty by the empire gave each citizen a strong

KORP and the Thinker

sense of belonging; it made them feel valued and accepted inside a social circle. They felt their lives were significant. The idea of an empire also gave them a deeper understanding of patriotism, so much so that they would defend the imperial cause under any circumstances and for the rest of their lives and not return. They felt like members of the organic imperial body because of that act and felt like they had climbed into a special place in KORP's heart, and he honoured them that way. His closest collaborators were comfortable with the One Way card gesture. They, too, received esteemed honours and recognition.

***

During the Nuclear War, he saved The Thinker, his stool of old books, newspapers and magazines. He put them in a box and took them underground. After the war, he had a replica of his room built. He hung the poster of his colleague, The Thinker, on the wall and his stool as it was.

Also, before the Nuclear War, KORP allied with the country where Kate lived, placing her under protection. It was a small, peaceful and geographically protected country. After the war, it played a significant role in the Earth's restoration. He knew Kate was well because his private agents cared for her. She wasn't under vigilance, but she was safe.

"There was a powerful reason Kate had to run from KORP's side. Still, she loves him as much as he does her. Is she hiding from something?" (The Thinker)

That is a good question. Who knows?

With each passing day, his mysticism gradually grew; perhaps this is typical when someone reaches maturity. Also, every human thinks more deeply about death. He frequently asked himself, 'Where am I going, or what is my destiny?'

"And what happened with KORP's conscience? Was there any change after the war?" (The Thinker)

That is a good question, too; he had a seared conscience. Therefore, inside, he was still the same figureless silhouette without facial features. He was still the dark man. KORP had involuntarily manifested some healing since he now smiled more frequently, especially when he saw a child's smile. Those angelic smiles brought tears of happiness and joy to his eyes. He attended birthday parties more regularly than imperial parties. He was pleased to see future generations of his empire develop in a happy family environment.

It is disheartening to know that he did not have the experience of laughing with someone close to him or sharing his intimate experiences with someone beside him. I speak of the company of a woman, of course.

Perhaps the woman who would live with him would not understand the way of life that he led, nor the way of thinking of him; or, to understand him, she would have to be someone who also, because of the bullying, had a dark soul like him. Then, just like that, she would know how he thought, felt and what he expected in his life, and they would both have the same need for affection.

Also, only then would they sit face to face to form an entire space of love where they would be The Thinkers for each other and promise to help each other erase the marks of that scourge. Area of love where both would be The Thinkers, but out loud, to help each other exist, to listen to each other, to cheer each other up with 'I love you very much' or with 'I can't live without you', or perhaps with some magic formula of love that only they knew how to invent, or simply just looking passionately into each other's eyes and, in silence, putting their lips together to drink the most sublime nectar that feeds the soul of humans.

KORP would look at the photograph of Kate with profound intensity and wonder what it would have been like. Many times he fantasised about having a family with her, only with her. Sometimes he caressed the photograph with his index finger and slowly slid it over her eyes to remember when they looked at each other deeply and passionately, in silence while their souls conversed, then slid it over her lips to recognise the scent of her kisses, which shook his five senses and left him floating in ecstasy. He refused to kill the memory of her passionate caresses, which gave him goosebumps; loved to remember the sound of her voice every time she called him by his name and said to his ear, with charming, soft and tender whispers, "I love you."

KORP took Kate's photo everywhere, which had exclusive space in his wallet. It travelled with him to all the ends of the Earth and the moon, so it escaped from prison in the wars with him. It was like his shadow, inseparable from him, and he would kiss it every time he had to go out on a mission, saying, "Hold on tight, we'll be right back."

Also, blood from his wounds stained that photograph; he drenched it in long nights of nostalgia every time he remembered her; it was wet because of his tears when he was sad; it was missing and then recovered from the lost and found items in the city; that photograph felt the blows of bullying. That photograph helped him gain strength when he thought everything was over; it accompanied him on his thousands of adventures, where she was always by his side as his faithful companion, beautifully dressed in 2D.[24] In that photograph, Kate seems determined to stay with him 'to the end of the universe'. She looked into his eyes with a deep, sweet, firm and sure gaze.

That photograph was his last sentimental good; it was his last wish, his last breath, his favourite corner, his indomitable strength to get out of trouble, the last drop of the antidote of life, the light of him.

That photograph still gave him hope to fight, to snatch the happy days from fate. Every time he looked at Kate in that photograph, it was visible that he still loved her so much, but it was even more visible how much he tried to keep this 'still' from dying.

---

24. **2D** means two dimensions.

8. Civilian life in the KORP Empire

Where there is no vision, people perish.

As the years passed, the KORP Empire built its power. It became the mighty and most prosperous kingdom in Earth's history. It had two main pillars as a foundation: freedom and respect. All the civil reforms and government programmes implemented in his empire reinforced his political campaign slogan. KORP's decisions appropriately protected them.

Equal prosperity reigned. From the most significant city's inhabitants to the minor corners, they had food security, power, wealth, excellent health care and the right to the most outstanding education. The empire used technology aggressively and impartially for the benefit of all its citizens; he wanted to take time away from death and give it to life.

KORP firmly believed that the size of his works in favour of his empire should match the height of his power: "It is my duty to do great works because my power is great," he expressed with great pride. He then devised strategies to make his power and influence catalyse the civilisation he was forming, then attributed a particular purpose to everything he possessed, as he did not want all that glory to end up in a bottomless sack. His mind brimmed with powerful and admirable good intentions.

He redirected the apparatus of the imperial industry by saying, "All technology in the empire must shorten the path so that prosperous well-being comes quickly into someone's life. Therefore, this scientific and technological giant must serve effectively to humanitarian logic, for they are the heart of this empire; therefore, we must take care of them so that this good life flourishes in fullness in each."

He improved the empire's socio-economic conditions to their highest level. Workers earned very well in their jobs, and that gave them stability. It also gave them access to a much higher standard of living than the rest of the countries or kingdoms. I repeat that the salary of one couple member was enough for the other to stay at home and care for the descendants.

"The offspring of the younger generation also have rights," he stressed.

Non-member citizens, those who had not got a One Way card, paid a tax but were free of specific responsibilities towards the empire; member citizens, those who accepted a One Way card, enjoyed significant benefits and privileges but also had many responsibilities towards the empire. Neither of these two civilian classes had any extra weight on their shoulders.

KORP reasoned many years ago that freedom was the most sacred right in a society and that guaranteeing it was the key to national social stability; he emphasised that principle as a constant reality. Despite the dire situation outside the empire, people here had what they always dreamed of: freedom and provision for their basic needs. The population needed nothing; they felt protected.

KORP de-commodified human beings first and favoured them with humanitarian aid programmes because they were the raison d'être of his empire. Then, he opened the doors of the borders to accessible business; in this way, he made trade fair and healthy, and honest to flourish little by little in all his domains. Fair trade was the basis for trading. By law, the empire didn't accept products stained with the deception of the 'Fountain of Miracles' financial theory, slavery or blood sweat.

People from many cultures came with their products from distant lands to trade with the empire, and, in return, KORP sold them manufactured technologies to energise the empire's trade with the planet again. It became closer, more fluid and more efficient, generating prosperity for both sides. The faster money moved around in the empire's monetary system, the more wealth and stability it developed. KORP knew this golden principle of trade and took care of it.

The five major cities were prosperous, majestic and safe. There was no need for crime. Citizens could get money with the One Way card if needed. The only condition was that they had to spend it within the empire.

If one lived in any imperial city, one could not leave it. Only the military or merchants who traded with the empire could leave because they carried special national and international trade permits for security reasons. Non-members could leave the cities but not return for safety reasons.

The Gerikos protected each city. These were lofty towers with wide walls, so cars could drive over them in both directions. "For their sake, they will come out when the right time comes," said KORP because he didn't want them to see the disaster his bombs had caused. The authorities were still cleaning up and rehabilitating the radioactively contaminated regions of the planet. The Earth's surface was still dangerous in vast areas like the Valleys of Death.

People promoted peace and harmony in the cities and within the empire under the principle, 'Respect others, and others will respect you'. They encouraged the younger generations with great intensity. Despite the difficulties of living together in human society, everyone, without exception, sought that common good, especially the older generations, who had survived the Nuclear War and knew the two realities – the two eras.

***

"When a seed carried by the wind reaches your hands, don't throw it into the sea; it will end up at the bottom, and you will never know what kind of fruit it will bear. If you sow it, it may bring solutions for humanity." (The Thinker)

Thousands of Time Traveller caravans arrive daily in the empire's cities, seeking refuge. They were survivors of the Valleys of Death. They came from different parts of the world. By law, the kingdom provided them shelter, clothing and food, and the cities' inhabitants were kind to them. Newcomers felt welcomed and well-treated. The citizens offered help when they saw them arriving at the city entrance, saying, "If you did it, I can too."

This saying became a creed, a principle of doing good, and a code of good ethics.

Upon entering the KORP Empire, newcomers signed a pledge of 'Respect others, and others will respect you' before being integrated into society. They could also become Citizen Members by obtaining a One Way card. Most people accepted the card almost immediately; it was easy to get one. They just had to freely and voluntarily pledge allegiance to the empire. Most of these people were victims of trade monopoly wars and injustices in their homelands or fled the miseries of the Nuclear War. The emperor ordered decent accommodation and food until they fully integrated into imperial society.

Their first job was to learn the empire's language. The aim was to speed up language learning at the beginning of their arrival, for which the government built learning centres and equipped and provided staff specialising in advanced tutoring.

Also, to integrate into society, minorities were legally required to respect the majorities' rights in all public places to facilitate relationships in the public's daily lives.

Some minority groups had grouped into small family clans of similar cultures: large families with their own and usually exclusive customs and unique language. These groups suffered the most from cultural clashes because of the significant cultural differences between the empires. When some minorities insisted on imposing their cultural rules on the majorities and changing the rules within the realm, there was a simple choice: either accept the empire's laws or move somewhere else where they could change the practices.

"It seems contradictory to say that freedom exists when minorities cannot exercise their rights in public places. For KORP, there were more critical things to think about and consider than cultural differences. These were still difficult times." (The Thinker)

Learning the empire's language was a race against time; therefore, adults and children had to attend language learning centres to help them integrate with minor problems. Adults had jobs once they learned the language, and children integrated into the school.

Speaking and writing the empire's language immensely helped people's daily lives, which was undeniable. Learning the language made people project their thoughts in one direction instead of spending too much time considering cultural differences. Therefore, KORP stressed, "Thinking about cultural differences at this stage is a non-essential luxury."

Many accepted the Cultural Differences Law reluctantly but had no choice but to save their lives. For KORP, speaking the empire's language was paramount.

"If they cannot see the need to speak the imperial language, what future awaits them here?" he asked.

Time Travellers occasionally tried to ignore the Cultural Differences Law and then caused chaos in the streets or public places because they felt unhappy. Many of these people came from closed, traditional and strict cultures and then, with a rebellious attitude, refused to contaminate themselves with empire civilisation by avoiding learning the empire language and civil law. Even the Cultural Differences Law did not threaten their existence.

KORP emphasised: "The law on the culture question is not a life-and-death situation, but language is."

It was vital to prioritise language learning to achieve social stability, which brought a lot of peace to the empire and was noticeable in the whole social and production chain. Once Time Travellers had learned the language, they were more open and willing to integrate. They developed deeply healthy human relationships with the empire's inhabitants despite not being culturally similar to them. KORP had created a third culture in the kingdom where all citizens felt neutral and equal. In that way, all citizens contributed to the same degree to their human relations and were not concerned with imposing their cultures on others. "I repeat, inside the house, everyone is free to be and think what they want," KORP said.

Within two years of their arrival in the empire, the Time Travellers were independent in their own lives. One could see them in the city interacting fluently with the mainstream because they were fluent in the language, and many had secured jobs.

Not speaking the empire's language excluded many people; some even became impoverished because of their self-exclusion. KORP hated it when people banned themselves because they did not speak the imperial language.

In a New Council reunion, the emperor stated, "It is unfair, and I will not tolerate adults feeling rejected for not knowing the language, let alone children in schools." He made the empire do its best to reach children with such a service. The children learned quickly because their minds were like sponges that absorbed knowledge easily.

KORP believed that excessive language diversification led to conflict and division. He was not against different languages, but did not want the empire's unity broken because of that.

"No offence, but the moment you cross those walls and enter the city, you embrace the new culture: the culture of KORP civilisation," he said.

He believed that creating a single path, a single direction in which everyone pushed homogeneously, would generate less social friction. Life would be easier. He said, "Seeking peace is better than war."

The multiculturalisation of the empire was beneficial and inevitable. Time Travellers came from different parts of the globe. They brought their careers, professions, science, medicine and mathematics knowledge, etc. Many worked in crucial places of industry, health and education; these human beings represented a vast and complex cultural world. Also, each individual arrived with an ethnic-social-linguistic package, so this multiculturalism enriched the empire culturally.

Some people who came to seek refuge in the imperial cities had over-inflated illusions and expectations about the empire, which created many problems. KORP was clear and firm with them and told them: "The world is big, and if you don't like it here, the doors are open for you to leave, but if you stay, nobody eats for nothing, least of all from my hands."

The One Way card also attracted many people from outside the empire. Out here, they called it the 'Almighty One Way card'. Charlatans told dazzling stories about it to pique people's curiosity. People naively believed these stories and joined Time Travellers' caravans. The charlatans charged a lot of money for a seat in such caravans. Over time, agencies and criminal groups of human traffickers formed. Without the slightest qualms and knowledge of the empire's reality, these evil people sold travel tickets called 'One Way Trips to the Cities'. Cleverly, they deceived with this argument: "When you arrive in the KORP Empire, you will be a multimillionaire from the first second you walk through its gates, thanks to the Almighty One Way card."

Some unwary people listened to these words and got rid of their inheritances; they sold their houses or gave up their jobs to pay for a seat in these caravans under the illusion of reaching the KORP Empire and thus getting their Almighty One Way card.

To shorten the route, many of these organised caravans had to cross clandestine ways, most of which passed through the Valleys of Death, where many lost the path along the way, and others disappeared. Only by sheer luck did people make it to the cities. As soon as they passed through the gates, these naïve people were the first to become Citizen Members. Once they got the card, they wanted to abuse it, withdrawing lots of money and intending to send it out of the empire. But they got incredibly frustrated when they couldn't do that transfer operation. They regretted getting the card as they could not return to their homeland with it, then realised the charlatans had tricked them.

Only sometimes did Time Travellers' caravans come from these smuggling agencies. Instead, the vast majority fled calamities.

KORP had implemented a quasi-secular imperial political system that offered equal opportunities for all beliefs. Anyone could practise their faith, religious beliefs or political thoughts and celebrate gatherings. The only requirements were to observe them in the empire's official language and respect others' ideas. For him, the only true religion in the kingdom was his god Time.

He built large clocks all over the empire to show that Time was his god: "Worthy of honour and worship," he stressed.

***

KORP retired to rest in the gardens of one of his islands, where no one disturbed him. He had a team of people who simultaneously acted as his security personnel.

As a young man, he bought islands in exotic parts of the world; some didn't survive the Nuclear War, but some remained untouched.

His favourite islands were those with high places, such as mountains or high rocks, where he could set up a telescope to observe the stars or anything that moved in space.

He also liked islands with caves, where he set up scientific research laboratories, especially for pandemics. Because of privacy, he recommended that these underground laboratories conduct medical-genetic research.

One day, when he looked at space, he saw a UFO crossing over the sea – a close encounter of the second kind.

"Closer than farther away," he added.

Every time he saw these objects, he took them seriously. He was very devoted to them because they were so fascinating. They had fascinated him ever since he was a child.

These flying objects aroused enigmatic curiosity and speculation across the planet. KORP did not want to be out of that. He thought these objects intentionally reached out to the line of the unknown or unknowable and, from there, influenced people's imaginations.

He said, "Non-identification is the right place to stay; only then are they even more unreachable."

The most popular speculation about these objects was that they came from other worlds and sought to colonise or settle somewhere in the universe. Others insisted that this was not speculation but the truth. KORP was also inclined to think that they came from other worlds and were inhabitants of some planet beyond our galaxy. These objects inspired him to colonise space. He heard about close encounters and even claimed to be abducted by aliens. Since he was young, it was his habit to talk about those events. True or false? From KORP, you could get all kinds of stories. Only he knew the truth.

***

"Youth is the horse on which the present's future rides." (The Thinker)

"Each new generation quickly assimilated their ancestors' pain and wounds. They did not forget it. However, that historical past did not prevent the younger generation from writing their history by improving the history of their ancestors. Humans are fascinating." (The Thinker)

What do you mean by that?

"For example, if the previous generation lived in caves, the next or after that would build something better than that, or if they used to hunt by throwing stones, the next generation would use spears, etc. Generations develop!" (The Thinker)

Yes, that's right.

"The blessed thing about human beings is that each new generation has its path, destiny and essence of freedom. We should never deprive, prevent or limit them from these vital elements in life. We should encourage, inspire and help them so their life journey is dignified, peaceful and accessible." (The Thinker)

It was the way, of course, the thinking of the upcoming generations in the KORP Empire. In these generations, in the deepest of their hearts, their self-determination rose with fierce passion and strength to carve out to be the owners of their future.

These young people wondered deeply and rightly, 'What will life be like behind the Gerikos?' or 'What lies beyond the horizon?'

Although the cities were very prosperous and they found everything they needed, even KORP built immense gathering centres and playgrounds so people of different ages could socialise, ensuring they could have good times with their families. The upcoming generations wanted to write their own story. They tried to write it beyond the walls or the horizon.

Being inside those walls represented the history of their ancestors, and they felt it was not their story; they had not forged it. They were born there and inherited that story. The desire to meet or jump over the wall to write their own story was a yearning, germinating delicately and powerfully in these beings' wills and adventurous spirits brimming with energy and desire. They longed to carve out a space in the electromagnetic field of time to plant the tree of their destiny and forge their future there. They wanted to grow by creating, generating and being the authors and owners of their legends and dreams.

It was customary for these energetic beings to gather to dream and travel into the future. In the evenings, as the day was setting, hundreds of young adolescent boys and girls perched on the high edges of the Gerikos. In contrast, the sun seduced them to discover the rest of the planet, and the horizon called them to try. They were like little migratory chicks, ready to fly in search of their destiny in life.

***

KORP incentivised the empire's inhabitants, members and non-members, to become even more prosperous. He opened the opportunity to invest in astro-space programmes, scientific, medical, hydraulic, agricultural, construction and other economic development programmes. One could invest from just a penny upward without a limit. He encouraged them by saying, "If you have a penny from the corner shop and it is resting peacefully somewhere in the house, save it; you will earn another penny in days." With this speech, he opened the door to economic prosperity.

"Everyone should have an equal economic opportunity," he stressed.

Anyone who wanted to invest a penny in the empire could do so in any of these fields. Interest rates were juicy, attractive and short-term. He designed this incentive to generate an industry workforce and economic resources, primarily for space programmes.

The city of Luz eventually became the mother of all astronomy programmes, leading to an aggressive race to develop them. A dynamic Mars colonisation had started thanks to his extra energy extracted from the moon. The voyage to the red planet took mere weeks.

The Intercity Space Research department found rare soils on Mars when fused with terrestrial minerals, allowing them to build lighter, stronger and larger spacecraft. So, they needed an increased influx of ships to import these raw materials from the Martian planet.

KORP also built two more helium-3 industrial plants on the moon, thinking of turning Mars into a cosmological base for future exploration missions to other planets; he thought it was better to look out into vast space than to look at his face in the reflection of the gleaming metal of the Gerikos. He hoped, one day, to find a planet equal to or better than Earth and optimistically promised to take everyone to live there. Many embraced this offer with deep gratitude because, for them, this promise represented hope for life. He was in denial about the idea that planet Earth was the only habitable place in the universe. Regular UFO sightings caused that denial. Under the 360° Space Programme, he built powerful telescopes at the tallest skyscrapers to view space from a 360° angle. Within hours of the programme's inception, clubs of space watchers formed throughout the empire, meeting to share their findings. Young people filled these observatories from sunset to sunrise the next day. At night, stargazing from these vantage points was spectacular and awe-inspiring. Anyone who stepped up to look at the sky from one of these telescopes would come down transformed, inspired and immersed in star travel ideas.

From the top of these lookout points, you could also see the city and the industrial centres where the empire had assembled more enormous spaceships – all kinds of spacecraft that could go to the moon or Mars and, from there, "to the ends of the universe," observers said. These industrial centres were the pride of the empire.

Various recreational environments surrounded the 360° Space Programme viewpoints; the designed atmosphere sparked the imagination of anyone who came to observe the space. The young visitors were insatiable galactic explorers, and with ardent enthusiasm, they shaped their futures as they travelled around observing.

Thanks to this astro-space programme, job opportunities in the space industry emerged and flooded with original ideas for space projects, some more ambitious than others. Bright and innovative minds looked at the universe from a different perspective; this made them forget they were inside the Gerikos.

He also created centres for technical space education, and the empire financed those who wanted to study or intern there. There was an urgent need for skilled technical personnel.

KORP sincerely believed that humans had a crucial role in this part of the universe: to administer and colonise distant worlds. They were suitable potential candidates; he said this because of his success on Mars and the moon.

In the years that followed, spacecraft left Earth for Mars frequently. From there, they sent space probes to various places, especially Saturn, the next target of this aggressive planetary exploration.

"KORP was wise to open up interstellar space to develop possibilities rather than close them down. If I had to praise him for anything, it would be his vision of the future; he always opened the way to new possibilities. He constantly asserted that there was always a way." (The Thinker)

For him, possibility was an unexplored and undercover path. He looked at it excitedly and delightedly because it was his most incredible opportunity. He said the possibility was like the universe's space, where the ideas of every human being on the planet, from the beginning of its history to the end of its days, could fit – a space where there was still room for millions upon millions more ideas.

In a matter of months, the industrial space environment grew.

Flying cars or flying ships propelled by energies based on lithium and helium-3 gradually replaced terrestrial vehicles.

Fossil fuels vanished from the market. And extracting them required complex logistics. They also destroyed much of the oil infrastructure in the Nuclear War, as were the primary targets to neutralise the enemy.

Residential buildings in cities were increasingly daring – always built upwards. This form of urbanisation saved space on the sides to grow food. These tall residential buildings disappeared in the clouds.

Thousands of health and construction professionals arrived daily at imperial ports because of labour shortages in those areas.

He also invigorated economic resource investment in major cities through a scientific programme called 'Ultimate Good'. Through this programme, the cities developed exciting ways of progressing in specific, strategic areas in a brief space of time.

The city of Luz was the heart of other cities. Every father of a family in the empire longed to send his children to university there. Here was the cradle, the centre of complete and advanced scientific knowledge.

Gradually, the empire annexed more kingdoms because of economic prosperity and industrial explosions at every level. There was friction between the empire's border and some ancestral domains, like the kingdom of the south-east, which was also a powerful domain. It demanded that their seized territories return. For that reason, KORP had his steel horse riders stationed in strategic locations across the globe to act in the event of adventurers challenging the empire's geopolitical hegemony. Despite this, the emperor said: "Peace is the most effective medicine for the sickness of war."

He was always unequivocal in his political and geostrategic relations with the countries he shared a border with. They knew that if KORP said it, he would do it. So, they avoided physical contact with the imperial Biodermatik armed forces. Instead of war, free trade agreements had to be signed to ensure imperial peace.

On the seas, he had his steel horse riders; on land, his Biodermatik armed forces; and in the skies, he had his angels of death. He was referring to intercontinental nuclear ballistic satellites. In the stratosphere, he had two interstellar ships capable of intercepting ships crossing his celestial domain.

"Knowledge is the light that helps one see amidst ignorance." (The Thinker)

Imperial schools were temples of knowledge. Children had all the facilities and didactic support, so learning was a pleasure and not a burden. Education was, therefore, enjoyable. Teachers had all the help they needed, both in terms of staff and teaching materials. KORP said: "The light of knowledge that flowed from the teachers and poured on the students must be pure and sacred."

He did not want to deprive teachers of anything they needed to teach, be financially vulnerable, or rest because he did not want to contaminate the light they carried within them with anything, so he insisted teachers must also relax and sleep well to stay focused in the classroom. He stopped them from being overburdened with educational work and refused teachers to take schoolwork into their homes.

"There is no need for them to do that," he said.

He remembered what a good job his teacher had done with him as a child, sometimes remembering her as if she were his second mother.

The empire built thousands of schools and training centres to ensure that all generations grew up in a world where knowledge gave them hope and confidence to face the future. He built great libraries where people could freely learn. Above all, he opened centres to update computer skills at all levels because it was the lifeblood of the new sophisticated cyber industry.

Before long, teachers could see the fruits of their labour reflected in their students. That brought peace to the emperor's heart. Educating the younger generation was his strategy to ensure his empire's robust and long-term future.

He promoted and never restricted information access. He said that "information is the food of knowledge". The only condition he set was: "Information must contain light and no deception, riddles, lies or darkness." He insisted that the information be understandable, easy to assimilate and smooth as glass. News with traps, misinformation or conspiracy hints had been filtered out. He destroyed this information that caged knowledge or put stones in the way instead of light.

"One must say bread to bread; wine to wine."

***

Of all the laws of the KORP Empire, the primary rule was: "With the same measure as you measure, they will measure you." Initially, he learned this rule in a religious society. It was straightforward: respect, and you will have respect. Up to that point, there were no jails in the cities.

In the empire, people could break laws like in any human society. However, the realm marked the offender for life without redemption or a second chance, or they faced exile.

As in any human society, there were also the clever and the cunning – the "cynical, clever people", as KORP described them. They wanted to take advantage of the imperial system without giving back. Or those who faked illness not to work and, in their audacity, abused the One Way card and then lived the life of a king. A person with this attitude was called 'Insolent'.

KORP was very harsh on the Insolent people. He said: "Nobody forced them to swear allegiance to the empire, and nobody forced them to stay either."

He wrote a law called Insolvency for the Insolent. Any Insolent person discovered red-handed in insolent audacity actions cheating the system became 'Insolvent' and faced extradition or lost his rights as a Citizen Member. Then, a court would apply the Digital Death law, so the individual had no access to the financial system. Ultimately, the Insolvent was nobody; his imprisonment was wandering the city, and he faced banishment if he did not publicly repent.

KORP ensured that the laws in all spheres of society in his empire made people happy; he saw they did.

**

Hospitals and health centres were temples to life. In the KORP Empire, dying was forbidden, meaning one should take care of one's body as a unique treasure. He went to extraordinary lengths to ensure his subjects' lives were benign. He emphasised that freedom was precious, and that life was the ultimate expression of his god Time.

Family and health were the top priorities at the empire's table. These two elements were the cornerstone of his 'well-living' logic. He said these two pillars defined the uninterrupted flow of the human species through the universe. For this reason, he believed ensuring his people's physical and emotional integrity was essential.

In the empire's health legislation, KORP wrote:

"Human beings are the supreme good of the empire. Therefore, we must protect them, so the generative process that runs through their DNA from conception is safe.

"Imperial law recognises and protects all the genetic information human beings carry in their DNA and declares it the priority for protection. The empire recognises that protecting man and woman's genetic manifestations is essential. It's the only guarantee of the existence of the human species throughout the universe. Therefore, it declares that their preservation is a priority. The empire shall provide all necessary and secure mechanisms for the human being in the imperial domain to fulfil his reason for being in the universe from conception, arrival in the family as a child, and growth and development in human society until his death. Therefore, the empire must protect the family, which it recognises as the number one subject of protection. Any act of harming, disrupting or destroying the physical health, psychological health or nuclear family of human beings in the empire disrupts the natural development of the human species. Such an act will be criminally punishable."

As you can see, KORP had no other direction to look at. He set his sights on improving the lives of citizens. He developed the health sector above all other projects with that in mind.

Hospitals had the most modern and sophisticated medical equipment; by then, he had developed nanotechnology and, with it, built micro-nano-biotech submarines for surgery in medicine. These tiny submarines dived through the patient's bloodstream and scanned the inside of the human body. They transmitted those images in situ and in real-time. They allowed high approximation to the affected sites, especially tumours, and from there, they delineated with high-resolution scanned images where the tumours started. With those images, surgeons could remove them more precisely. They also helped maintain blood quality, reporting any abnormalities they found while diving. They were medicine's greatest allies.

He first used the micro-nano-biotech submarines to manufacture the symbiotic suits; seeing their effectiveness, he also opened the possibility of their use in medicine. He called them 'my invisible allies'.

Also, throughout the empire, entire communities of doctors and nurses were the visible faces of the national health programme. They were big-hearted people with caring spirits. Many of these guardian angels came from distant lands.

Biodermatik science became an invaluable ally in reconstructive medicine for doctors. Also, it made the empire its cradle. The technology he developed to extend human life was innovating daily. He opened avenues for research into cures for everything, from simple coughs to the strangest diseases and rare viruses. These viruses included the coronavirus and its variations, which ravaged the entire planet in the previous era. KORP even lost one of his best friends to it.

He created battalions of doctors, nurses and health workers to scour cities and villages looking for sick patients to help. He wanted to defeat death.

Thousands of individuals were highly grateful because they had another chance to exist through implementing the free

National Health Service.

Medicine in the empire had a single purpose: to take time away from death to convert into life for humans.

***

Civil unions were entirely human-to-human relationships. He recognised civil unions between humans within established parameters, such as age, to prevent underage marriages.

The legislation did not accept any civil union other than one human being with another as legal.

For example, he did not recognise the civil union of a human being with an animal of any species as a couple. He was unequivocal about that issue.[25]

On gender preferences, he was open-minded because he said: "A human being does not cease to be human just because he likes to consume something different or think differently. You can't judge or force someone to conform to a certain taste. If someone likes to eat chicken, let them eat it. Everyone must live in whatever way makes them happy, full stop."

He said absolutely, "Concerning this issue, the law of 'respect others, and others will respect you' should apply."

He wrote a law regarding unwanted children to prevent abortion that said, "Unwanted children belong to the empire. Therefore, women must give birth in the designated places. Once the baby is born, the mothers can leave them there, but they can have them anytime if they change their minds."

KORP built centres where these children were born, cared for and educated. As they grew up, they integrated into imperial social life. Most of them became great people in society. He had a special affection for these kids and respected them.

---

25. **Animal partner**. He did so because some religious cultures in the empire believed sincerely in the civil union of humans with animals. Sometimes, humans married animals in those cultures, so they also asked for governmental economic benefits for their animal partners. He did not prevent it but did not include it in legislation; therefore, that kind of union did not receive government financial support.

Many mothers went to these centres intending to give birth, leave the baby there and disappear. But after they gave birth, they realised the baby was too precious, so they kept them and received support from the empire to look after them.

"KORP's affection for these kids raised a suspicion in my head. Perhaps his mother left him at the nursing home doors in a box when he was a baby." *(The Thinker)*

I was thinking the same. I hope it was just a market woman's gossip. No one knows the truth apart from KORP's parents.

***

In the empire, no one could monopolise finances. The emperor dictated the law of the 'full cup': "If a person makes enough money, he may not send the extra money to any fiscal paradise island outside of the empire. They had to invest in the empire first to open new enterprises to create jobs for future generations; I repeat, first within the empire."

He said that his companies were to the benefit of the empire. Therefore, other companies must follow that path as well. Greedy citizens left the empire or, if they stayed, needed to respect the laws or risk 'insolvency'. In the previous era, such people condemned humans to destitution. KORP felt disgusted whenever he thought about it. Many of them built their wealth by stealing during pandemics. The empire kept a close eye on them. He always suspected them.

He enacted thousands of laws to carve an imposing empire in the image of Victorious Cultures.

"KORP's attitude towards his empire was like a man's attitude towards his brand-new wife, whom he wanted to please in everything, and so he did his best to make sure that everything made her happy and nothing would spoil her. He loved his empire, and the people of his empire loved him too." *(The Thinker)*

9. KORP and The Thinker

In solitude, even talking to the wall has its benefits.

The Thinker was his source of ideas. For KORP, that thoughtful man was full of patience; the one who couldn't get enough of him was always there for him, and he expected to be there. That man on the wall was his best friend, father, mother, pillow and confidant. The Thinker was his piece of heaven, in whose presence he felt unconditional love and by whom he felt accepted and loved, whose hug was like that of a loving father.

That man who did not grill him with thousands of questions, which he could refuse to answer, run away from, or felt forced to respond with lies, did not look at him frivolously.

KORP did not have to worry about dodging his gaze scanner in his presence because he felt supported, and his acceptance was free of conditionality or thirst for control. He trusted this naked man so much that he could undress himself and his soul in his presence because he knew The Thinker would never disclose his secrets and did not doubt that if there were more to reveal, he would gladly show it, but only to him. Like him, he felt The Thinker was a black hole star that swallowed his secrets like biscuits.

The confidence and strength of spirit he had developed in himself through the presence of this thoughtful man were his greatest strengths. That force sustained him when he faced daily life and gave him self-assurance. The encouragement that had helped him out of bullying came from that mysterious man. He had given KORP the green light to do whatever he wanted. The one to whom he did not report his actions but willingly shared them; the one with whom, to reach his presence, he did not have to make an appointment or stand in line for a minute; the one who accepted him regardless of his social status. For this thoughtful man, taking up his precious time to listen to KORP was exciting. There was no long list of requirements or conditions to meet because the doors of his attention and heart were open twenty-five hours a day, if any.

Likewise, in KORP's presence, The Thinker was happy. He was not ashamed of being naked. To him, KORP was no longer a child. He now saw him as a grown-up young man whom he described in this way: "The grown-up young man who enjoyed eating pain like a cookie without shedding a tear."

It sounds like a sadomasochistic description of KORP, but it was the truth, and nothing was more accurate.

The Thinker remembers when KORP was a child in this way:

"There were days when I felt powerless when he cried in my presence. When that bullying problem started, he came home crying almost every day. From then on, he bit his fingernails."

The Thinker recalled with awe how KORP overcame this scourge. He saw him holding his countenance repeatedly and getting up after falling over day by day. Until one day, he stood firm and fought with fate to rip out his right to be a fortunate man.

"I remember that when KORP was a teenager, more often than not, he would come to me with a nosebleed; then tears stopped flowing to his eyes until the day arrived when he would no longer cry when bullied at school but would instead give half-sarcastic smiles full of determination, saying: 'Ignorant people, you will never bend my will and knees.' And, bending down, he would ask me for permission to sit on his stool. When he came bloody-nosed, he would wipe off the blood and suck it from his fingers; it was like his ritual, increasing his determination."

For The Thinker, thinking next to this now-grown-up young man was also sublime; it was the existence of the most religious experience on the face of the Earth. This mysterious man also felt special when he was in the presence of that unique human being. They both lined up in their minds and talked about their plans and how they could tackle them.

He knew every gesture and every movement of KORP's face, and could tell by the tone of his voice when he was lying or telling the truth. He knew what muscles moved in his face when he was happy, eating or in pain. As soon as he entered that room, that thoughtful man did a body scan to determine exactly how many blows he had received and to what parts of his body.

The force that came out of this surreal relationship affected KORP's life because it was so strong; The Thinker knew him in his innermost being and had cradled him since he was a little boy. He had watched him grow up and transform from a child into a teenager and then a young man. Now, he was a dashing, grown man of whom this mysterious man was very proud, just as if he were a happy father.

"I've never seen him happier than the day he fell in love with Kate. That day, he came home from school and sat next to me. He would have been about seventeen years old. KORP's face showed overwhelming joy. As soon as he entered that room, he did an adorable dance that I had never seen him do before. After singing a few melodies, mimicking a talented opera singer, he lay on the bed and stared at the ceiling for long seconds without saying a single word; he rarely blinked but stared into infinity as if hypnotised. He exuded an indescribable joy. Then he told me vividly what that moment was like when Cupid's crush magic happened. It's worth telling you about those details. I am not being nosey, am I?

"'It was love at first sight,' he said, smiling. 'She came to my table looking for an answer to a chemical formula problem; we were both in biology class. When I helped her find the answer in the book, I saw the most beautiful eyes I had ever seen. Then our eyes crossed, and magic happened when her gaze struck me; my heart filled with warmth and joy. It was the sublime moment of that gaze, injecting the sweet feeling of special attraction, tenderness and comfort. It was the instant of the look that magically supplies that kind of warmth that slowly melts the soul, then destabilises the body's senses, and then quickens the heartbeat to shake the emotions in the soul and finally fill everything with the feeling of first love – that pleasurable feeling of indescribable happiness. At that moment, I discovered beauty in all its glory. It was the day I carved her image into the depths of my spirit to immortalise her, where she will dwell forever.

Now, I cannot stop thinking about her for a single day, and for a single minute of my life. Every moment I am looking for any excuse to see her and catch her glance,' he told me."

That mysterious man also remembered the day KORP came into his room carrying Kate's photograph. He would have been eighteen years old. He put the picture next to him and said, "Take care of her, please."

He also remembered that day when he arrived home broken.

"KORP felt mortally wounded in his soul and wept constantly. That was the day when Kate left. He begged me — on his knees — to show him how to turn back time, fix everything and fix the mistakes he thought he had made, and how to bring Kate back to him and stay by his side forever. He was twenty-two years old; they were both studying at university." (The Thinker)

That was the only issue in KORP's life where his colleague, The Thinker, could do nothing to help him. He did not know why Kate had left so suddenly.

"He never told me how he had lost her, but I could see how much he loved her. The only thing KORP feared was the emptiness Kate's absence created in his being. So, to compensate for that and ease that emptiness, he carried Kate's photograph in his wallet. Through that picture, he remembered and felt the intensity of the words she whispered into his ears many times. He clung so tightly to that photograph that there were moments when he seemed to want to tear from it some molecules of hope that would make her return possible."

That photograph was the only witness in the universe of proof that someone loved him. For him, that truth still existed inside that photo. It was like his secret spring, from which he drank the water of life daily: love. In that photo, Kate looks happy; it is her happiness to love him too. He took the picture the day they kissed for the first time.

"He told me it was a beautiful day, and they walked along the beach as they held hands. She whispered in his ear, saying, 'I love you so much, KORP.' And every time he remembers those words to the ears of his soul, they are like ASMR."[26]

26. **ASMR**: Autonomous Sensory Meridian Response. It is commonly triggered by auditory or visual stimuli close to the ears or by caresses on the scalp or neck. It is distinguished by a static or tingling sensation in the skin, usually beginning at the

That man on the wall, whom **KORP** adores and respects so much, also knows how to respect the results of the 'wars of love', where sometimes one can win or lose. Wars whose outcome The Thinker preferred to say, "That's none of my business."

---

scalp and running down the back of the neck and upper spine. It is an experience of euphoria characterised by intense positive feelings.

10. The Ultimate Good

Power of knowledge.

The clocks continued worshipping the god Time in the KORP Empire, and the emperor continued to command admiration from neighbouring countries and kingdoms worldwide. He aroused passion and respect from the population. His leadership was unquestionable.

He promoted peace and harmony wherever he set foot. Likewise, his imperial geopolitical influence pushed from the inside out regionally with dominant force, globally and extra-territorial. Nothing stood in his way of global glory.

The residents of his empire were happy and protected. They did not suffer from a lack of necessities in any sense. They felt like chicks under their mother's wings. Any place within the empire's jurisdiction was ideal for raising a happy family in freedom. Citizens would support him as emperor at any cost. He devoted himself to extensive lengths to make all affairs in his empire click in complete harmony, like a clock ticking.

In his office, sometimes he closed his eyes to listen to the clicking of each gear on his cuckoo clock and admire its precision. Each click was like an orchestra playing a complex but eloquent melody to his ears; it made him understand time complexity more efficiently; it brought back to his memory the situations resolved that day and made him feel productive. Above all, it brought him closer to time with gratitude and awe: Time was his god.

He instituted one day of the year to celebrate a special feast in honour of his god Time. The main ceremony for his god happened in the Cathedral of Clocks, whose architectural reconstruction was exquisite, as beautiful as the original, and whose interior housed over ten million clocks of all kinds and from all periods in human history, from the very practical, like the sundials made of stone, to the most complex and challenging to understand, like the clocks that worked in a vacuum, also known as quantum clocks. He said that quantum clocks came directly from his god Time because they had zero error.

In that cathedral, each clock had a special meaning and story; some belonged to soldiers who died in wars; others belonged to great factories that had contributed centuries to humanity; others came from the tombs of prominent personalities; and so on.

An army of so-called Clock Priests celebrated the central festival in honour of the god Time. They came from a sect called Majhia,[27] they wore long robes of bright and multicoloured phosphorescent. People throughout the empire held these priests in high regard and revered them.

The central ceremony in the Cathedral of the Clocks had two parts. First came the Thanksgiving ceremony, followed by the Forgiveness ceremony.

In the Thanksgiving ceremony, the central tower bell would ring twenty-four times, representing the day's twenty-four hours. After the twenty-four chimes, the Majhia priests offered fragrant incense on the main altar inside the cathedral to thank the god Time for its bounties. At this moment, the crowd would constantly repeat 'thank you' in a solemn, almost inaudible voice for half an hour, and, as there were thousands of people, the whole murmur sounded like a swarm of bees.

Then, after an hour, they held a Forgiveness ceremony; at that point, the bell tolled again, but only once. That toll symbolised the twenty-fifth hour; it represented the longing of people who wished a day had over twenty-four hours because they felt they had not done enough in the day's twenty-four hours. At that moment, people repeated sorry and forgave us for half an hour as a murmur.

The Majhia determined that longing for the day to have over

---

27. **Majhia** means 'Those who converse with the god Time'.

twenty-four hours was a terrible offence to their god Time. They interceded that Time would turn a deaf ear to that longing. They hoped people would be content with the day's twenty-four hours and stop longing for such things. Then, on that last chime, the Majhia would symbolically compile the people's apologies, from the emperor down to the previous imperial employee. These priests addressed their prayers to the god Time, thus: "Never grant us the twenty-fifth hour, for, if you do, humans will ask for the twenty-sixth hour, provoking your wrath."

The priests taught that the twenty-fifth hour was the darkest space that existed in time and the universe, which walked differently; they said it was the space where time lost its rhythm and moved slower and angrier, an area where every second became an hour and an hour a day and so on; a space where beauty lost its essence, its strength, and its energy; where happiness was too bitter, and weariness begged to die.

They also said that when a person entered the twenty-fifth hour, he did not find happiness because that space produced bitterness of spirit and much anguish and became frustrated with life because it gave him the feeling that it was a burden that caused more regret than satisfaction. Because of this, Majhia said, "The twenty-fifth hour becomes an endless torture instead of producing happiness. To live in the twenty-fifth hour would be the end of everything, since it would take everything out of its place."

There was also an exciting reason behind everything that happened in twenty-four hours, and a new story began on a new page. The priests called the first hour 'the blessed one' because it was the hour when humans could redeem their actions.

From the book *Temporal Creatures* by the senior Majhia WFK,[28] the following is an extract by the Majhia priests:

"At the hour known as 'the blessed one', humans can erase their past mistakes and write another page in their lives if desired. This principle is called 'The Disc of Life', which spins as it

---

28.   **Majhia superior WFK**: Walter Frank King, founder of the sect or religion dedicated to time study. He was an expert in astrology. He wrote hundreds of books. For him, time was a creative force.

collects and fulfils the wishes and decisions of the creatures in the universe."

Many books in the empire's libraries discussed humanity's history, closely linked to time. They also emphasised that time was a creative force. The text says:

"Time is the central axis around the universe. Both life and death compete to get the most outstanding amount of time for their ends. Time is like a bargaining chip in the fight for life and death; humans must decide which side to take."

On the day of the feast for the god Time, people from all corners of the empire came to the capital city and joined the central clock craft priests' procession; then, they stayed to celebrate the festivities for a few more days. All festive, artistic, sporting and social activities revolved around time.

The empire organised a giant clock-making competition and rewarded the most beautiful, complex, sophisticated and extravagant clocks. KORP awarded prizes to the ten most outstanding and exquisite designs. The competition winners received a substantial amount of prize money. The winners had a place in the Cathedral of Clocks reserved for their art masterpieces.

Hundreds of Watchmakers Dance troupes also came to the capital city and held parties late into the night. At three o'clock in the morning, they would gather at the pantheon, a mysterious place for the doubly mystical people. They believed the god Time should receive more than ceremonial dances, so they sacrificed living beings and even human babies.

***

The space industry in the KORP Empire developed extraordinarily thanks to the 360° Space Programme. Brilliant minds showed off their new inventions, such as interstellar spaceships, space vehicles, etc. The younger generations fully understood the concept of looking at the universe instead of just the Gerikos.

Once a week, the industrial centres, universities, schools and other public places held a planetary exhibition where many people gathered. Through these fairs, the visitor's gaze turned beyond the walls. This event showed the new reality of this part of the universe.

World leaders came to this space exhibition to find innovative space technologies. These revolutionary inventions gave humanity great hope for world conquest.

"It's only a matter of months," said KORP.

He proudly walked around the exhibition fair, talking to everyone and explaining where he planned to take humanity. These futuristic 'astro-space horse riders' would sail the endless seas of outer space in a matter of weeks. Progress transformed from the distant, utopian future to the real, near future.

KORP also developed the next generation of warfare weapons that fired laser beams, electromagnetic heat and ultrasound waves. This weaponry was mighty.

He continued to produce his symbiotic suits, which contained even more technological applications to protect soldiers and were even more sophisticated. He said to his advisers, "We must always be cautious when facing aliens in some newly discovered world."

All five cities developed at the same speed. They experienced unparalleled prosperity. Cities existed on their merit and effort and wealth were clear on the streets, in commerce and in urban infrastructure. They stood proud, burying their ancestors' memories. These cities polished their identity as KORP imperial cities: they were cosmopolitan, modern, technologically sophisticated and, above all, wealthy and clean, for they were highly conscious of recycling.

KORP encouraged their development, promoting industry and self-consumption at all levels. He said: "First, my empire."

Years ago, he organised a scientific competition between the five cities – a healthy competition in the best sense – to stimulate industry technology. The match was that each city had to reach the top of the imperial system pyramid carrying the torch of the unique common good. It comprised scientifically developing a common good that would contribute positively to the development, coexistence and subsistence of human beings across the empire. A common interest that serves the well-being of humans and elevates their quality of life. The emperor called this common good 'The Ultimate Good', which had to fulfil these three essential aspects: to be an elementary property that human beings needed to live; offer an efficient service to improve the quality of life for human beings; and should have an effective result for the immediate future of human beings.

Any discovery achieved in this scientific competition that did not fulfil these three elements did not make up an Ultimate Good. KORP said: "The city that places its Ultimate Good at the top of the social structure pyramid will receive more money for its achievement and declared a City of Merit, with more autonomy, fewer taxes on the central government, and a seat on the New Council. The city will also be able to make its most significant decisions internally."

This scientific competition aroused the interest of the inhabitants of the five major cities. Because of it, their inhabitants developed efficiency and professionalism from childhood. The aim was also to secure the empire's future technologically in the long term.

KORP believed that education made a nation strong. To promote this belief and awaken a thirst for knowledge, he displayed the slogan 'Knowledge is power' on giant banners and placed them at different viewpoints throughout the empire. He also put them in places where people congregated to socialise to encourage this scientific marathon.

Because of this scientific marathon, a natural and positive inclination towards education was born throughout the empire. People developed a genuine appetite for learning more.

It contributed significantly to the decline in school dropouts amongst the younger generation because education was pleasurable, well-rewarded and purposeful.

After years of work and patience, each city reached the top of the imperial pyramid, carrying its torch of the Ultimate Good.

As a result, each city complemented the other to form a single organic human geographical body. It was fascinating how well they connected through the Ultimate Good.

In the White City, medicine was the Ultimate Good. They developed technologies that may regenerate the cells to combat illnesses, which reduced the number of deaths. In Green City, agriculture was the Ultimate Good. They developed technologies that may help grow food in different environments. The Ultimate Good of Crystal City was hydraulics. They developed technologies that may extract water from natural resources, even from the moon's rocks. The Ultimate Good of the Golden City was construction and urban development. This city developed technologies that may help recycle construction materials. It built the most beautiful places to go on holiday in the empire. The town of Luz specialised in cybernetics, astronomy and manufacturing all kinds of macro- and microcosmic cybernetic devices, from interstellar spacecraft to micro-nano-biotic submarines that ploughed through the bloodstream of the human body, which had become strategic allies of the doctors. The capital was home to the world's finest universities, libraries and research centres. As the empire's capital, it enjoyed a privileged economic position, giving it advantages over other cities. Still, it never flaunted, starting with the emperor.

***

KORP's Ultimate Good challenge was intensely studying human beings to reverse death. The idea he had to die one day was a struggle for him. However, he wanted to do so for experimental purposes, but just for a few seconds, then return to life again. He and his co-workers spent years conducting in-depth and severe research on the biological life of humans. What was his aim? He wanted to extend the life of 'mere mortals' as he referred to humans. The emperor was still in awe of the hero who had defeated death and believed he was a demigod or a survivor of the ladder story linking heaven and Earth. He had heard this story years ago in the land of Victorious Cultures. Truth or fable, it always impressed KORP and he kept the statue of that hero in the Cathedral of the Clocks.

While researching in his laboratory one afternoon, he swore he would also defeat death one day. Whenever he worked in one of his laboratories on this matter, he shouted his famous saying, 'If you did it ...' Referring to the hero who defeated death, the rest of the staff would reply by calling, 'I can too.' It reminded the team that they were in a war against death. He assembled all the empire's health science and genetics scholars and mandated them to work diligently on the issue. He made it a national priority to find the genetic code of immortality; the empire built sophisticated laboratories only for that purpose. He charged the White City with being at the forefront of the project, with him at its head.

Being in the same position as The Thinker, he wondered if there was some blood whose DNA contained immortality information somewhere in the universe.

He also wondered what blood this hero, who had defeated death, would have had. He conjectured he must have had different, perhaps flawless blood and that this blood had to contain the key to immortality.

"Where is that man? What happened to him? I want to meet and talk to him if he is still alive," he wondered.

"KORP asks the million-dollar question. If someone claims to have defeated death, he has eternal life. So where is he? I am also practical in my questioning. The presence of this hero that many speak of is something that even I would request as proof that he defeated death." (The Thinker)

'If that immortal blood exists, its DNA formulation surely holds key information. Perhaps it is blood whose DNA differs from that of mere mortals, and if so, how did it become different? Has it undergone genetic alteration or mutation? Could it possibly have had immortal parents from conception onward? Perhaps it is a child of the gods?' KORP wondered.

He based his conjecture on the human body's current DNA data, which contains forty-six chromosomes: twenty-three from the father and twenty-three from the mother. He concluded that this combination of chromosomes is going to die at some point.

"Hence, to achieve immortality, it is imperative to undertake reformulating, reprogramming, re-engineering, regenerating and re-editing blood from the DNA gene or the genetic information encoded inside the chromosomes." He said this to his collaborators.

The question of how to overcome death led KORP to conduct various genetic experiments in search of answers. For him, it was a key, essential question – the positive response that could affect humanity's fate and would mean we would be immortal.

He did not enjoy living out his last days struggling with illness, as with everyone in old age. He felt humans should live longer, not for such a short time. This feeling added to his determination in his quest.

He was reading in the holy books that many people had lived almost a thousand years in ancient times and longed to be one of them with a profound illusion created in his mind.

In the same pose as The Thinker, he spent long hours trying to find the formula, the antidote to stop death; he even came up with the baffling idea of making robots that would run on human blood. He thought he could preserve someone's life in an immortal or more resistant body; then wrote that idea down in his book because he knew that the key to life was in the blood.

The empire set up substantial underground experimental laboratories in the building next to the palace to capitalise on this knowledge. Then, he equipped them with sophisticated and unique technologies. Sometimes, he would inject himself with elements compatible with his blood cells to reverse ageing. Then, he immersed himself in the universe of human biological, botanical and inorganic microcosms, seeking answers.

He built a micro-nano-submarine named Leviathan-01. It was approximately thirty micrometres[29] long by seven micrometres wide. Sitting metaphorically in it, he immersed himself in liquid elements to study the microscopic world, looking for answers. For example, in a bathtub of non-purified water, he would travel thousands of nautical micro-miles, and, on the way, he would

29.   **Leviathan size** is 0.030 mm by 0.007 mm.

encounter all kinds of weird, fantastic animals, unimaginable micro-creatures, and aquatic monsters invisible to the naked eye but real. He also had a well-equipped blood bank for his research, and, sitting in Leviathan-01, he travelled through different people's blood to study cells. Leviathan-01 almost always had problems travelling in the blood with high cholesterol levels. One day, while navigating through a person's bloodstream under stress, as it passed the person's brain, this tiny submarine suffered an electric shock that destroyed its electrical functions because of the high electricity voltage in this body. Poor Leviathan-01 had to be evacuated through an emergency operation and rescued as it passed through the veins of the patient's arm.

KORP also reached the depths of matter: the molecule, atoms, neutrons, protons and electrons, trying to find the borders of life and death and thinking he had reached the bottom. Traditionally, science understood 'matter' based on these elements. However, at these depths, he corroborated his suspicions that protons, neutrons and electrons had sub-atoms, which were even more minor elements. He realised Leviathan-01 was a gigantic vessel in this fascinating world of sub-atoms. These findings surprised him so much that, as the fathers of science had said years before, 'Certainty could no longer define matter'. Because of the depth yet to be reached. Then KORP said in amazement to his team, "Studying sub-atoms is the genesis of another era, which requires more time and technology to reach those deep dimensions. The microcosm is still deeper. I don't know if I will have enough time to get to the bottom of it, but I will try!"

One discovery that dazzled him significantly was learning biological elements like cells could emit, absorb and process light.

Scientists called this discovery Biophoton,[30] spontaneous emissions of low-intensity electrical light, which was essential.

---

30.   **Alexander Gurwitsch**, a Ukrainian Soviet scientist, discovered the existence of biophotons in 1923. During the 1970s, **Fritz Popp**, a German biophysicist researcher, revolutionised our understanding of biophotons and their importance. Nearly all living cells, including those of plants, animals and people like you, produce light particles known as biophotons. Amazingly, you absorb and emit millions of biophotons daily. Millions!

KORP corroborated DNA-produced biophotons, or biological electricity, in quantities necessary to run its biological industrial machinery. "Fascinating!" he said. This discovery supported his theory that cells were superior industrial micro-hubs that originated from an intelligent mind. Scientists regarded this phenomenon as 'nature's greatest miracle'.

KORP was determined to crack life's code. Inside Leviathan-01, he dived into the deepest recesses of the human body in search of clues about life's origins or the boundary between life and death. However, the deeper he dug, the more intrigued he became by microbiology. He realised that life was more complex than he had once thought.

Some of his co-workers suggested that the human body's biological functions work perfectly, can live forever, and adjust at 'the zero point', where no imbalances or fluctuations cause death. However, in the past, something destabilised that harmony, causing changes, inequalities and clashes in their biological functions, resulting in his death.

He also validated the partial compatibility of animal DNA with human DNA. He made mixtures that contained both human and animal DNA. For example, he grew human organs using animals in laboratories. Sometimes, one could hear him talking with his rat because it was developing a human ear on its back. It was fascinating to look at, but also creepy.

For him, this quest was a war for life, arguing that the end justified the means. Genetic material mixing experiments end in catastrophic results.

Sometimes, he cut his finger or body to study the regenerative process of cells. Then he would meticulously film the entire process of the wound healing. He admired how, in the shortest time, these tiny biological factories, called cells, could produce reconstructive parts at the wound site at the speed of light.

He hoped these cells would produce more durable components to extend the lifespan of vital organs.

KORP didn't want to go a day without learning more about human microbiology. The more he knew, the less he thought he knew. He said to himself, "There is so much to discover and research."

He decided his next step should be to amalgamate human biology with robotics and cybernetics by creating cybernetic bodies using Biodermatik science, which would function based on human blood. He said, "Perhaps in this way, I will find the zero point, where no such fluctuations create biological disharmony. So perhaps," he continued eagerly, "I can preserve a person's life for longer."

He imagined soldiers with these cyber-biological characteristics fighting in wars.

'They would be invincible to the enemy,' he thought.

He argued that the human body was too fragile to face war in this day and age. Even though soldiers wore the symbiotic suits he had designed, he saw they were still weak. He felt that soldiers should have more substantial bodies.

He envisioned astronauts with bodies that could cope with harsh conditions on other planets.

"That would be a significant advantage," he said to his collaborators.

He would call such a mixture of human and cybernetic bodies the 'Humbrids'. This idea of amalgamating biology with cybernetics was his next strategic step.

"Perhaps the closest thing I've ever seen to immortality," he muttered.

His discipline and ability to study microbiology were dazzling. Sometimes, he would only eat and drink coffee once he found something new, and even then, he barely ate a piece of bread. He stored this valuable information on hard drives.

KORP wanted immortality to be his Ultimate Good. He longed for it very much.

"If I find the formula for endless life, it would be the most sublime sacrifice I have ever made to my god Time, and it will be proud of me," he told his colleague, The Thinker.

He also established a battalion of male and female experimenters who used their bodies, or the women's wombs, as genetic research laboratories. He performed various genetic tests on his army of volunteers, with whom he conducted multiple experiments, driven by curiosity and dressed in his noble cause, 'For the good of humanity'. One, in particular, was a well-known experiment: mixing generic genetic material from a man and a woman, seeking to produce a third human gender. He was tired of trying. It was impossible.

Many of these test participants were professionals and experts in various sciences. Years later, they would occupy critical positions in imperial scientific development if they survived.

The dedication these experimenters showed to science and KORP civilisation is admirable. They didn't mind paying the price if they could reverse death. To die for the good of humanity was a sublime sacrifice for them.

11. A little more

Where the will has hijacked, desires rule.

They say the glory of fame lasts fifteen minutes, but I say that the glory of KORP's fame seemed eternal. Because of his extraordinary circumstances, it should last forever, or at least over fifteen minutes. The glory of the emperor extended to the ends of the world on the back of his weaponry industry and Biodermatik science he had created, to the moon with his helium-3 energy industry, to Mars with colonies on the brink of independence – including food and water – to the cosmos, sending dozens of space exploratory vehicles, and to the microscopic world by building medical micro-nano-biotic submarines to aid in medicine, and so on.

KORP established a commercial bridge to transform rare soils from Mars at an industrial level so that, when mixed with the Earth's minerals, they could strengthen the space industry and build strong and larger interstellar ships capable of carrying and bringing products beyond Mars on an industrial scale. These were thanks to his 360° Space Programme, which bore fruit. Across the empire, people unleashed a fierce race to develop the space industry in pursuit of universe colonisation.

In just a few months, the number of new industrial astronomy companies in the empire had increased, accelerating the construction of immense technological centres to manufacture more complex and sophisticated spacecraft and space equipment. This industry needed a large workforce. With remarkable wisdom and patience, he got the empire's inhabitants, instead of looking at the Gerikos, to look into space. Thanks to this, fantastic ideas for space exploration in any direction of the stratosphere are born every day.

A group of astronomical scientists discovered signs of life on one of Saturn's moons, which was promising news for space exploration lovers. They were waiting to confirm that news.

The emperor fed the upcoming generations all kinds of reports relating to space; this gave them security and hope for the future. Those thirsty for new experiences – dreamers of travelling to the stars – did not stop investigating.

The new findings, published in the 360° Space Programme news magazines, powerfully nourished people's expectations for their immediate future. The lookout points also became favourite astronomical observatories for families and their children. There were interactive viewing platforms for mothers and young children, provided with all kinds of educational materials. However, adolescents and young people were the target audience in these places. Little by little, space became their longing.

***

As the years passed, KORP's power grew through his influence as an emperor. His kingdom aroused admiration and fear for the four cardinal points. The memory of the pain inflicted during the Nuclear War died in the memory when the old generation passed away or forgot it.

When KORP took decisions, science and wisdom appeared peacefully in his mind.

Within the empire, some societies seriously believed that KORP was a demigod, an entity. They even held small gatherings around his image in some places, lighting candles in his honour. They protected him through their prayers and entrusted him to Providence so nothing would hurt him. He was still the all-time hero to the masses, their paladin, even for the younger generations. They thanked him, felt safe and walked, holding high their countenance. They were very prosperous at any level under his shadow.

His image grew so much that his followers surrendered themselves to him. He became, in some ways, the father of his empire.

Not only did they look at him as an emperor, but they also admired him as a father. Some people knelt before him when he passed the streets, calling him 'an honourable father'.

Although he was cold towards them, people still loved him. For many, there was no life outside the Gerikos; cities were the perfect places to live. People found meaning in their existence and felt they had reached the glorious paradise every human hopes to see after having been on a pilgrimage.

Many kingdoms and countries asked the empire to annex them. Some were kingdoms contiguous to imperial domains, and others were not necessarily contiguous, but voluntarily asked to be annexed.

It was impressive how many people kept arriving in the caravans of Time Travellers; some were still fleeing the miseries caused by the thermonuclear bombs because the land to cultivate was dying and had condemned them to die of thirst forever. They needed to shelter under the shadow of the emperor's good father.

KORP's heart seemed bottomless; he received any Time Traveller. He sheltered them generously in cities or anywhere the person wanted to live. Throughout his empire, he cared for and provided for humans, saying, "Humans first, always, humans first." He insisted humans were the reason for the empire's entire existence.

Sometimes, he stood atop his palace and inhaled deeply, trying to smell every corner of his domain. He did that every morning because he wanted to be sure everything was under control. From there, he made a wish through this prayer: "I hope everything is fine and in order."

Entire flotillas of his steel horse riders loaded with KORP technological products and weaponry set sail from the ports of the empire and returned laden with exquisite foodstuffs from distant lands. Many kingdoms, countries and people traded freely with him because he was fair in his business. Merchants searched for or contacted him because they said, "The Emperor KORP has ethics and morals in his prices."

Merchants held him in high esteem because his business motto remained: 'Above all, the right price.'

Because of this attitude of justice in business, many merchants gave him an extra portion of the products they sold him called 'Yapa'.[31] It was a symbolic way to say, 'We appreciate you very much, and we sincerely hope you will return soon to negotiate with us again.'

Slowly, the scars of the Nuclear War faded away. The new generations knew nothing about that war. KORP ordered them not to discuss the subject with the upcoming generations, neither in public places nor in educational centres, so as not to put the weight of sadness on their shoulders; instead encouraging them to look into the future. He succeeded at that, too.

The new people born into the empire carried a futuristic vision: a space migratory gene. They were children for the conquest of the galaxy.

They did not talk about anything except travelling to the stars. These kids aimed their ambition towards colonising anywhere beyond the walls and into space. The empire brainwashed and robotised them.

***

"In this part, maybe it's time to talk about what was going on in the pit of the Emperor KORP's heart." (The Thinker)

Yes, it is true. Strange changes are about to take place in the emperor's heart. We would never have thought these changes could affect him because of his lack of conscience, but how wrong were we?

Perhaps if an average person were the emperor, he could be one hundred per cent happy with the glory he has achieved; instead, the idea of being 'almost satisfied' was rounding KORP's

---

31.   **Yapa**: If you buy ten oranges, they will give you eleven. The eleventh is the Yapa.

head, and he wasn't pleased, so he wanted a little more.

"Dissatisfaction is not evil if you know how to feed it because sometimes it contributes to self-improvement, but there is a different dissatisfaction, and that different dissatisfaction had reached his heart and was about to wake up." (The Thinker)

It's true; thanks for clarifying. Despite all the glory and power of Emperor KORP, there was a small abyss of dissatisfaction deep within his heart. That innocuous hole was like a larva that initially seemed harmless but carried the tastiest but most deadly poison.

One day, that larva came out of its incubator to roll until it rested in the garden paradise of the monarch's heart, then it transformed into a stunning microscopic plant; it had branches made of gold, its leaves made of glass, and its roots made of the most sublime diamonds on the face of the Earth. It was a beautiful plant. That beauty had put down its microscopic roots, and it was growing. It seemed harmless at first, and it looked stunningly beautiful.

From that day on, whenever KORP looked at himself in a mirror, he started saying unfamiliar words, and people heard him speak. He would say in English, "Why not?" suggesting there was no reason not to do it. It was an answer to that question. The answer to a question or suggestion popped into his heart and went to his head.

What was that question? Without a doubt, this question arose from that beautiful tree. Even his advisers heard him saying those words every time he passed by a mirror and looked at himself carefully.

In weeks, the microscopic tree in his heart grew unimaginably, so much so that it became robust and manifested as a question-answer-wish.

Months later, the small tree transformed into a gigantic, beautiful tree whose essence was dark, as dark as a black hole. It fed on that other black hole called KORP. It devoured the taste of the bread of victory from the emperor's mouth and caused dissatisfaction. Also, it ate away at the satisfaction of the emperor's accomplishments. That new black hole was called vanity, whose hunger was voracious and impossible to satisfy.

"Vanity is the most corrosive thing in nature; is the force that pulverises the toughest rock and the element that sends the first to the last place; it is the essence that transforms freedom into prison; it is the black hole that destroys the beauty of the most beautiful and transforms the wisdom of the wisest into foolishness."
(The Thinker)

Soon, vanity built its throne in the emperor's heart and ruled his mind, spirit and will. Its gigantic, unfulfilled desire finally imposed its rules and demands on the monarch's will.

At first, those demands were small, and KORP faithfully met them. Every time vanity's orders came up, he answered with a question such as, 'Why not?' Its needs gradually became bold, cynical and cunning until it caught him in its web.

As the days passed, vanity demanded powerfully from the eager garden of the emperor's heart. It was like an insatiable black hole that never satisfied itself. Poor KORP, he quickly slipped off the rails like a train running off the rails fully because he was bound to fulfil only that parasite's wishes.

Vanity demanded a little more power, wealth, dominion, knowledge and glory, bit by bit.

***

"Whenever vanity sweeps away a person's convictions, they end up deposited in the middle of an infinite haystack; it will be a miracle to find them again."
(The Thinker)

Before long, vanity claimed its first victim in the emperor's heart and mind: his convictions. When he built this great empire, he worked and fought hard on those principles with his colleagues, people and friend, The Thinker. The vanity had chewed and swallowed like delicious chocolate bars on these principles. It went even further: it reached KORP's subconscious, so much so that he dreamed of that tree with crystal leaves, where he heard voices that told him he was that majestic tree that the world admired and whose crystal leaves reached everyone to the ends of the Earth while looking at the tree and seeing how it grew. Even in those dreams, he answered with these words: Why not? It was bizarre.

Because of vanity, he also developed a kind of auto-hedonism that made him divert his gaze from objective reality to a subjective reality that contained a solid desire to fulfil only his desires. Amazingly, he justified every pleasure he gave himself with a 'Why not?' In a greedy, urgent way, as if the world would end that afternoon.

Quickly, the effects of vanity on his life became public and more prominent. His slogan was the next victim, which vanity erased with its destructive force, cynicism and cold ease to bury and replace with another saying. For example, this motto, 'Humans first in the KORP Empire until little more shows up' replaced this other principle, 'Humans first in the KORP Empire'.

All cities had reached the top of the imperial pyramid on equal terms based on their rights and merits and had earned the title of Imperial City Merit. They were proud of that achievement and wouldn't settle for less. They had reached that position through diligent work and effort as a community. Achieving the Ultimate Good was no small thing; it was the maximum expression of dedication and effort that any society could achieve within the empire. For that reason, certifying the Ultimate Good was a source of great pride and celebration. Still having reached the top of the pyramid of his empire and achieved the glory he boasted, the emperor felt it was not enough. Therefore, he was determined to do anything to get a little more.

Little by little, the emperor lost the satisfaction of achieving anything. That happened in winter when the capital city had to dress in thick clouds that produced gloomy days. The saddest thing about that winter was that the darkest day had come and was to be the longest and darkest night ever seen in the empire's life. They were to be caused by the thick grey cloud: Emperor KORP.

"Once more, dangerous days were approaching for the inhabitants of this prosperous empire. The inhabitants would have prepared for the coming long night if someone had read these warning signals. They would have stored forces of all kinds to strengthen their hope because they would need all the willingness, all the courage, all the wisdom, and all the bravery to endure that dark darkness." (The Thinker)

***

With each passing day, it was more evident that KORP was brutally puffing up in vanity. His way of managing time had transformed, and this became his double god. Now, he frequently mentioned being swamped and emphasised the importance of not wasting even a single millisecond of his dual god Time.

He repatriated the misers he had expelled years before. With them, he founded a society called 'Platinum Card'. These people taught him to worship money properly. From them, he learned to love money. Since then, there was the 'One Way Platinum' card, which became the maximum expression of the monetary value of his empire, and from then on, it was the most coveted because it granted superior status to whoever owned it. It wasn't easy to get one unless the emperor delivered it. It was superior to the well-known One Way card.

Vanity also put in KORP's heart a desire for fame that had never existed, appearing daily in the press with small KORP tips. These were tips on anything; they had neither head nor tail and needed to make more sense. The press had to tolerate these writings because he was the emperor.

He also loved absolute control of his empire, so he became more of a perfectionist every morning. Suddenly, when he found the utensils on the breakfast table in disarray, he sorted them out and refolded the napkin again. He ordered the kitchen staff to put a magnifying glass next to the silverware on the table. With this glass, he observed the food on his plate to ensure it did not contain impurities.

Suddenly, his rules, methods and laws had to be followed to death without a margin of error because mistakes needed to be eradicated and replaced with perfection. What did that imply? It implied that the surrounding humans had to be flawless in their ways and impeccable in everything they did for him. If not, one error would end up in prison. In months, he had dozens of prisons built where the imperfect ended up.

He developed kicks in the air as tantrums. They were sudden

outbursts of temper and mood swings that hurt his relationships with the surrounding people. Those tantrums made him more eccentric, unrecognisable and unpredictable. Doctors called them 'vanity tantrums'.

"Inevitably, KORP had passed through the door that led to intolerance, to the space where heroes die in life, to the place where the best intentions float inertly, to the world that our passions adore the most, to the space where our real emotions vanish, to the space where freedom dissipates. He stood within that circle mortals fear most: vanity." (The Thinker)

Thanks to his vanity, he sadly removed his convictions on political matters, with which he regulated his empire, from their place. However, it was not for the better. In the short time since he fell into vanity, he took his empire to an area in time and space where only he understood it. He took it to a place where only he knew how it worked and how to manage it to provide solutions.

His obsession with absolute control of his empire had reached unhealthy levels, so he declared his love for distrust, who became both his confidant and favourite friend; through it, he suddenly stopped trusting his closest collaborators, friends and relatives. These were those who had been by his side since the previous era, had supported him daily, and had bet on him, risking everything, even their lives.

In this solitary space, away from his friends and relatives, he satisfied voraciously all of vanity's appetites, his arrogance, and all with ease. There, with a wink, he fulfilled his wishes in seconds. Everything he wanted, he got through that one magic eye movement. When he wanted something, he did that mystic movement in his eyes to get his wish. For him, his wonderful wink had become like Aladdin's lamp.

His callousness had transformed into a rock whose essence was solid, tenacious and difficult to penetrate. He knew how far he could push the limits; as we saw earlier, he was stubborn, very proud and determined, but vanity added a double portion of all three. It was like a double force that helped him lose his fear of danger. He believed unthinkingly in the possibility of the impossible.

KORP knew life's weaknesses and strengths: he had overcome the most fearsome challenges, such as bullying, and had defeated them. But vanity made him feel like he could be and do more than that.

With this new magical feeling, if something was challenging to overcome, he just needed to grit his teeth and shout, 'Yes, I can!'

In this way, he got what he wanted for his overall satisfaction.

With that extra determination, he also gained twice as many resources as he possessed: political, religious, social, academic and, above all, military, to where he thought of war as a game. He frequently played in battles, thanks to that new permissive power he had attributed to himself. He enjoyed knowing he was the strongest in regional military conflicts. If there wasn't a war in the area where he wanted to play, he provoked or invented one. Sure, he could beat any enemy.

The fantastic biological factories he had once admired with passion had now become his favourite targets. The emperor invented even more lethal weapons; he perfected the destructive power of his Toys, with which he now revelled in destroying human cells with efficient brutality. Also, showing his teeth like a rabid dog, he pointed missiles skyward to defy any deity who dared watch over him.

Here's a sample of the way he now saw things in his mind: he changed the name of the war to 'Existential Games'. With that new name, he glorified the way his victims died, and that fact – ever since he became vain – gave him a lot of pleasure. Also, he ranked death and named it Holy Death.

He travelled to the ends of the Earth to get involved or start some war. In his pocket, he carried his own rules for his existential games. Most of all, he liked the opponent to be his size so that it was appropriate for his expectations and lived up to his standards.

"Only in this way is a victory worthy," he said after becoming a fearless warrior.

He transformed one of his previous laws into a lethal weapon of mass manipulation and renamed that weapon 'insolvency'. That deadly weapon allowed him to terrorise humans' lives and hearts.

To his empire's inhabitants, he stopped calling them citizens, members or non-members. Also, he claimed the property of everything that breathed within the kingdom – even the humans – to whom he gave the name of adepts, better said, 'My adepts'.

Insolvency was his favourite deck for hitting someone efficiently. He used it in all areas of politics under the pretext of 'Order'. For example, if there was a public fight situation where he wanted to intervene, he waved his hand like a windshield wiper. People fell silent and stood still, afraid of insolvency. He said: "Order is the father of freedom."

He also deduced, "If I don't control the masses, there would be anarchy." He said it justified the use of 'insolvency'.

To ensure total control of the masses, he ordered the Gerikos to be double-reinforced when entering and leaving his domain. He then forbade his followers from escaping his cyber system and the walls, wanted them to stay inside these. He mused his subjects were too dangerous outside his imperial system and those walls.

His distrust grew along with the changes in government, so overnight, he flooded the streets of the cities and every town with Biodermatik soldiers. These soldiers were elite armed forces soldiers trained for extreme conflicts. What could a defenceless civilian do against a soldier who had a thousand more technological advantages? Nothing was the correct answer.

His mind transformed like over-leavened bread dough. His mistrust grew unchecked, mortally wounding his empire.

In a matter of months, the vain **KORP** devised how to create a single path, rule and law. He concluded that a tamed horse was more straightforward to mount, so he developed a single path, rule and law to tame the people, now known as savages, and imagined himself riding a mounted horse like a conqueror, raising the sword of vanity and repeating, "Why not?"

***

Shortly after falling into the pit of vanity, he also proclaimed himself 'the giver of life', wielding the power to decide who lived and who died. KORP appropriated that pretentious gift. It was an arrogant right that he kept to himself.

According to the 'Boomerang principle', he redesigned his government system so that all the empire's freedom and decision-making authority should belong to him. He signed these newly adopted laws with a golden pen filled with gold ink.

The sages of the empire met and wrote him a memorandum letter, saying that, "The ability to give or take a person's life is an arrogant decision that a mortal human can attribute to himself. Only fate has that supreme power."

After reading the letter, he became furious and had a colossal vanity tantrum. He responded with another brief note, saying that if they continued in that position of sedition, he would apply the law of insolvency to them to teach them a lesson for having had the audacity to send him a letter in that way. This situation is just one example of the extremes he had gone through day after day.

When he discovered that a national leader had executed someone for a crime, he would get furious with that leader, so much so that the emperor would have him arrested and executed.

He went out to invade any town or nation under any pretext. In those invasions, he caused thousands of innocent fatalities, so he justified it by saying that no one could claim the rights of those innocent victims. After terrorising and destroying those towns, he would come out of those razed places as cool as a cucumber, saying, "Oops, that was a slight mistake!"

After all, he was the only one with the right to give or take their lives because those were his rules.

KORP transformed into a cynical, dark and ruthless individual.

***

Freedom's flame of light in the KORP Empire had turned into a fleeting light from an asteroid, destined to disappear if nobody did anything urgently. The glorious years of peace, progress and freedom his followers had enjoyed at the empire's beginning had ended.

"The light of spring was concise for this empire, perhaps the most powerful and prosperous in humanity's history. However, for now, the KORP Empire was still the most powerful. From here on out, the emperor would hold his glory on the shoulders of his followers. Now, the ultimate question was, at what price?" (The Thinker)

***

Despite having a vain emperor, the cities in the empire continued their daily lives towards both progress in freedom and peace to become more powerful. In particular, the capital of Luz continued to be the most sophisticated in knowledge related to science and astro-spatial cybernetic technology, with the condition that, by order of KORP, it had to speed up its space programmes. For this it had received an extra budget from the National Treasury, thus condemning the city to perform miracles to satisfy 'little more' the vanity of its emperor at any cost. He rushed to extend his glory beyond Mars as soon as possible, insisted that they build the most significant number of spaceships in the shortest possible time, and sped up matters related to Martian soil exploitation.

He sped up the construction of taller skyscrapers, so tall that between heaven and Earth, stainless steel metal structures hung in the clouds. On top of those buildings, he stationed more telescopes with sophisticated resolution, part of the 360° Space Programme. Double-equipped them to track spacecraft when they travelled to or from Mars or the moon.

***

Suddenly, he emphasised the word 'victory', but obsessively. He started filling his galleries and museums with various sculptures that recreated the spirit of the Victorious Cultures. He placed considerable emphasis on the symbolism that urban constructions should convey. In his orders, he instructed architects to include any historical forms of victory in the architectural projects of public buildings and monuments in the imperial territories.

"Each block, each brick, each wall, each building and each ornament must signify and make victory's glory shine. Nothing should reflect the bitterness of defeat because it is bread for the weak. Walking through the city, one must feel the victorious gladiators' spirit, strength and wisdom in each cubic metre of urban construction," he said.

KORP liked the idea of having sculptures of lions because of how strong they were, snakes because of how cunning they were, and owls because of how wise they were. He ordered Egyptian sphinxes to be built because they reminded him of the glory that the Egyptian empire had held, and he also longed for that glory to keep shining in his kingdom. The imperial architects had the order to build Egyptian obelisks and place them outside his palace, also replicas of the Egyptian pyramids built in different parts of the empire. According to KORP, the Egyptian empire was the only victorious empire whose light from its torch and eye of knowledge continued to shine.

One day, he ordered the Majhia priests to hold a big ceremony in the Cathedral of Clocks to honour the memory of the Egyptian empire. That day, he kneeled at the altar, wishing that the victorious Egyptian glory embodied in his empire would continue to exist.

The emperor also developed strange ways of looking at the objective world; some were disgusting. In the blink of an eye, imperfection, weakness, critics, free thought, freedom of expression and art became objects of political persecution. Their destiny was to be in jail or be an Insolvent. All this was because of his extreme mistrust of others. From the depths of the Earth, he unleashed the political persecution demons; they were dark beings whose work method uses True Lies.[32] He sent them to every street corner and every corner of the empire to denounce the seditious who had

---

32. **'Lying Truths'** or 'True Lies': You must pay attention to the second word of these phrases. For example, in the 'Lying Truths' phrase, the second word is Truths, meaning they are truths disguised as lies; the second phrase of 'True Lies' refers to lies disguised as truths. Across the empire, the media used this technique to fool people. Since he got puffed up in vain, KORP also used it a lot, intending to cover up corruption in the empire.

committed acts that cast doubt on his decisions. He infiltrated calls, emails and social meeting places, all kinds of instances where his subjects freely communicated with each other. The first victim to enter the newly built prison was liberty, then trust; later, thousands of imperfect human beings whose sin was to have different opinions or think differently.

As his misconception of glory grew, his vanity grew faster, too. However, his tantrums and eccentricities increased even quicker, which became more apparent after an explosion of vanity. A vanity tantrum was sudden, usually hitting him at the least expected moment. These vanity outbursts or tantrums triggered his desire to think, expressed as 'Why not?'.

When people heard him say, 'Why not?' they discreetly or surreptitiously withdrew from his presence because they knew he would dismiss them from the activity. Every time he had his vanity tantrums, they were warnings he would need to reflect later. At that moment, he would order that lunch, dinner, walk or business meeting to be suspended because he had an immense desire for something and needed to think deeply.

For example, suppose he had a vanity tantrum at lunchtime. In that case, he'd call off lunch and send everyone out of the building within a three-hundred-metre radius. He would order to bring his stool and place it on the table, and being alone, he would take off his clothes, sit in the position of his colleague, The Thinker, and review the amount of knowledge that he had harboured in his mind, in the galleries of his mind. For example, while thinking, he would go into his financial gallery to ensure that all the formulas and rules about making money were exceptional, including the magic formula that helped him achieve that 'bit more' at light speed: fraud. Then, if he concluded everything was in order, he would move on to another gallery, and so on. Therefore, when he had reviewed the sciences and mathematics or had reached the depths of the human body, he would move from that position. He would take notes in his book if there was ambiguity about something.

In addition, sometimes, while thinking, he travelled in his

mind to the farthest stars and visited strange extraterrestrial worlds, where he saw weird creatures and imagined himself strolling in those places. Likewise, imagine hundreds of humans descending from their interstellar ships into interplanetary colonies. He also imagined climbing the golden staircase and arriving at the abode of the gods, where they welcomed or greeted him by making a corridor and throwing streamers and blankets along the way.

At the end of all this magical thinking, he would say, "Yes, truly, I know a lot."

12. An unpredictable emperor

An empire without people is like a luxurious but empty building.

In the blink of an eye, vanity led **KORP** through hundreds of extreme situations and contradictions, so much so that things in his empire were beyond his control. The most significant counterweight or pen that unbalanced the socio-economic stability that prevailed until now was to prioritise his space projects over the empire's inhabitants.

Because of the speed with which materials wore out or oxidised on Earth, the Star Trek Society, or STS,[33] of which he had become a member many years ago, advised him he wouldn't get very far if he didn't start an aggressive plan for urgent economic investment in his astro-space programme. Until then, he had built several interstellar ships, almost ready to be sent into space. However, **KORP** needed more financial resources to launch these gigantic space horse riders; they needed that final push. These types of projects demanded a lot of financial investment.

Since he was in a hurry to expand his glory a 'little more' towards cosmic realms, he ran at it full pelt instead of going little

---

33.   **STS**: Star Trek Society. They were very experienced galactic explorers in the KORP world. They became the right arm of the empire when it came to space matters, thanks to their knowledge of astronomy, astrophysics and subatomic physics, also called quantum physics. They knew how to move objects from one place to another over time. They discovered it was impossible to travel to the future because there were no traces of activity in the electromagnetic spectrum of space and time but to the past or other dimensions.

by little.

"I think KORP misunderstood the recommendation to inject urgent economic resources. The advice of STS was to put the built ships into space first." (The Thinker)

I think so, too. But the emperor ordered the manufacturing of these spacecraft to triple and put the ships ready to launch into space. To finance this decision, he had to restructure the entire empire's economic system, which cost him an arm and a leg. Overnight, he stopped funding essential national programmes in the imperial production chain, such as microenterprise and self-consumption, health and education; above all, he could have explained those decisions, but he didn't. Because of this, many domestic goods and services companies had to be closed because of a lack of money in these areas; they were strategic, small, service companies, an essential part of the food sovereignty chain. Practically, these supported domestic consumption, and millions worked there.

He also invented all kinds of taxes to drain the economy of people who had passed the stage of poverty; for example, he removed many benefits Time Travellers received upon arrival in the empire and benefits for adult education and eliminated the One Way card rules. Because of this, people suffered shortages of goods. Two or three in ten people had to begin in the streets or practise informal trade in the squares. Chaos was everywhere.

Imagine that at this very moment, you receive a call from your boss, and he says, 'Mr Croketa, I have fired you.' Surely your reaction would be, 'Excuse me?' Then confidently, you tell your wife, who is desperate because of this terrible news, 'Don't worry, my love, we have the powerful One Way card!' Then you withdraw money with your One Way card. The machine gives you a receipt with the balance of the money you must pay as soon as possible plus interest.

All the money that KORP collected from taxes and benefit cuts poured into his space programmes. Knowing the economic imbalance he had caused, he did not care; enlarging his glory towards the galaxies was on top of any earthly priorities from now on.

He won the favour of the Platinum Card society and the elites, with whom he built a straitjacket to protect himself from those who criticised him. He sought refuge within its shadows after forming a symbiotic political suit with his space society. They helped him bring order to the chaos that had set in. They tried but couldn't because they needed to understand the politics KORP had implemented, and they weren't politicians.

In several days (because of this sudden breakdown of the imperial economic system), terrorist cells, rebel cells, rescue cells, humanitarian aid cells and food supply cells emerged to balance that imbalance. These reforms suffocated the most vulnerable economy, threatening the empire's harmony.

"What do you mean by 'the sudden breakdown of the imperial economic system'?" (The Thinker)

When KORP laid the foundations of his empire, human beings were the masterpieces, the cornerstone of the political constitution, and dignity played a key role; both catalysed socio-economic life. It was a fundamental reality that these concepts were constant. The emperor said from the beginning, 'Human beings first'. He made no difference in gender or civil status. That truth guaranteed the respect and integral unity of the empire. However, since he became vain, he suddenly displaced the human being from that primordial place, thus causing a vacuum and, therefore, a rupture. That rupture created a government crisis, so KORP only governed his space projects now. He had forgotten entirely about human beings in his domain.

"If the emperor stepped down the accelerator, he could get more resources for his space projects without affecting most people. Sacrificing millions of minutes for fifteen minutes of the glory of fame is a terrible waste and a bitter contradiction for me. What a pity!" (The Thinker)

Not only was the empire suffering, but the emperor was also, as within himself, becoming more unpredictable, so much so that he neglected himself.

He slowly put his empire's inhabitants on one side. He replaced them with his space programmes and subjective ideologies: strange philosophies and inconsistent conclusions buried the most precious thing he had in his empire: human beings.

Also, in months, he replaced the people according to the order of priorities in his mind; he replaced them with his delusional love of knowledge and his sick passion for his rules, rules that were increasingly dark, heavy and difficult to comply with. Those kinds of subjective rules were like stones chained to the shoulders of their governing.

In his mind, he competed with those who worked at his side, mainly with his closest collaborators. He was unattainable and unpredictable in that race by staying one step ahead. What was his fear? Remember, he was never afraid but was vain and because of that he wanted to; he had to, and he would be the first in everything. He developed toxicity in his relationships, starting with the people he helped daily, including his collaborators, so their newly located place would be one or two steps behind him. In this way, he turned his collaborators into modern servants.

His collaborators no longer enjoyed his confidence. Many people who were by his side from his political beginnings, who had helped him build the empire, seeing the sudden changes in his actions, moved away from his presence and preferred to work in other fields of industry, although still within the kingdom. Those people could do the work for him. Before they enjoyed his complete trust, they sometimes spoke on his behalf or decided on him at his request. However, all that changed. They could no longer do so because KORP's word became sacred and canonised. Now, there was only him, and he did not want anyone to represent him.

In this way, he had placed himself in an unreachable and unpredictable place where the kings of the Earth lived in the past era.

"And what happened to his long-awaited freedom?" (The Thinker)

Good question. The emperor caged it with his principles, which he used to defend his country and the most vulnerable and needy.

"And what happened to his catchphrase, 'For the sake of humanity'?" (The Thinker)

That is another good question. The emperor made it into an excuse – a very subtle one. When he came out to give his speech, he repeated his catchphrase with a passion that gave the feeling that he was doing things according to it. However, deep down, he had also imprisoned it in the same prison of his convictions.

"The Emperor KORP didn't need to distance himself from people to become unreachable. Unfortunately, when vanity reaches the heart of any human being, it destroys the fundamental principle of human relationships: trust." (The Thinker)

He also instructed significant changes for those who worked close to him. He first ordered changes to the entry rules for newly hired staff, especially those working as Counsellors.[34]

The magnitude and depth of these ongoing changes are worth mentioning. For example, if there was an applicant for the job of Counsellor, the applicant had to first, study the manual book *The Private Life of KORP* in college, and second, pass the exam. It was the first fundamental requirement that applied to everyone, including his former collaborators and those close to him.

Before continuing, it is also worth clarifying something here. There was a lot of informative material (primarily scientific) in *The Private Life of KORP*. It contained chemical and mathematical formulas, biological and astronomical contents, and fantastic knowledge to build Biodermatik, robotics, nanotechnology and artificial intelligence. They elevated that manual book to a university curriculum and declared it a national asset. In addition, he meticulously documented the entire history of his life up to that point, organising it into 'blocks of work and time' that included seconds, minutes, hours, seven days of the week, twelve months, years and decades. Then, each decade had the same format as the beginning: it repeated its entire agenda in the new decade that began.

For him, the 'Wheel of Life' began every ten years; thus, the first working day of the new decade had the same format as the first working day of the previous decade, and so on. That was

---

34.   **Counsellors** replaced the role of the advisers; most of his advisers left him, so some had to do that job. Counsellors were expert politicians and great statists.

the way he organised time in his mind's avenues. He applied that principle to all of his daily actions.

He called 'blocks of work and time' the hours he spent producing or working, what people would call 'hours of work in the office'. Each working day enclosed ten hours for him, divided and grouped into 'blocks of work and time'. Each block had a specific designated colour and a particular time measured in seconds.

For example, if he divided a workday into five 'blocks of work and time', he would organise them in this order and with this colour system.

Block one, red, with 1,500 seconds. (That is 25 minutes.)

Block two, blue, takes 2,100 seconds. (That is 35 minutes.)

Block three, grey, takes 3,600 seconds. (That is 1 hour.)

Block four, yellow, takes 7,200 seconds. (That is 2 hours.)

Block five, green, takes 10,800 seconds. (That's 3 hours.) And so on.

The colour helped him distinguish the time on each block. KORP did not measure blocks by hours or minutes, but by seconds. Therefore, 'he commanded time with inhuman precision,' as people said. In his mind, his biological clock learned to calculate time in seconds because he was obsessed with time and lack of conscience. However, since vanity entered his life, he could calculate time in milliseconds – a diabolical double precision.

For example, if it were a Tuesday, at 2:15 pm of the first week of the month, which had thirty-one days, KORP exited one 'block of work and time' and entered another. If, on that day, an applicant was taking the exam for the Counsellor position, the applicant acted as the official Counsellor for those two hours. As I explained above, those two hours could hold three 'blocks of work and time'. The applicant had to know in advance what number of blocks they were or what colour to prepare the papers for the emperor.

The emperor was interested in something other than how much the applicant knew, where he had studied, his academic level, or anything else. He only hoped that the person would serve him efficiently, ideally without mistakes, and, above all, that he would do nothing wrong to waste time on unnecessary things in the office because the emperor came to that place to be productive. KORP expected the applicant formatted all documents perfectly, efficiently drafted and sacredly arranged so that reviewing them was easy to sign. He emphasised that 'each letter must be at home', in its space; it was part of the ongoing demands for perfection in that job.

Before signing, the emperor reviewed the papers; then he signed the contracts of the new staff in the factories; then the emperor signed the life sentence cheques for five minutes; for another five minutes, he signed sentence cheques for 'thumbs-down';[35] for another two minutes, he signed legal judgement executions; and so on. He did office jobs for two hours.

As the clock struck 4:15 pm, his feet were already at the door, ready to head out and into his next 'block of work and time'.

The applicant waited for an answer in the corridor, standing guard and looking straight ahead like a soldier. If he were suitable and accepted for the Counsellor position, KORP, passing him, would wink and give him a thumbs-up. However, if he were inappropriate, the emperor would glance off to the side, coolly ignoring the applicant and leaving without explanation, in complete silence. He didn't enjoy wasting time explaining his actions; because of his vanity, even the clock ticking meant wealth.

The conditions of the Counsellor contract stipulated working twenty-four hours a day, five and a half days a week, for six years. To the applicant who got the job, he gave his well-known 'incentive cheque' as a salary. The incentive cheque was a blank, signed cheque with a tiny thumbs-up hand drawn next to his signature.

The payment was a single blank cheque for six years of service; the amount had to be written by the Counsellor and spent entirely in the imperial territory.

"That way of payment, it's weird. Don't you think?" (The Thinker)

---

35. **'Thumbs-down'**: KORP took the responsibility to execute prisoners sentenced to the death penalty from the judiciary system. In time, that became like a game to him; he found delight in doing it. He sent to the victims before he executed them a cheque signed with a golden pen where he drew a tiny thumbs-down beside his signature. Sometimes, he wrote the amount; sometimes, it was a signed blank cheque.

That's right. No Counsellor reached the end of six years. If anyone reached the end of six years, the empire forbade them to speak about what it was like to work for the emperor for the rest of their lives. If the Counsellor revealed it, they faced insolvency. In this way, KORP trusted his mistrust.

When the empire offered the Counsellor position, they advertised it in such a way that made anyone feel trapped by the salary.

***

Love for his god Time became a delusion that exceeded incoherence. He wasted no time at all. Every second of today was more valuable than yesterday's. Time was like his sacred cow. He tamed the seconds and transformed them into a wealth of ways and means under his motto, 'A little more'.

In weeks, imperial authorities filled prisons with inefficient Counsellors and imperfect people at work daily. He hated being late for his appointments. He would retaliate against his Counsellors if they made him late for his activities.

When invited to parties, he dressed in extravagant outfits, adorned himself with precious stones and wore gold jewellery, which he had stolen from gambling houses in his youth. He sometimes wore his favourite ring, embedded with a rare stone, saying it was not a terrestrial stone. Perhaps an asteroid? Maybe. With the press behind him and in the middle of the cameras' flashes, he walked along the catwalk he had ordered to have deployed. As he passed, he looked at the models, who were also looking at him anxiously in the eyes, wanting to elicit the well-known wink from him. He would arrive at his table with two or three models, whom he would dismiss as soon as he took a seat.

When he arrived at his company, where he had to promote the worker of the week, he made all the workers stand up. Then he walked down the line, looking the workers in the eye without knowing who the worker of the week was. Randomly, he winked at someone and would be happy with it.

When he had business meetings with prominent people in business, he listened to them for two or three minutes; after those minutes of conversation, he would stand up, and everyone would get up, forming a formal half-hour farewell greeting. He wouldn't have accepted the offer if he hadn't winked when he left.

If he felt like buying something, he would explore the shops in the city. When the shopkeepers discovered it was the emperor's shopping day, they made the finest products to seduce him with all kinds of articles. If he winked when leaving a store, it was the most popular store of the week.

***

Gradually (and unfortunately), darkness reigned in KORP's Empire. People walked expectantly at his feet, waiting for the emperor's approval in every event of their lives. The inverted pyramid fed him approval-hungry souls, who fell at his feet, agonisingly waiting for him to wink. KORP reduced the value of the humans in his empire to a ridiculous, mean, hypocritical, calculated, hollow and cold wink. But with his magic key of 'Why not?' he opened the doors of his hedonistic personal passionate paradise, where he paid homage, worshipped himself with the luxuries His Majesty always dreamed of and did not deprive himself of anything while still stealing the bread of the people he governed.

The emperor would also rush to the ends of the Earth, looking for valuable pieces of archaeology and art for his collection. Passionate, he savoured the taste of gold, especially from places rich in history or where pirate ships battled and sank with the treasure they carried. There was nothing he longed for more than that.

***

"The speed, voracity and viciousness with which he lost his scruple in business was impressive." (The Thinker)

I would say the same. The emperor got to where his shamelessness fled into exile out of the shame it felt for the emperor.

KORP no longer negotiated and paid a fair price. Now he stole.

He brazenly renamed his stealing acts 'Necessary Business' and dressed them in lofty financial theories to justify plundering. I will explain those details later.

Making his creative business ideas a reality was never a problem; he only had to wink to fix everything. He developed various financial theories to multiply that 'little more' at lightning speed. His sixth sense played a significant role, as he knew how to sniff out and find riches.

He always left his mobile phone on mode ON because he unthinkingly believed some business ideas floated in the electromagnetic field. He thought his device knew how to catch them from there, so this way, he didn't waste time either. Sometimes – or almost always – he would walk around staring, mesmerised by the screen of his mobile phone while gasping for some business idea, with such concentration that he forgot to watch where he was going and sometimes stumbled into utility poles, street trees or the gates of his palace. He was struck so hard that he cut his face severely from the impact and was bandaged for many days.

Once the nasal septum had broken, they had to bandage his head like a mummy. Thus, he walked the streets looking like a real mummy that had escaped from the museum; seeing him, children ran away from him in floods of tears.

His obsession with amassing money became an indomitable force – his reason for living. His vanity still needed to be complete and satisfied; it always wanted, asked and promptly demanded a 'little more'. That longing for that 'little more' wouldn't let him sleep.

The paladin moved further and further from objective reality. He didn't care now because he had more significant priorities to attend to and had little time to talk to anyone. In a piecemeal manner, he lost that habit he had learned through a lot of work: being empathic with human beings.

KORP also claimed that every electronic communication device launched on the market could reduce the distance between 'space' and 'time'. The more space one uses, the more time he reduces or saves; that way, time could hold more space. KORP convinced himself that one could be doubly productive in this way. He explained with grand passion how this new financial theory worked:

"If I give one worker one hour to pack a thousand books and another worker two thousand books to do the same job and time, applying that innovative financial equation, we can reach this conclusion: the one that packed two thousand books shortened the time in half compared to the one that seals a thousand books in the same time."

He believed this innovative financial equation was a tribute to his god Time, then baptised his factories with the new name 'Guardians of Time' and doubled production to cut time in half. He then enacted a law throughout the empire called 'Creating Space in Time' and said, "Each factory has twice as many spaces to create to reduce time by half."

When asked, "What about the workers who do the factory job?" he replied, "They are not indispensable." He replaced them with robots, which he said were better than humans at Creating Space in Time; robots didn't complain about working. He no longer liked that humans in his factories complained about producing twice as much simultaneously. With this enacted law, people needed to make more in less time. Then he ironically questioned, saying, "I do not have to be responsible for my workers' moans."

From then on, the law forbade workers from leaving work until the next day. It had to be finished by statute on the same day; otherwise, he would replace them with Time Travellers.

"Time Travellers will do the job without complaint because they have no alternative," he told his advisers.

He had secretly changed the immigration laws for all the

Time Travellers as well; now he called them Third-class Migratory Agents, whom, as soon as they set foot in the imperial territories, he declared them Undocumented Insolvent, for which they no longer had rights (not even humans, absolutely not in his new empire). They had no right to a living wage, a roof over their heads or help; it turned them into a freely available productive force.

In this miraculous way, while his workers worshipped his god Time, he filled his pockets at lightning speed with gold. Of course, that thrilled him and made him feel incredibly successful.

All the money he generated from his companies using his 'original finance new theory' would enlarge his space projects, which aimed to continue to expand his glory a 'little more' beyond the galaxies.

It was admirable how, with a brief wink, he monopolised fair trade globally and turned it into unfair trade. His sixth sense had discovered another business philosophy called the Gift Horse.[36] With that theory, he eradicated the factories (which fed his fellow humans in the land where he was born and which had provided him when he was little) to establish them in territories where, according to him, time cost the value of the Gift Horse, that's to say, crumbs. According to his sixth sense, time could hold thousands more spaces on these lands. To ensure that the 'hairs' of the Gift Horse remained unseen, he hired children, adolescents or anyone who, by nature, didn't question him. He regarded these people as third-class humans. Therefore, he paid them for their work with the norm of the old financial principle of the Fountain of Miracles, crumbs. Then he sent these tainted blood products, which these people made on miserable salaries, to his shops in imperial cities. He sold them to his fellow men at diamond prices.

With this sudden change in attitude towards the objective reality of his empire, KORP had dug a deep well – an abyss beneath his own feet. He fell with nowhere to stand.

***

---

36. **'The gift horse'** means cheap labour.

He was still unsatisfied with his empire, so he set his sights beyond his domain's limits to travel to the ends of the planet, looking for ways to amass even more wealth. One day, in those latitudes, he was desperate to size the riches of these countries because he saw large quantities of diamonds that interested him. He did not apply his 'time and space' or 'sixth-sense' economic theories here. He invented another formula, which he baptised with the innocent name of 'Open Societies' to justify pillaging the free and sovereign nations to seize illegally their wealth, human rights and even the souls of their inhabitants through this kind of 'economic equation'. This new theory or approach gave him the green light to thieve.

Since then, whenever he came to a country and saw some wealth that he wanted to have, he stopped negotiating to gain it illegally. He did it this way. First, he disguised his espionage agencies as humanitarian aid agencies, investing millions in spying on those countries while making Machiavellian plans to attack them. Once he set the goal, he infiltrated the political reality of those countries to sow his True Lies through his angels of lies, the press. These were the media close to him, from whom he bought stellar spaces to publish his True Lies, paying them a lot of money. Then, he divided its inhabitants by imposing fraudulent elections through which he set leaders he could manipulate. After that, he provoked internal wars and divisions among the population so that they devoured each other to cause chaos and confusion. So, amid that confusion and chaos, he seized the riches. He fled those countries, leaving behind division, death and destruction while loading the loot stained with terror and innocent blood on his steel horse riders, then took the swag to the so-called 'Fiscal Nirvana Islands' to hide it. He left those looted nations as cool as a cucumber, as if nothing had happened. In this way, he became rich but infamous in the eyes of both countries and heaven.

Almost every country or kingdom that saw his steel horse riders arrive hid and closed their maritime or land borders to him because they were terrified of him since, in his steel horse riders, he carried his Toys, whose bellies brought death and ruin. Anyone who dared to discuss and challenge his allegedly legitimate actions, protected by his Open Society law, showed his teeth like a rabid dog.

***

His promotion of war was admirable. He provoked wars left and right mercilessly. To him, they were his favourite existential games. He was looking for any pious excuse that would allow him to show his vain power.

He invented another pious excuse in his cunning behaviour: 'Secure the world's security.' That excuse gave him the green light to justify the atrocities committed by his angels of death or Toys on the planet. When KORP saw the news of the disasters he had caused in some country, he would sarcastically smile and say, "Oops, a hair saved me!" His teeth looked like Dracula's because of the wine he was drinking.

He equipped his steel horse riders with all kinds of war material and sent them to the ends of the Earth, proclaiming he would secure the world's security. Aiming to find the ideal world enemy for his existential game, he knocked on the doors of each nation, inviting them to play his existential games with him. He knocked on the doors of the Victorious Cultures, looked for enemies on the coral islands, and crossed the deserts, the mountains and the jungles. He was eager to use his latest Toys for the first time. If he couldn't find the ideal world enemy in the sea, he would dock his steel horse riders to head into the continents on foot. If he did not find the perfect world enemy there, he would make one and provide it with the same Toys he possessed, thus entertaining himself for long months and even years.

Those 'existential games' were the right place to test how destructive his latest inventions and technological discoveries were. He convinced himself of how lethal his Toys were when destroying humans. He had forgotten what it was like to protect them; now, he would look for them, and when the emperor found them, he would use them for target practice. Now, his priority was to improve the destructive efficiency of his Toys; as he did so, he sarcastically swore, "For the sake of humanity, I must secure the world's security."

"What a contradiction! It seems he thirsted for innocent blood." (The Thinker)

That's right, and the Earth, with overwhelming pain and tears, received lifeless human cells or micro-factories, into its bosom.

The paradox was that he should win at the end of those existential games because it was his game, his rules and his Toys. At the end of the existential game, he shamelessly asked, "Do you like my Toys?" and insisted, "I'll leave them to you, but you pay me little by little on one condition: only buy them from me."

As a result, he created allies with technological and financial dependence worldwide. With that attitude, he spread terror everywhere. What right did he have to do that? He had no right.

"Why was KORP so insistent on playing existential games?" (The Thinker)

Wars were his favourite factories for creating space in time, so he got rich faster. It was the most efficient place to apply his sixth sense.

"I don't want to be the one having to do it, but I have to tell him that his time playing his baffling existential games is ending. He wouldn't believe me if I told him, poor vain KORP, he's so sure of himself that he still thinks he can do anything. However, I feel compelled to warn him regarding his behaviour." (The Thinker)

13. Above the top

Twinkle, twinkle, little star.

While KORP lost significant space in his battle against vanity, much was happening underground in the capital city, Luz. Some of those loyal to him or his close collaborators formed a parallel army of Biodermatik soldiers and secured areas within the cities in alliance with some members of the New Council. This group leaked top-secret scientific information from the empire to create a side project. These were not part of the resistance; they were part of the same government but wanted to take complete control to govern at some point.

"This group handled the argument that KORP had no offspring and, at some point, that power must remain in their hands." (The Thinker)

This powerful argument would set a big problem; there will always be people caressing power, even more so if it is an empire. Little by little, the empire lost its presence in many places outside the major cities. In these places, unhappy people had cooked up many ideas to do something about this crisis.

Meanwhile, the Emperor KORP lived a life obliterated by the reality of the empire; he kept descending into the abyss of confusion.

KORP developed a strange habit of getting up at midnight, especially true on those nights when the stars reigned and the moon was conspicuous by its absence. He would leave his house and walk hurriedly towards hills or high places to observe the Earth, the sky and the space between them. Before leaving his house, he wore a long black cloak with a large hood.

Being there, in the gloom of those lonely places, he became a wandering silhouette of the night. As he walked, he caressed the wooden pyramid he carried. He repeated words to himself as if conversing with someone.

Sometimes, he lit his oil lamp to cross small hollows where there were bushes and small rocks. After crossing, he turned off his lamp again and slowed down his steps until he reached open places, beautiful dense meadows of delicate grass, and there he desperately surrounded himself with the gloom of the night plagued by millions of stars in the sky. In the middle of that procession, he spread his cape on the grass and lay down on it, looking at the stars. In that position, he extended his arms and pointed his fingers at some specific constellation to connect it with imaginary lines to another constellation. During those walks, he composed a series of prayers or lyric poems in an almost inaudible voice, almost murmurs filled with lovely melodies.

Also, in that stillness, he made pauses in his movements to create moments of stillness in which he could hear the silence sound. He wished some stars would communicate with him through a twinkle as a sign of acceptance of his prayers. When any star twinkled, he reacted with a radiant smile because he was sure it had heard his prayers. After a while, he would get up again and walk towards other high places with the same stealthy anonymity until it was time to return to the palace.

His vanity for wanting a 'little more' led him to think and sense that 'little more' hid in that depth of the universe up there in some constellation or star or beyond in a different dimension – as a super glory; he called it the 'True Glory', where the five senses could not feel but only through the supra-senses.

One day, when KORP was in the middle of those ceremonies, he felt a strong need to get or be at the True Glory, which people considered was above the top of the reality where one lived. He wanted a 'little more' of that True Glory because he was unsatisfied with all the glory that the emperor possessed at that moment. So that feeling of insatiable need turned into a decision so fatal and stubborn that he said one day, "I will reach the True

Glory no matter what it costs me."

He took that decision as a challenge and a goal. It was as if he wanted to climb to the top of the last rung of his pyramid to find that little more of True Glory, a 'little more of the ultimate above', but he would look for it through the hidden sciences.

"I sense now that KORP shoots in any direction, I think he has completely lost his compass course or North Star." (The Thinker)

A few days later, he walked towards the unknown world like a sleepwalker. Since he was very stubborn, he hastened the matter by summoning his advisers (the few who stayed) and asking them how to reach the True Glory or the Ultimate Above. His advisers convinced him to do it through the hidden sciences.

Excited, he contacted a centre or school specialising in the hidden sciences. They assured him he would dominate the supra-sensory transcendental reality if he entered the True Glory or the Ultimate Above. Only then could he escape the limitations of the simplicity perceived by the five senses and explore life in its entirety. He would possess absolute powers that gave him extraordinary advantages over mortals.

This news shocked him a lot. Some of his advisers studied those hidden sciences and were attentive to helping him.

They also assured him he could reach the last step by being disciplined and fulfilling all the requirements demanded by those sciences. Then would cross the dimensional portal to meet the Source of Everything from whom the emperor would receive all the extraordinary knowledge and all the supra-sensory powers that His Majesty wanted, and at the end of it all, like the cherry on top of the cake, the long-awaited immortality.

He felt overjoyed upon hearing all these incredible offers. Crying with joy, he accepted the conditions without hesitation; he was very excited when he heard the word 'immortality' and enrolled in a school that day.

They emphasised he would need much discipline and to surrender his will to the rules and conditions established along the way. Then, and only then, would he get that sublime supra-sensory knowledge to help him understand the reality of living in the True

Glory or the Ultimate Above. To hear this news overjoyed him. That morning, he headed to the store, bought a sportswear set, and gave away several winks and thumbs-ups. He wanted to start the disciplinary training process as soon as possible, so he returned from the shop to the palace, jogging in his newly purchased sportswear.

Being in the school of hidden sciences, he developed camaraderie or brotherhood with his classmates in a short time. There, he learned incredible things about this science and trained with care. He asked to be treated like another student and not like the emperor. So they did. He felt comfortable in that school of disciples.

Each lesson he received made the hairs on his skin stand on end and profoundly affected him. There, he had hundreds of sessions and rituals that eradicated his beliefs about the objective world of life. He replaced them with these new teachings, like brainwashing. His conversations focused on the knowledge he was learning so much that he sometimes confused his interlocutors with a talk from the telepathic extra-dimensional quantum world. In short, the emperor enjoyed his sessions and put much effort into them. At the end of his training, he looked different. He didn't look like the KORP everyone knew, but seemed more docile.

After many long days of training, the day of his graduation or ascension to True Glory or the Ultimate Above finally arrived; he had to cross the dimensional portal to meet the Source of Everything, as they told him. From this source, he would receive absolute super-sensory powers and immortality.

The dimensional portal was a magical door supposedly forbidden to mere mortals. However, as in the eyes of mere mortals, caressing prohibited things is a pleasant bitterness. KORP accepted the challenge, arguing that now, for all the new knowledge he possessed, he was more than a mere mortal.

"I dare say that he felt like he was almost a demigod or the chosen one. Why was he so eager to reach True Glory or the Ultimate Above? What were his needs?" (The Thinker)

It's a good question. In those moments, the emperor felt his power was insufficient; he thought he needed more super-powerful abilities. Because of that concern, he was so disappointed by the natural world around him. KORP felt fragility had enveloped common sense and could not reign like that. He concluded he needed another more powerful force – powers that he considered essential to rule – that would give him the ability to have absolute control over everything. So, the new teachings he received brought him closer to the honey of 'the true knowledge' and infinite power. Those lessons made him daydream.

"If I achieve these extrasensory powers, I will communicate by telepathy, read people's thoughts, know what my enemies are thinking, make someone obey me without asking them out loud, and move things with my mind," he explained with excessive passion.

He became insatiably thirsty to learn more about the metaphysical, extrasensory, super-sensory and supernatural worlds. In a short time, KORP transformed (with the help of his influences) into a mystical eminence. He became known and respected in the world of hidden sciences through the Count of the Heights.

He offered lavish ceremonies to celebrate his invocation rituals. With these ceremonies, he sought to prepare the way for the most momentous day of his encounter with the Source of Everything. During his invocation prayers, tears of devotion flowed from his eyes.

His mentors were proud of their apprentice disciple KORP but also highly concerned about the profound transformation in their emperor's personality because they had never seen such tangible results in their schools. It was the first case of true conversion.

After finishing his lessons, he got into the habit of carrying small gifts for his colleague, The Thinker, and took light scent sticks for him.

One day, after consulting with the principal of his school, they assured him he was ready for the great day of his meeting with the Source of Everything. He planned to wear some splendid heavenly clothes for such an event.

He hired the most talented fashion designers in the empire, asked them to design hundreds of samples for the leading actor in a celestial realm-related play, and gave them a few weeks' notice. He thought of Michelangelo's ancient paintings in Saint Peter's Cathedral in Rome.

After a few weeks, he asked the designers to organise a fashion show where they could exhibit their creations. At the end of the event, they decided which clothes they liked the most. He planned to wear those unique clothes when crossing the portal.

Sponsored by the big fashion chains, the designers organised the most prominent fashion show with the heavenly clothes of the year. They put so much effort into designing and making these divine clothes that they had trouble deciding which was the finest. Also, catwalks in cities to reach the masses; streets of every populated centre had transformed into streets inhabited by celestial beings. As expected, the public added spirit to the event by designing and wearing heavenly homemade clothes. In addition, they attended the biggest fashion event of the year. Those kinds of events restored cultural life to the empire; in them, the public took advantage of the time to socialise, and, in addition, it was an opportunity for families to meet again. Because of the suffocating control of the empire, many had lost contact with relatives.

After the big fashion show, the jury chose the most outstanding clothes.

KORP had his outfit, and the cloth merchants had their profits – only the exact date of his long-awaited meeting with the Source of Everything needed to be decided.

***

Meanwhile, his Counsellors tried to keep civilian life afloat in the empire. They put a straitjacket on finances, reassuring the population financially for now. With that action, the entire productive system in the kingdom started moving again. The empire entered a political parenthesis. Little by little, the rebellions ceased because the Counsellors reduced taxes and sought funds from other areas to ease the burden on the most vulnerable. They did this behind KORP's back since the emperor lived on another planet.

The Counsellors were brilliant politicians who knew how to handle the masses with good empathy, especially when KORP was not in his right mind, almost since he had fallen into vanity. They were people with high conscience and knowledge of the empire's internal and external politics. Also, they had to redirect the emperor's political-diplomatic relations at the governmental level.

Working as a Counsellor to the emperor was an enormous responsibility. They knew how to handle imperial reality objectively. The Counsellors were like the hinges that supported the emperor in his relationship with the multitudes.

"Thanks to these remarkable thinkers – his Counsellors – KORP could have made his parallel or double life possible. He would have fallen as emperor long ago without these brave imperial warriors. Some Counsellors loved the emperor and were very loyal to him for doing their work, despite how dark he was with them." (The Thinker)

***

KORP anxiously awaited his graduation. While he waited, he paced back and forth, longing for and cherishing the unknown with the attitude of a caged lion. He wished for a shred of opportunity to fulfil his desire to reach the True Glory, the Ultimate Above. Meeting the Source of Everything was the last step. Still, this event mysteriously remained delayed, and no one could explain his reasons.

There were days while waiting in which the emperor's impatience and desperation threatened his supra-sensory project. However, he clung on and patiently waited for news. As the days passed and weighed on him, he worried more about the matter.

He would review the meeting protocol when he went to bed at night. He would also memorise what he would say when appearing before the Source of Everything. Whenever he had doubts, he immediately contacted his mentors to ensure he would say nothing imprudent or make any mistakes. Before hanging up, he asked if there was any news about the exact date of his meeting. At first, he called his mentors every hour, then every two hours; after a few weeks, every six hours; and after a month, every twelve hours. His mentors answered his calls infrequently.

KORP's wait was tense. Several months passed, and not even his mentors spoke to him. He spent entire days dressed in his heavenly clothes in the palace. Then his suspicions grew that something was wrong, but he hoped, trying to think positively. While he waited, he researched and studied books related to this topic. He still attended classes with his former classmates, despite finishing his studies. His thirst for more was insatiable. He was determined to atomise those limits to get a 'bit more' of enhanced power and glory.

***

The waiting was so long and endless, so he installed ceremonial altars invoking the Source of Everything on the buildings of his government palace to shorten the waiting time. At those altars, he begged the favour of the Source of Everything because they made him believe that those places of invocation also served in the search for blessings in the unknown dimensional world. He spent many hours at the altar at the top of his palace. From there, he made unimaginable efforts to capture the attention of any source that could guide him. After making some offerings or sacrificing some animals, he insisted he was ready for his big meeting.

He arrived worried in the presence of his colleague, The Thinker, suspecting something was wrong. Sitting next to him, he took out Kate's picture to talk to her and explained his plans for her and why he had taken this path; after kissing the photo and returning it to his wallet, he rushed to find another altar. Sometimes, he would also inflict minor wounds on his arms and pour blood drops on the altar, saying he would give his life to find the Source of Everything. While spilling, the drops of blood repeated, "I am the chosen one."

"Where did he get the idea that super-sensory knowledge grants someone immortality?" (The Thinker)

Since he fell into vanity's trap, he read and listened to more of this type of literature. He did not want to be ignorant next to those hermetic scholars. He wanted to be among the first.

The emperor waited so long that his frustration mocked himself; finally, his impatience killed his patience.

As his mentors assured him, he thought it would be easy when he began this pilgrimage. However, one event would mark a setback in his frustrated supra-sensory project. One day, while in the tallest building in the city, he looked into space from one viewpoint of the 360° Space Programme through the telescope. The night was starry and the sky was clear. He spent long hours looking at specific constellations and stars, as was his custom. He hoped a star would twinkle at him to assure him he was on the right path. Suddenly, a solid and icy wind unleashed itself in the night's quiet. In a few minutes, this wind brought clouds loaded with rain that unleashed a fierce storm. KORP was out in the open and did not move from there. Angry, he screamed madly at the wind to clear the sky of the clouds it had brought and continued on its way. The wind became even crueller, swaying the building like a tree. Desperate, he held on tightly to the telescope as the wind whipped at his body and the rain scrubbed his face. He shouted again to the wind: "Clear the sky and go your way!"

After hours of getting wet from the relentless rain, he did not move and clung to the telescope like a tick. At that moment, he felt heaven was unwilling to listen to him. It had forever closed the doors on the day of his magnificent encounter with the Source of Everything. He slumped down, frustrated, sad and shivering with cold; the skin on his face and hands was purple from the cold. The next day, he got pneumonia so badly that he had to spend nine days in the hospital.

Lying in his bed, he was weak, pale and emaciated; he ordered medical personnel to cure him quickly. Connected to the intravenous feeders, he meditated and talked to his regenerative cells in the middle of those tubes.

"Speed up your work."

He was hoarse, too. The disease prevented him from seeking his longed-for encounter with the Source of Everything.

His patience and interest in the occult sciences died of disappointment and hopelessness. After ten days, the doctors released him with strict instructions: "You must rest." From that day on, he felt discouraged and regretful about not reaching the True Glory or the Ultimate Above.

The emperor was furious; he felt deceived and suspicious of those who advised him. He also wondered if the literature he had read was proper.

It was not the fault of the literature that he had read. Still, the emperor read that information because whenever he found words like 'possibly', 'perhaps', 'allegedly' and 'maybe', or words that etymologically expressed doubt, he intentionally ignored or changed them so that they were true, as he desperately hoped they were true.

Until that moment, he had invested a lot of energy, force and time in the illusion of reaching True Glory to get the ultimate absolute power. He clung to those expectations so much that he broke into a thousand pieces when his fantasies shattered.

He was angry because he had no tangible outcome from that encounter. That disappointment broke his spirit; he returned to the corner of his bedroom to swallow the pain of an unfulfilled expectation.

Seeing him broken, his colleague, The Thinker, responded to him silently because he saw the pain he felt in KORP's face. He said, "Another lost battle," while watching him cry with the same intensity as when Kate left.

The emperor did not like things not happening the way he wanted. Because of vanity, he carried a double portion of expectations and felt a double dose of disgust. From that corner (in tears), KORP talked to his colleague, The Thinker. He asked him for advice or the key to getting True Glory, which he deeply felt he lacked.

In the following days, he resolved to bury the matter and meet with people who assured him that 'possibly' a dimensional portal was the key to True Glory or Ultimate Above. He felt shocked and suspicious of the people who looked at him like he was naïve after having tried everything but to no avail, and suspected that they had bullied him. It always amazed him when someone took him for being innocent. It was the last thing he expected from human relations.

For all these reasons, he decided not to insist on the matter any further, and since then, he has never spoken with that school again. He took refuge in silence and walked away from them, looking to the side.

With that experience, he realised the limitations that mere mortals face. He also felt that sometimes you can only have what you want. His new friendships with his classmates were the only salvageable thing from that experience. He thought, 'It's not that it doesn't exist, but there are barriers, limitations that prevent its access,' and added with great disappointment, 'Perhaps I am still a mere mortal.'

"I understand his disappointment at being as limited as a mortal, but I disagree. Vanity is fooling him into believing that life is not enough, so there should be something more relevant than life itself. What a pitiful way to waste time trying to find something more relevant than life rather than enjoying it." (The Thinker)

14. Dilemma

When vanity hijacks a person's will, it turns his life into a prison.

Since vanity kidnapped KORP's will, he kept falling into a void, into the most bottomless abyss of confusion. He reached the level where greedy philosophical conclusions reigned, which produced great anguish, thirst for power and unlimited lust in him. There, he visualised his new destiny: fulfilling all his unique desires.

From then on, his vanity and desires imprisoned him. He wanted to escape that prison once but couldn't; he tried twice but sank deeper. There, he lost what bit of sensitivity he had left, the one with which he organised his avenues to walk coherently. Vanity pillaged his natural principles and values in that place until he became a lawless monster.

The emperor no longer cried when he saw a child's smile; even if he wanted to, he couldn't. He did not seek the welfare of human beings in his empire anymore; even if he tried to, he couldn't. He no longer reasoned objectively; he couldn't, even if he wanted to. His life was in the colossal prison of vanity, which was dark and had high, thick walls like the Gerikos.

Inside him was sometimes a voice calling for help: his real KORP, which had become so small, almost invisible, and only he could hear himself; that place become wholly isolated and sealed. No one else could listen to him there; even if they wanted to, they couldn't.

He didn't enjoy looking at himself in mirrors because he had lost track of his face. He had lost track of himself. It was difficult for him to remember who he was or what he was like. Vanity had transformed him into a completely different person, with other ambitions and another gaze. He suddenly became very suspicious of everything, especially mirrors. Seeing himself in a mirror may have brought him closer to terror. Whenever he came across a mirror, whether on the wall of a building or in a public place, he panicked. He immediately hung clothes over the mirrors to cover them. He ordered his staff to ensure that there would be no mirrors wherever he walked that day.

By covering the mirrors, he sought to disprove the absolute truth and reality that they reflected. The emperor said, "The reflection of a mirror is pure and reflects facts and keeps nothing for itself." He didn't like that the mirrors revealed his newly gained identity, he felt mirrors stripped him of his thoughts and made his true intentions public. What were his true intentions? Get absolute power without a doubt; this was his big desire and ambition. "Why not?" he said.

"This insatiable desire to achieve absolute power and immortality was the product of that feeling of disappointment because with each step he took to reach True Glory, he met immense obstacles impossible to cross. So he decided that His Majesty's KORP needed other superpowers to help him overcome those obstacles; he returned to the biological and cybernetic sciences to find them there." (The Thinker)

It is true. Up to that point, the emperor had made remarkable strides in the biological sciences to his credit. However, there was still no sign of finding immortality, and nothing was concrete because of the depth of the microcosm. So for him to beat death (it was still Pandora's Box), as you say, he thought he lacked superpowers.

In the study of the supra-sensory world, the most significant obstacle was certainty. No one had entered and exited the dimensional portal, making one think this was the true path to absolute power and immortality. So, the million-dollar question was: What was behind the dimensional portal? No one could answer that question for sure. Poor KORP was at a point where there was a 'Y' end, and he didn't know how or which way to go. Even his mentors at occult science school had assured him they all handled their hypotheses based on possibility.

Whenever he thought about this dilemma, the image of the hero who defeated death came to his mind. He asked himself again, 'How did he defeat death? What did he do? What was his secret? Was he a wizard? An entity? A creative or regenerative force? Who was he? Where did his power come from? What force propelled him to return from the dead? Did he attend training like I had? Was he a practitioner of the occult sciences? Who was his mentor? Did he receive that resurrection power from the Source of Everything?' He desired to feel that energy, that life recharged a corpse's cells to start their biological production again. He passionately and vehemently wanted to feel that sensation of victory over death.

Like a sixty-foot-high wave, vanity pushed him through its 'Why not' sting, seeking desperately urgent solutions to its unsatisfied, infinite demands because dissatisfaction was its nature. Then, those vanities' desires and needs made KORP even more brutal and added a new set of dilemmas, making him lose his mood more easily. There were days when he was irritable and didn't want to stop talking to anyone, not even his advisers or Counsellors. He was like an angry, wild beast.

The emperor also did not like to look at himself in the mirror because, every time he did, he also found another grey hair or small indentations in the skin of his face, which were undeniable signs of ageing, and that meant that he had less time to live.

"I can also assure you that, with much sadness, he also lost the sense of the simplicity of life that was to accept and delight in the simplicity of the things of the objective world." (The Thinker)

Yes, sadly, that is true. People heard him questioning the why of everything with the sole intention of inflicting harm. He regularly invented philosophies that served as guillotines to destroy natural laws and replace them with unnatural ones because the objective reality surrounding him annoyed him.

In time, he became an expert philosopher of the existence of the human being, but at psychopathic levels. For example, he lost the elementary concept that the 'sun rises for everyone'. When this beautiful principle passed through the sieve of his machine to philosophise, absolutely nothing fitted in his mind. He would say, "This beautiful principle has an error: not charging a tax for the solar rays emitted by the Star King." Then, his wise conclusion about that principle was this:

"We should collect taxes for each megawatt of solar electricity that the Star King pours on the Earth" (wishing to leave in the dark those who did not contribute to that service). The emperor had forgotten that nature was supportive and was only interested in the excellent care of human beings rather than worrying about how to get easy money from them. He insisted it was unfair that people did not pay a tax on solar rays; then he said, "If I were the Star King, I would shine only on those who pay their tax for my solar rays."

However, for KORP (according to his revolutionary new philosophy), 'it is not fair to receive something for nothing,' like, in this case, the sun's rays. We know it is the Star King's personal and sovereign decision shining upon the righteous and the evil people, upon the poor and the rich people, upon the greedy and the unsympathetic of character, upon the meek and the humble, and the peacemaker's hope-seeker or bloodthirsty nature.

He filled his heart and mind with the strange philosophy to encrypt them into ideologies to turn them into his modus vivendi, becoming cunning by binding the truth with lies. He no longer called 'bread to bread' or 'wine to wine'. He taught his subjects to dig up the truth with obscure, twisted philosophies. It wasn't necessary to do that, but he did it.

Wandering in his mind one day, he decided that humans in his empire should also pay for rainwater. He was tired of humans in his kingdom being able to collect water for free. He then wrote a 'Spatial Hydraulic Rights' law, claiming he owned the rights to clouds and rain.

In the empire, there were regions where it rained a lot during the rainy season. Strangely, however, the water disappeared entirely from the Earth's surface in those same regions in the summer. This situation brought instability to the people who lived there, who, naturally inclined to survive, collected rainwater. For this reason, many dug reservoirs in the ground, like pools, and others built large tanks to collect enough water to hydrate throughout the dry season. Also, people had to do so because, since he became vain, the cost of drinking water rose, and in those regions, it cost twenty times more than before. KORP also monopolised transportation and water services in his greed, so buying water cost a lot.

From the beginning, the emperor underestimated people's survivable instincts and ignored that fact; it also rained a lot in the rainy season.

When he discovered people were collecting rainwater, he stood in horror and started investigating the case. Among his gallery of dark and greedy philosophical ideologies, he had one that said, 'Everything has a price, and nothing is free'.

He then asked if people from those regions paid the empire for rainwater; the answer was obvious. They told him that people paid nothing because it was a gift from Providence. When he heard that, he had such a vanity tantrum that he ordered recruiting a legion of people. After he appointed rainwater ambassadors and called them to fix that situation urgently, he sat on his golden chair, preparing for his lavish lunch. He was getting fat and slow. Those rainwater ambassadors rushed to those regions and carried the law in one hand and the receipt book in the other. They inspected each house and calculated the amount of rainwater they had collected. They appraised it per cubic gallon and issued a receipt with the cost people should pay. He also built specific offices where inhabitants could pay for their rainwater.

Helpless people had to accept their immense debt. Because of the size of the water collector tanks they had built, some had no choice but to mortgage or pay the bill with their houses. Because of this, thousands ended up on the streets.

The emperor amassed much money from rainwater after making all that scandal because, for him, 'Everything has a price, and nothing is free'. He became so greedy that he looked for a way to get money from people doing nothing.

He didn't need the money; I repeat, money was never an issue for KORP. He still had his inheritance money, alongside thousands of safes filled with jewels and gold deposited in the vast underground cellars of the palace. So why did he do it? He had vanity and wanted to show off.

KORP went deeper into this abyss. He put his wicked hand into people's pockets, applying his sneaky frog-in-the-pot principle. It works like this: put a frog in cold water, light a fire, and gradually increase its hit. The frog adapts to the water temperature as time passes, noticing nothing. Finally, the heat of the water rises so much that the frog's fate is tragic.

At first, people said little, but KORP gradually and deliberately increased imperial taxes. His empire became a laboratory for financial-economic experiments like this, so much so that, in his kingdom, he saw human beings as a kind of currency – anything but worthy human beings. He became very skilled and cunning, like a snake.

He no longer reasoned; vanity turned him into a delusional psychopath. For him, the simplest things became even more complex to understand; the noble became a barrier to breaking down, and human dignity was dying in his empire – thanks to the disproportion of his vain mathematics that emerged from his modus vivendi and arrogant way of seeing the world.

Little by little, he also changed or updated the names of his empire's inhabitants. For example, suppose someone is called Peter Pereza. In that case, his updated name was '59-three barcodes-Peter 2787-P5-two barcodes-Pere-V-z-a V'. When Peter Pereza got to a store to buy a loaf of bread, he had to recite all those numbers and barcodes before purchasing the bread.

Peter Pereza had lost his human position to become a barcode number in the modern imperial system, as KORP had proclaimed. If '59-three barcodes-Peter 2787-P5-two barcodes-Pere-V-z-a V' got sick and perhaps, by mistake, the nurse mistyped a number or a character of that infinite name in the cybernetic imperial health system, they left him in the hospital corridor without treatment – until he tasted death's bitter bite.

"I wonder why the hell KORP wanted absolute superpower and immortality when, even if he could, he didn't want to ease his people's pain?"
(The Thinker)

The emperor was stepping backwards instead of pursuing true 'freedom in peace and progress', as his motto used to be. Perhaps his new slogan should be this:

'For the good of the empire, let us transform human beings into an unlimited source of financial resources.'

Although humans' dignity and rights must always be above any ideology, and any ideology must be at the service of the human being, in his empire, this equation was backwards. The value of his doctrines counted more than people.

"KORP had crossed the limits, and he is walking beyond the limits away from reality permits; he had inverted the natural poles. By putting ideology above human rights, he had broken down and assaulted the barriers of rightness. Nature will show resistance and antivirus. History has shown that when an ideology becomes cynical, Machiavellian, and crosses the line of dignity and human rights, justice comes in favour of the human being, and from then on, that ideology dies." (The Thinker)

15. Gene of Life

The higher an object rises, the heavier and more tragic its fall will be.

At the beginning of the KORP Empire, the inhabitants put all their trust in the emperor's hands. They voluntarily deposited their destiny on the imperial plans. However, faced with the dramatic change in life's rules, many felt betrayed, disappointed, frustrated and rebelled.

Quickly, all kinds of conspiratorial groups arose throughout the empire in pursuit of destroying it or changing the rules of the government. Among all the resistance, three influential groups stood out. These groups became the ones who challenged and fought against the Biodermatik military forces – which we will discuss later – but the rest of the population tried to free themselves as well. Unfortunately, because of their 'One Way, Only One Way' vow, although they wanted to, they couldn't. If they did, they faced the miserable life of an Insolvent. Despite it being the empire that broke the agreement, many people were not willing to surrender. They took the risk of going against the imperial system. Imperial authorities called these rebels the 'Curious'.

If someone retracted the One Way, Only One Way oath, the empire registered them as Curious and retaliated against them. If the kingdom could not convince the Curious of his betrayal, it would torture his family. The emperor recited this pretext: "Well, what does it matter? Along the way, there are always necessary sacrifices."

If coercive tactics didn't convince the Curious, they sent him to the hands-free prisons, which were even more effective. They isolated the offender from the financial system by cancelling his One Way card; the empire declared him insolvent and expelled him from his job. This way, the Curious could not access any essential imperial services; they would not have access to the health system, couldn't pay their rent, couldn't send their children to school, could not do business of any kind, could only do nothing, and little by little, the Curious man dried up economically and psychologically – to the point of wandering the streets until he reconsidered his betrayal.

The weak endured insolvency for a week, but in the end, they accepted their guilt and re-joined the empire against their will or despite their dissatisfaction.

Many Curious people passed through the traumatic experience of insolvency, so they decided it would be the last time to rebel. However, those who determined not to go back on their decision to leave the empire condemned themselves for two things: to leave the city by climbing down the Gerikos wall to escape, or to remain there and find a place to take refuge because the hunt for Curious rebels was a public spectacle broadcast live on television.

Sometimes, when the nights were dark, one could see tiny figures slowly lowering themselves down the four hundred and twenty-six feet of the Gerikos' height to escape. They did it with long ropes or pieces of material transformed into makeshift ropes. Those who got to the other side of the tall walls joined the merchant caravans, travelling to the south of the continents for food.

The rebels who stayed in the city opened moral, material and psychological support centres called 'Shells'; they were places either hidden or far from the KORP civilisation and well camouflaged – safe and secret – even in someone's house, or they could be inside the city or outside the Gerikos, in substantial underground caves. Some subterranean Shells housed up to twenty thousand people.

Most of the Insolvent and Curious took refuge in the Shells. There, too, the non-Insolvent rebels met. They healed their wounds and strengthened their spirits after wandering the city, begging.

Couriers called the Moths77 connected the Shells, the first group of the resistance, made up mostly of teenagers. Those youths organised themselves into rebellion cells as they had high expectations for their future. They did not want their lives ruined by the emperor's vanity. KORP did an excellent job educating the upcoming generations to ensure the coming end of the empire. These young people were an obvious example of that strong future.

The name 'Moth' derives from the effect these insects produce on wood when it is useless or old; they consume it and force change to occur. In reality, it was these teenagers who started rebellion throughout the empire. They were brilliant young men and women unwilling to let their emperor's vanity take them for fools. They sought to prevent that infection from jeopardising their future. The Moths77 wanted the journey of their precious genes to be happy; they wanted to build a barrier preventing this plague from reaching far into time. In the distant future, they wanted to live in an ideal world where, as adults, they could exercise their human rights in peace and freedom, just as KORP had promised years ago.

Apart from being intelligent, they were also full of vigour and life; they were so strong that they could crush even the most complex rock.

Across the empire, several legions of Moths77 infiltrated public offices to spy and collect information, especially classified information; they delivered it to J3CeXteens.

The J3CeXteens were the second resistance group. They came from religious societies whose beliefs did not allow them to have more than one deity, so from the beginning, they resisted the One Way, Only One Way vow. Only one authentic, One-Way path defined their citizenship for them – it wasn't the KORP Empire. They believed that their emperor's vanity was a manifestation of the personality of the Source of Everything, who, for them, was the true enemy of humanity.

The J3CeXteens believed in the existence of a Cosmic Proportions War. In this war, the powers of the universe – good and evil – as gladiators disputed for a treasure of incalculable value: human beings.

When they talked about the reasons, they did not accept the One Way, Only One Way vow, they told this story:

"In the genesis of everything, His Majesty, who established everything from the beginning, put a garden on Earth – a paradise. That piece of heaven on Earth was the most beautiful place in the universe, so beautiful that it fascinated the heavenly creatures, too.

"One day, because of their free will, all the heavenly creatures in the council volunteered to administer the paradise created on Earth. Among them was one who was the most beautiful of all, even by his name: Morning Star. Besides being beautiful and having an excellent reputation, he thought he was wise and clever. He believed, in advance, that he would administer paradise.

"All the heavenly creatures eagerly approached His Majesty one morning because they wanted to be custodians of the brand-new paradise. They asked who among them would be the stewards of the new heaven created on Earth. Morning Star had already decided it would be him. The answer His Majesty gave them that morning was this: 'I will leave the humans there; they will administer the paradise I've created on Earth.'

"Hearing what His Majesty's will was, Morning Star filled with rage and had an epic vanity tantrum, which was heard in the heavens as thunder and felt on Earth and made the mountains tremble. Morning Star arrived on Earth to strike his first blow and leave his first mark on people, driven by hostility and vanity. Disguised as a snake, he appeared in paradise under the name of the Source of Everything. He found perfect and obedient humans doing their jobs as administrators of the beautiful garden. By trickery, he enticed humans to eat from the 'good and evil' tree, which His Majesty had commanded from the beginning not to eat. In this way, he corrupted humans' perfection.

"Not content with this and completely blinded by his vanity, Morning Star also corrupted the animals, the plants and everything in the beautiful paradise, thus leaving the beautiful garden and the humans destined to die. Finally, before leaving from there, he commissioned Death to administer paradise.

"When His Majesty heard the news, his heart ached so much

that in that instant, he vowed that one day he would restore paradise as it was at the beginning. He also promised that in the future, he would send an extraordinary being, the Gene of Life, in whose blood he would carry the antidote that would destroy paradise's administrator – Death. Then His Majesty commissioned Genesis, a mighty creature in his kingdom, to be the guardian, the watcher, and the protector of the plan until the day of the promised fulfilment came.

"When Morning Star discovered this plan, he had another vanity tantrum so big that everyone could hear it as thunder in the sky. However, it was so loud that every corner of the universe could hear it. Furious at that moment, he ordered his heavenly followers to track down and destroy His Majesty's plan for human life on Earth with the cynical intention of avoiding the unavoidable. He also asked them to use any destructive and aggressive method about any sign or evidence leading to fulfilling that promise. He also dared to alter humans' genetic code to prevent the promise from coming true, which is why there were giants on Earth in those days. Fortunately, the giants did not get very far.

"His Majesty expelled Morning Star from his realm for what he did and changed his true name to the Supplanter. Over the years, His Majesty's promise came true despite the obstacles created by the Supplanter and his henchmen.

"In a small town, at the appointed time, a child was born whose blood proved he was the Gene of Life. However, as stipulated in the plan, his life and blood needed to be poured into the Earth to make the impossible possible.

"When the Supplanter learned of the Gene of Life's arrival, he sought him out and found him in the streets proclaiming His Majesty's plan. The Gene of Life was already a handsome young man whose face flowed with justice, love, forgiveness and compassion. In that meeting, the Supplanter wanted to negotiate the non-negotiable with the young man. Taking him to a mountain, he offered to give him all the kingdoms of the Earth if he avoided 'the unavoidable'. The young man, determined and knowing his destiny, rejected that offer. The Supplanter had another vanity tantrum so strong that it made the heavens and the mountains tremble. He knew he could not convince the young man and, in his impotence, called his faithful collaborator – the administrator of paradise, Death – and ordered him to kill the Gene of Life to avoid 'the unavoidable' and to chain the body in its abysses for all eternity. However, the Supplanter recommended not to spill the young man's blood on the Earth.

"Death – obedient and doing the only thing he knew how to do – killed the young man in a brutal death. Butchering his body, he ripped his beauty from him, intending to leave him unrecognisable.

"After Death killed the young man, he tied him up and buried him in his abyss, where he guarded the body. He did not realise that, in his clumsiness, he had spilt the blood of the Gene of Life on Earth, thus fulfilling His Majesty's promise from the beginning.

"On the third day of the event, Death was walking happily in paradise, thinking it had done a fantastic job when he suddenly felt someone pierce his heart with his sting, the same sting with which he dealt his blows to mortals. As he fell wounded to the ground, he came to terms with his mistake in trying to avoid the unavoidable.

"With Death out of the way, the Gene of Life's first job was to restore humans to perfection so they would never die again, then to restore the Earth to what it was at the beginning – a beautiful paradise. Seeing that he had lost the battle, the Supplanter had to eat the Earth's dust and drink the bitter wine of defeat. However, not content with that, to this day he still seeks to ruin the lives of those most precious to His Majesty: humans."

***

The J3CeXteens began their rebellion the first day they learned **KORP** sought the Source of Everything. They met for interception sessions at the same time that the emperor sought his long-awaited meeting. Hence their name, J3CeXteens, or spirits that operate in the invisible world.

J3CeXteens were experts at interpreting the invisible side of life, the world of spirits. For them, visible reality is a small portion of the true magnitude of reality in the universe. They believed in the existence of the parallel world, whose domain was spiritual and where all kinds of mighty creatures operated that influenced the world of human beings – an invisible place but as accurate as the visible world. They were also well-known experts in cyber-information technology.

The information J3CeXteens collected passed to the Arktxts, the third operational arm of the empire rebellion. These people are those who were and are no longer or those who are but soon will not be; they were part of the elite or KORP's straitjacket. These rebels operated with the same technology as the empire because they knew a lot about weapons and logistics, from how to design them to how to make the kingdom's very weapons. They set up small factories for war weapons to use in their fight against the powerful Biodermatik armada forces. They also developed invisible symbiotic suits. With them, they formed a small army of invisible soldiers that kept the imperial soldiers at bay when they approached areas the resistance had already controlled.

"The scientist who designed the invisible symbiotic suits made them from a small sample of soil taken from Mars. That is why there were so few of them. But this expert man who had invented them was the scientist who once discovered rare soils in Martian rocks. He had led the Mars mineral exploration before imperial problems started. This man was an important figure who stood by KORP's side for many years. Like him, many people were helping the resistance because they thought KORP must stop somehow." (The Thinker)

These people, too, were weary of their emperor's follies and thought that by resisting him, they would change the course of their emperor; they still loved him and believed the monarch's disgrace was temporary. They hoped that the empire's glory would shine again one day and the logic of the well-being of humans, as was the empire's motto at the beginning, would come back.

Those three groups of rebels worked together in that civil war, putting their heads on the chopping block in pursuit of restoring their beloved empire. A single motto united them: 'Let it be what once it was.'

16. The scent of love

Conquered conquerors.

One day, around noon, KORP walked quickly towards the upcoming gallery he was building. On his way, he had to pass outside the kitchen fire exit due to snow melting in the passageways in front of the palace. It was hazardous to go through the key passages, although it was the shortest and most direct way. It was winter and close to lunchtime; he ordered the lunch to be ready at 1:30 pm.

Passing through the kitchen, he suddenly froze like a statue, staring into infinity. In that position, he closed his eyes and took a deep breath. Moving his head back, he slowly filled his lungs with air mixed with the exquisite smells from the kitchen. He exhaled and inhaled again, not caring that he was doing this in front of his team. Three of his advisers, five Counsellors, two bodyguards, some construction engineers and the press accompanied him. His companions looked into each other's eyes in astonishment. They discreetly shrugged their shoulders with surprise gestures as if to say, 'What's going on?' But nobody said anything; they couldn't say anything unless he asked them, and they were constantly obliged to answer.

KORP inhaled a familiar and exquisite fragrance. That scent was so powerful that it forced him to stand still like a statue. That fact was so striking to him that at that moment, he asked himself this question: 'What does it feel like walking into the middle of food's flavour molecules?'

So, from the reaction produced by these flavours, he forgot he was heading to the new gallery building site. Instead, the emperor looked inside the kitchen, seeking the answer: the effect of food flavour molecules on his will shocked the emperor.

His Counsellors had no choice but to enter the kitchen with him. Already in the kitchen, it surprised the chef to see the monarch and the rest of his assistants, as evidenced by his facial expression. He was a tall man with an Anglo-European physiognomy, a white complexion and grey-blond hair whose face colour, surprised by his unexpected visit, had changed from white to pale red.

KORP looked at the chef, winked and gave him a thumbs-up. The gesture thrilled the chef, and, as a sign of reciprocity, he wanted to shake his hand, too. He quickly wiped the excess water from his fingers with his apron, eager to shake hands with his emperor. In those microseconds, one Counsellor cleverly got behind KORP's back and looked directly into the eyes of the chef, who was still digesting the emperor's wink and thumbs-up. Thankfully, just in time, the chef caught the Counsellor's gaze. Surreptitiously and slowly, the Counsellor nodded, saying, "Don't try it." The chef discreetly glanced at the Counsellor and took in the message. The chef, fortunately, did not extend his hand to his emperor that day. He said, "I hope my Lord enjoys his lunch today."

"If the chef had offered his hand to KORP, he would have faced ridicule for not receiving a reciprocal gesture from the emperor and embarrassment if the news broadcasted in the empire." (The Thinker)

Imagine this scandal appearing in the headlines of the national press. As you already know, the emperor never extended his hand to anyone to greet, let alone reciprocate with any such gesture.

Indeed, the kitchen overflowed with exquisite smells. The impact was so overwhelming that, at that moment, it aroused the hunger of all visitors, including KORP. It was understandable, as the finest chef in the empire was in charge of the place; the people who worked for him were the most excellent staff members and created the most delicious foods made with the highest quality of meat. It came from the most magnificent farms in the empire.

In silence, the emperor strolled around the enormous kitchen table, completing one lap. For a few more long seconds, his eyes did not glance away from the food on the table. He fixed his gaze on the roasted meats; he scanned the rest of the delicacies with a greedy eye. Treats and exquisite flavour molecules flooded the table.

Delicately, he closed his right hand into a fist and stopped walking; gently and thoughtfully, he tapped the table twice and wondered, 'What does it feel like to walk amid these delicious molecular flavour scents?' Then, at that moment and suddenly, he ordered the chef to clear out all the staff in the kitchen – including the chef himself – to come back after three hours, to leave everything as it was, and to make sure that any fire was off. He stressed again that they must return in three hours.

At that moment, all the kitchen staff were so terrified after hearing the emperor's orders that they left in silence. But, just as they got outside, murmurs began and continued as they walked away. In seconds, the areas out and inside the kitchen were silent, with only the sound of a few timid drops of water falling from the kitchen roof due to snow melting.

The chef, who smiled at first, changed his smile to deep concern. Poor chef; not even he understood what was happening. This equation ran through his mind: wink, thumbs-up, and everyone out of the kitchen? That hadn't happened before, least of all in the kitchen. Confusion and worry overwhelmed the chef. Some women harassed the chef, saying, "Please have mercy on us because we have families." Seeing the chef's plight, one Counsellor said, "Do as the emperor says and don't worry about a thing. Everything is fine, and remember to come back in three hours, as he ordered."

KORP then ordered his Counsellors to bring his stool and put it in the middle of the table so that all the food in preparation would surround him. He asked to be left alone.

He took off his clothes, sat in The Thinker position, and, closing his eyes, inhaled deeply, again and again, the exquisite smell of the flavour of these foods.

After meditating for long minutes while enjoying those sublime smells, he made several conclusions about those tasty flavour molecules.

He concluded they were super-intelligent and operated in some remote part of that sacred place called the kitchen, from where they subdued humans. It shocked him they had so much power and made him want them himself, and he said, "To make someone want you, you have to be on the same level as the food flavour molecules." For that fact, he declared them worthy competitors. Then, he included them in the list of Victorious Cultures in the gallery of his mind. Then he imagined the powerful influence those molecules would have had on history and thought of the battles they would have won by conquering the conquerors.

Because of his imagination of the enemy surrendering, begging to appease their hunger, he declared them strategic allies.

Also, he deduced they were like scars, difficult to erase, and heavier than gold since they remained in the depths of memories and feelings.

KORP concluded they were free as air, and no one could stop them. Sitting on the breeze of the wind, they travelled across the world to reach places impossible for others. He stated they were so interesting that they broke the will of the most powerful human being and left him immobile for a moment – he was talking about himself.

He also concluded that they were generous because they gave back the hungry person the will to live, healed broken hearts, helped to conquer lost loves, restored broken relationships, strengthened friendships, made new friends, united families; and congregated with neighbours, broke down the walls of resentment; broke down cultural barriers; guided nations to peace and created good political relations; made one forget the bitter days of war and strengthen stability; softened human connections; and they opened the doors to good business.

He concluded the key was not how big or small the animal the meat came from, but its taste.

The emperor deduced that those manipulating food flavour molecules were extraordinary beings, perhaps angelic, because only they could bend the will of those molecules so that they made them obey them. He felt very grateful for the chef he had employed, for everyone who worked in the kitchen, from the one who cleaned to the one who produced the food. For the entire productive chain of food, he had formed to supply his empire and his palace.

As the emperor navigated his thoughts, tears ran down his cheeks because the scent he felt at that moment reminded him of his mother, father, brothers, friends and the smell of the land of his people. It reminded him of those happy days when he was little; he sat at the table with his parents, and while they ate, they admired the tenderness and beauty of the fruit of their love, whom they had sworn to love and care for the rest of their lives: their little KORP.

In that instant, he wanted to return and sit at the table with them again. Back then, he felt safe, loved and protected by them, too. His mind moved to the day his mother prepared a meal with that same flavour: roasted meat – his favourite dish that his mother lovingly cooked for him.

While still in that position, he searched through the galleries of his mind for other flavour molecules. He then thought, 'What smell does the business taste of?' After long minutes, he concluded it was dark and had the flavour of a polarised world; it was ambiguous to the point of being obscure and tasted intrepid fear. It had a calculating fragrance. Cold, startling and above all, pleasant but disloyal.

After a long minute, KORP opened his eyes. He had spent over two hours in that position. A death silently dressed everything outside this building, and he was still sitting on his stool, surrounded by food. His advisers ensured no one interrupted their emperor, so they periodically walked around to prevent the unsuspecting from entering the kitchen.

The emperor held a handful of food that reminded him of his childhood. He cut a piece of roasted meat, dipped it in meat juice, put it in his mouth and sat back down, scooping another bit into his hand. As KORP ate, more tears fell. The memories became so real that he remembered his mother's arms, the warmth of her lap, and the days she held him and told him to behave and not fight at school. He wiped away his tears again.

Finishing his bite, he picked up a dessert of raspberries and cream. He ate it and then immersed himself back in his thoughts, searching for the scent of love.

The first thing that stuck in his mind was the image of his beloved Kate, the sweetness of her voice, the tenderness of her hands, the taste of her kisses, the softness of her skin, and the scent of her hair and pillow. Then came the image of his mother, father, brother and sisters. Then came the portrait of the older woman who greeted him from her window when he left for work; also the image of Mel, the boy who once shined his shoes and made him laugh like he had never laughed like that in his life, the pictures of a soldier going to war to defend his nation; the image of the one who builds an illusion; the photo of the family of the police officer who died while protecting him from a terrorist attack; of the firefighter fighting fiercely to save the older man; the image of the people who had sheltered him and his whole family one night when the owner of the house had thrown them out on the street for not paying the rent; the image of his first teacher and how she would patiently sit next to him to help him finish his homework and encourage him, saying, "That's great, little KORP; you've done great. Now let's play; it's recess time," while the other children waited in the classroom because they had already returned from break.

The image of the family that had rescued him from the prison during the war flashed through his mind. This family had risked everything and hidden him to save his life while his enemies waited to kill him. He also visualised thousands of parents willing to do anything to make their families happy.

Likewise, the image of the gardener mowing the lawn of his house passed before his eyes. He sometimes showed him the chicks of birds that had fallen from the nest, saying, "Look, little KORP. Aren't they cute? Their feathers have dishevelled like your hair." Returning them tenderly to the nest.

When he thought of the scent of love, only images and memories of human beings flashed by, and then he wondered, 'And where am I? Where am I?' And he also asked what the scent of his love was. He tried hard to make that fragrance pass through his mind, but it wouldn't.

Four hours had passed, and he was concentrating so hard on understanding the scent of his love that at that precise moment, someone knocked on the kitchen door and it shocked him so much that he almost fell off the table. KORP got mad and had a big vanity tantrum, shaking the kitchen. At that moment, he ordered that person to be stripped naked and made to sit in The Thinker's position, but outside in the courtyard, in the open air. They shouldn't, they couldn't and they didn't have to interrupt him like that. Enraged, he spent the rest of that day in the kitchen. He didn't even ask what the man who interrupted him wanted.

KORP's reaction in the kitchen reached the ears of all the palace staff and left them both perplexed and scared. Some wondered why the emperor hadn't come out of the kitchen yet. That day, he did not realise that this way of reacting was the scent of his love. He also did not come across his elemental molecule flavour scent: love, which was darkening because his ambition, power, glory, riches and strength had become too heavy to handle, and everything he touched died.

The poor guy who interrupted him in the kitchen that day was lucky he didn't die of hypothermia. They rescued him with the excuse that he was indispensable in his workplace; many jobs had delays in the upcoming gallery without him.

The construction contractor had to send that man because the emperor had not yet arrived at the newly built gallery and had informed him that the three sculptures His Majesty had ordered and placed in area 'C' were collapsing. The snow had eroded its foundations. In the first place, the first builders who placed those sculptures there had done the work in the summer, and that year was the driest in decades; they needed to put more concrete in the foundation, too. That man wanted to ask the emperor if he wanted to leave the sculptures in the same sandy, muddy and wet place.

The Counsellors warned the contractor not to tell the emperor that repairing the foundations would cost lots of money because KORP would ask them to put the sculptures in the same place and write a blank cheque to pay the repair costs. The contractor found a small water tributary under the foundations of these three sculptures that filled with water and produced humidity in rain or snow; it was an unavoidable whim of nature.

So, if KORP said to put them in the same place and pay the repair costs, the contractor would be in serious trouble. The water flow would not stop. They knew the emperor did not enjoy discussing the same subject twice and would sue him for damages.

Or he would eventually have the builder's company shut down because he hadn't done an excellent job. But if the contractor told the emperor that repairing it would take a long time, the emperor would say, 'You better move it somewhere else not to waste time.'

"In such situations, his Counsellors never said fixing something costs money. Because of his vanity, KORP was so sure he had so much wealth that he said, 'If it's for money, it's not a problem.' The emperor used this phrase as a dirty rag to rub in the face of his opponents or someone he considered inferior. He also used it to show off the power that his money gave him." (The Thinker)

That's right. Counsellors carefully considered every word they said to the emperor because of the suffocating perfectionism he demanded; he also became disgustingly demanding in how people addressed him.

Being in his presence in those moments of vanity was unpleasant, let alone when you talked to him. It was sinister how he dissected the words when his interlocutors spoke to him.

Days later, when his vanity tantrum had passed, he asked what the man who interrupted him in the kitchen had wanted. After hearing the case, he stepped out to look at the situation in the gallery. The construction area was an open space covering over fifty soccer fields, decorated with beautiful gardens and gigantic sculptures of Thinkers.

From the gallery, the view of the capital city was impressive, and vice versa. The place was in a geographically sloping area with gently rising hills that, from a distance, looked like a prairie. It was ornamented exquisitely with lush trees and exotic bushes brought from all corners of the planet, and there were paths and hundreds of passageways. The passageways connected with twenty-one gigantic sculptures of Thinkers spread out across the field, surrounded by beautiful gardens that gave off exquisite fragrances. On the sides of the paths were Persian rug-style patterns, with flowers and bushes in all colours. They looked fantastic.

The gallery's design had a 18th-century baroque style. If you visited that place, you involuntarily closed your eyes to inhale the scent of the flowers and plants. That aroma invited you to rest, meditate or think. The site was full of butterflies and thousands of birds that had agreed to share the beauty of the environment with squirrels and wild animals. It was a beautiful place.

KORP built this magnificent gallery inspired by his colleague, The Thinker, as he had helped him create this glorious empire. For this, he wanted to honour him.

He also built the gallery for the city's people to visit and have a good time there. That place provided the strength of decision to the indecisive mind, peace to the oppressed heart, space for the creative mind, light to those who walked in the darkness of ignorance, certainty to the one who had doubts, conviction to those who wandered, determination to achieve the impossible to achieve, wisdom to the foolish, and rest to the agitated mind. In this place, deciding would be more reasonable.

He also wanted his advisers to spend some time thinking in that place because he felt they could not conclude it on their own, and it bothered him they always did what he told them. So he said, "Maybe this place will help them think for themselves and draw their conclusions about things."

He wanted people to have the same experience he had with his colleague, The Thinker. KORP believed one could communicate with the minds of these enigmatic sculptures of thinkers by looking closely at their faces.

Thus, one travelled with them to the depths of ideas, where infinite springs of wisdom flowed, from which one could better chart one's destiny.

"Only by being in that depth can one find the answers to any question, from the simplest to the thorniest and most humanly difficult to solve. Great minds, brilliant minds whose ideas created more spaces for life, more spaces where time and humans came together to be creator gods," he affirmed.

KORP also hoped that when a person entered that gallery, they would not come out the same but different, impregnated with the fragrance and flavour of the enlightening ideas of those enigmatic thinkers.

At the entrance to this gallery, there was an enormous sign welcoming visitors, written in many languages: 'Thinking is healthy.'

The twenty-one sculptures of Thinkers were majestic. They were one hundred and twenty to one hundred and forty-five feet tall from head to toe, delicate and finely carved in white marble, and had strong gladiators' bodies and angelic teenagers' faces. Only some sculptures were in the same thinking pose. They weren't all naked either: some were half-naked, others wore tunics covering their entire body, some looked to infinity, and others looked at the horizon towards the city.

The gallery had exclusive garden-like spaces where stools were for visitors who wanted to think without interruption. That gallery was like a sanctuary, like a temple for the gods on Olympus, where they worshipped ideas and wisdom.

KORP had a good sense of smell, a high and incredible taste, and a unique touch when building something; he attributed it to his money but never to his ability to appreciate something. Sometimes, he underestimated himself because he unconsciously suffered from the aftermath of bullying.

In the middle of the gallery, he had a special place built where he placed a copy of his colleague, The Thinker, sculpted in white marble in its original size, with a woman to his side. They sat next to each other on a bench; he had one hand on her hip, and she hugged him around his neck as they kissed. Very romantic! According to KORP, this sculpture expressed the genesis of the first kiss, unforgettable innocence and the first love's purity reflected in one's thoughts and, when remembered, had the taste of the freshest water that feeds the soul or whose trace is, sometimes, like an open wound that bled and hurts when that love is dying or is missing. Through this gesture, he didn't want his colleague to feel alone.

***

After inspecting the place that day, he found the three sculptures tilted; the emperor found the ground wet and muddy. Their type of foundation was seriously affected; the material the previous builders had put in for the foundations needed to have been more extensive and abundant. The damage was noticeable, so a tiny puddle formed around each sculpture. Because of their enormous weight, they leaned dangerously at an angle, like the Leaning Tower of Pisa.

As KORP observed this situation, this question gently settled in his mind: 'What would happen if, because of the lack of material in the foundations of my imperial system, it also collapsed?'

17. Thinking is healthy

Déjà vu.

Every year, at the beginning of spring, the emperor invited celebrities from all over the world (whom he called 'my allied friends') to celebrate with a party in their honour. They were world leaders and mega-entrepreneurs with whom the empire successfully traded. This time, he made the party coincide with the opening ceremony of the Gallery of Paradigmatic Thinkers, the original name of the newly built gallery. He wanted to show to the entire world the extent of his empire's glory.

Next to that gallery, he built a hangar in the shape of an oval planetarium. Inside it, he had a cinematography room set up where his guests would see the future of humanity. There, he would project a documentary on all the technological advances in pursuit of galactic space conquest, which the empire had achieved. KORP would allow those celebrities to invest in those new space technologies and their upcoming futuristic plans. These were real and fantastic business plans. The emperor also desperately sought more financial resources to put the interstellar ships he had built into orbit – a long-overdue project.

When his guests arrived at the gallery, the whole place looked majestic, impeccable and brilliantly ornate. The sculptures of the twenty-one Thinkers were so terrific that celebrity artists could elevate them to the 'First Wonders of the World' rank. The event symbolised the birth of a new era in humanity's history: the colonisation of new worlds.

It amazed visitors when they walked through the gallery

gardens; the gigantic sculptures watched over the capital city from there. That place reflected the empire's prosperity, glory and power. He released hundreds of peacocks and fawns so they could roam free to add elegance and colour to the event. He asked his guests to come dressed in 17th- and 18th-century baroque-style clothing from the time of the French monarchs Louis XVI and Marie Antoinette, the last frivolous and wasteful queen.

Seeing his guests dazzled by this masterpiece gallery and how much they admired him, his heart rose even higher. In that moment of glory, he thought he was the fundamental piece in the foundations of the universe because his guests said beautiful things about him. As they toured the gallery, they commented on the documentary they had seen. They praised his colonies on the moon and Mars with profound admiration, and above all, they admired his bold plans to colonise planets in space.

They ate the most delicious delicacies of the empire brought in for lunch, and KORP advised his chef to satisfy his guests with delight, and his chef did not disappoint.

In the middle of this lavish lunch, unexpectedly, he made a peculiar toast: "Friends and allies, the day has finally come when the world is born a redeemer." He was talking about himself.

All his guests shouted at the top of their voices, most under wine-induced euphoria: "KORP, KORP, KORP!" With that toast, he merged his idea that he was the fundamental piece in the foundations of the universe. This toast lifted his spirits, and so he was once again overjoyed. However, his face reflected something else because, every day, it was increasingly difficult for him to smile because of vanity.

The food served at lunch at that remarkable event substantially influenced his commercial decisions that day; he convinced his guests to form a network of strategic commercial alliances with him. He also closed multi-million contracts for the empire. So the emperor, in public, recognised all the kitchen staff. The chef, this time, took the recognition with a pinch of salt.

Immediately after the banquet, he organised a walk through the gallery. That walk was the icing on the cake for that party. Undoubtedly, it was a party of business and costumes unprecedented in the empire's history.

The cherry on top of this imperial party was when he asked for an aerial parade of the new imperial-developed flying vehicles (the Skydiggers). They were flying motorcars for civil or military use, similar to jet skis. He dazzled his guests with that aerial parade, and some of his guests ordered thousands of Skydiggers. These vehicles could move in space and levitate along the ground like air motorcycles. They worked based on the extra energy he had achieved on the moon. They were light and fast, so they defied time.

After the air show, he persuaded some guests to use the Skydiggers to avoid walking through the gallery because the place was so vast. The Gallery of the Paradigmatic Thinkers was magical and dazzling in the spring's reflecting sun, inviting people to think amicably.

One of his guests, from a kingdom across the Arctic, invited him to walk with her through the gallery. He unbelievably accepted her invitation. With music playing in the background as they walked, she took his arm and asked him questions; they were comfortable in each other's company. Dressed in those lavish baroque clothes, everyone looked extravagant; it was like travelling back to the 18th century, a time of daydreams and excesses.

The emperor, as part of his elegant attire, wore a white wig with a bulging braid at the back; a coat; a jacket; baggy breeches, which were golden with olive-green and flecked; and shoes with high heels, whose square buckles were prominent and far too elegant.

The invitation highly flattered KORP, and the beauty of this young woman impressed him. As they walked, he told her stories about himself, his exploits in the war, and how he had escaped alive. Each of the emperor's words dazzled the young woman, and she excitedly clasped his arms.

"The emperor never accepted invitations, least of all from strangers. Still, somehow, he had opened up a space in his attention, and strangely, the young woman brought Kate to the forefront of his mind." (The Thinker)

As they talked, he felt comfort in her presence; above all, the girl's hair, eyes and smile reminded him of Kate, so much so that he could almost see in her the honest look and smile of his beloved. Every time he looked at her, his heart leapt with indescribable joy.

As minutes passed, the young woman revealed that her parents adopted her. Whenever he heard her speak, KORP only thought of Kate's voice.

"My adoptive parents told me my mother was a single mother originally from these lands. However, because of serious family problems, she had to flee her home and take refuge in the city where I am from. She tried raising a family there but could not because of economic problems. Eventually, the family she worked for adopted me, and she joined the Expeditionary Scouts. I was two years old then; I haven't seen her since then."

"The Expeditionary Scouts?"

"That is so, my Lord."

"The Expeditionary Scouts were originally from this area. They were a legion of experts in environmental condition research. We sent them to find likely places to establish a colony to rebuild our society in case we lost at the Nuclear War. As you can see, we didn't have to go down that route; none of them came back. We assumed everyone had perished. Do you remember anything else about your mother? Or have you been told something else about her?"

"No, my Lord. I was lucky to have an adopted family. My adoptive mother only told me that my mother was from this capital. That is precisely the reason for my trip: to learn more about my parents' and my ancestors' history."

"We can help you in that regard. Here, we have the most advanced DNA archive centre in the world. A small blood test will suffice. Immediately, you will know where and how to contact your relatives if you have any. It will take up to five minutes."

"Your Highness?" The young woman blushed with excitement. "That fast, my Lord?"

"One hundred per cent; of course, yes. I guarantee you. I was the promoter of that system, and it is infallible. Through this programme, we have found and reunited families separated by wars, and today, they are happy families. The empire carried out DNA tests to identify everyone. As simple as that."

KORP felt deified when discussing his findings and inventions with the young woman. His contributions to science gave hope and stability to humanity. His empire was his guinea pig, where he did all his experiments and sold his findings to the rest of the planet.

"Of course! I want to, my Lord; of course, I want to!"

The young woman was extremely excited to know she would find a relative that afternoon; she wanted it to be her mother or father.

"I am also so captivated by the glory and history of this empire, my Lord. I have heard so much about technological advances in astronomy and space matters in my homeland that I am fascinated by everything I have seen and heard today. The hope you offer humanity, my Lord, will make my father happy."

Suddenly, the young woman stood up and took a deep breath. She had no sense of shame or fear at being in the presence of the most significant man in the empire. She was relaxed with him as if she had known him forever.

"What a pity my parents could not come on this trip. This technology and also to hear about your plans for humanity could fascinate them, remarkably. Bless them, they are too old to make trips of this magnitude. By the way, they are deeply grateful for your invitation, my Lord. Um, the scent of these flowers and this atmospheric call for freedom!" said the young woman, closing her eyes and inhaling the aroma of the flowers in the passageways.

"What is your name?"

"Celest, my Lord, it comes from the name Celestial."

"What a beautiful name."

"My parents gave me that name because they said, as a child, I would point my fingers to the sky and count the stars. Believe it or not, my Lord, I have three telescopes in my bedroom. I like to look at the sky and the stars. My parents often joke that I'm weird."

***

After the magnificent party, maybe around midnight, KORP reminisced about the good times that day while lying on his bed. He remembered the cheerful faces of his guests, how great the weather had been, and the significant economic contracts he had signed for his space projects. However, he particularly enjoyed talking with the young Celest, whose face resembled his beloved Kate. Amid that pleasant moment of recollection, the existential question he had had days before, as nocturnal butterflies, came back: 'What would happen if, because of a lack of proper foundations, my empire collapsed too?'

Everyone had left, even his Counsellors. KORP was still stunned by that question. That day, in the presence of his guests, he reaffirmed to himself that he was the foundation on which the existing world rests: he would lead humanity to universe colonisation. He was so pleased that, at last, he had the world in his hands and could direct it all at his will. He now had the financial resources to extend his glory beyond Mars and the moon and set his sights on a moon of Saturn because the SST reports of life on that planet were extremely promising and more. Besides, he had his galactic fleet ready. However, before continuing his fantastic galactic plans, he needed an answer to that annoying question.

Days before his guests arrived, he had a horrible dream. In his dream, he saw that the sculptures in the Gallery of Paradigmatic Thinkers were collapsing because of the lack of proper foundations. Since then, he hadn't been able to sleep properly.

At that moment, he got out of bed and stepped out to tour the palace, trying to stop thinking about the damn question. It was a profound and severe question: challenging, existential, crucial, disturbing and pragmatic. It felt like a night butterfly hovering in his mind's light.

This moment was the first time he had ever asked himself a sincere question that made him sit at the desk of his mind in front of himself. He had to answer as his Counsellors had to answer when he asked them a question.

He had avoided this moment for many days, but no longer had a choice; it was inevitable.

KORP was afraid to face the truth. He feared answering profound questions. For him, answering those questions was like a medical check-up for his convictions or looking in a mirror from which he would have to run.

"This explains why he did things his way, fabricating the circumstances and impregnating them with his truths – truths that sometimes he fabricated to create a world where it was easier or more familiar for him to walk – a parallel world that was easier for him to adapt to his needs." (The Thinker)

***

Eventually, the time came when he wanted to end this annoying, existential question. After several hours, he finally searched for an answer. He was determined to face the truth.

Picking up the first blanket his fingers could snag, he slung it over his back and walked towards the gallery.

He was barefoot and in his underpants; he had no pyjamas on, but it was a warm spring night. His footsteps led him to the beautiful open field. Along the way, the shadows of the majestic and gigantic Thinker sculptures welcomed him. They hugged him amicably under the full moon's light. He crossed the Fountain of Mars' Sirens to reach his chosen place. He was near the sculpture of his colleague, The Thinker, called Genesis of the First Kiss. It was a beautiful place – the most intimate in the entire gallery. In that place, there were several stools and silence reigned supreme.

It required much care to walk through the passageways because of the abundance of delicate and exotic flowers lining the walkways. The gallery gave off a solemnity in that stillness. KORP said, whispering to himself, "In this silence, one's mind is better amalgamated with these Thinkers."

Above the dimly lit sky, it was possible to see the clouds, some running and others riding on the wind, all trying to cover their tracks and escape with a suspicious attitude because they were fleeing from a crime scene where they had been the key witnesses. They didn't want to get involved, but the moonlight gave them away. Others tiptoed away from where two thirsty souls for love were drinking the most sublime nectar that fed the mortals' living souls.

After KORP arrived at the scene, he, with a gentleman's bow, greeted those he considered his colleagues with a gentleman's bow. He sat in their position to align or merge with their minds.

Deep in thought, time quickly slipped away; minutes became seconds, and hours became minutes. KORP searched his mind for the answer he had needed for a long time. At about two in the morning, he finished browsing through all his mental galleries. He was happy because everything was, or at least seemed to be, in order. At four in the morning, he reached the following conclusions. These conclusions held answers and truths he did not expect. He concluded that:

- The entire universe stands on a solid foundation; the Almighty One who established all things from the beginning.
- The Original Architect who drew the plans of the universe and built it.
- The Only One who formed the Earth, the stars and the galaxies.
- The Powerful Energy that warmed the soul of the Star King.
- The Lord of Clocks, who set his watch to the eternity rhythm.
- The Loving Hands poured freshness into the crystalline water of the springs.
- The Force that made the sunshine for everyone and did not charge a penny.
- The Spirit runs throughout nature, nourishing and protecting.
- The Power that created matter, space and time and feeds them with harmony.
- The Source of frequencies, vibrations, sounds, music and rhythms.
- The Physicist who injects drive into every molecule that flows in the universe.
- The Divine Hand that sets limits on the sea, the sky and the earth.
- The Super Designer who hung up the stars and the moon to light up the night.
- The Loving Lap provides shelter and warmth.

- The Amazing Father who clothes every human being with dignity.
- The Creative Artist who paints children's faces with innocence.
- The Good Shepherd protects all who come to Him.
- The Mother who treasures each of her children's tears and comforts them.
- The Romantic Cupid who brought Kate into your life to be your companion.
- The Guardian Angel that carried you when your enemies hunted you down.
- The Doctor who injected you with the antidote of life when a snake bit you.
- The Intrepid Bodyguard outside the casino who saved you from the killer gun.
- The Engineer who set up the sophisticated-complex biological factories: cells.
- The General who destroyed ninety-five per cent of nukes in the Nuclear War.
- The Fantastic Scientist who can talk the hurricanes into calmness.
- The Water of Life springs from the Earth's depths to quench thirsty lives.
- The Entrepreneur who trades fairly and does not monopolise the rainwater.
- The Provider of sap on the field's grass that transforms into refreshment.
- The Wise Master who sticks to the truth no matter what.
- The True Friend to whom your life matters, and he would give his life to you.
- The Great Sculptor who carved the most glorious piece in a human's heart: Love.
- The Invisible Geneticist sent the Gene of Life to regenerate human DNA.
- This foundation is not KORP but Origin.

Suddenly, KORP opened his eyes in fear and shock. His hands

shook with nerves. He remained in that position for many seconds. With the darkness of his soul, he stared into infinity, and his eyes were wide open and bloodshot. His fingers tightened with hatred around the blanket, and he wanted to tear it to pieces. His face turned angry. Extremely angry and showing his teeth, he shouted with brutal force and disgust as he grabbed his head. He got up and profaned Origin while looking at the moon, which quickly hid behind the suspicious clouds.

His jugular veins were large. He rose from the stool and made a threatening gesture, clenching his fists tightly and raising his arm skyward. Then he spat on the floor sticky and dry saliva from his gall; much remained stuck to his lips, which he cleaned and rubbed against his half-naked stomach. He lowered the blanket to his midriff and, raising his fists to the sky, launched more foul words of a higher calibre again into space. He walked around the place, disoriented, while screaming in anger. Not looking where he was heading, and while his bitterness overflowed from his being, he cried and cursed Origin.

KORP had transformed. Like a solitary beast, he was angry and dazed in that big gallery. In that instant, amid his fury and without a second thought, he declared war on Origin. He instantly gazed at the endless sky, swearing he would not rest until he had defeated his new enemy and removed him from his place at the universe's foundation.

After a few minutes, with the voice of an angry seducer trembling with rage, he approached the foot of one of the gigantic sculptures. Kneeling, he begged it to show mercy towards him. This time, he expected these Thinkers to align with him.

He sat down on the wet grass and leaned against the sculpture's foundation, gesticulating with incomprehensible words that reflected his extreme discomfort. As he stared at the sky, he continued spraying insults repeatedly. After a brief pause, he gestured incredible and rage-filled words again. After a few minutes of sitting, he got up. Large mud stains on his feet and legs reached his buttocks, which stained his underwear. Still disoriented, he kept walking. He wandered alone through that heavenly, beautiful place like a wandering spirit in pain.

He shouted, always looking at the sky and raising his fist to threaten. In the distance, one could hear him screaming. They were the screams of an angry man spewing loud fury. Even the crows withdrew from the place, angry at the shouts of the irritated man who wouldn't let them sleep.

He turned to another sculpture and, like a beggar, knelt in front of it. It was a female sculpture whose long dress reached her feet. With his arms open wide and looking into her face, he implored her, "Please wish me luck." KORP knelt until he reached the foundations and caressed the feet of that gigantic and striking sculpture, trying to arouse her feelings of compassion towards him. He stood there praying to win her favour, then got up from the spot, grabbed a stool, and carried it for several minutes. He threw it against the feet of another sculpture; however, it didn't blink or look at him out of the corner of its eye because it was thinking. Seeing that the statue did not react, he grabbed the same stool and threw it at its feet again. This time, he used ruthless force and evil intention to produce pain or some reaction and got the same answer. Then he turned around and roamed; at that moment, he felt he had finally found his perfect enemy, one that would ignite his most vibrant war and one he expected to defeat easily.

After that, he also concluded that he was more determined to fortify the foundations of his empire. He resolved he could defeat Origin and make him kneel before him, just as the food flavour molecules could defeat the most powerful. Again, in an uproar, he kicked at the bushes that formed patterns like those seen in Persian rugs. The bushes flew into the air as the flowers and whatever ornaments his murderous feet had hit.

He ran from place to place, screaming. Angry, he climbed to the top of a tree, and from there, he looked up at the sky again. With threatening fists, he shouted at the moon, hiding once again behind suspicious clouds. The emperor got down in a hurry and looked exhausted. He headed back to the palace, mumbling angry words. On the way, he picked up his blanket and covered himself in it, stained with mud and water dripping from one corner.

Upon his return, he kicked the beautiful flowers in the passageways and cursed everything in his path. Those homicidal kicks happily didn't reach a curious little kitten hiding behind the bushes, thanks to an owl that alerted it of the presence of this crazed man.

"KORP had realised an indisputable truth. He was not that foundation, power, wisdom, patience, tenderness, shelter or perfect clock, but Origin. I still don't understand why he declared war on Origin. He could have done something else, but not something as monumental and baffling as that. He could have cursed from the roof because everyone curses in frustration, right? But this time, I think KORP got out of hand." (The Thinker)

18. The Second Opinion Principle

Free will is not absolute.

KORP was angry with everyone because of his experience at the Gallery of Paradigmatic Thinkers. His vanity tantrums lasted for many weeks. He locked himself in the palace. His Counsellors left him food and clean clothes in the main hall because he had ordered them not to let anyone in and to do as he told them.

He ordered that they invent some story to justify his absence from official commitments. His advisers told him not to worry; they would do as requested.

The news reported: "The emperor suffered another terrible terrorist attack, and Providence saved him. Now, he must rest for several weeks."

Knowing someone stood above him and he didn't control everything upset him. 'Someone who, if he wanted, could change the course and circumstances of my life and my empire,' he thought. He lived believing in absolute free will.

Then he asked himself, 'What is the point of deciding something if Origin comes later to change the decision?' He felt a deep bitterness, knowing he had no freedom to act because Origin controlled everything, including his free will. He wanted to think that he was the absolute master of his destiny, even after death. For that reason, he unleashed an obfuscated campaign to defeat death, resorting to unconventional means – even for humans. He wanted his own KORP Empire. He desired to feel that his glory was the product of his work.

KORP was so sure of himself that it was like a hard slap in the face when he learned the truth. He judged Origin to be an intruder who had invited himself to the party of his life and the empire he had designed and built. Although this had opened his eyes to reality, he didn't accept it.

"It cannot be true, and my empire will not have two foundations. I will not allow it. My life is mine; I decide what to do with it, and this is my empire," he chanted. Each square inch of that enormous, deserted palace that surrounded him echoed the words of frustration and rage. He evacuated all the staff, even caged exotic birds, from the palace corridors.

He had always believed and had grown up believing that he had originated from controlling and manipulating the circumstances of his life and filling them with utter pleasure. Still, the revolutionary truth in front of him shocked, derailed and disoriented him.

This truth – a new truth for him – became like a bucket of cold water poured over red-hot glass: his heart broke into a thousand pieces. Who can rebuild or repair it? Who can make sense of the disaster inside his mind? But he decided not to share the glory of his position as emperor with anyone other than himself.

He wanted to clarify that the Origin's presence was unnecessary in any space of his existence, empire or the universe. In anger, he screamed, shouting and swearing from his room: "I don't need anyone's help because I'm enough on my own!" He was angry and screamed from the balcony towards the deserted palace gardens.

Later, after exercising self-control, he created a more robust KORP government system as the first step in his war against Origin. He thought that with this stubborn decision, he would fortify the foundations of his chief authority. So, he resolved to strengthen his empire's foundations by expanding his powers and glory through omniscient control. Then, his second step to crush Origin in his domain was discrediting him and sowing doubts in people's minds and hearts. He said to his advisers, "He is not the only Origin in the universe. I will show this to you."

Immediately, he propagated falsehoods by promoting and showing the existence of more than one Origin creator of the universe. To achieve this, he mounted a mighty horse in a philosophical war. They called that horse 'the other point of view'; it was his favourite. He always thought he would never use it because of his self-confidence. Still, as His Highness was in a tremendous mess, he said, "In war, everything is valid," to justify his decision.

This war aimed to dismantle and obscure the absolute reality of Origin's existence and his role in the universe. KORP aimed his missiles towards his newly discovered enemy and was determined to do anything at any cost.

He immediately called his advisers and planned a sophisticated machinery of disinformation with them with the pure, perverse aim of banishing the word 'Origin' from the minds and hearts of the inhabitants of his empire and all the people of the planet. It was his goal, and he would only rest once he had achieved it – if KORP said so, he would, no matter how much collateral damage it would cause.

"This picture sounds familiar to me, but this time, his determination has a double portion of force, energy and destructive character. It is important to remember that he is egotistical and vain." (The Thinker)

As a scientist, he embarked on scientific research to prove the 'There is more than one Origin in the universe' theory. He frequently travelled to the Mediterranean. "Perhaps my colleague's ancestors will reveal something relevant to this matter to me," he said. He had decided that getting a second opinion about the universe's origin was worthwhile.

"I think this time, KORP is in a colossal mess." (The Thinker)

Being in those lands rich in ancient stories of daring sophists, he walked through every space and every ruin of those geological sites. He also knocked on every door of the place where they taught the possibility of the existence of more than one Origin in the universe. There, he filled all his pockets with informational material for his campaign.

Upon his return, he brought enough literature to find a 'second opinion', thinking there was always a way. Upon his arrival at the palace, he ordered material to be brought to him, whether from scientific, religious, philosophical sources, fables, or whatever on the subject.

By then, the Intercity KORP Federation had brought rare soils from Mars. His Majesty ordered the Federation to collect dust from Mars and analyse its origins. He also commanded them to take dust from the moon and study its origins and any asteroid found to understand its origin. He was determined to find any hint to prove that a source other than Origin had created the universe to justify and validate his second opinion.

The emperor asked the empire's most famous thinkers to come and give exclusive talks that would reveal the existence of different inceptions of the universe other than Origin; they would also air on television.

These people were scholars, scientists, religious, non-religious and magic storytellers or preachers, but they needed to know the universe's history perfectly. He would pay them very well. The condition was that the discussion, talk or debate must be convincing. His strategic advisers held the lecture in the palace's main hall.

Within a few days, celebrities, teachers and famous thinkers gathered in the imperial capital city to teach their truths about the universe's origin. In their position as scholars, they were both respected and genuine individuals. There was nothing else they needed to do except their job.

The empire declared the days of the talks bank holidays, and everyone had to see or listen to the speakers for 'mankind's sake'.

He decorated the palace hall with scenes related to the lecturers' historical explanations. KORP adored the Greek philosophers; they were his primary reference and the key feature of that imperial awareness event. On the first day, he arranged the palace hall as a forum with various elements, like marble busts of historical heroes and Greek gods and goddesses, Thinkers on pedestals, and other statues, creating a Greek atmosphere. They dressed KORP elegantly as a philosopher and sat in the middle of the bleachers among his advisers, Counsellors, members of the New Council, and all the empire authorities who also dressed as philosophers. They inundated the place with television cameras, journalists and make-up artists, trying to give the final touch to the panellists before their talk. He stared straight ahead without blinking as he passionately digested the talk. He wrote in his book if there was anything important to mention; the atmosphere was more surreal than real; it was magical.

If you sat in this hall, you would experience a powerful atmosphere that made you feel you were in the time of the Greek philosophers. At the end of the talk, he paid the lecturers and waved them off with his traditional wink and thumbs-up sign of approval. He was excited.

In the intense weeks that followed, scientific club talk activities were abundant, from which the entire empire received much information regarding the universe's origin. After each debate, KORP returned to his house strong and doubly convinced that there was more than one Origin in the universe, which made him happy. In the evenings, he organised banquets in honour of the speakers.

He displayed giant posters in cities with the critical points from the previous day's talks. He worried people would quickly forget the lectures they received. After all, the emperor had led the empire into an all-out war against the Origin. He needed to convince his subjects and have them on his side at any cost.

So he decided that the general population should also participate in the talks and perform them live, so the lectures became interactive and participatory. He also asked to air the public's participation on television, which became an influential factor; it was a matter of media strategy. Some participants expressed their points of view in the live broadcast and felt that their opinions counted.

"Of course, they only permitted phone calls, which supported KORP's position." (The Thinker)

The following month, the emperor requested to change the décor of the palace hall into a Roman palace and, in the middle, put a massive table with maps of the Roman Empire displayed where some generals were planning the next annexation battle. As part of the scene, he would also be one general, while the speaker would talk about the victorious Roman army. He called himself Marco Antonio, considered one of the most outstanding Roman generals, who had Cleopatra as a lover. The atmosphere in the palace was also engaging, so authentic that the smell of a Roman war was almost lingering in the air. Roman music and war drums excited and dragged the entire empire into pursuing a war against the enemy.

He also asked the speakers to emphasise the gods' role in the Roman armies' victory. He gave the lecturers a long list of the gods to whom the Romans had attributed their victories; these gods' names were Hercules, Jupiter, Invictus Sun, Divus Julius or Divine Julius Caesar, etc. The lecturers did so, emphasising that victory was certain when these gods were on the side of the Roman armies.

On the day of the talks, he also dusted off a theory that he had once considered capricious, stubborn and nonsensical: the relativity of good and evil.

However, he had always doubted that theory, arguing: 'If someone defeated death, being the maximum expression of evil, then evil is not relative to good, since without death on the way, evil has no power over the good, whose maximum expression is life.' He based this conclusion on the story of the hero who defeated death and turned out to be the Gene of Life. He learned it from his mentors when he was involved in the occult sciences, who had assured him that, for them, in the cosmic war, the true enemy was the Gene of Life. However, to discredit his now enemy and win over public opinion in front of the cameras, he had to sell this nonsense theory as a True Lie. To symbolise his new strategic war position, he had the chessboard (his favourite game) drawn on the floor of the main hall of the palace, in the Cathedral of the Clocks, in the parliament, and in every vital meeting place across the empire marked with the number ten a symbolic number that represented absolute power and absolute control. With this drawing, he taught that 'in the universe, there is more than one absolute power, and this other power is also similar but has unique essence,' thinking of the cosmic war between the Gene of Life and the Source of Everything. He wanted to rub Origin's face in that chessboard symbol and show him he had decided which side he was on.

He had read carefully the story about the triumph of the Gene of Life over the Source of Everything. That truth added more concern to his war against Origin, so whenever lecturers gave talks in the palace, he unfurled the gigantic chessboard-patterned flags throughout the empire. He subtly encrypted this chessboard symbol in television commercials, including scenes from movies, soap operas, etc.; they were part of his strategic media, psychological warfare.

But, despite his efforts to crush his enemy in the depths of his heart, he felt that the protective circle he had built around him was closing little by little and suffocating his much-loved freedom. The space of his free will was reducing in size.

The day the lecturer explained the Roman war strategies, he moved the pieces on the maps of the table where there were small ships, soldiers, catapults, horses and camps made of wood. He took in every detail of the explanations and carefully wrote everything. The talks took long hours, but without a doubt, they were rich in historical content. He was happy that other gods, but not Origin, had helped the Romans defeat their enemies. The press highlighted how valuable this historic cultural contribution was.

Finally, the following month, he ordered the city's main square to be transformed into a scene of the Continent Nuclear War. He called his advisers to make a giant world map and place it in the middle of the square, as they did for the Roman lecture. He also asked to display a colossal screen for a movie about that war. It was the war KORP won. With this, he wanted to show Origin that he had won the mother of all wars. He was unafraid of him and would celebrate his newly won victory as soon as possible.

Setting the scene for that diabolical war took months. More details needed to be put in place. Finally, after months of work, everything was ready for the big talk. The general in charge of the talk hired three film companies to advise on the set design. They used 3D television images to add realism to the explanations. The media handled special effects very well; they were magicians creating a reality (which did not exist) and creating an immaculate scenery of the capital's central square. It looked genuine; the hard work of all those who set up the decor paid off; he paid them triple and then dismissed them.

On the day of the last talk and exhibition, the emperor, for the first time, called for a minute's silence to express tribute to the victims of that horrendous war and had hired hundreds of weepers to act distraught in front of the cameras.

The strategists who were to execute that atrocious war were lecturers. Before the talk, one of the principal generals spoke with him.

"My Lord, in that war, the enemy never had the slightest chance of reacting, let alone win," he said as the other strategists boasted of that fact with sarcastic laughter.

Then KORP asked the general strategists if they had a record of the nuclear bomb explosions. How many exploded on the day of the Nuclear War? The general strategist took him aside to explain something to him alone.

"Here, between us, my Lord, what happened in that war was a miracle."

"What do you mean it was a miracle, General?"

"We won that war with only five per cent of the detonated bombs, my Lord. We don't know how, but the enemy sabotaged the rest of the bombs before the war. That day, many strange things happened, my Lord. Some launch bases couldn't launch the bombs; some bombs never left the ground because of technical failures. When our technicians opened some devices to check and repair the problem, they found a rare acid that had entirely turned off its control systems. Also, most of those launched from the steel horse riders and ballistic beasts of space mysteriously never reached their destination; they all disappeared into the sea. After the first hour of the conflict, everything was in chaos, my Lord," said the general strategist, who was very proud of the victory.

"Knowing where the bombs are and why they didn't explode is no longer relevant, General. These are different times, and those were other times and circumstances. That was a glorious victory; we must feel proud of that. However, we are on the winning side, and that is a significant fact. I congratulate you, General. Go ahead," KORP replied in a subdued voice. Clapping him on the shoulder, he winked and gave him a thumbs-up.

'I'm not giving my enemy credit,' thought KORP between smiles.

Hours later, the strategist generals started talking about how the most significant events in that horrendous war had happened. They organised that talk very well. There was a sense of enchantment in every word the strategists spoke, a sense of patriotism that inspired the masses. The realism that the special effects showed and broadcasted live throughout the empire was fascinating. It had to be.

As the strategist generals explained and explained and explained the events of that dreadful war, they always came to the same conclusion: there was no other way to wage this kind of war without resorting to nuclear bombs.

That talk and demonstration disappointed KORP. He paid triple what he had promised but didn't wink or give a thumbs-up. He left the place quietly and looked to the side. The strategists, thinking the explanation needed to be more precise and comprehensive, reacted overwhelmed. Even though public opinion was positive, the emperor was unconvinced, and the citizenry was proud of their mighty victory.

"Still, he does not believe that his current war will defeat his new enemy. Perhaps he wanted to use nukes against Origin in this current war?" (The Thinker)

It's an excellent point to consider his frustration.

He locked himself in the palace to inquire again. Because of the excessive reliance on nuclear bombs, the strategist's last speech overwhelmed him. He barely entered his room; a vanity tantrum had affected him so greatly that he angrily threw the books on his desk out of the window. He screamed helplessly. Like thunder, his screams exploded inside the palace and beyond.

He needed a more effective strategy, something more tangible that would twist Origin's heart. He needed something to quench his presence and pulverise his power because he concluded nukes were an appetiser for his enemy.

***

"If you don't find solutions to your problems in the present, you will find them in history." (The Thinker)

He paced the newly opened gallery with his hands on his hips, baring his teeth like a rabid dog. He waited impatiently for those paradigmatic thinkers to reveal another formula – some way to twist Origin's arm to defeat him. By coincidence, a miracle happened that day. When he looked at one of the gigantic sculptures, he noticed it was staring at an area of leafy trees that had engulfed a building, which caught his attention. Accompanied by his Counsellors, he hurried to get to the place mentioned.

There, he found an old complex of buildings for various uses, including camping. He found many books stacked in the open air in the camping area under some roofs. There were tonnes of paper as books and magazines. They were the first shipment of books he had ordered to study the strategies of war in other countries. He also called for more books on Victorious Cultures.

Many of these books referred to the war strategies as Victorious Cultures designed and used in their military campaigns. There were powerful, exquisite, strange, naïve, simple, complex, unheard-of, ridiculous and admirable strategies.

As he read those books, he tried to understand how they had defeated their enemies and what objects they had used or considered. One hundred per cent of the strategies alluded to divinities in their armies. These divinities had broken the human world's protection paradigms with their supernatural powers and had made victories possible.

Those references mesmerised KORP; he repeated this in his mind: 'There is always a way', trying to align himself with these paradigmatic thinkers' ideas while digging into the strategies.

After finishing the books, he concentrated on the building engulfed in foliage. It was an old building with two parts. The second part was a matchbox-shaped construction covered with black-tinted glass, making it impossible to see inside. At the entrance of that building, there was a space with seven steps, like a forum.

Decades ago, KORP banned entry to that building because it held too much sensitive and dangerous information about the empire. An express order read, 'No one except KORP can enter this place'. There, they kept all the data (collected without authorisation) from the telephone calls of each individual on the planet before the Nuclear War. It was part of an espionage war then. It contained all the infiltrations of private calls and business conversations, which was how KORP got inside information to always be first in business.

He ordered that building to be opened in that desperate search for a strategy to help him defeat his enemy. So it was. Inside were hundreds of old computers with screens arranged in rows that covered almost the entire space. Compared to the cybernetic system in the empire, those computers were archaeological relics. However, they still worked. They were like an army of well-trained and disciplined soldiers. The military strategists used those machines to elaborate on strategies before and during the Nuclear War.

KORP knew that at the heart of these devices were hard drives, and at that moment, he ordered them to work, and they did. With a click, the place lit up where it had once been dark and musty.

The emperor wore an ancient Greek philosopher's costume when he read strategy books because he believed that by dressing like this, he would draw out the victorious spirit of the warriors in the books. He had learned this mysticism from the occult sciences, and he wore a white robe and a scarlet red cloak partly hanging from his arm because it was so long, and a crown of laurel leaves on his head, which was correct for the period.

Sitting politely, he touched his crown to stop it from falling. Although distant, the tunic and the computer became close in that magical and surreal moment.

He looked at it civilly and turned it on. Immediately, all the shortcuts to the programs appeared on the screen. He moved the cursor to the internet shortcut and clicked it. He pressed each keyboard button reverently because he didn't want to upset the device or cause mechanical failure or an explosion. After all, those devices were from wartime. 'I hope no explosive has a connection with it,' he thought. Once again, he clicked his cursor on a search engine and typed, 'How to defeat Origin with a single strategic move'.

Five million, two hundred thousand responses immediately emerged, with different ways to defeat Origin, from most effective to naïve. Occasionally, advertisements would appear in the middle of the computer screen. They were prominent in type, inevitably forcing the reader to read them because they covered almost the whole screen. When KORP was young, he would look at those pages from the first page to the end. Then he clicked on the list's last page, and the previous page and a story appeared. With carefully written information in great detail, recorded in gothic-type font, it read:

"There was a war between two gods where ... "

At that very moment, propaganda ran through the screen. It read:

"KORP Cyber-Smart Condoms, For Worry-Free Satisfaction-Guaranteed. Don't worry, be happy!"

Following this announcement, a scene showing a man dressed as an executioner with a Ku Klux Klan-like hat and holding a fishing net followed. The executioner ran after some terrifying fleeing sperm – the advertisement was hilarious. Seeing that, KORP laughed very hard, causing laughter to erupt amongst his advisers and the other people there because catching the emperor's laughter was inevitable, and everyone – absolutely everyone – laughed.

It was the propaganda he had made when he was young, when he first started his company. That product had brought him fame and money in the military but had almost cost him the closure of his company; this was the product that had helped his business grow. In that instant, he remembered he had been on the streets once, looking for opportunities to prosper, so he knocked on doors that way.

At that moment, he realised that once in his life he was like those adolescent people who had stood on the edge of the Gerikos looking at the horizon, like migratory chicks ready to fly in search of their destiny. This ad made him remember that when he was young, he tasted life as a young man, tasted his personal space and freedom, was happy in his way, and did baffling things like this.

He dried his tears as he thought to himself, 'This is already history, and the times are different.' He picked up his robe, hung it on his arm, and straightened his tunic.

Then he continued to read the story.

"One god was more powerful than the other …"

He quickly decided that he was the least potent god. He kept reading:

"The contest winner was the least powerful god."

He appreciated the words in that paragraph so much that he clicked on the 'like' image – he liked the thumbs-up idea. He continued to read the story.

"To defeat his enemy, the least mighty god took action and killed the only son of the mightiest god."

KORP was even more appreciative, commenting in the comments section: "What a pity this kind of information is on the last page – I ordered it to be moved to the top. Signed: KORP."

He continued reading the story.

"The mightiest god was so devastated by the death of his son that it gave him very severe depression – so deep that one day he plunged into an abyss, hanged himself and died. Thus, in this way, the less powerful god put an end to the enemy of him."

Before closing the computer program, **KORP** clicked on the 'like' image again but did not want to read the end of the writing where the explanation or source came from, so he closed the program.

At first, that story seemed implausible, but although it sounded logical and suited his needs, he took it with a pinch of salt.

Leaving the building, he walked to the Gallery of Paradigmatic Thinkers, concluding that this was the strategy he had been searching for.

19. Erasing Origin's marks

Do not erase love's traces; there is no life without them.

After KORP had found his strategy to defeat his enemy, he decided first to have a euphoria bath at the Hades Arena before implementing his plan. So that night, the city held an Ascension Ceremony attended by the most prominent people in the empire. The emperor asked his staff to prepare a seat for him there.

"It would be an excellent idea to explain to our readers what the Hades Arena and the Ascension Ceremony entailed." (The Thinker)

Yes, you are right.

Years ago, KORP commissioned each business (an institutional and human organisation in the empire) to be structured pyramidally. By doing so, he intended to enhance his glory and refinement in management and efficiency via competitiveness in the workplace.

Those who reached the top of the pyramid would occupy the position of an executive, and to recognise that effort, the empire awarded them with the One Way Platinum card. Those who held this card were exclusive members of the KORP civilisation. It was one of the most valuable privileges offered by the empire to those who successfully climbed to the top of that pyramidal socio-economic structure, and it made them believe they were exceptional citizens. Some of them dared to suggest they were of a superior race.

There were only three ways to reach the top of that structure: by direct appointment from KORP, where all you needed was a wink or a thumbs-up from the emperor; by succession, when the one who held the top position had a son, then only that son could occupy it when the time came, despite being an act of discrimination against daughters. Finally, through the Ascension Ceremony; terms, rules and many inhumane conditions accompanied this method of racing to the top, because of how fierce it was to compete. Each rung the competitors climbed received incentive prizes, rewards and more privileges to improve competitiveness. Even women could reach the top without impediment, restriction or gender discrimination.

People considered the third way the most worthy and honourable of these three. However, it had to be done in a duel behind closed doors because it was an act of cruelty when candidates performed it.

The empire held the Ascension Ceremony when two candidates for executive positions held equal qualifications, aptitudes, academic qualifications and merits. In the ceremony, candidates had to partake, unconventionally, in a duel called The Single Opportunity to win a single position. The emperor suggested this method since his vanity considered it more civilised. They didn't choose the candidate by finger or by dice rolling. The duel occurred in Hades Arena – an area similar to a Roman Circus Arena – to honour the god Zeus (considered the god of the sky in Greek mythology and to whom they worshipped with many offerings, including human lives). The candidates had to compete in different competitions, which sometimes involved physical strength or mental capabilities.

"Remember, KORP must highlight the existence of any form of supernatural power because of his war against Origin; so, this ceremony to the god Zeus fitted like a glove." (The Thinker)

The Ascension Ceremony had many symbols: on the day of the event, they flooded Hades Arena with exquisite aromatic perfumes in vast quantities, so the smell flooded the capital city, Luz. That smell symbolised life and glory for those who would ascend to executive positions, but an offering to the god Zeus for those who will suffer defeat.

This event sparked a great deal of admiration and euphoria.

Also, the ceremony sometimes lasted days because there were so many candidates to get the position. Thousands of people attended it secretly, including the emperor, when he needed to bathe in euphoria, like on this day.

Days after he had bathed in euphoria, his heart still beat faster than usual because he wanted to end this war as soon as possible. This time, he felt like he had found the formula for his victory. He picked up the phone and asked the executives to come to his presence because he had some plans to execute urgently.

The next day, thousands of executives arrived in his presence. These people were all faithful copies of **KORP**: they dressed like him, had the same hairstyle, had immaculate clean shoes, and wore the same type of after-shave perfume.

In front of these executives unfolded an endless list of 'necessary reforms'[37] for the empire's labour and civil laws. They had to be applied urgently, immediately after the meeting. He wanted to deliver his vengeful blow as soon as possible.

The reforms he applied from that moment on intended to reduce human dignity in his empire more than it already was, dismantling the money and human rights that every imperial member possessed; this was a way to press his thumb down on the crown of the universe and said, "Who else but a human bears the marks of Origin?" He had digested the strategy he found on the internet extremely well.

In that meeting (with cynicism and bullying), he deployed a dystopian[38] society or Orwellian policy on his government – to implement a governmental system solely intending to destroy human civilisation from its foundations, starting with the family. He would apply brutal, repressive control – with suffocating

37. **Necessary reforms** refer to KORP's plan to destroy a human society from its foundations.
38. **Specific indicators can point to living in a dystopian society.** For example, citizens constantly fear and have limited access to information, with their thoughts controlled. A single leader is unthinkingly followed by much of the community, creating a sense of constant surveillance. Individuals are dehumanised, with only the collective being valued. Conformity is highly valued, and society may appear perfect but is deeply corrupt.

surveillance and persecution – to those who opposed his reforms and decisions.

After the meeting with his executives, the emperor called a press conference where he read his updated government programme disguised as 'necessary reforms'. However, deep down (strategically encrypted), it had the dreadful purpose of eradicating human rights for all citizens in the empire. And on the entire planet as well.

First, he ordered mirror manufacturing to be prohibited, and all mirrors removed from public and private places, including homes. With this action, he wanted humans to forget that they had the marks of Origin on their faces.

He then ordered his Counsellors to ensure that the crown of the universe – humans – challenged everything, absolutely everything, under the excuse of 'the other point of view'. I am not referring to questioning something to get a suitable response because it is natural to doubt. I am referring to that of challenging for questioning's sake, which has as its essence a toxin that kills convictions. It is that kind of inquiry that transforms free thought into prison, that kind of destructive questioning that does not have the slightest intention of hearing any response but whose sole purpose is only to confuse, divert, disorient, distort, obscure, litigate and argue for the sake of arguing – to silence the truth. That type of questioning points the finger and makes one feel guilty, even about the air one breathes, guilty of the decisions one makes, guilty of the human relationships that one builds, guilty of the number of steps that one takes in the day, guilty of the family that one raises, of the beliefs that one has, of the cultural customs that one inherits, and of the intensity and sincerity with which one loves. That questioning leads one from being an heir to the fantastic universe to feeling like an intrusive and undignified object under the sun at the level, perhaps, of an insignificant cockroach with no purpose or destiny in life. Hostile questioning leaves one seized with fear, leading to being on the brink of insecurity, a nervous breakdown and dying from stress.

Here's a very mild example of questioning: 'Which came

first, the chicken or the egg?' Or, 'Can Origin create a stone he can't lift?' And thousands of other vague questions like these are just alphabet soup – nonsense, a flock of vultures hungry for convictions.

He disseminated and infiltrated this questioning in schools, colleges, universities and educational centres. With that, he sought to confuse people, causing them to blame Origin for the confusion and the evil in the world, and then accuse him of it.

KORP wanted to leave humans in a labyrinth of mental anarchy where they couldn't get out and would curse the Origin.

Substantially, he emphasised questioning those elementary issues where marks of Origin were more evident. These issues included family, children, gender issues, faith, religion, the natural relationship of a man with a woman, marriage, etc. He sought to open gaps in those issues to destroy them.

For example, he opened a gap in the entire concept of family with the sole intention of being bullied. He suggested children should originate anywhere but in a mother's womb. To support that suggestion, he had enormous genetic complexes built where he reproduced children serially (clones). He justified this by saying that having children this way was more manageable and less painful. He established a discounted payment plan and printed catalogues where one could choose what children to have and then order the purchase online.

Now, he felt nauseated every time he thought about how beautiful a man's relationship with a woman was and that both formed a couple whose fruit of this love was children. To destroy that natural fact, he invented unnatural concepts and teachings to question the gender of couples, young people and children. He encouraged this doubt by creating ideas, such as the third gender, even knowing that it was a genetically proven impossibility from DNA. For many years, on his way to building his KORP superhuman soldiers, he had travelled down that avenue without success. He tried to mix the two human sexes (or genders) biologically, male and female, to form a third sex (or gender) of both. He tried to do this, supposedly to strengthen the genes of these two bodies into one body. Although he tried desperately, he couldn't achieve it and did not fit his theory of 'There is always a way'. Through those experiments, he discovered that the genetic information of humans had already been pre-established, and there was no way to reverse or alter it. There was no way to create a third sex gender; he got inhuman specimens with that experiment. It was clinically and genetically a disaster.

"This man is completely insane and blind, to where even his 'sixth sense' doesn't function anymore; his vanity eats away at his mind and will in gigantic bites." (The Thinker)

He maliciously forced, by law, two people of the same gender to form a family. Then, he provided them with children from his factories, with the sole and cynical aim of replacing the concept of motherhood. He sought to erase the irreplaceable truth that mothers give birth to children.

"Here, perhaps it is necessary to clarify the respect our readers deserve: we want to exempt people who, because of fortuitous circumstances or for medical or humanitarian reasons, have taken the brave step of being adoptive parents to form inclusive, alternative families to protect and care for children at risk of abandonment. You are heroes." (The Thinker)

But I'm not referring to these kinds of alternative families. KORP's attack aimed to destroy (defying reality) the naturally established families. On his agenda, he was after happy families, couples who already had children – most of the empire – to be ridiculed and mocked as an act of bullying on Origin.

Dear readers, you remember that gender equality was never an issue in the empire. The previous law had protected all citizens' rights; then, each could decide what kind of life to have in their private lives because there was space for everyone, and people were living respectfully with each other. KORP used to say: "If someone likes to eat chicken, he is free to eat chicken. For likes, there are no dislikes."

But now, where there was no need, with mania, he raised his questionings (and supposedly modern new teachings regarding family and gender) to the rank of a binding law.

By law, he forced every educational centre, every teacher and every tutor to teach, indoctrinate and emphasise how dubious it was to be a male or female and how dirty the relationship between a man and woman was.

He also offered free aesthetic surgery to change the appearance of gender to form distinct class families under his philosophy called 'Modern Open Societies'. He also provided this new type of family with children from his factories because they couldn't procreate biologically. But at what cost? KORP never had an issue with the price. He had within his reach the technology, economic and human resources and the power to impose them. He then promoted those supposed achievements through his press as technological advances. Many accepted and supported these teachings and changes with glee because they had no children yet. However, when they had their children naturally, they realised the truth and their mistake in helping with the emperor's suggestions and new teachings.

Because of these lies, many had to degenerate themselves or dress up against their will to appear a different sex gender because of the suffocating media pressure KORP had imposed and the constant bullying of anti-family and anti-sex gender groups supported by the empire and its media to anyone who didn't go along with them.

KORP walked into the streets to admire the new family he had established in the empire. The family concept fell like dominoes. The emperor was delighted with his success over his enemy through these 'necessary reforms'. His media system was one of his strategic allies through which he had achieved these successes.

Little by little, all life in the empire fell to the bottom of its inverted funnel-like pyramid. Deep down, the vain emperor awaited his victims with vicious cynicism and bullying towards Origin.

He also destroyed free, sovereign human groups who rarely questioned but lived with gratitude. To achieve this, he sent his steel horse riders to travel to the ends of the Earth, carrying with them destruction and death. He intended to destabilise these free and sovereign peoples and nations to exploit them until they ate the earth's dust – so that they would deny and curse Origin.

He declared insolvent those seditious who publicly promoted beauty, art and music or expressed admiration for nature. These things also reflected Origin's marks. His distrust grew so much that he couldn't stop it; he closed the schools of art, music, theatre and cultural activity, apparently maintaining order. He banned public sports and social gatherings, arguing that the people were plotting against the empire in those places. His reforms carried the sick paranoia of someone vain and in trouble.

It made him sick whenever he saw the man who made peace, the supportive one, the one who showed kindness to others, the one who fought for a noble cause, or the one who held the genuine truth. He forced them to work long hours to shut them down before they could get home and fall asleep.

He also diverted the natural flow of life for the people he ruled by creating reforms that would alter that fact. For example, he wanted to stop a child from forgetting he was a child. He also decided that adolescents should forget that they were adolescents and that the young should forget they were young. To achieve this goal, he ordered that children play less and should go to school at an earlier age – supposedly to create more space in their minds. He thought that by doing this, these children would behave like adults when they reached adolescence.

"In this way, they will contribute their taxes to my imperial system at an earlier age," he mused with a sneer.

He ordered that his 'sixth sense' economic theory be mandatory in every job throughout the empire. Through this, he tripled factory work over the same period, resulting in workers becoming enslaved people, his enslaved adepts.

He also ordered smiles to be ripped from human faces and replaced with stress. To do so, he increased the price of groceries, cut wages to half the minimum wage, cut One Way card loans and quintupled interest rates.

In some places, the resistance stood against his gender and anti-family agenda by boycotting the industry of his favourite drink, making him lose lots of money. Because people deliberately stopped drinking this product, hundreds of trucks stacked up on the country's main roads. Knowing this, KORP had terrible vanity tantrums. Also, people carried out peaceful marches, claiming their rights as citizens of the empire. To silence them, he savagely repressed them with his Biodermatik soldiers, perpetrating brutal massacres against the demonstrators, where silence, in conspiracy with death, mocked the lifeless bodies.

Little by little, he erased dignity from the faces of the humans in his domains. They dressed in clothes of indignity and walked with fatigue from their debts and lack of freedom.

What was happening to humans in the empire was a mystery. They wondered if they had done something wrong. Why did the emperor behave this way towards them? The emperor never said he was at war against Origin. Events in the empire just happened without explanation. The laws were changing, and the empire forbade people to appeal. They couldn't appeal because the entire judicial system only benefitted those who were friends of the emperor or were his close associates. KORP had transformed his government into an executioner carrying a whip and a sword.

***

Resistance against this humiliation and dehumanisation of humans in the empire was also present on the streets. The Moths77, the J3CeXteen and the Arktxts now controlled vast strategic urban areas where the imperial law did not apply. These were big citadel islands that KORP no longer had access to. These human groups sought to cause a revolt at the imperial level; they sought to provoke a rebellion of such magnitude that it would be irreversible and irresistible. Many rebels stationed themselves in strategic places along commercial routes, where they caused blockades, which infuriated KORP to his core.

To warn Time Travellers not to become empire members, some J3CeXteen stood at the entrances to large cities and put ceramic tablets in their travelling bags with the words 'Don't do it' written on them. There was also a drawing of the One Way card on the ceramic tablets, with a cross in the space where they had signed it.

The resistance also encouraged people to disaffiliate from the imperial cyber system, take refuge in the Shells, or flee to the Southern Hemisphere. They distributed small maps of how to get south of the zero parallel by evading the empire checkpoints and the Valleys of Death. Slowly, the resistance provoked a civil war, in which more human groups joined them.

***

The repression against the J3CeXteen was cruel because KORP believed they were the authors of the rebellion throughout the empire. These people had profound reasons to resist the One Way, Only One Way law and to believe in the cosmic war of the Gene of Life against the Source of Everything. The emperor sought to erase that belief from their minds and hearts and teach them a lesson so they would change sides and move away from Origin.

He would go out hunting J3CeXteen in the city, and whoever he caught would sit in the Scorner's chair. It was a public chair in the main square where the inscription read, 'The thief'. When people passed by, they could see the thief sitting on the chair and eating the people's shame. It was an unfair punishment. If there were not enough reasons to expose them, he invented more falsehoods and published them in his press. Usually, they were lies related to some sexual scandal. KORP was an excellent father of lies.

Sometimes, to gain the trust of the trapped J3CeXteen and use them as informants, he blackmailed them by offering significant financial credits to calm them down and gain their confidence. To the rebellious J3CeXteen, who accepted his monetary credits, he gave them all kinds of honours in public. Still, once a week had passed, behind the scenes and in complete anonymity, he would block the financial credits again, keep the data of those people, cancel their One Way cards, declare them insolvent, and send them out on the streets. Then he would say, "There is no forgiveness for betrayal."

KORP hated the Shells because they represented the antithesis of his newly established imperial project and 'necessary reforms'. He knew that people with ethical principles had taken refuge there. There were families, young people, adolescents and fortunate children who strongly reflected their marks of Origin. He sought to destroy them at all costs because of their explosive growth; they were becoming more secret and profound. Some Shells had to be built in tunnels dug under the Gerikos and connected with the underground Shells outside the city. From there, one could flee beyond the parallel zero to the south.

The undercover J3CeXteen were like sponges, sucking energy from the Shells and causing divisions. They were effective Shells strangler parasites. Some J3CeXteen worked for KORP and took refuge in the Shells to control their growth.

But nothing discouraged the J3CeXteen; the more he chased them, the stronger they became. They also discovered that the emperor was at war against Origin and was using humans as bait. They published this news in the alternative press that the Arktxts had put into circulation. This news united and strengthened the resistance, which, joining forces, enlarged their army of invisible soldiers and sent them to blow up vital imperial buildings such as banks, weapons and robot factories and cause collapses in supply routes for food. They would not let the emperor have it easy; the civil war was growing.

One day, the Biodermatik soldiers caught a J3CeXteen delivering ceramic tablets to the city gates. They brought him into KORP's presence because they had previously seen him in the same act of sedition. People called him JJ, and he was from the White City. They got him to the palace, and KORP immediately recognised him because they had taken him months ago into an interrogation room, but he ran away.

But this time, this interrogation system was unique and filled with questions poisoned with trickery and hate; after it, the interrogated person supposedly left this room cursing the Origin.

This room had installed hidden microphones and cameras.

During this interrogation, JJ answered each question without hesitation, but they expected a different way. The last question was an order to curse Origin with a 'Why not?' and they would broadcast the answer on television.

KORP was watching behind the glass window and, impressed by this man's resilience, went inside.

"Jonny Jair Thompson. From the most outstanding general of the White City to the most rebellious citizen in the empire. What made you change your mind, Jonny? I trusted you so much, and you paid me this way?" said KORP, furious, looking at him.

"You trust me a rank, but I trusted you my life, and you can take it if you want; that is the size of my trust. My family believed in you. You were my old-time champion hero, but you have broken your word and gone too far! No one wants the poison you carry inside to reach their future generations. Your Highness."

KORP was furious after hearing these words. He left the place, asking the personnel to proceed.

After asking JJ the poisoned question, they eagerly awaited the answer, but JJ sang instead of answering it. The response surprised everyone. Enraged, they asked him again.

At that moment, the man fell silent and closed his eyes to recite some prayers in an unknown language. After a few seconds, smoke came out of the lie detector and electrified the wires; several luminaries burst into flames, panicking those present, who fled wrapped in fear.

Behind the hidden glass, KORP watched in amazement at what was happening inside the interrogation room. The scene was like something out of a science fiction movie. When the staff returned to the stage a while later, JJ was still in the same position. They tried again but could not get the answer they hoped. On this day, doctors realised this man had intrinsically linked to Origin: his answers reflected his indescribably intense and so powerful relationship with Him, and with each question, he grew stronger still.

The case of that man aroused great concern and curiosity

about KORP and his team. They wondered in astonishment, 'How can this man regenerate the Origin's marks?' They called this phenomenon 'Origin Mark Regeneration' a discovery.

Days after that incident, he captured other J3CeXteen and subjected them to physical-psychological studies. He inserted various micro-nano-biotic substances into these people's circulatory bloodstream. Leviathan-01 and Leviathan-02 also went on a reconnaissance mission to a J3CeXteens' brain; KORP wanted to know what that force was like. He wanted to film inside these people so he could study it. He discovered it was not a physical object or tangible. It was like invisible software that didn't have weight, but it was there. Then, it noted that these Origin marks were an extraordinary force that became powerful words when they left the J3CeXteens' lips. He offered them money and privileges. He did everything humanly possible to change their minds, but it was impossible. Nothing moved them from their convictions.

He wondered, 'What is this invisible force? What power makes them stand firm in their relationship with Origin? Could there be anything better than riches? Anything better than pleasure?' He had no answer. He had always thought that money changed people, but that day, he realised that only money changed some people. The J3CeXteens showed they would do anything to maintain their principles and refused to succumb to his pressure.

That day, his desperation grew even more because he faced an authentic but inexplicable phenomenon that powerfully stirred his ego, and he felt jealous of that case of regeneration of Origin marks. He felt jealous that his subjects did not feel the same way about him; he felt rejected, betrayed and frustrated, so much so that His Majesty lost his temper and had a big vanity tantrum so intense that, screaming, he hit a table, and it broke in two. Except for his Counsellors, everyone fled the place out of fear.

At that moment, he realised he was losing this war. His most effective pressure weapons weren't working.

He left the place, showing his teeth. He spat out sticky, phlegmy, dry saliva that landed on his clean, shiny shoes and kicked hard into the air to clean them, which made them worse. His shoe flew off like a missile, flying so high and far that it broke the palace glass and ended up in the garden.

Days later, he meditated on this issue. The strength of the Origin Mark Regeneration phenomenon surprised him. 'This force comes from the inside out. Is this the power that links these people with Origin? Why do only some people have it?' he thought. He wanted a logical explanation for this illogical phenomenon, but no rational description existed. It was an unknown phenomenon to him. He had never experienced such an experience and was so close to feeling it. From that day on, he concluded that J3CeXteen carried an invisible DNA, which produced that force inside them. He deduced that this link or point of contact united the J3CeXteen with Origin. Then he noted in his book: "This link is like an invisible and mighty piece of software, a force perhaps more powerful than freedom."

***

In his mind, KORP had devised thousands of ideas to find hope for winning this war. One afternoon, at six o'clock, he looked out the window at the infinite horizon. The window covered the entire front wall, and the city looked beautiful. Skydiggers and new flying cars filled the city space; from there, it was possible to see the Gallery of the Paradigmatic Thinkers, distinguished because of its impressive size. Beyond this was the Cathedral of the Clocks, which also stood both proudly and majestically, a rich piece of architecture and a living witness to the glory of the empire.

The sun's rays retreated from tall buildings minutes later, swallowed up by the late-night shadows; this was the emperor's favourite time to watch the city.

From a delicate crystal glass, he drank his favourite whisky. He looked thoughtfully, without blinking, at infinity with his cold, deep and abysmal gaze. He gently lapped the liquor with the tip of his tongue, still clinging to the glass. At that moment, he softly whispered, "Why not?" with deep concern while digesting the taste of the liquor. It was his vanity.

He felt disappointed. In his desperate state, KORP bit the rim of the delicate crystal glass and broke it, cutting his lower lip, which bled slowly. However, KORP, still looking into infinity for a solution, did not notice the cut. Seconds later, one of his Counsellors entered the room to tell him dinner would be served. When KORP turned around, his mouth was bloody. The Counsellor, in desperation, took a tablecloth and rushed to his aid. As he cleaned it up, he realised his emperor was in a trance as he stared into space in deathly silence. The Counsellor noticed his emperor seemed possessed by something inexplicable. After a moment, KORP came to his senses and cried in the Counsellor's arms. He cried like a child, with deep sobs.

The emperor's blood stained the Councillor's shoulders.

He could only speak with long sobs. "I'm sorry, I'm so sorry." The Counsellor embraced and stood in that position for a long time until he fell asleep. He was drunk and exhausted to the point of exhaustion. After a few moments, the Counsellor called the doctors, who stitched up his slight wound. On that day, the Counsellor discovered an unknown KORP who was fighting inside the emperor, could not escape, and, on that day, had reached out from inside, asking for help because he was drowning. The Counsellor kept what had happened to himself and went to the Cathedral of the Clocks early the next day. He held a long prayer session there with some priests for his emperor. He loved him very much.

***

The resistance made alliances with some kingdoms in the south. From there, they sent humanitarian aid and supplies for the civil war that originated in many parts of the empire. Fortunately, the press did not report such news because they were in cahoots with the emperor. Otherwise, they would have discovered these alliances. The resistance formed several more regiments that prepared to take over critical political institutions in the capital city. They had increased the number of soldiers and war supplies. Casualties were considerable on both sides.

***

Meanwhile, the emperor stood in his stubborn war against Origin. He came up with one last option: find the single particle that makes up Origin. Desperate, KORP returned to the ancient building where the old computers were. Inside, he turned on the one he had used long ago. He opened the internet browser and typed in, 'Where do I find Origin particle?' The correct information soon emerged.

What was his plan, or what was his goal? The emperor claimed he could become an Origin from a single particle. He prepared his steel horse riders and assembled an expedition to follow the tracks of the information he had found.

He sailed for several days until he reached one of the twenty places on the planet. There, they searched incessantly to find the elusive Origin particle. In that place, they claimed to have found a particle, but after a bomb hit this place during the Nuclear War, it disappeared. With much haste, the experts rebuilt the machines to continue the search. The traces of bombs made by KORP were also there. It was a fantastic place, with incredible technology, but half destroyed. Also, in that place, KORP found books and magazines that revealed amazing stories of quantum physics discoveries, the physics study of sub-atoms or the study of matter and energy at the most fundamental level.

The article spoke of an artefact from the past. This artefact could open dimensional quantum holes through which time travel could be possible. That excerpt moved the emperor to tears. He took every word of the article as truth. Once again, he ignored the words 'could', 'perhaps', 'possibly', etc.

Poor KORP, in his desperation, had committed kinds of abuse that later cost him tremendously or had terrible consequences. That was him: when he was desperate, he would take bits of words and form his ideas, supporting his ideological position. He often used this trick, especially with religious books, and sometimes took excerpts out of context. He interpreted them to mean what he wanted, so they supported his ideological position. Therefore, he interpreted many things his way.

On that day, without hesitation, he said he had found what he had always dreamed of travelling through time and to the underworld.

He ordered the people who worked there to come to his presence, baptised them as 'Trackers' or 'Seekers', and asked them to teach him more about quantum wormholes – and also requested to bring for him a tracksuit. He immediately put his hands on rebuilding the site with the help of hundreds of people dedicated to this science.

At the entrance to this technological complex was a statue of the goddess, referred to in an excerpt from a magazine; KORP ordered for it to be restored and taken to the Gallery of Paradigmatic Thinkers to be honoured "just in case," he said.

He returned happily to the capital city, and even though the reconstruction of those machines would take longer, he was super happy researching quantum wormholes.

The emperor found information about the existence of free energy in the electromagnetic field, which was infinite in quantity, and from where, by injecting a specific vector into that field, one could extract enough power to produce the famous wormholes, dislodging matter in time, just as the Trackers had claimed. He believed this process could be possible and would revolutionise time travel, allowing humans to move through time and space. He was determined to make this a reality and dedicated his life to the research and development of this technology.

This information gave him hope he could win over the Origin. He asked the Trackers to teach him more about this science. They gladly led him and assured him he might even alter reality to where Origin existed with this science. They explained to him that Origin was a spirit. He immediately thought that, thanks to this science (which was all new to him), he would soon reach Origin's domain and face him in his own home. While he worked, he repeated,

"As on Earth, so in heaven." He was super excited, so he repeated to himself, "I told you so. Can you see it? I told you I was right. Right? There is always a way."

"Poor KORP, puffed up with pride and vanity. If someone told you at this moment that your war of tantrums and nonsense against Origin was ending, you would not believe it. You would still believe that you could do anything you wanted to. I respect your decisions and your chosen path, but I disagree." (The Thinker)

It was admirable how much power he held. He was about to be the absolute owner of the planet, thanks to his geopolitical doctrine of One Way, One Planet, in which his Biodermatik forces were diligently planning the territorial expansion of the empire to the south of the continents – beyond the zero parallel to where thousands of drones departed every day to collect geographical information.

The emperor was so powerful that he no longer needed to sit on The Thinker's stool to know where his power lay or how he would achieve True Glory. He was already there! He only needed to desire and wink to achieve something. Through his insensitivity, vanity buried the power he had once enjoyed and wielded.

He didn't realise that, at that very moment, thousands more died in the civil war unleashed by him. However, he felt jealous because one J3CeXteen told him he loved Origin. Even though out there – in the KORP Empire – millions admired and loved him so much, but he ignored them. He could no longer tell how much admiration and respect his followers felt for him. He did not appreciate that people in his empire would give up their lives for him.

"Vanity had ravaged this man who lacked conscience, so much so that his blindness blinded his blindness." (The Thinker)

With all the power he had amassed, he could reverse his decrees and restore life to human beings in his empire and across the planet; could have built shelters for older adults who died every day, tormented by cold and loneliness and also have made factories to provide decent jobs for future generations; could have banished the monstrous monopoly and restored fair trade throughout the planet and knocked down the Gerikos and embraced the Time Travellers again. He could have, for the value of a nuclear bomb, helped to industrialise some countries lacking in technology – to offer job opportunities for their future generations; could have used his sixth sense to restore the humans' dignity that he had torn apart, but no, poor KORP, he preferred to look the other way.

Damn vanity!

20. Elusive particle

The mysterious and illogical paths.

In the restored laboratories, the Trackers worked inhumanely to locate the Origin's particle. Emperor KORP, urged on by urgency, rode his steel horse riders across the globe, searching desperately for information on his enemy. He also surrounded himself with dozens of Trackers to learn more about quantum physics. Despite being a scholar in the atomic sciences, he felt that the more he knew, the less he knew. From those wise people, he learned thousands of fascinating things about sub-atoms through quantum physics, which studies the nature and behaviour of matter and energy on the atomic and subatomic levels, also called quantum mechanics.

Inside his mind, he sensed this was the last card up his sleeve in this war because he could smell it in the air, feel it in the wind and read it in the stars; nothing must fail. Sure enough, something big was coming.

"KORP had entered a different space in his mind. Something had pushed him to think that he must stay prepared. Sometimes, looking at the sky, he wondered if Origin would appear with an army of thousands of soldiers or cosmic forces. He would then have to face his Biodermatik soldiers and galactic fleet." (The Thinker)

That's right; he frequently climbed up to the 360° Space Programme viewpoint to see if there was any unusual movement or something abnormal in space.

So, lest his enemy surprise him, he ordered the intercontinental ballistic satellites to remain on high alert. He called his generals from his five forces: air, land, sea, cyber-armada and space, ordering them to do regular pre-emptive deployment tests and enter an orange-red alert status. Hours later, after giving that order, the entire empire activated on orange-red alert by an order from the emperor.

Suddenly, and without explanation, the Biodermatik soldiers guarding the streets vanished from the streets. They retreated to their barracks in complete anonymity.

Across the empire, there were moments of heightened tension. In the sky, warplanes, drones and Skydiggers made loud noises when practising.

Before the Nuclear War, people experienced this tense atmosphere. Even the resistance had to fall back and enter a state of red alert because the imperial alarm was so severe that many thought another Nuclear War would break out at some point.

"I hope no-nonsense political news prevails at this moment of alert in any information media outlet. Otherwise, it would be sufficient for a wicked person to spread false information through any channel or suggest conspiracy theories because this would likely push the population to stampede over any food supply centres to get food and water; as a result, it would kill more people by the human avalanche than the civil war waged at this moment." (The Thinker)

During this emergency, he finally finished creating his 'KORP-made soldier'. They were half-human, half-robot soldiers. He called them 'Biobots'. They were humans amalgamated with robot bodies. They had conscious bodies but also mechanical bodies. He made them from human bodies, whose heads were intact but had suffered from terminal diseases. He claimed that he had saved someone's life. These human machines worked on human blood fused with intelligent bio-cybernetic elements and lithium, which, according to him, was the ancestor of immortal blood.

Most of those Biobots were giants built to reinforce the military forces made of steel hulks. They could also walk in space and fly.

KORP hoped, with positive thoughts, to come out of the supposed confrontation with a glorious victory; he was still too sure of himself in that regard. Until now, he had not lost on the battlefield.

He held periodic meetings with his generals to learn about the situation because they had two battlefronts to consider: the Origin and resistance armies. The armada downplayed the resistance because they were under siege but concerned about Origin's military forces. The empire deployed more spaceships into sidereal space, and more guards took their place on the 360° Space Programme viewpoint telescopes.

***

Waiting for the last battle, the emperor, in his eagerness, invented a tax called 'Let's clean up the atmosphere' to support his astro-space, travel to the stars, his subatomic, time travel of matter projects, and all his military campaigns financially. He argued for this tax:

"Each human being produces carbon dioxide; therefore, as a taxi paid for carbon dioxide emissions, humans should also be subject to this tax.

Signed: The emperor."

Decades ago, when people thought it was impossible, they made this joke: "The day KORP charges for the air we breathe …" Unbelievably, that day had arrived for the empire with the invention of this law.

The White City stopped paying for the said law and published the protest in the empire's press. It was the only city that bravely expressed discomfort at the abuse and extremes the emperor had reached.

Learning of this, the emperor sent Biodermatik troops. He militarised the White City, apprehending rebel leaders and publicly executing them as a warning. The city was under siege for many days and gradually received fewer provisions of food flow so they could strangle it. Nobody challenged, let alone appealed, KORP's decisions. Since then, the White City had also organised a massive rebellion, and it was only a matter of time before it broke out.

***

On one of his trips back to Luz, the capital, his steel horse rider, Neptune, suffered severe damage at sea by waves and storms; the ship dropped anchor for several days. KORP, seeing that the gigantic boat was not moving, ordered his evacuation to be imminent. After the wind died, they evacuated him to a smaller ship than the Neptune to continue his voyage.

Along the way, they helped a fishing boat the storm had fiercely hit and almost destroyed, and KORP ordered its crew to rescue them because they were in danger of death. Those lost sailors were vigorous men – brave warriors of the seas.

He walked down to the accident scene and talked to one of them. Those people did not know who he was. One of them told him about how they had arrived in that region. Throughout his conversation, he mentioned Origin.

"We are fishers in our native land, sir. Every year, we return to the land where Origin dwelled with humans, and we pay a tribute of reverence for everything he did for us." The man said this while taking a hot drink with numb hands.

"What did Origin do for you?" KORP asked, surprised.

"His blood opened the way to endless life for humankind."

Hearing this news, KORP admired the reverence the warrior of the seas had for Origin. In addition, he perceived the same force that had emanated from the J3CeXteens' software. He was deeply shocked by this news.

"Isn't death the direst enemy of humanity? Don't humans expect someone to defeat death? Isn't it a longing or a fulfilment to know someone has overcome death? Does it not bring joy to the reader when the fictional hero defeats death? Of course, it does." (The Thinker)

Some tears of emotion came out of KORP's eyes, which he hid with a small, tired yawn. He immediately recovered from his thoughts and continued talking to that man. He retrieved relevant and valuable information for his war interests from that conversation.

The narration of the warrior of the seas coincided with the information one of the J3CeXteen had given him. The emperor was visibly desperate, shocked and confused by the data. He wondered what Origin would be like in person. He gathered his historians and verified those facts.

"It is true, Majesty. The texts show it was precisely in that Magical Land to which the warrior of the seas refers that Origin lived among humans," one of them told him.

Wasting no time, he planned to sail to the Magical Land. His plan was straightforward: 'Maybe if I find something belonging to Origin, maybe there I can find his particle, and from it, I can become Origin, too.'

"KORP is sure that he can be and do whatever he wants. To this point, he learned to manipulate molecules to apply to humans, so he can apply Origin's molecule to himself to become Origin." (The Thinker)

Yes, it is true. KORP hoped he would soon become an Origin; he was now an expert in human and artificial blood manipulation. His plan was simmering. His Majesty was so happy about this plan that he ordered his chef to prepare a special meal night to celebrate his historic victory. He spent a lot of time talking to the head of the Trackers, who explained that if they opened a wormhole with their device, the emperor could enter Origin's presence in the blink of an eye. Then he could confront him face to face. And in his heart, KORP was planning to take with him the last generation of nukes to destroy his enemy. But he needed to find this elusive particle first.

Sitting at his office, in a hurry, he made a long list of the equipment for this last expedition. He met with his experts, who advised him to build unique safes to store the objects he found on those lands. He ordered glasses with three-dimensional lenses to see super-sensible things.

'Perhaps some vestige of his presence in electromagnetic space has remained in those lands,' he thought. He now understood the extrasensory universe as well. He seemed like a demigod because of how much knowledge he possessed. KORP knew it all.

***

In the central city of Luz port, on platform 77, there was a secret operation in action. Hundreds of soldiers and civil personnel were working. That platform anchored a sophisticated steel horse rider called the Hercules. Cranes loaded containers with safes and supplies. An army of scanner drones, Skydiggers and war aircraft sat at the bow.

The Hercules carried an army of Biodermatik soldiers and their newly developed Biobots. Also, KORP ordered a convoy of seven sophisticated warships, several nuclear submarines and the intercontinental ballistic satellites in space to be alert. He armed his military forces to the max for this expedition – intimidating!

"In case something happens," he had said to his advisers.

The emperor set sail at 00:05 on the fourth day, the third week and the seventh month of that year. He hired the sea warriors to be his guides. Whenever KORP set sail on the Hercules or Leviathan, he stood on the apex of the bow with open arms to feel the sea air, exposing himself to a dangerous situation.

'It's a powerful feeling,' he thought.

He spoke with the ship's captain and instructed him to arrive at the Magical Land at night. At KORP's request, the Counsellors ordered the most luxurious hotel to be reserved. They also demanded that large banquets be prepared for each meal and accompanied by the most exquisite wines. Those banquets had the purpose of misleading local security: he would be in another hotel.

***

Upon arriving at the Magical Land, he unpacked all his search instruments. The next day, he gathered ten of his most notable scientists: anthropologists and archaeologists. He sent them to tour the land and fill the safes with objects related to the Origin. They all looked like noble, prominent and harmless tourists.

This land was so special and its inhabitants were friendly. Getting up early, KORP left the hotel in a hurry when it was just the beginning of the day. He did not want someone to see him go or accompany him, so he went alone without his Counsellors, who disguised themselves and followed him from afar.

No one knew that Emperor KORP was visiting those lands.

Locals only knew some illustrious and notable tourists had arrived.

He carried a camera, a small backpack and an Indiana Jones-type hat. Instead of a whip, he had a water canteen strapped to his belt. He wore a scarf tied around his neck, shorts and heavy-duty expeditionary shoes. He looked like a Boy Scout.

As he walked through those magical lands, he visited villages; he talked with people through the streets, showing a deep interest in knowing more. People loved him. They had never seen a charming tourist so interested in Origin's stories. Some flattered him by saying that he was a holy man.

During his search, he was looking for traces, footprints and archaeological remains. He walked into small or large towns, talked to people to gather as much information as possible, and wrote it down in his book. The people of those lands were friendly. Those who conversed with him sought to satisfy his thirst for knowledge.

In return, this friendly, charming tourist rewarded locals for every tiny piece of information he received before leaving for the next village. The guides explained to him about the places where Origin had been, where he had walked and what actions he had taken. He put his feet on the supposed footprints Origin would have left behind and inhaled the air deeply, again and again, to feel his presence, just as when he inhaled the essence of the flavour of food in the kitchen. The emperor replicated the movements and actions Origin would have performed and then wrote them down in his book.

They told him that Origin had transformed water into wine. He immediately thought this wine could have been the tastiest and most expensive wine in the universe. Then he conjectured it was wine at the gods' table. Looking at the blue sky, he dreamed he would soon drink that wine with them, but up there.

He bought bits of material or objects that supposedly belonged to Origin and kept them in reinforced safes. He surrounded himself with local archaeologists, who declared they knew the closest historical facts. Some charged him a lot for a small piece of information because they saw that this kind and charming tourist would pay anything.

He bought several gold and silver vessels because they told him Origin had used them the night before his death. They also said to him that those vessels had magical powers. He kept them in safes so no energy or molecules would escape; he wanted to catch particles, hair debris, or anything containing his DNA.

People sold him pieces of cloth they claimed were from the shroud they wrapped his body in when he was in the grave. He purchased some sandals that supposedly belonged to the Origin. With them, he would have visited each town, each city and each village of those magical lands to deliver his message, and they had never suffered wear.

They told him fantastic stories about the Origin. Those stories were so incredible that he thought people had made them up to get money out of him. The most impressive thing was that he had raised the dead. That story excited him because he thought he would do something like that soon.

They told him Origin restored sight to the blind, multiplied bread and fish to feed thousands, healed the sick and freed the demon-possessed. However, sadly, one day, they betrayed him and cruelly tortured him to death, but on the third day, he rose from the dead.

When KORP heard all this, he thought people were exaggerating. However, deep down, they reminded him of the story of the Gene of Life, which was similar. So, since he was in a war, he had no choice but to consider the thousands of stories they told him about the Origin. He reluctantly wrote it down in his book.

"It may be worth mentioning the reason for his reluctance. He was super excited at the idea of his findings, and it filled him with positive energy. His reluctance was because, in those lands, nobody complained or said anything terrible about the Origin. He wanted someone to speak ill of, say negative things about his enemy, or question everything. What he heard contrasted with the prejudices that blinded his mind." (The Thinker)

It is true. The emperor filled twenty safes with various things in the first few weeks. He closed a safe and rushed to find more objects, leaving one camera inside one safe and going with another new camera. He felt he could have collected some Origin particle in one of those objects.

Meanwhile, his entire security arsenal watched their emperor's every move from the sea and from space to ensure that nothing disastrous happened to him or that he was the target of a terrorist attack.

Hundreds of bee drones arrived and departed from the steel horse riders with information and videos of all the emperor's actions. They were both agitated and calm moments for the military. Likewise, they were vigilant against the Origin's cosmic forces.

21. Cheque mate

It only takes one molecule of conscience to transform the world.

Even since he had arrived in the Magical Land anxiously searching for the Origin's particle, whenever he stepped out to find artefacts or objects or visited an unfamiliar place, he returned with even more intrigue, concerns and questions about Origin instead of answers.

One morning at the hotel where he stayed, he got up at dawn to have breakfast on the terrace. He had planned to draw another route for that day. A teenager interrupted him with an anonymous message during his early morning meal. The note read: "Dear Mr KORP, would you like to know the place where they killed him?"

Surprised, he asked who had left that note. All the hotel servers told him it was an anonymous note, and he only had to send a message with the answer if he wanted to know the place. Taking his golden pen with shaking hands excited, he wrote a reply to the note, saying "yes". He opened his chequebook, signed a blank incentive cheque, and put it in the envelope next to the message. Then he sealed the envelope and wrote, "URGENT!"

Signing a blank cheque like that was like a gamble – a game of chance for him. By the way, it was his favourite game. The anonymous person had to go personally to withdraw the money from the cheque. It was the only way because he had designed it like this. He hated it when somebody wanted to take him for a fool.

Hours later, when he was preparing to leave, another message arrived. Hastily, he sat down on the terrace bench and read. The note read: "Dear Mr KORP, Thank you for the cheque. I used the money to buy a loaf of bread and coffee and deposit the rest for the Nuclear War victims. Do you want to know the place where they buried him? Just answer yes or no."

KORP thought that was funny and replied with another message saying "yes". He looked excited. He forgot why he was visiting the Magical Land because these games caught up with him. Immediately, he opened his chequebook and wrote on the cheque, "Five million". Smiling, he then sealed the envelope and wrote, "URGENT!"

He waited for the reply at the hotel, eager to receive the answer. He thought the game was exciting. At mid-morning, he stepped out to the terrace again, and they offered him the appetiser menu. There was so much to choose from that it took him a long time to decide.

He opened the menu of fine wines, whose bottles cost thousands of pesos. Still thinking of the wine that Origin had transformed, which he surmised would have been the tastiest and most expensive wine, he assumed he would soon be an Origin. He laughed sarcastically, and the server looked at him in surprise.

Out loud and laughing, he said, "Why not?" Again, in silence and with a few signs, he called the server and pointed with his tiny finger at a wine whose cost per bottle was forty thousand pesos. It was the most expensive wine on the menu. He had concluded that he deserved the most expensive wine on the menu because he was almost a demigod already. Again, he said, "Why not?"

As the server took his order, the messenger arrived, saying, "A message, sir."

Without thinking, he snatched the envelope from the messenger's hand and, without saying thanks, opened it and read it. He was super excited. The note read: "Dear Mr KORP, Thank you for the cheque. I used the money to buy a glass of water and a sandwich. It was delicious."

KORP laughed openly, thinking this player had a good sense of humour. At that moment, the server brought the wine he had ordered. Accompanied by the sound of wine pouring into the glass, he continued reading the message: "Do you want to know where he defeated death? Answer yes or no, and then I can take you to all three places."

Immediately, he pulled out his chequebook, and with his gold pen, he wrote, "Thirty million", but next to the signature, he drew a small hand with the thumb down. He took ecstatic delight in signing those death warrants. He drank a large gulp of red wine and his white teeth turned red. It was time to arrest this anonymous, curious, daring, opportunistic and seasoned gambler so that they could execute him.

"After he became vain, killing someone gave him pleasure because it made him feel like the owner and master of the universe. No one ate for free, at least not from his hands – absolutely no one. And nobody received something for nothing – absolutely nobody." (The Thinker)

Hastily, his hand trembling with excitement, he wrote the reply, saying "yes" and put the message and the cheque inside the envelope, sealed it, and wrote, "URGENT!" He then got up and walked around that terrace, laughing sarcastically at the anonymous gambler's fate. He thought he had found someone worthy to play with and admired his boldness. Still, KORP would never let the unknown player win the game because the emperor always imposed his own rules, so this time, he decided to end this game in this tragic way.

Three hours after sending the note with the death sentence, KORP asked to serve lunch while waiting to hear how the anonymous person he had sent to kill had died. Amid the clatter of utensils, a young messenger man wearing unique white clothes appeared on the terrace with another note; he looked like a messenger from a far, far land, and his white clothes shone so much that they caught his and the staff's attention. The emperor was expecting the teenage messenger. The message came in a gold envelope that shone like a mirror. It was exquisite and stunning. It had written "True Freedom" in elegant letters in front of it. KORP didn't thank the messenger, snatched the envelope off his hands, and opened it; he was so excited. When he touched the message note to pick it up, an intense heat shook his entire body, completely regenerating his conscience in a second. It was like an electric shock. He thought it was the effect of the wine. The heat and the impact made him get up. He filled his glass with wine, picked it up and strolled through this immense terrace, whose sea view was dazzling. He walked to one corner of the deck while the staff were preparing the lunch to read the note, took more giant wine gulps because of his enthusiasm, and read the message. The ink of the message was blood and read like this:

"Dear Mr KORP, thanks to your money, my execution was possible. I was looking forward to having lunch with you today and having a good time. I'm sorry I can't fulfil that wish, but I'm sending you this gift of love. This card is called the 'Gold Unlimited Life' card. Do you want to meet me in person? You only need to sign the card with the pen I sent you. That pen contains my blood, enough to write your name once and forever on the card. You should know that the card will only become effective once you apply my blood by signing it. Otherwise, it will be impossible. Signed: Origin."

In that instant, he dropped the glass of wine in his hand. It crashed onto the marble floor, leaving thousands of micro-shards of glass swimming in a sea of wine.

He dashed to the railing at the edge of the terrace to look out onto the street, expecting to see someone who looked like the messenger, wearing gloomy white clothes, running or escaping in a strange, alarmed manner, but he only saw a crowd walking. Then, he rushed down the emergency stairs at incredible speed to find the messenger, and when he reached the street, he looked around. There was just a crowd walking by. He wanted to see someone different in public, maybe someone wearing a spacesuit or dressed like a Tibetan monk or someone who looked like a priest, an Indian monk, or a shaman, someone who had the image of a holy being with white clothes, like the messenger.

At that moment, many photographic images of holy people or priests about whom he had inquired and of people who resembled those extraordinary or space beings flashed through his mind, and he compared them to the messenger. On the street, only ordinary people walked by.

In desperation, he ran to the other corner of the street and saw the same thing. He waded through the streets, pushing pedestrians to move, hoping to find him. He desperately searched for him. His heart rate rocketed. He turned back to return to the hotel as soon as possible. He sweated in anguish because of the impact. On the way, because he had been so many blocks away, he thought about the card he had received. He had an instinctive nose for gold and concluded that the card was genuine gold; he also knew very well when blood was blood and concluded that what was inside the pen was actual blood.

Shock and fear took KORP's soul. He immediately called the bank to ask if anyone had withdrawn the money from the cheques. They told him yes. He wondered how many times they had done it. They answered three times.

"The first time was a young man, a shoe shiner named Mel. He withdrew much money, my Lord. He said he served you in the main square of your palace, my Lord. The young man took fifteen pesos and deposited the rest to help needy people. The last time, the person withdrew money with his face covered; he seemed to run away. He took thirty million, sir, and said it was to do the job; I didn't understand what he meant by that."

"And who withdrew the second time?"

"Ah, yes … I'm sorry, my Lord. Let's see. Yes, here it is. The second person was a carpenter named Emanuel. He withdrew the five million, of which he kept ten pesos, and the rest he deposited to help the patients affected by the Nuclear War, my Lord. That man was remarkable, sir. All the bank staff agreed that the man's gaze emanated from love and compassion. He said he was on his way to accomplishing a special mission on your behalf, my Lord. You choose your clients well. I congratulate you, my Lord."

Finally, he called the people in charge of the execution, and they told him they had done what he ordered.

Three hours had passed since the execution, so KORP saw where they had executed him. There were traces of fresh blood on the spot. Then he asked where the body was, and they hurried to where they had left it; it was empty.

"He was a thin, tall individual – taller than average – had long hair, maybe in his thirties. He did not resist, my Lord. Despite the torture you ordered, he didn't open his mouth. It was a savage execution. He said the sacrifice made on your behalf was complete before he died, my Lord. We do not know what he meant by those words."

"Where is the body, then?"

"It was here, my Lord. We assume they took it to the morgue. Rather, we don't know, my Lord. That is no longer in our hands, sir."

KORP couldn't overcome the shock. Everything had happened so fast that, at that moment, he wanted to turn back time to tell him he, too, would have liked to sit down to eat together.

On the way, he sat down next to a closed door and, being on the ground, leaned against the wall. He felt his strength leaving him. In that instant, sadness at the news of the young man's execution consumed his insides. When he looked at his hands, they had blood. Terrified, he touched his body to see if he had wounds, then looked at his hands again, which were bloodless. It was a vision.

As his advisers and Counsellors rushed towards him in concern, many watched from the hotel terrace, wondering what had happened. A multitude of curious people crowded the place. Nobody understood what was happening. They could only see a man sitting, leaning against the wall next to a closed door, who had touched his chest, screaming and desperately crying as if he had received the bad news of a loved one's death.

Immediately, dozens of Biodermatik guards arrived and mounted a security operation; they held heavy weapons. From the Hercules, several Skydiggers and Biobots crossed the air space around the hotel. Security forces surrounded the area and some buildings and arrested some onlookers, but shortly after, they released them. They had nothing to do with the matter.

KORP put the card in the envelope with the pen and the notes and put everything in his shirt's pocket. Wiping away his tears, he sat up and dropped the scarf around his neck. The wind blew it away before the crowd. He asked all of his staff to leave him alone

– even his Counsellors, who, being disguised, looked like strange tourists among the public.

Ambling, he headed for the hotel. He looked tired and looked around again to find him to apologise and say sorry for his actions. He sat down again in another closed doorway because he felt exhausted from all his pursuits and achievements, tired of fighting for everything.

KORP lamented that he had missed the moment he most longed to be in the presence, in the place, in the time, and in the exact moment Origin existed. He thought everything he had differed from the experience of looking him in the face and talking to him.

From there, sitting, he looked at the crowd, and, in his soul, he cried out for mercy. He ached from every look directed at him. Each face was like a dart that pierced his heart and caused pain. At that moment, he remembered the humans of his empire, and his heart ached so much that he cried out in regret: "I'm sorry, I'm very sorry for what I did." He rested his head on his drawn-up knees, and from inside, he could hear his voice begging for mercy.

At that moment, his conscience took control of his life, and heat as light illuminated his mind, united his common-sense neurons, restored his beliefs, ideals and the principles for which he had fought so hard and restored his will. Through his body ran an intense light that reached the space of his factories or cells, which immediately shot up like a dry tree in spring. The light of his awareness emitted energy so strong that it dried up the gigantic tree of vanity. This tree slowly collapsed to the ground, shattering its crystal leaves and precious stones, causing intense pain in his torso, forcing him to touch his chest because he believed he was having a heart attack. After a few minutes, paramedics arrived and rushed him to the hotel medical facility.

***

Hours later, the phone would not stop ringing in his room, but he left it. Everyone left messages. Most were messages from those close to him, invitations to attend entertainment places at night. He held in his hand the card that Origin had sent him. Lying awake on a bed, he looked at the ceiling, seeing puzzle-like geometric figures.

After thinking for a few minutes, he returned to his senses and realised he was no longer the one who made the rules. Tears slipped down his face and crashed onto the pillow. He repeated the words he would have written: "I would like to have some time with you, too."

Sorrow and sadness at the young man's execution filled him. He had disowned his gold pen and tossed it somewhere in the room. He was ashamed of what he had done. A moment later, he picked up the gold envelope and reread it: "True Freedom." Those words provoked fear in him and clashed with his concept of freedom. Then he looked at the card and slowly slid his fingers over its surface to check again if it was genuine gold. He realised it was gold; this time he didn't doubt its authenticity for a second.

The card had an embossed DNA genetic code following the name KORP. It was beautiful and perfectly made in every detail.

Over and over, his fingers rested on the characters as he brooded. He looked at the card and ran his fingers over the surface again. As he watched it, he read the characters: *KORP DNA 23 + Y, Unlimited Life.*

After several hours of shock, KORP finally got over it. He thought of using the Unlimited Life card because he wanted to know if this card worked on his empire financial cybernetic system. He compared the format with the type of One Way cards he had made for his followers in the empire. Undoubtedly, the card had the same size and format, but with one difference: it lacked a signature.

At that moment, he took the pen from the envelope and considered signing it. He took off the cover to sign it but told himself it was his One Way, No Return ticket if he did it. At that moment, he thought about this hypothetical question:

'What happens if I sign it now and after a while, I regret it? Will they declare me insolvent for retracting this decision?'

He wanted to figure out how it felt to have the Unlimited Life card if signing it, but he wondered if he would regret it later. Poor KORP faced a dilemma again.

"He never accepted when people would back down from their vow to his empire, so he measured his hypothesis against his own rules, and I think his conclusion is obvious." (The Thinker)

He was silent for a long time as he gazed worriedly into infinity. He thought: 'Perhaps I never should have started this journey.'

He realised he seemed like a tiny insect trapped in a gigantic and powerful web that struggled to extricate itself. Still, it couldn't, even if it wanted to. He felt trapped. Slowly, he calmed down to find a solution at this critical moment. Trying to enlarge the seconds in his favour, he searched to do something and step out of this powerful trap. At that moment, he thought taking risks was the only way to escape. So he picked up the pen, determined to sign the Unlimited Life card. He pulled off the pen cap, and when he almost signed it, he remembered the J3CeXteen were straightforward people. They were not interested in hoarding earthly goods.

'Perhaps the ultimate good for them is not on this Earth, but in the realm of Origin; if this is so, it makes sense: the riches of Origin are millions of times more than mine,' he thought.

After a long time, he collected himself again, thinking, 'Perhaps it would have been better if the Hercules had never left the port.'

So he pulled out his One Way Platinum KORP card, the mother of his cards, the ultimate expression of his glory in his empire. Then, through his renewed conscience, he compared the two cards. He wanted to assess what advantages they offered his followers. Still thinking that his One Way Platinum KORP card had no comparison, and based on that presumption, he contrasted the two cards, saying, "I offer gold and money; Origin offers unlimited life." After comparing them that first time, he was utterly silent, so much so that anyone could hear his heart beating in the room. In a cold, long moment of silence, he stopped comparing them.

Sure enough, there was no comparison – not in this equation or algebra; it was an incomparable comparison that produced deep frustration inside him. In that instant, KORP felt he was the poorest of humans. His silence told him that his comparisons, presumptions and conclusions did not stretch the value of the One Way Platinum KORP card against the Unlimited Life card that Origin had sent him.

In the solitude of his mind, he slowly descended from his pyramid. Each comparison he made lowered him one step further, and he painfully ingested the bitter taste of the bread of defeat. Within seconds, the roles reversed. As he walked down the steps of his glorious pyramid, he kept repeating, "While I offer bitter life to the people in my empire, he wants to spend quality time with me. Since I provide death with my bombs, he offers unlimited life. While I offer jail to the imperfect, he gives the flawed true freedom. While I submit them to insolvency, he deposits money in their accounts. As I propose to wipe the smile from their faces, He smiles lovingly at them."

He cried as he walked down the steps. He felt very ashamed of himself.

"While I attempt to discredit him, he offers me his compassion. While I offer …"

At that moment, KORP ran out of the hotel towards the beach, where he kept running and running and comparing: "While I offer destruction with my Toys, he offers restoration of things. While I offer thirty million to execute him, he offers me his pardon."

He kept running until his feet couldn't stand anymore. Tired, he fell to his knees in the sand, where, raising his arms to the sky, he spread his palms open and shouted, "Okay, you've won. I no longer control anything or know anything. I want nothing more than to be with you, and I'm sorry for what I did. Have you heard me?"

KORP kept utterly silent while the sea caressed his soul. Then, with great sadness, he wanted to hide or keep running to escape. He felt he was naked and realised he was now the candidate and

Origin was in control.

His actions had caught up with him and they demanded justice.

22. Please do as I told you!

It is always possible to dress people with dignity.

KORP felt disoriented. He had a profound and unbearable unease in both his mind and heart. He spent many hours lying on the bed, his head on the pillow, in brooding shock.

Perhaps unfamiliar, a question arose inside him: 'What are you doing?' The light of his conscience sent signs that things were not right in his life and his empire.

His Counsellors were concerned because the emperor endured days without eating and did not leave his room or come out. They saw him struggle to escape confusion and pain.

As the days passed, KORP wanted to turn back time and wished he hadn't signed the last cheque with his thumb down. He longed not to have drunk that lunch wine, and suddenly decided that it was the most bitter he had ever drunk. He repudiated it with great disgust because he felt embarrassed by the notes he had sent and wept at the confusion in his mind and heart.

Regret squeezed his heart, tearing from him the residue of vanity's deadly poison that still lingered in his veins. Pulling out the photo of his beloved and kissing it through tears, he wished Kate was there right now to comfort him. After hours of sitting there and looking at Kate in the photograph, he felt like he was leaving a giant prison in an abyss of darkness where he had spent many years. Slowly, KORP breathed the air with the essence of entirely different freedom that had transformed the corpse floating inert in space into a conscious being. He had a terrifying feeling of being hunted; he felt he was a fugitive. The guilt of his actions was too heavy, and he wanted to run to escape, to hide in the depths of the earth.

***

One afternoon, he finally exited his confinement and went out for a walk on the beach. His Counsellors were more relaxed about the whole situation. He asked the hotel personnel if they could *please* prepare breakfast at nine o'clock, then returned to the same place where he had been on his knees days before. Sitting on the sand, looking out to the sea. He was calmer and more at ease, but he was still shocked.

He looked more closely at the sea border on the sand, showing him this truth: 'There is a limit to everything.' After walking for several hours, he came to his senses and concluded that he had reached the limit of his wrong actions.

Origin had cleaned the darkness from his conscience and returned him to the light. Now, his awareness had illuminated his conclusions and outlook on life. He accepted that things in his empire were not right.

Immediately, he acted and wanted to fix them. He walked to where his Counsellors were and asked them, "What would you change in the empire if you were the emperor?"

He remembered at that moment the tiny letters he had written in his book when he was concluding about the algorithm of conscience:

"If I had a single molecule of conscience …"

He suddenly felt the deep pain in his torso again. It was a pain like depression, which often comes and goes without explanation. He couldn't stop crying. It was regret's pain.

He put on his dark glasses so they wouldn't see him crying. At that moment, one of his Counsellors told him: "My Lord, if I were the emperor, I would ease the burden of my subjects by annulling all the decrees that make their lives miserable."

The second said: "I would eliminate the ridiculous rainwater law and the oxygen tax."

The third said: "I would build a time machine to travel back to the beginning of the empire's glory days and start from there again."

He quickly returned to the hotel, thinking there was still time and that this wasn't the end of everything. He thought he could do something about it. After all, he was still the emperor and held all the power and glory he possessed. His three Counsellors were stunned by the emperor's approach to them.

In his hotel room, he looked everywhere for paper to write on and found none; then he took all the toilet paper rolls available, including those in the warehouses instead. He wrote reforms, laws, mandates, amendments, explanation notes, annulments, confessions, etc. He used up dozens of rolls of toilet paper while he wrote the list, along with the minutes, hours and days.

His restored conscience made him realise that the world he had created because of vanity was a whole of falsehoods, and he wanted to amend it. Quickly, the emperor wrote plans, ideas, calculations, strategic situations and everything he could to untangle the things he had tangled up with his fruitless decisions. With those things, he had made human lives miserable in his war against the Origin.

As desperate as he was, he wrote the things he wanted to fix first. There were thousands of situations. Until this point, he had filled over five dozen rolls of toilet paper in the days of writing, spending hours in the afternoon and long nights until dawn. Exhausted from writing all night, he fell asleep on the desk.

***

That week, he suspended all his activities in the search for Origin's particle. He ordered the Hercules to return to the capital without him on board. He said he would return to the capital on his presidential air vehicle. A considerable stir arose among his advisers and staff, especially among his scientists, because they believed KORP had found an Origin particle.

In a hurry, they packed everything. They loaded the safes and excitedly weighed the anchor. They dismantled the entire military convoy and the prevention operation and returned to the capital city.

KORP thanked the hotel for its services, paid the employees an appropriate tip, and said goodbye with a "Thank you sincerely".

***

As he flew home in the presidential aircraft, he looked out the window and saw the Earth he had destroyed. Traces of his Toys were everywhere. There were traces of destruction, misery and desolation, and he saw long caravans of Time Travellers heading for the cities.

He closed the curtain because he felt embarrassed and put on his dark glasses so no one would see him crying. At that point, a female staff member approached him and offered him something to drink. She was faking an attentive smile. Her skirt was very short, and the neckline of her blouse exposed almost all of her. KORP felt very embarrassed and said, "Miss, tell everyone to dress with dignity."

"Sir, but ... You ordered us to dress like this and ..."

"Yes, I know, and I'm so sorry. Please do as I told you."

The young woman, with a hurried step, disappeared into the bar. After a moment, she picked up a crystal glass and, opening a bottle, poured water into it, half of it falling to the ground because her hands were shaking. Her face flushed with embarrassment. While the young woman drank the water, she thought about what to do when arriving at her destination if the emperor declared her insolvent.

"In his war against Origin, KORP poured fear upon those poor souls in the empire, which moved them to live double lives." (The Thinker)

At that moment, the flight attendants arrived and found the young woman crying. Tears of helplessness dripped down her cheeks.

"By the emperor's orders, we dress like this and …"

"Look and listen to me, little one. Don't worry. Let's do what the emperor says."

Soon, they all put on decent clothes.

Throughout the flight, the emperor acted strangely. None of the staff wanted to walk past him because they feared he would come out with something strange until they reached their destination. The emperor's actions were mysterious and unexpected, which confused everyone. Before leaving the vehicle, the emperor addressed the crew with another, "Thank you sincerely."

Along the way, he decided to clean his own house, but a prominent gentleman already lived there: his pride. It was the first knight he would have to defeat under the cover of his new conscience.

23. Untangling the tangled

Even the mightiest empire can accept a contrite son who begs forgiveness.

Various people transcribed from the toilet paper rolls onto the empire's digital system KORP's new decisions. They were in the palace's main hall. It was tedious work. There were thousands of notes to copy verbatim, and they had to ensure everything was word perfect.

They could ignore nothing. In addition, they had limited time, and if necessary, they worked in shifts since it was urgent.

***

The radical change in the emperor's conscience and personality immediately affected the life of the empire and the palace. It also affected his relationship with the New Council.

He eliminated the phrase 'Why not?' from his daily speech and replaced it with 'Thank you' or 'Please'. He also extended his hand to reciprocate when somebody greeted him as an act of empathy.

"This last gesture surprised everyone so much that the press took a picture just as he shook hands with his chef." (The Thinker)

The emperor's reforms surprised the New Council and aroused suspicion that he had become mad, so they doubted he was telling the truth. Behind closed doors and the emperor's back, they called an emergency meeting of all the leaders representing all the social structures of the empire. They wanted to replace him because of the royal family's need for a natural successor; this fact was a great excuse to rid him of. This meeting was brutally heated. Different opinions arose, even reviving old enmities between clans and power groups in the empire. Some suddenly produced inheritance papers from vast regions that supposedly belonged to their ancestors, and they considered independence or autonomy for those regions if the mad emperor continued to rule. The final decision from this meeting was that the New Council must take over the government and reign as soon as possible.

In the Central Military Command, the leaders of the Earth, Space, Marines, Biodermatik military forces and the Academy of Counsellors decided whether their emperor had turned mad. Also, one member of the Nanotechnology Society ignited an intense debate about the integrity of KORP's experience in the Magical Land. In those situations, the Counsellor's word was vital.

The Academy of Counsellors made all the military forces understand that the emperor's experience was an absolute real miracle. As proof, the emperor had the objects that proved that fact: the message inside the envelope, the pen and the Unlimited Life card.

For the Academy of Counsellors, the emperor returned to life. That news brought hope for the empire's restoration, which was vital. At the end of that meeting, all the armed forces supported their emperor, as they had never done before. They united against the New Council's political pressure on society.

Another magnificent piece of news was that the emperor's transformation had reached the ears of the resistance. They initially took it cautiously because of the infiltrators' fake news. They deployed a group of spies to investigate. After verifying the integrity of the emperor's transformation, the Arktxts, who had waited for this moment, agreed to stop their rebellion. They also appeased the resistance. Moths77 participated in the empire's reconstruction, and J3CeXteen helped the most vulnerable.

KORP asked for an immediate meeting with the resistance to stop the civil war, which brought tears of hope to the population. The White City held this meeting. From this day, the White

City became the protector of the emperor because of the New Council's plans.

But the New Council sought to replace him as soon as possible. They had many excuses to put their plans into action.

"Those leeches – the New Council – wanted to leave intact all the reforms the KORP had implemented until then, because they benefitted them the most. So they started their rebellion, supported by the eminent authorities of the capital city before the emperor unleashed the new reforms." (The Thinker)

Agitated and confusing days filled the empire. Fake news circulated with all kinds of convincing lies, like these: 'The empire will divide into smaller kingdoms'; 'Is this the end of the KORP Empire?'; 'The emperor abdicates because of madness'; 'The New Council has taken control of the capital city'; etc. This news appeared and disappeared from the website as if by magic. Still, it left traces of confusion among the most vulnerable people.

The New Council, learning that the military would support the emperor, intensified its campaign to boycott the new reforms about to be enacted. For them, the emperor had turned mad; therefore, a healthy leader did not write these recent reforms, and, according to the current law, they were not legal. However, they faced the big problem of proving that KORP was mad.

"Understandably, any change brings its consequences, but no one will be the same after that. Overall, the New Council must remember that KORP is still the emperor." (The Thinker)

***

In a beautifully decorated room was a neatly pressed bed on which a goose-down pillow rested placidly. On the wall in front of the bed was a giant poster of The Thinker, covering almost a third.

On television, the presenters were excitedly reading the latest news about the reforms the emperor would apply to the empire within a week. They hoped that this news would bring joy if they implemented it.

"In the coming days, the emperor will announce deep and radical structural reforms that will benefit all empire inhabitants.

Will these reforms signify the long-awaited return of the true Emperor KORP? Undoubtedly unprecedented news in recent years. The Academy of Counsellors will submit these laws to the New KORP Council for debate," the newsreaders said.

In the room was a man dressed in black who walked from one side to the other with the haste of a caged lion. As he watched the news, he turned off the television with one hand and reached for a gold card that looked like a One Way credit card with the other. The security cameras stopped filming at that point. He lay back on the bed, examining the characters on the gold card.

"*KORP DNA 23+Y Unlimited Life*. What does this mean?"

With his fingers, he traced the relief characters, trying to decipher the code's magnitude, scope and value.

"What does it mean?" he wondered again.

"Who can live with that many chromosomes? He is male and has a human mother, but he is also someone else. Who is his father? Where does he come from? Was his father one demigod? Why is he so significant? Is he related to the hero who defeated death, or is this the genetic code of the Gene of Life? Is this the formula to defeat death? Will it be the path to infinite cell regeneration? It's a unique blood type!"

Then he read the message written in blood.

"*You should know that this card will only become effective once you apply my blood by signing it. Otherwise, it will be impossible.*"

He read the note several times, and the rule was undoubtedly clear; it was Origin standard rules. KORP rules do not have space here. However, his pride was looking for a way to evade that rule because of a hypothetical fear that originated from comparing the card to the regulations of his empire. The emperor didn't want to sign and then retract to be declared insolvent. Then he thought and repeated, 'I would have liked to meet you too.' Deep in his heart, he thought of how to get Origin to come back and spend time with him or play with him again, but this time, he would win the game and send the cheques to KORP. He felt that all his possessions – his Ultimate Good – were tiny compared to a minute, a second, perhaps a microsecond, to spend time in the same place, time and space of reality where Origin existed.

Firmly, he wanted to be with him in that present reality – not after, not before, not in the distant future, but in that same present. His presence, energy, essence and eternal real life beckoned him. Overnight, Origin became his last reality. He longed to meet him in person but was still in his way without respecting the rules Origin pointed out.

KORP looks transformed, although, in the back of his mind, he still clung to the 'there's always a way' on which his pride had once ridden; instead, considering his new awareness, he yearned to be in the presence of Origin. He wished to see him now because he admired him greatly.

"Human beings also have the option of 'on my terms'; they often succeed and get used to that idea. Also, they need the option to break the rules when they want. They do and get used to that idea, but I would like to know if these options are compatible with Origin rules; otherwise, he would have clarified it in the fine print if he had one. The rules were clear. KORP only has one way to meet him in person: signing the card. These are the rules of Origin. How the rules worked was not a mystery to KORP. He knew perfectly well the meaning of a pact or agreement and its implications." (The Thinker)

***

Once they had finished transcribing the reforms from the rolls of toilet paper to the imperial cyber system, the emperor sent them to all media outlets for publication. He read the reforms on the empire's radio, television and websites; even the colonies on Mars and the moon could hear him via holograms.

Every reform and word brought rest and joy to the empire's inhabitants. Happily, the sun of hope shined again in the sky of the KORP Empire. It took many days and time lapses.

The Academy of Counsellors didn't allow these reformed reforms to be sent to the New Council for debate because they found the plot they were cooking up. After all, he was the emperor, and the empire still owed him allegiance.

"I think it is worth mentioning just a few of the thousands of reforms to

our readers or his new will so they may understand the magnitude and scope of the profound change he had in his life." (The Thinker)

Of course! You're right. The empire's infrastructure became abandoned because of the prohibition of social activities on the streets and in public places. Thanks to his renewed conscience, the emperor opened an aggressive reconstruction campaign to restore it to what it was at the beginning of the glorious empire.

The first thing KORP decided was to declare all the Insolvents to be Solvents legally. He ordered the closure of prisons filled with thousands of imperfect and Insolvent people. With each one he saw coming out of jail, his torso ached. With profound sadness, he said, "I don't think I can restore the time they lost inside those dark and cold walls, and I don't think I can heal the pain I inflicted on their souls and restore the happy times those steel bars stole from them."

Then, the emperor stood at the prison entrance with his dark glasses on so no one could see him crying. He extended his hand to those who left and recommended that they reflect the mark of Origin they carried in their hearts: love.

He restored the first law: 'Respect others, and others will respect you.' Then, he immediately ordered to close the cloning programme and to destroy the baby factories so people would decide when and how to have their babies to strengthen the concept of a mother and father. With this law, he restored human relations to a high level of respect.

"I would like to shine a light on this matter. Respect for others is the key to opening the Pandora's Box of human relationship rights. By doing that, there will not be secrets, no running away because of criticism, no hatred, no living inside a closet; there will be no more 'True Lies' or 'Lying Truths'; instead, there will be more shoulders to rest and trust on; will be extended soft hands to ease any suffering; will be more opportunities to shine; will be freedom of opinion; there will be humans who will think differently and not be ashamed. There will be humans who will help each other beyond their beliefs to get to the last corner of the universe in peace and freedom." (The Thinker)

He ordered the destruction of his printing presses. He burned all the papers he had carefully written to make life impossible for those who rarely questioned but lived with gratitude. Instead, he asked people to examine his imperial system and promised to amend his wrongdoing.

As a symbol of this new way of thinking, he built the Cathedral of Mirrors, a stunning structure covered entirely in glass and mirrors. He believed this cathedral represented the importance of love, truth, the need to overcome fear, the ability to experience joy and the opportunity for change. Ultimately, it was a symbol of the existence of Origin.

He decreed to hang mirrors in all his domains, beginning with his palace and continuing through the streets, subway stations, airports, etc., and that they be enormous and beautiful to reflect the Origin's mark. He could now look at himself in a mirror without fear or shame.

KORP was excited and convinced that, in this way, he could build an enormous mirror over the empire. These mirrors would make Origin descend to look at his face, and when he saw him, he would say: "Yes, and I would like to …"

He locked himself in his library for long hours to investigate the history of the gods of the Victorious Cultures, to find any clue of Origin's whereabouts or some situation in which he played the sending notes game just like the one he had played with him. He read many legends, tales and stories, seeking clues about where he would have been. The emperor also read how often Origin participated in or what army he would have led to victory.

In one of those history books, he read that on the Emerald Continent, there was a place called the Mirror of Origin that caught his attention, and he consulted his historians and found it to be true.

"It is true, my Lord. It was a gigantic white mantle – a salt lake that, after receiving rains, transformed into a magical natural mirror of monumental proportions. This mirror was so great that its reflection reached anywhere in the solar system, my Lord," said the historian.

"This lake existed in the high plains of the Blue Mountain range, whose mountains disputed with the clouds to reach the skies of the Emerald Continent. The natural mirror was beautiful –

astonishingly beautiful. According to legends and historians, from time to time, Origin descended to look at his face. The site was a strange natural phenomenon because of the type of energy in its subsurface, my Lord," the astrophysicist said.

"What about today? Does this site still exist?" KORP said, agitated because they were talking in the past tense. That day, he also discovered that his bombs had hit this Mirror of Origin in the Nuclear War, so they left only traces. As he read that, he put on his dark glasses. KORP was so sad when he heard this news he walked around his room, thinking: 'Perhaps if I could build a time machine to get to that place, I could wait for him there, and, when he comes down, I would tell him I would like to …'

He locked himself in the design laboratory to design a time machine, and the happy Trackers helped him with that project because it was their speciality.

'It must be a machine that moves on the dimensional rails of time; only then will I be able to reach that magnificent natural mirror. A machine that will take me to a time when the whole place looked so lovely, to an age where I didn't have to feel ashamed of its destruction,' KORP thought.

As his fingers wrote mathematical formulas and drew graphs of a time machine, his heart erupted excitedly at the thought of preparing to meet the Origin. They programmed him to travel thousands of years into the past.

After putting the project on paper, he returned to one of his technological complexes for study matter: he gathered his most competent army of scientists. He put Commander Sarah Hope at the head of the team, and they built it.

After many days of meticulous work, KORP and his team had finally finished building the time machine he designed. It was a fantastic, complex machine, and with it, they also made some prototypes of tracking devices that would accompany him on that trip; there were twenty-five very sophisticated robotic machines, which he called Biortan. Five could transform into humanoids or animals or any creature; these would travel with KORP to track Origin's presence there.

The Trackers told him that in the Emerald Continent also inhabited creatures of saurian proportions and, further north, apart from humans, giants. He also considered that factor and included it in his designs. The rest of the Biortan would travel to other continents. That was the original plan.

To construct the Biortan, they applied nanotechnology and biological-human artificial intelligence. These were machines as complex as the time machine, with the difference that these were independent and transformed according to the situation to interact. When they transformed, they had almost identical human functional characteristics. They talked, laughed and interacted with each other, humans, animals and the biological environment. They equipped them with various devices to navigate through space, time and to immerse themselves in the spirit world where those cultures existed. He thought, 'Perhaps they could have seen him go down to the spirit world and find him walking among them.' He had heard that Origin owned the spirits.

In his quest for immortality, KORP performed thousands of genetic-cybernetic operations to get different blood types for various purposes. The Biortan were the prototypes of robots that carried human blood fused with lithium in their operating systems. This blood type harboured intelligent molecules like human red cells, which could perfectly interact and communicate with human biological cells.

The Biortans weren't just robots that could transform, they also had a conscience – not as developed as humans, but something more than simple instincts – so that they could distinguish good from evil, justice from injustice, truth from lies, work from laziness, admiration from apathy, and humility from pride. However, they did not possess the most essential element in the universe: love. They could not love.

"Love is a human-defining quality. It is the irrefutable proof of the existence of Origin embedded in the heart of each human as the extension of his glory – the mark with which he sealed each human being making them capable of loving." (The Thinker)

A tradition says: 'The day Origin gave life to humans, he took a knife and cut out a small piece of his heart and implanted it in the souls of each one, and that love was the original mark making each one unique. Without love, a human being is incomplete and ceases to exist forever.' KORP and his team could not encrypt love in the Biortan; although they wanted to, they could not.

**

KORP kept reading about the reforms. He decreed they destroy factories where they make robots to employ as many humans as possible. They would also earn a decent wage so that, when working, they would not complain, but reflect Origin's marks. He said this to his Counsellors: "Origin will be glad my employees don't complain and can earn enough for their families."

He ordered each factory to produce an extra ten per cent for people experiencing poverty and to make mirrors. He was determined to fill the entire world with mirrors.

"The more Origin marks reflect, the more likely he will return," he said.

He transformed his steel horse riders into messengers of peace. He dismantled the destructive poison weaponry they carried and filled them with specialised people to reach the ends of the Earth, having a single message: 'Reflect the mark of Origin.' They were legions of people who brought hope wherever they put their feet while helping to rebuild the destruction across the empire and the globe. They also asked people if Origin had been in those lands because KORP wanted to know if he inhabited elsewhere. Also, they identified those places where famine existed and, at the cost of building a nuclear bomb, developed industries in those towns because, he said, "Perhaps this will stop migration, and we will no longer need to be Time Travellers."

Also, the emperor ordered all citizens in his domain to be declared first-class citizens as the only social status class in the empire; he outlawed racism and slavery in all their forms.

He ruled factories should destine a percentage of time to process food for people experiencing homelessness and clothing to cover them with dignity instead of making his destructive Toys.

KORP asked to eliminate unfair trade. Also, he ordered the factories to return to the places he had eradicated so that his fellows could have jobs for generations and employ the most significant number of people and fewer robots.

In the eyes of the New Council, those first new reforms were too radical and incomprehensible. The New Council disliked the reforms because they believed they would affect their pockets because these reforms proposed fair redistribution of the empire's wealth among all citizens through fair trade.

For those people who came from fascist political parties across the empire the reforms were too romantic-humanistic; they said they took away character and arrogance from the empire. Some of these people were rapacious speculators and opportunistic mercenaries with illegal wealth. They wanted to live in a powerful, solid kingdom that exuded pride and fear. Simultaneously, according to them, governing was easy when fear was your ally.

"Fear is temporary because humans can overcome it. They quickly assimilate, overcoming fear, because the love within them is stronger than fear, and where there is love, there is no fear." (The Thinker)

Some of his political supporters did not agree with the reforms either. They were worried that the emperor had turned mad. They confronted him, saying, "What are you doing?"

KORP responded to them: "Do as I tell you."

With the new reforms, the empire turned 180° in every direction and aspect of its governmental structure, abolished the pyramid system and said executives should rotate.

Next to his office was a gigantic warehouse full of decrees, laws and contracts he had signed with his clients. With those documents, he tipped the scales in his favour in the past because they were all written in subtle and fraudulent terminology, so he conned and swamped his clients with terrible viciousness. Each document was like a knife with which he aimed for the jugular of his victimised clients; it was his vanity. His clients called it 'the small print of the contract'. The emperor wrote it in all those apparent legal papers: "Executed." With all his soul, he wished he had not executed them because he realised how easy it was to destroy with a signature what someone had built with so much sacrifice and love. He spent months sorting out those documents with the affected people.

He woke up each day feeling that he could untangle more and wore thick clothes to avoid getting sick because he said getting sick was a waste of time. The emperor's behaviour impressed his Counsellors; he didn't sit down to eat but brought sandwiches to eat on the way. He crossed mountains to reach small communities, passed through towns, untangling and repeated, 'twenty-two per cent'.

"When he was writing these reforms on the toilet papers, he considered every situation that needed to be untangled and numbered them; then KORP made a device called 'Untangler', and every time he untangled one situation, he clicked on the 'Untangler' app,[39] and it was telling him what per cent he had already untangled." (The Thinker)

His mind tortured him with the same philosophies he had once invented to destroy others, but now he wanted to reformulate them. Where he had said that "time has valued the gift horse", he said: "I invented it. It was an excuse to employ cheap labour."

And he argued that time has the same value and weight here, there, or anywhere on the planet.

Returning to his factories, where he brought products stained with blood and sweat at the price of a 'gift horse', he ordered them to be rebuilt and technologically developed until they became factories of dignity.

He destroyed the fraudulent financial equation of the Fountain of Miracles with those actions. He said, "This economic equation was the invention of the sixth sense of a baffling miser man who involved many in the infamous world of ill-got riches."

His Majesty recast his Toys and turned them into specialised medicine machines, saying, "If I properly care for the sick, the old and the homeless, then maybe I can extend their lives a few more years."

He revoked his proud formula law of 'Creating spaces in

39.　An **app** is a shortened version of the word 'application'. It refers to a software program that performs a specific function for the user.

time'. He changed the factories' names from 'Guardians of Time' to 'Factories of Dignity,' saying, "People work to bring dignity to their families."

He remembered that Origin wrote "Dear Mr KORP". Those words made him feel valued; despite mistreating him, Origin had treated him with respect until the last moment, and now he wanted to show respect to everyone by saying, "If you did it, I can too."

He ordered that they buy bottles of wine from the street for the palace, which cost five pesos, and pay forty thousand pesos for them. He wanted street wine to have the same fair-trade flavour as brand-name wines sold in exclusive venues. According to some, such a purchase was asymmetric.

"It doesn't add up if one wants to be fair," they said.

"Don't you think that paying forty thousand pesos for a bottle of wine that costs five pesos is an exaggeration on KORP's part? What was the reason behind this action? What was he thinking? It's difficult to tell." (The Thinker)

***

KORP spent many years untangling what, once, by his vanity, he had tangled. With each reform and decree, he restored and improved the quality of life of humans in his empire and outside of it, which was notorious in every corner of his domain. The light emanating from his conscience molecule often perplexed him. It was as if he had seen the morning light for the first time.

The emperor strived to unravel the dark things in his empire, so much so that his health had declined because of the many nights spent sitting on his stool beside his colleague, The Thinker. He longed for the return of his empire's glory to the state before falling into vanity's disgrace. With the amended reforms, he wanted Origin marks – love – to shine forever on the faces of the empire's inhabitants. It was a sign of the glory they inherited from their creator.

Above all, he hoped to find Kate and bring her by his side. He still loved her too much. He realised that her love helped him to cross the immense river of life to this point.

***

After years of darkness and oppression, the humans in the **KORP** Empire rested from the calamities of modern slavery they had suffered at the hands of their vain emperor. Thanks to life, the sun of consolation shone again and more intensely on the humans in that corner of the universe. Of course, they quickly healed their wounds. Their minds and hearts were full of joy, and they hoped to rebuild the empire and the planet in the challenge's face.

There were two things that **KORP** could never forgive himself for, two things that, although he wanted to, he could not remedy, and that is why he thought that life, heaven and destiny looked at him with contempt. The first was Kate's absence by his side, and the second was losing the opportunity to meet Origin in person; those drinks were too bitter. It was difficult for him to sign the Unlimited Life card because it was a matter of principle for him. He spent days wrestling with this dilemma. His pride was too overwhelming.

"It's worth telling our readers that, one day, heaven showed him the most beautiful side of its face amid all that bitter bitterness. I am referring to the news that made him understand that, whoever he was, whatever he did, and wherever he is, Origin would always show his most beautiful face to him: his compassion." (The Thinker)

Of course! He had just returned from the most memorable holiday of his life and was tired of the trip to the moon. One afternoon, as he prepared to leave his office, a group of geneticists from the Academy of Counsellors came into his presence and urged him to speak with them. The geneticists insisted on the emperor because they had very revealing news to share with him. Faced with such insistence, he could not deny them his time.

"Indeed, my Lord, DNA evidence confirms that the young woman is your relative, sir."

"Are you saying I am the girl's father?"

"The evidence does not lie and is irrefutable, my Lord. You know better than anyone else that this test does not lie."

"What certainty is there, aside from these DNA tests?"

"The girl's mother, sir, only her mother could reveal the truth. But without a doubt, the young woman carries your genes in her blood, my Lord. That is irrefutable proof."

"That's impossible!"

This news overwhelmed him.

He ordered the geneticists and doctors to leave the place. Then he sat down with an eerie stillness. He was pale, thoughtful and motionless for a few minutes. That news was like turning the page to enter a new story, different and with other actors, starting with KORP, who had to be a family man. However, the reality at that moment was different, and that news surprised him.

Another unresolved issue came up with that news: Kate. She had dropped out of college and disappeared from the emperor's life because one of KORP's executioners had abused her. The day that misfortune occurred, she was a few days pregnant. Kate was carrying the heir to the empire in her womb. Still, as she plunged into a chaos of worry about what had happened and believed that the child she was expecting was from the executioner, she fled out of fear and shame that someone would find out.

Not even Kate knew the absolute truth: KORP was the birth father of the baby she was expecting. Kate had escaped to the kingdom of glaciers on the other side of the Arctic, where she found refuge; her father's sister lived there.

In those frozen lands, Kate finished her education and found a job as a biologist for a big company. The owners of this company didn't have a family, and Celest would sometimes stay with them. They were familiar with Kate's story through her aunt. One day, they proposed to adopt her little girl, promising they would never reveal 'the truth'. Kate accepted the idea so that her daughter could be safe there.

After giving up her little girl for adoption, she joined the expeditionary legions. This organisation handled environmental protection projects. Kate had commanded an environmental ship searching for endangered marine fauna, like the blue whale. She travelled the oceans of the entire world. Sometimes, when her boat encountered Leviathan or Hercules warships at sea, Kate used to yell over the loudspeakers at this baffling soldier standing on the ship's bow with open arms. One day, annoyed, she took a picture of this madman and said, "Who the hell is this baffling soldier?" The marine safeguard body posted this picture on the 'Extreme Risks' webpage, in the section where some people expose themselves to danger in the sea. She never came across the fact that the soldier was KORP.

Kate always loved him. He was also the only man in her life. She called him 'Naughty pixie porcupine' because, every time they were together, he would launch his nose into the pool of her blonde hair and dive into it, inhaling the molecules of her perfume essence as a porcupine does on earth when looking for worms.

She also kept a photo of him and carried it with her everywhere.

Finding out Kate's whereabouts was a never-ending story in the middle of nowhere. Although detectives found her once in the city where she lived, they soon lost track of her again because of the work she used to do.

Shock washed over KORP. A heightened feeling filled his gut with indescribable happiness and overjoyed. He said, "Am I a father?"

He had the DNA test results and compared them with his. There was no doubt the evidence was irrefutable.

That moment was monumental in the emperor's life. Never had news of this magnitude shocked him from being so powerfully. He couldn't compare to the feeling that had been born within him. There is no comparable moment to the feeling he had when he had won the election; this one was more intense, so ardent that not even he could contain it, and it made his heart overflow with joy. That news brought reason back to his existence.

He had always felt that fate had shown its sad face from the day he was born. Therefore, he had to fight to bring happiness to his life. He lived with the idea that fate had cursed him. Even as an emperor, he had to gamble to prove destiny was by his side. However, that news was like a unique and sublime gift he would never have dreamed of receiving; it was a gift of love, grace and compassion.

He looked at the two photographs and saw that, without a doubt, it was a complete family reunion. The young Celest was a beautiful girl with a smile like Kate's. He was radiant. In that instant, his heart plunged into happiness, reminding him how beautiful life is. As he laughed, he let the tears flow; they were tears of joy and said, "Celest, my daughter!"

As he digested the news, he wanted to scream and tell the universe that he was the father of a beautiful young girl.

***

Two things brought happiness to his life: the news of his daughter Celest and the project of his trip in the time machine to the Mirror of Origin. He imagined meeting Origin in person, though in his own way.

AT THE END OF PART ONE
TO BE CONTINUED

24. Author's notes and discussion topics

1. Writing this work was an extraordinary and profound experience – a trip down memory lane. Some areas and scenarios in this story are based on real life, whereas for others, I had to stretch my imagination to get to places where it would be impossible to travel. Some areas and stories in this story are genuine.

As stated, I started writing it on the train to London for my Spanish classes. Because of my previous job, I made periodic trips to different parts of the country, and the train was my primary means of transportation, which also became my desk. In addition, I wrote in some places in Diss to soak up the atmosphere. Also drew various sketches to give it realism and had to get involved in multiple situations to feel the mood. Sometimes I had to walk around in KORP's shoes – to feel and think how he thinks – this was the most complex but fascinating part. I also had to put aside fear and worry about what people would say. Also, I drew many scenes from my lived experiences. I'll tell you a little more about them now.

2. In January 1992, I arrived in Ecuador, where I had the privilege to meet and live with wonderful people. I got involved in community social aid projects and humanitarian institutions with a fantastic team of humanity-lovers. Together, we helped hundreds of low-income families with assignments that gave them a better quality of life, e.g. running water, health care, etc. Also, in many places, I saw the monster of monopoly (in the agriculture business and poverty) enslaving families and communities. I also got involved in politics.

3. In August 2010, I arrived in England with my wife and two young daughters after living, serving and working in Ecuador for eighteen years. Despite having previously visited the country as a tourist, my new reality welcomed me with a big hug and a slap. Even for my wife, being British, her country's reality had changed so much since she left for Ecuador that, for her, too, it was an almost new experience to arrive and start over. We found a nation discussing whether to leave the European Union, the famous Brexit, and debating with concern about the new wave of migrants from the Middle East. Amid all that, little by little, we integrated and moved forward, although not without some setbacks.

4. Living in this first-world country has always been challenging from the start. It was like sitting in the Formula 1 champion's race car for the first time and driving; many things were new! To this day, I'm still in second gear and trying to use third on the gearbox. I'm slow, I know. Before one can run, one first has to learn to walk. That is the golden rule. As a newcomer, the new reality pushes one to swallow whatever it serves you to eat, and you should eat it without asking too many questions because 'then you'll understand'. For me, the success of emigrating depended on four things: papers in order, language, job and integration into society, which I've learned after all these years. I worked in various places here, and now I teach Spanish. These experiences became material for writing as well.

5. For example, I wrote the KORP kitchen scene in the restaurant where I worked when I first came to Diss. It was winter, where there was snow everywhere, and it was Christmas Eve. I took my laptop and went to have coffee and write in that restaurant. After several hours of being there, I returned home with many words on my computer and a lot of caffeine in my blood.

6. I took the scene of the cultural minorities from my experience of learning English. We were a group of immigrants from different countries learning English at the Diss Youth and Community Centre. During the break, we shared our life stories about how we got to Britain and how we were doing. We all agreed that learning English was essential to having a 'normal life' here in Britain. It was fun!

7. I based the story of Time Travellers on the sad scenes I saw in airports when emigrants had to say goodbye to their loved ones. And also on the circumstances of the thousands of immigrants from the Middle East who arrived in Europe and, in many European countries, people prevented them from passing by the iron curtains put up to stop them; and also on the thousands of emigrants who embark daily on dangerous trips from Latin America to reach the United States. I have been an emigrant since I was eighteen, when I left my beloved homeland, Bolivia, in search of my destiny. Since then, I have lived as an immigrant in some countries, until today. For this reason, I know first-hand the experience of an immigrant, from extortion, racial discrimination, mistrust, misunderstanding and rejection, to the warm embrace of someone who welcomes you with no prejudices into their country and offers you help or their home to stay in. This last part makes you forget all the bad things that being an immigrant entails and how beautiful life is. I have several fathers, mothers and dozens of adopted brothers and sisters in those countries. My thanks go to them for everything they have given me!

8. I took the scene of the rainwater tax from real life. When in 2000 Bolivia sought to refinance the public water service of its third-largest city, the Financier required that it be privatised, which is how one big global corporation gained control of all of Cochabamba's water, even that which fell from the sky. Among its laws there was one which prohibited people from gathering rainwater without paying for it. This situation ignited the Water War – a common good against privatisation. People from Cochabamba expelled this global corporation from Bolivia.

9. The scene with the immediate restoration of KORP's conscience is the story of my parents, the only difference being that they signed the card of their lives, with the blood of the *Gene of Life 23+Y* = Jesus. That signature was enough for alcoholism to be defeated and eradicated from their lives forever. I witnessed the miracle that happened when they believed in Him. I was nine years old at that time. Since then, my family has lived in the light of hope. After all, true miracles that transform lives still exist!

10. One thing that, even now, I can't get over is seeing the poverty that exists around the world. It shouldn't be like that; there is no need. Everyone should have equal opportunities because we row in the same direction on the same ship: life. I experienced poverty at home until I was nine because of my parents' alcoholism. Honestly, guys, it's not pleasant to be in that situation. I plead with you, parents, to avoid putting your children through the pain that comes with alcoholism. After my parents experienced true freedom, they realised how wrong they had been and they recognised all that had happened with my family was an unnecessary evil.

11. I've found many fascinating things about cells in my research. They are sophisticated biological mechanisms that work in perfect harmony to sustain our natural bodies. For example, some suggest that whoever designed our physical bodies did so with functional biological characteristics, if not too much to say, timeless or perfect state because of how complex and sophisticated cells are; this may explain why the ancients existed for hundreds of years, some reaching nearly a thousand years of life according to sacred texts. Why do we die, then? It's the million-dollar question. Somewhere in the genesis of humanity, someone introduced death. Because of this, we are still suffering from that misfortune. However, I believe death is not a supreme or absolute end, but life.

12. On the spectrum of all the existing things in the universe, the absolute end is life, and that plan has not changed. Life continues to be our 'Ultimate Supreme Good', giving value and meaning to our existence; also, love continues to be our Ultimate Infinite Good, which provides beauty to our lives. I believe that Origin was the one who, because of humans' deaths, provided us with the Gene of Life which, according to the sacred texts, makes our perfect regeneration possible to take us back home – to a place where there is no disharmony in the functioning of the cells that produce death. I am not religious, and that is not a requirement to believe in something. (Is it?) I believe in the miracle of life.

13. Each human being carries within himself his own KORP, which, by nature, can have unique characteristics. For example, he may be the noblest and most pious knight who seeks meaning in his existence in this life. The most ruthless individual who lacks a conscience, or he can be someone who wants to leave his noble mark when passing through this life to change the course. The one addicted to selfish hedonism and only cares a little more about himself or the one who is prone to take care of others. That one who fights to take from life the right to be happy. The one who is forced to create a parallel reality to exist in because of the rejection and the misunderstanding that he suffers from those surrounding him. That one who wants to reach the goal but does not know how or where to go because he has lost his way and resorts to strange means to return or someone who knows what he wants and is determined to face life despite the current against. Someone who is wildly vain and seeks by any means to control others, for which he invents excuses, methods and Machiavellian ways to achieve his goal or someone who has learned to manipulate circumstances to live at the expense of his innocent victims. Someone who is crying out for help or someone who has lost their conscience and needs to be regenerated. The one who has experienced the regeneration of his conscience and knows the difference between living in true freedom or someone who has learned to love passionately to the ends of the universe.

14. As long as the sun rises, the rain continues to fall; the earth continues to produce its fruits, and the stars rock the night our purpose of existence stays intact. We are not the product of nothingness. We have a purpose for existing and a conscience that guides us in that direction.

What if I told you that the Formula 1 champion's race car appeared out of nowhere, like a big bang? Would you believe me? How about I teach this nonsense to the thousands of spectators watching me sit in that fantastic car? Indeed, that teaching would offend the engineers who created that super-outstanding racing car. So much so that they would sue me for slander, and the public – booing me – would take me out of the vehicle and expel me from this racing stadium for teaching nonsense, right?

15. Oblivion is still a bitter drink. We cry out when left inside a box labelled as forgotten. We love hearing people say, 'I still love you.' We have a hard time coping when someone says to us, 'I already forgot you', and we cry out that this disgrace would never have happened, and it's worse if it comes from the mouth of the one we love. It hurts a lot.

We always cry out to be remembered as the Victorious Culture. It is our tendency, as human beings, to leave memories or small footprints as we pass through this world; it is like the blood of our human relationships. We wish people remembered us through our actions. In a certain way, we yearn that, through memory, our essence continues to exist in time. Am I lying?

16. We have a tendency to find solutions to local and global problems beyond the galaxies when the simple solutions are right in front of our noses: a change in our conscience. The world would be a beautiful paradise if we only had a molecule of conscience.

The solution to local and global problems involves a personal decision. It is difficult to accept that we must be the first to take a step towards change, but easy to hide behind any excuse. Many people say this country is part of the first developed world. Still, if one could wear the shoes of its leaders, one would realise that they scream to heaven for the government to occupy not the first place but the second place because not every one of them wants to be the first of the first to face the profound changes in the country and less the global ones. They hide behind this excuse: 'You give me the example first.'

Sometimes, Origin has to bend our knees because it has become heavily complicated for us to be the first to change. We have become accustomed to looking at the objects of our circumstantial reality as flat carpets without height, depth or length, on which we walk without the slightest sensitivity. Or we may have to think about emigrating to another planet because we don't want to look out of the window of our presidential vehicle and accept that we need to fix our conscience to produce significant changes in the world. If so, we may have to ask KORP and X-man to speed up their space programmes because they will have thousands of passengers who want to have a seat on the interstellar spaceship of Interplanetary Time Travellers' caravans.

17. Origin has left traces of his existence in every corner of the universe, and the most sublime, extraordinary and fantastic imprint he gave us is love. Every time a human loves and respects others, they manifest this legacy.

However, remember that he does not need us to leave our imprints for him to love us or to keep us in mind because, from the first microsecond that our little heart pumps blood through our circulatory system, he loves us and remembers us 365/24/7 constantly because we are his precious 'Ultimate Good'!

For this reason, no human being has the right of possession over another human being, much less to take advantage of any kind. It cannot and should not be the case because the day this happens, it will violate the possession rights of its proper owner. No matter if you are a moralistic, religious, atheist, philosophical, scientific, agnostic, gnostic, liberal, democrat, socialist, capitalist, anarchist, conservative, person in business, movie star, diplomatic, or whoever, to love and respect each other has been our right since conception.

18. Once, I went to see the exhibition of a sculpture called 'The Kiss' by the same creator of The Thinker, Auguste Rodin, a French sculptor. That piqued my interest, so I included it in the Gallery of Paradigmatic Thinkers' scene. However, the name of KORP came not from that work; it comes from …

"Orlando, maybe you should save that information for the end of this saga, don't you think?" (The Thinker)

About the author

Orlando was born in Cochabamba, Bolivia, and raised in the Andes Mountains in a small mining town, where he lived until he was fourteen. At eighteen, he left his country to get involved in a life of community service. After his studies in Argentina, he lived and worked in Ecuador for eighteen years with charitable institutions in community development projects. He has also been involved in politics and music.

Since 2012, he has taught Spanish in Diss, in Norfolk, UK. He is passionate about writing stories for his students; that's how he wrote this KORP saga.

Printed in Great Britain
by Amazon

40478040R00182